ICE HOUSE

Tim Clare is a writer, poet and musician. He won Best Biography/ Memoir at the East Anglian Book Awards for his first book, *We Can't All Be Astronauts*, while his fiction debut, *The Honours*, was longlisted for the Desmond Elliott Prize. He has performed his work at festivals and clubs across the world, on TV and radio. Tim has also written for the *Guardian*, *The Times* and the *Big Issue*, and presents the fiction writing podcast *Death Of 1,000 Cuts*. He lives in Norwich.

@timclarepoet | timclarepoet.co.uk

Praise for *The Ice House* and *The Honours*

'Told in rich, allusive prose, *The Ice House* is a leisurely meditation on good and evil'
Guardian

'Darkly compelling'
Financial Times

'Riotously entertaining . . . Delightfully twisted'
Sunday Express

'To say Tim Clare has a way with words is a bit of an understatement . . . Tim's writing is full of poetic pleasure. A joy to read, fast and closely, for the story and for the mastery in it'
Jess Kidd, author of *Himself*

'Irresistible'
Huffington Post

'An incredib ensive ode
to the Engl ost on the
b
Nac ies

Also by Tim Clare

The Honours

THE ICE HOUSE

TIM CLARE

CANONGATE

For Suki

This paperback edition published in 2020 by Canongate Books

First published in Great Britain, the USA and Canada in 2019 by
Canongate Books Ltd, 14 High Street, Edinburgh EH1 1TE

Distributed in the USA by Publishers Group West
and in Canada by Publishers Group Canada

canongate.co.uk

British Library Cataloguing-in-Publication Data
A catalogue record for the book is available on
request from the British library

ISBN 978 1 78689 482 3

Typeset in Baskerville MT by Palimpsest Book Production Ltd,
Falkirk, Stirlingshire

Printed and bound in Great Britain by Clays Ltd, Elcograf S.p.A.

A man burns.

He stands at the foot of a mountain. Ropes of flame lap up his naked body. Fat drips and smokes. As he burns, he heals.

Hagar watches from the shadow of the church. She registers his torment with a slight tightening of the jaw. Her three centuries have not numbed her to suffering, but it is a familiar pain, a punch working the same bruise. Still, she has never seen a peer with gifts quite like his.

'Who is he?' she says.

The angel stands beside her, his slender body wreathed in vapour. He smiles winsomely.

'My dearest friend. His name is Gideon.'

The angel's calmness makes her belly clench. There are bodies in the river. Blood gluts the shallows. How can he be so serene?

'And Sarai?'

'Gone,' says the angel.

'What? How?'

'Her kidnapper fled with her into the jungle. He managed to evade all our troops. He's very ingenious.'

'Then it's over.'

The angel chuckles softly. 'How quickly your faith evaporates.'

'But everything rests on her! Arthur, we *need* her.'

The angel lowers his gaze. The mud around his bare feet stiffens, glistering with frost.

'It's not yet the time.' The angel seems irritated, almost petulant. 'You of all people ought to understand the value of patience.' His expression resets, his composure returning. 'Don't worry. He loves the child. You'll track her down within the decade.'

'How?'

'I don't know exactly. Oh, don't look at me like that. I don't mean to be cryptic. My god dreams out of time. I see fragments. Possibilities. But I know we can win.'

Hagar tongues the hole in her gum left by her missing eye tooth. Her skroon, Räum, is tethered to an olive tree, his canoe-shaped beak clop-clopping as he feeds on the corpse of a soldier. His feathers are dulled with road-dust, but the wet ridges of his long, straight bill shine like the pearlescent ribs of a seashell. Grey skin bags around his double-jointed knees. His legs are muscular, the middle toe of either foot extending in a wicked, blade-like talon. He glances up, fixing her with his big hazel eyes. His lashes tremble with droplets of coagulating blood.

She turns to the angel. 'Tell me what happens.'

'But you already know.'

'Tell me again.'

'Very well,' says the angel, indulgently. 'You face your master in Fat Maw. You die, twice. Explosions rock the spire and the city burns. Grandmama is there, and dear Gideon, of course. Sarai is with us too, but she's no longer a child. She's old. She has grown into her talents. You must take care of her until then. You must take care of all our charges.' He glances towards the doorway of the old stone church. 'Each has a role to play.'

The cornices and window arches of the church are edged with black rope, greasy snakes shrivelled and tightened from years of rain and heat. Filling the entire doorway is a golem, armoured gauntlets bunched into fists at its sides. Its breastplate is incised with an eight-pointed star and it stands beneath the archway, supported by its own armour, inert.

Hagar pats its chest. The armour is searingly hot beneath her palm.

Within the recessed helmet, two blue embers flare into life.

'Excuse me, please,' she says.

The vast armour oscillates, producing a tone like an organ pipe. Black fluid flows through the armour's sealed joints, filling in limbs, flexing the articulated fingers of the gauntlets. A burnt, hoppy musk seeps from the visor slit as the golem rises, steps aside.

'Thank you.' Hagar walks into the church's cool interior. Its glassless lancet windows cast narrow blades of light across shattered pews. Thorns have pushed their way through the flagstones. They fill the room with a heady, resiny perfume that opens the sinuses.

At the back of the room, slumped against the wall, is a boy.

She is glad he is alive. The golem must have subdued him with a blow to the head before retrieving him – a crudely effective tactic, but one which might easily have killed him. He is not the boy she sought – the one who holds the child – but perhaps this mistake is providential. Perhaps, if the angel speaks truly, there are no mistakes.

The boy's face is tanned, one side discoloured by a big mauve welt. An oversized vest hangs from bony shoulders. Hagar draws her stiletto and holds it up to a sunbeam. The blade bisects the light, forming a cross.

'His name is Henry,' says the angel. 'He came from England by accident.'

At this, the boy stirs.

'I ought to kill him,' says Hagar. 'To be safe.'

'No, no. He's no threat.'

'But anything that might—'

'Hagar. We're not monsters. Isolate him if you must, but remember what we fight for. We must be merciful. Henry never meant to get mixed up in all this. He was trying to protect Delphine.'

The boy moans.

'Who?' says Hagar.

'Gideon's girl, back in England. She just killed my father and grandpapa. She'll be there, in Fat Maw. She helps us, though I don't think she means to. That's why I saved her from falling.'

'How long till she arrives?'

'Not for a good while, I should think.' The angel's image becomes foggy at the edges. His voice fades as his god calls him back. 'She'll be kept busy by the war.'

'You said the war ended decades ago.'

The angel darkens to a silhouette. Ice crystals form in the vapour rising from his shoulders, hardening into wings.

'Oh Hagar.' His voice shrinks to a whisper. 'War doesn't end. It sleeps.'

73 YEARS LATER

Spartacus911
Truth seeker
New member

New Topic: HELP SEARCHING FOR OBSCURE RECORDS
<< **on:** January 12, 2009, 12:18:02 PM >>
I am looking into the Neo-Pagan/Druidic rituals of Britain's ruling families & wondered if anyone could point me towards records of bloodlines of UK nobility/banking elites? Particularly any illegitimate offspring that might not appear on official documents? Interested in members of (hugely under-researched) pre-war Mithras cult SPIM (1932–35) (poss. linked to British Thuleans). They were based in the East of England, on the site of an ancient medieval grove renamed Alderberen Hall (from the German *Öl die Beeren* [lit. 'oil the berries'] referring to the anointing oil & the elderberries symbolising witchcraft & the harvest – classic ritualistic elements in ancient druidic human sacrifices) where they reportedly conducted various occult rites, mainly symbolic tauroctonies (a survivor account describes human participants dressed in horns & ritually murdered). Known members included:
Lazarus Stokeham, 4th Earl Alderberen [DROWNED SELF IN LAKE]
Graham Burchfield, 1st Baron Wolfbrooke (newspaper magnate with financial links to the Rothschilds) [REMAINS RECOVERED FROM FIRE]
Ivanovich Georgi Propp (33rd degree Freemason & White Russian émigré, underwent initiation w/ Blavatsky, occultist) [VANISHED]
Would appreciate any help investigating. Thanks.

'Solitude is the school of genius.'

Rob Pettifer
LP bountyhunter
Moderator

Re: HELP SEARCHING FOR OBSCURE RECORDS
<< **on:** January 13, 2009, 08:39:06 AM >>
Spartacus, please stop posting these. This is a vinyl collectors' forum.

Shellac addict, Deadhead and Beefheart, no YOU'RE a hoarder ;)

Spartacus911
Truth seeker
New member

Re: HELP SEARCHING FOR OBSCURE RECORDS
<< **on:** January 13, 2009, 10:18:58 AM >>
'I can only show you the door. You're the one that has to walk through it.'

'Solitude is the school of genius.'

CHAPTER 1

ABLE WAS I

Delphine woke up and remembered: Thompson was dead.

Her spectacles lay upside-down on the bedside table, beside an ashtray of polished green alabaster. Her dressing gown still hung from its peg on the door, yellow silk brocade with black satin cuffs. The world was trudging on, callously normal. She lay there, letting the fact of his death sit on her chest, heavy, invisible.

Eventually, her bladder forced her up. She unhooked her stick from the end of the bed. Her knee wobbled. Bugger it all.

In the bathroom she wetted a comb under the hot tap and hacked her white-grey hair into a vague semblance of a side parting, wincing as the teeth snagged in tangles. She took satisfaction in her discomfort – each tug at her follicles felt like a little reprimand.

She dragged some clothes on and rode the stairlift downstairs. The kitchen smelt of roast lamb. She carried the coffee pot to the sink and flushed the previous day's grounds, flinching at the cold water flowing over her swollen knuckles. A sunbeam lit a slow blizzard of dust. The little TV was still on, muted, yellow Teletext subtitles flashing up under footage of jet fighters banking over the Gaza Strip. A tangle of maroon wool lay nuzzled up against the bread bin, capped with a plastic crochet hook. On the kitchen table was a heap of threshold correspondence she hadn't replied to – physical letters and printed-out emails, some marked with post-its. Cranks, mostly – a man from Arizona who believed the human genome had been corrupted by a race of biblical giants, a Portuguese student who kept sending her articles arguing that the moon was hollow. The remainder were folklorists, historians and archaeologists – friendly, sincere people who didn't mind her peculiar questions about bat-people or gateways to other worlds. Of course, she never told them what she knew. How do you explain that when you were a child, you stopped an invasion led by an immortal aristocrat from a world that should not exist? How do you explain your memories of humanoid bat-creatures with fangs and leathery wings, of towering minotaurs armed with flintlocks? How do you explain the insect that appears in your dreams – the dark hornet with a sting that turns people into something less and more than humans, the godfly? And how do you explain that one of those people was your father?

It was, quite obviously, too much for an email. Better to stick to her cover story. She was just an eccentric old lady, writing a little volume on comparative mythology.

Spread out across the rest of the table were OS maps of parts of Venezuela, the Siberian steppe and Canadian tundra. Her magnifying glass lay in a red leather slipcase. A lovely, weighty one it was – mother-of-pearl handle and a grooved brass pommel shaped like an urn. An eighteenth birthday present from Mother.

Delphine walked to the back door and slid off her blue-green Carmichael tartan slippers. She unhooked the long cedar shoehorn from its spot next to the coats, rested a palm on the jamb and slotted her feet into a pair of calfskin brogues. The ritual mollified her a bit – it was rather like turning a fried egg – her fallen arches expanding and relaxing as they settled into the contours of the orthopaedic inserts. Not very practical for gardening, but she had a weakness for handsome footwear – a vice she called shoebris.

She shuffled outdoors. The dawn air was chilly, fragrant. She stopped at the edge of the patio, one hand tucked inside her suede waistcoat, feeling like Napoleon on St Helena.

She lit her pipe and took a few contemplative puffs.

The sky was a bright, uniform grey. Off in the east, the smudged gem of the sun. She gazed out across a havoc of weed-choked soil beds, brown puddles, a few sickly primroses, pebbles, pale grots of bird muck, cracked snail shells oozing cables of mucus, wet moss and a Frazzles packet snagged on a twig, opening and shutting its wet mouth in the breeze.

Peas and broad beans soon. Turnips too. Maybe this year they wouldn't bother. She tapped a clump of speedwell with the tip of her stick, watched the little purple heads shiver. Gardening was a siege. You held out as best you could, but the city always fell in the end.

On a green garden trolley, wrapped in a Union Jack flag, was the corpse of a Labrador.

Her heart sank. There he was. And there he wasn't. Gone forever. Death: the absence always present. Oh Thompson.

As she watched, the trolley turned and began rolling down the garden, towards the trees.

Delphine stood in the elm copse, puffing on her pipe to keep warm. She gazed into the gravemouth. Half-buried roots threaded spine-like through the uneven, clayey soil. Thompson's eyes were closed, his coat a glossy, velvet black.

'Are you warm enough, darling?' she said. At her side, light was bending round an astigmatic smudge the size of a small suitcase. She took a hipflask from her waistcoat pocket. 'It's just a nip.' Her jaw contorted as the toffee-and-cinders taste broke over her tongue and the booze vapour hit the back of her throat. Good shooting brandy. She took a second, more committed nip.

A stream cut across the northeast of the copse, swollen with run-off. The water passed beneath a wire fence into the neighbouring field. She squinted. It was hard to tell without her distance spectacles, but part of the fence looked like it had been ripped up where it crossed the flow. It was as if someone had shoved or dragged it into the air. The wire was twisted; a fencepost hung in it, unearthed. How long had it been like that?

Birdsong seeped through the constant, dissonant ringing that underscored everything. She had a hearing aid but it rubbed and the sound was rubbish. From the adjacent meadow came the *chak-chak-chak* of fieldfares amongst the blackthorns. Overhead, she fancied she could make out the high, sweet song of a coal tit.

Perhaps she was just wishing. The old garden used to fill with them. Mother would hang feeders from the conifers. Algernon had liked to scatter sunflower seeds around his deckchair while he read. If he stayed still enough, one might perch on the end of his book, an improbable wonder of white cheeks and biscuit-golden belly.

'I suppose I ought to say a few words.' She looked down into the grave and tried to sound appropriately solemn. 'Thompson Venner, you were a patient, noble campaigner and a gentle, loyal companion.' She took out his retractable lead. It was green textured plastic, with a silver clasp. 'Um.' She had meant to toss it in after him, but she held on. 'Sad to see you go, old man. You met your fate with a stoic mien.' She breathed in, the air cold against her teeth. The plastic felt rough beneath her fingers. 'Um.' Her hand was shaking. Why couldn't she just let the damn thing go? 'Would you like to add something?'

The arthritis in her wrist had returned with the insistence of a deep, radiating bruise. She pulled deeply on her pipe, sighed smoke into the breeze.

'It's all right,' she said. 'No one will see you here.'

The smudge at her side began to fill out, becoming a distinct shape with edges. It was like watching mist clear, or a camera come into focus.

The last of the blur washed away, revealing a wine-red scarab, eighteen inches tall, standing upright on two thick legs. Moisture had condensed on the segmented plates of her waxy carapace. She flexed the black palps either side of her mouth in a yawn.

'Well?' said Delphine.

Martha's jointed antennae sniffed the air, their two comb-shaped heads shivering. Dew had collected on the soft, club-like tips of her outer mouthparts, and with a gentle rippling motion she conveyed the droplets into her mouth. The smoked-blue centres of her eyes shifted upwards, suspended in pools of bright ghostmilk.

Martha tramped towards her little green trolley, hooked feet knifing through a slime of brown clay. The trolley was heaped with oddments. She liked to roam the meadows, collecting things, governed by no discernible organising principle: a sheep's jawbone, a thumb-sized hunk of porous basalt, bog moss.

She reached into the trolley bed, sifting through twigs, damp magazines, a tangle of old washing line. She retrieved something small and soil-clumped. It looked like a dead shrew.

When Martha held it up, Delphine saw it was a tiny stuffed toy, no bigger than a fist – a grey bunny. All its fur had been rubbed away. One of its ears hung ragged.

Where on earth had she found that? It must have been very dear to someone, once.

Martha spoke three ratcheting upstrokes at the limits of Delphine's hearing. She tossed the toy into the grave.

Delphine looked down. The little rabbit lay beside Thompson in the mud, its head resting on his jowl.

'There,' she said. 'You finally caught one.'

Slowly, she allowed her fingers to uncurl. Thompson's lead slipped from her grasp.

Delphine leant on her stick and finished her pipe. 'Back to the old people's home today.' She tapped out the bowl. Black ash drifted down into the grave. 'Ah, what a bloody mess.' She slid the pipe into her coat pocket and let her hand hang by her side.

Martha came and stood beside her. Together, they looked down at Thompson.

'Yet still we go on,' said Delphine. She exhaled. Strong, bristly fingers closed around her palm.

Outside the care home, a great monkey puzzle tree rose from the black soil. The flat triangular spikes lining its trunk and branches were brown from the winter. In France, the name was *désespoir des singes* – 'monkeys' despair'.

An old lady sat by the window in an ivy-green armchair, watching it.

Delphine put her book down on the table by the door. She sat opposite the old lady, on the crisply made bed. Her chest felt tight and she took a moment to find her breath before speaking.

'Hello, Alice.'

Alice squinted at the jagged tree with a look of mistrust. She was hunched over, her flesh dry and scored like old firewood. She began turning her head very slowly, juddering with a clockwork tremor. They had known each other since Delphine was thirteen and Alice was seventeen. What a queer, pernicious magic age was. To transmogrify so profoundly, yet so invisibly. To swap out tiny granules of a person's being while they slept, to grow a second body over their first until they peered out from within, swallowed whole.

She eyed Delphine suspiciously. 'Where's my squash?'

'On your tray, dear.'

'Ah.' Little hands, bulbous-veined, purpling at the knuckles. She clasped her orange plastic beaker. It rose, shuddering, to her lips. She sipped.

The weak sun shone in the pinks of her eyes. 'I shouldn't be up here.' Her words were halting, distant. 'I'll get in trouble.'

'I won't tell anyone.'

'I'm just having a little rest.'

'And so you should. You work very hard.'

Alice sipped from her beaker. 'I do.'

Delphine glanced at the white plastic radio alarm clock on the bedside table. Beside it was a Bible with a crocheted cover of powder-blue cotton, and a box of tissues, and an ammonite fossil set in a mosaic frame of razor clams and cockle shells. The room smelt of lemon disinfectant and witch hazel.

Alice tutted.

'What is it, darling?' said Delphine.

Alice nodded at the double-glazed window. 'He shouldn't be doing that.'

Outside, a gardener walked amongst neatly clipped hedgerows and borders with his backpack of moulded green plastic, spraying poison. It did seem rather zealous for March.

'They've probably had an infestation,' said Delphine. 'He's just doing his job.'

Alice shot Delphine a scornful look. 'I've never seen him before in my life.'

'I see. I'll instruct the staff to have him shot.'

A little puce wedge of tongue emerged and slid along Alice's dry blue lips. 'No. That's too much.'

'Perhaps he's an admirer.'

Alice broke into a smile. Tiny and hunched in her big green armchair, her neck jutting forwards, she looked rather like a tortoise.

'Oh no, I don't think so.'

'You haven't found rose petals on your windowsill? He might have come to whisk you away to the Riviera.'

'No, not for me. I don't think Reggie would like that.'

Delphine glanced down at her hands. She still had grave dirt under her nails.

'I saw . . .' She paused to clear her throat. 'I saw a kingfisher in the garden last week.'

'John lets him borrow his boat. We take it out around the harbour.'

Delphine's chest tightened. 'I see.'

'He pulled his shirt off and went swimming. Then he came at me with a, uh . . .' She formed her bands into a pair of beaks and flapped them open and shut. 'A snappy one.'

'A crocodile?'

Alice's mouth worked with silent laughter. 'A crocodile? Whoever heard of a crocodile at the seaside?' She gazed out the window, pursing her lips in scornful wonder. 'Have you been drinking?'

Delphine could still taste cognac on the back of her teeth. 'All right. A crab.'

Alice half-closed her eyes, beaming at the word. 'Ah. I like crabs. I used to play at being a crab. When I was very small. Mum and Dad'd be shouting, and I'd be in the corner, a little crab. They can't go backwards. Only sideways. Hmm. Reggie came at me with a crab once. I didn't scream. He says he'll teach the baby to swim, once it comes.'

Delphine felt a cold tightness in her gut. Poor Alice. She didn't remember.

'That sounds nice, darling.'

Alice lifted a finger to her mouth. 'Shh. You mustn't tell anyone yet. It's a secret.' She mumbled something inaudible, shaking her head. Then she chortled in her dry, gentle way, full of secret mirth. 'Crabs have edges like a pie crust.' She looked up at Delphine. 'What are you still doing here?'

'Watch your manners. I'm visiting you.' Delphine fished a packet out of her satchel. 'Now, would you like some chocolate buttons?' Alice eyed the chocolates sceptically. 'Don't pretend you don't because you always do. I'll put some on a dish for you.'

Delphine hauled herself upright and went to the bedside cabinet. She felt breathless, buffeted by all the non sequiturs. She took out a white china dish with a picture of a sailboat on it and put it on the tray table. She used a tissue to wipe off the dust. The dish jangled as she shook out some buttons.

'There.' Delphine lowered herself back onto the bed. She dug about in the packet for the last few buttons and popped one into her mouth.

Alice peered at her. 'I know you.'

'I should hope so. I visit you every week.'

'The builders keep switching things around.'

'I'm sorry. You're quite right. It's most inconsiderate.'

'You don't know whether you're coming or going.'

'Next time I see them I shall give them a piece of my mind.'

'Good.' Alice nodded, apparently mollified. 'I shall have to go back soon. My break's almost over.' She stirred her buttons with a fingertip. 'Elevenses is in the smoking room.'

'Alice, there is no smoking room.'

'I know!' She shook her head. 'Terrible, isn't it?'

Delphine dipped her head and massaged her closed eyelids. Sometimes she wondered if dementia was infectious. The longer she spent with Alice, the more weary and confused Delphine became. She could feel her ageing brain cells expiring. With its ramps and neutral colours and identical rooms, the care home was a machine for forgetting. Really, a machine for being forgotten.

'Alice. Are you in there, darling? Do you remember me at all? It's me, Delphine.'

Alice did not look up, but her expression brightened. 'Ooh! I know a girl called Delphine.'

'And what's she like?'

'Oh, very queer. I think because of her poor father.'

Delphine sighed. 'You might be right.'

Alice did not seem to hear. She was shuffling buttons around the dish with intense concentration.

'I shall have to go soon,' she said.

'Yes, Alice.'

'He's going to come for me. After the sun goes down. Reggie and me are getting married. We haven't any money but we're going to go away. It's a secret. Oh. I suppose I've spoilt it now.' She blinked and tears dropped into the dish. Buttons slid towards the middle.

Delphine got up and took a scented tissue from the box on the bedside table. She bunched it up like a rose, and dabbed at Alice's cheeks. Alice closed her eyes. Delphine gently touched the tissue to either eyelid. She leaned in and kissed Alice through her sparse white hair, on her crown. Her hair was soft and smelt of apples.

They sat for a while. Out in the corridor, somebody was shrieking for Tony. A pair of grey wagtails settled in the upper boughs of the monkey puzzle.

Alice nibbled on a chocolate button. She pulled a face.

'These are wet.'

'Oh, never mind, dear. Here have mine.'

Delphine held out the rest of the packet. Alice closed a blotchy purple hand around it and snatched it back to her tray table. She ate quickly, getting chocolate on her chin.

'I'll have to go soon,' Alice said.

'Me too. We're the last ones left.'

Alice tutted again. 'So they've left us to tidy up.'

Delphine had to cover her eyes to stop herself from crying. She felt odd and adrift. She took a couple of slow breaths, straightened her spine.

'You've done quite enough tidying up for other people. You relax.'

Alice nodded, her mouth full of buttons. Delphine smoothed her trousers, readying herself to stand. A pressure settled on her heart.

'It's been good to see you, Alice.'

'Mmm,' Alice said into her squash.

Delphine rocked forward, and with a splintering pain in her elbows, hoisted herself upright. She massaged her wrist.

'Goodbye.'

Alice did not respond. She was like a fortune-teller machine after your penny runs out. When she reached the door, Delphine noticed an old hardback sitting on the dresser. It was Volume VI of Gibbon's *The History Of The Decline And Fall Of The Roman Empire*.

'Oh,' she said, picking it up. She turned to Alice. 'Reading Gibbon's?'

'Yes,' said Alice, vacantly. 'I suppose we are.'

'She doesn't remember she has cancer.'

The drapes were drawn, the air thick with dust. Martha was

perched on her cushion in front of the hearth, knitting. She had lit the fire and the front room wavered in its dim, faintly aqueous glow.

'She doesn't remember anything.' Delphine glanced across. 'Martha, are you listening to me?'

Martha finished the row she was on. She set down her yarn. She extended a fist and bopped it once for 'yes'.

Delphine blew on her coffee. 'I wish they'd do more with her in there. She's alone most of the day. No wonder she's going batty.'

Martha took a couple of maple candies from a dish and dropped them into her coffee one at a time, stirring with a teaspoon. The table was heaped with books – tattered hardbacks with torn, faded jackets and dog-eared self-published paperbacks on geology, geomancy, folk legends, cave systems and cryptozoology, swollen with damp, each spewing crumpled strips of paper bookmarking passages Delphine must have thought were relevant to her research at some point. The covers were coated in a heavy patina of dust.

The books sat there like a reproach. She looked at them and felt sick. Were there others out there like her, who knew about the existence of a world besides our own? She had searched for so long, found so little.

What if there was no one but crackpots? What if she had run out of time?

She took a sip of coffee and clenched her jaw, blotting the thought out. Mustn't dwell. Lock it away. Onwards.

'Did you see the fence? It looks like someone's torn it up.' She pressed her tongue against the backs of her incisors. She felt a bit odd – residual brain fog from visiting Alice. 'It wasn't you, was it?'

Martha made her fingers into the shape of a beak and snapped it closed for 'no'.

'Right. Well. Very mysterious. Perhaps it was our friends from Cottingley.'

Martha picked up her knitting. The plastic needles clacked softly. Delphine closed her eyes and listened to their gentle, percussive music – *tak tak tak*.

No. She wouldn't doze through yet another afternoon. She had work to do. She rose with a grunt and marched down the corridor to the War Room.

She drew a key from a retractable lanyard on her belt and unlocked the door. A naked bulb lit a snowstorm of dust. Freestanding galvanised metal shelves took up three of the walls; against the fourth were a computer desk, a PC and a large dry-wipe whiteboard, covered in red and blue smears. Scanned and photocopied images were Blu Tacked around the board's perimeter: passages from library books; a photograph of ancient Syrian pottery depicting horned figures surrounding a pool; a newspaper article in Spanish from 1956, with a loose translation biroed into the margins about sightings of humanoid bat-creatures near a village; and sundry other scraps, hints and half-clues of another world, gathered over decades. Arrows on the whiteboard linked bits of evidence to web addresses and categories like UNVERIFIED and EUROPE.

In the bottom-left corner, held in a clear plastic sleeve, was a folded piece of paper covered in intricate writing and tiny diagrams: the notes of a man called Edmund Kung, who had drowned trying to reach the other world.

Around the rest of the room, shelves were crammed and top-heavy with coils of fence wire, a two-ring camping stove, a skeleton gun, a Mamod steam engine, a ribbed plastic bottle of methylated spirits, a silver-plated cigar guillotine with the legend *Tout Jour Prest* engraved across its stainless steel blade, a Crawford's shortbread tin stuffed with stiff chamois leathers and oily J-cloths, three colours of shoe polish (black, maroon and tan), grub screws in an old marmalade jar, a pair of hiking boots, a flare gun, a partially dismantled clay pigeon thrower and a small folding knife with a scrimshaw handle featuring a rather crude rendition of a giant squid assaulting a galleon.

Delphine lowered herself into the leather swivel chair. She opened a drawer and took out her pipe. She loaded it, struck two matches and puffed until smoke billowed out of her cupped palms. In the open drawer was a small, grey-brown hardback with a hole punched through its cover – A. Prentice's *Transportation And Its Practice.*

It was the only copy she knew of – the only printed text she had ever encountered that openly acknowledged the existence of thresholds, and the channel, and the black fluid called godstuff that connected worlds. She could conjure the image of it just by closing her eyes, even now. The churning pool. The hot stink of peat, hops, bitumen. She had doubted so many of her memories in the decades since. Never that one.

Much of the information in the book was skewed by prejudice or superstition – the author called the non-human sentient species 'lower creatures', and had an obsession with phases of the moon and cleansing one's spirit through fasting and prayer – but there were also lucid accounts of the author's journeys between worlds, including frank descriptions of the changes his body underwent, through which he tried to calculate precisely how many years younger the trip had made him.

She nudged the drawer shut and switched on the computer. She was remembering why she hated coming in here. Some of her notes on the whiteboard were years old. Probably permanent by now. There were copies of letters written by Algernon, each closing with one of his trademark elaborate, faux-fawning valedictions – *I remain, Sir, your humble servant in Christ*, etc. The place was a shrine to folly.

She swigged brandy from her hipflask. She had always held back from publicly sharing what she knew, partly to protect Martha, partly so she could distinguish those with genuine knowledge from cranks. What if other people were doing the same? What if there was someone else out there like her, waiting for a signal?

In the beginning, after the business at Alderberen Hall, after Father disappeared or died, she and Mother and Algernon and the lanta had all lived together. There had been twelve lanta in all: Abel, Esther, Ezra, Gabriel, Immanuel, Isaiah, Joel, Martha, Matthew, Naomi, Thomas and Timothy. People assumed Mother and Algernon were living in sin, which was easier to accept than the truth.

Delphine remembered the row the night Algernon told her that he and the lanta intended to look for a threshold in Venezuela. How he had broken the news that she could not go with them. She was too young. It was too dangerous. She remembered how furious she had been with him. For leaving them. For tearing their family apart. Most of all, she remembered her inability to tell him that she could not bear for him to go, could not bear to lose another father – and how it had only made her angrier.

In the end, it was Martha who had announced she would stay.

Delphine had never understood why – at the time, the two of them were not especially close – but for that act of loyalty, she would be forever grateful.

But Algernon was gone. Mother was gone. The lanta were gone. And now Thompson was gone. If death wanted you, escape was impossible. And death wanted everyone.

She and Martha were the only ones left. What would Martha do when Delphine died?

Why, after all these years, was she still holding back? She filled herself another pipe and fetched more brandy from the cupboard. What did she honestly have to lose that time wouldn't snatch anyway?

Delphine opened her email client and clicked New. She wrote:

vesperi
avalonia
the honours

If any of these terms mean anything to you, please contact me immediately. Replies will be received in the utmost confidence. If not, I apologise for the somewhat abrupt and cryptic tone of this email and wish you a fulfilling and productive week.

Cordially,
Ms Delphine Venner

She went through her address book and dropped every name that wasn't a business into the BCC box. She checked her spelling. She hesitated. She clicked Send.

Delphine sagged back into her chair. A thrill prickled the nape of her neck, as if she had just turned a launch key. It wouldn't achieve anything, of course. She had received similar emails herself, full of code words: Agenda 21, HAARP, Majestic 12, Nibiru, Derro, Project Grudge. It was like calling out across the sea for a drowned lover – not because you expected a response, but just to hear their name.

Delphine blinked and lifted her head. Her mobile phone lay on the desk. She groped about for her spectacles, which were folded up in her breast pocket. She must have dozed off. She still had her coat on. Had she been wearing it in the front room?

Her eyes were watering. God, how long had she been out for?

She found Martha in the kitchen, sitting in her converted high-chair, watching News 24 with the sound off. It was already dark outside.

'You all right there, old girl?'

Martha shuffled round to look. Her complicated mouthparts rippled with the slow precision of a loom.

Rik-ik-ik.

'I was wondering . . . I mean, we don't have to, but I thought . . . you know, because of everything. Would you like to shoot some faeries?'

Martha held out her fist. She rapped the table twice. Emphatic yes.

A hint of wing flashed in the beam of the infra-red lamp. Through the night vision scope, the treetops were a spectral, underwater green, blooming like weird coral.

The night was moonless, the meadow a wilderness of waist-high, fragrant grasses. Their sweetness tickled her nostrils as her finger settled on the trigger. She swivelled the rifle on its mount, easing the crosshairs towards the tiny figure perched in the old hornbeam.

The faery stood on tiptoes halfway along a branch, back arched coquettishly, delicate butterfly wings spread.

'I've found one,' Delphine whispered.

She let the sights settle on the upturned head. Using the monopod felt a bit like cheating, but she hadn't the strength to hold a rifle straight for more than a few seconds, especially with the scope and the IR lamp. Anyway, her degrading fine motor control added enough of a tremor to make things sporting. The faery's eyes and wingtips winked.

In the old serials, snipers became one with their guns. They tasted the wind, waiting, then squeezed the trigger between heartbeats. She tried listening to her heart. She couldn't feel it, had a crazy panic that it had stopped.

No, there it was: the angry pounding, the old habit, the boiler room. She was surprised at its vigour. Each heartbeat roared in her ears.

Martha sat beside her on the mobility scooter. Delphine focused on the T-shaped outline trembling in the breeze.

The faery fluttered, its eyes burning impossibly green-white. The crosshairs dipped to its thigh then rose towards the face.

The air rifle kicked gently – *ptfff* – as the CO_2 canister discharged. The sound was like someone spitting into a gutter.

The faery stayed poised, unsullied, glinting where she and Martha had hot-glued acrylic gemstones from the hobby shop. They had scanned and printed dozens of them from a charity shop deck of faery cards, backing them with cardboard during one of their long autumn crafternoons. She was surprised how many had survived the winter. After a storm she usually found a couple facedown in the dirt, the colour leached from their translucent dresses, their faces a Munchian smear.

'Now just look at that.' She lowered the rifle. The booze was making her head tingly. With the shush of the trees and the heavy smell of wild grass it could have been any time in the last fifty years.

She missed the recoil of her old break-barrel spring-piston rifle – the sureness of it. Her body still expected the kick of the mechanism, though the gun had long sat in useless pieces in the attic. She missed the whipcrack report of her Winchester over-and-under, the sweet bacon smell of the spent cartridges and the heat-shimmer rising from the barrels on cold days as she tracked a moving target. She missed collecting unbroken clays on the top field and the clanking, shifting sound they made as she carried them in a cardboard box back to The Pastures. She missed the rustle click of knitting needles as a dozen wine-red scarabs sat beside their yarn balls, the silent shining pull and plunge of darning by firelight, the spinning and the measuring and the snipping of the thread. She missed Mother's steady, affectionate gaze when she thought Delphine was not watching, the smell of woodsmoke in Mother's hair after woofing the fire with the bellows, the way she closed her eyes whenever people sang in church. She missed the framed sketch above Mother's last bed, Father's characteristic stark, vibrant lines showing Mother watching Delphine paddle into the sea. She missed doing the crossword together and Mother scolding her if she asked for a word's spelling ('You know perfectly well. Just think for a moment.'), the feel of Mother's hands, soft and slick from the ointment, so swollen that she had to wear her wedding ring on a silver chain round her neck (and she still wore it, right to the end), the smell of dried lavender and a hint of something like soured milk – yes, she missed even that. She missed the thumping in her chest after a long hike, the glowy torpor in her limbs and tingling skin after a sunrise dip in the ocean. She missed sleeping for eight hours at a stretch without having to get up to urinate – or worse, just to lie there with her churning thoughts. She missed watching Daddy smoke as he painted. She missed hot tea and log warmth with her dear lost Henry. She missed knowing what to hate and what to love, and loathed herself for wanting to, for caring, for the grubby futility of it all.

Martha was staring, eye-glow frosting her crushpincer mandibles. Delphine took a moment, the rifle stock snug in the soft flesh beneath her shoulder.

'Sorry,' she said. 'I missed.'

Martha took the air rifle. She pressed a huge domed eye to the scope. Her antennae shuddered, tasting the wind speed.

Delphine unscrewed the cap on her hip flask and took a slug of brandy. 'Oh, do get on with it. You're not assassinating de Gaulle.'

Ptfff. Martha lowered the rifle. She passed it back.

Delphine peered through the scope. Every time she inhaled, she felt her diaphragm come up against an aching resistance in her solar plexus.

'It's no good. It's not the same. Would you be a dear and get out the real one?'

Martha unzipped the slipcase on the back of the scooter and took out the SMLE. Delphine took the vintage rifle tenderly, running her fingers over steel and English walnut. She put on her head torch and loaded the strip-clip with .303 British. 'There.' She handed the filled clip to Martha, who knelt in the long damp grass and pushed the rounds into the magazine. 'Grab the torch.' Delphine shoved the bolt forward, chambering a round. 'Shine it on that tree.'

The big torch threw a beam like a floodlight. The trees at the meadow's end danced with a mesh of shadows. Amongst the hooked bare branches, faeries flashed and blazed.

Delphine licked her lips. The beam wobbled, stabilised. She glanced at Martha. 'Ready?'

Martha bopped her fist.

'Right.' Delphine flipped the safety catch forwards from its little notch in the stock. She squinted at a vague glint in the trees. Lined up her sights. Squeezed.

A thunderclap rang across the dark field.

She chambered another round. Squeezed.

The shot boomed flatly. She chambered another. Squeezed.

She lowered the rifle.

Martha shut off the torch and they took it in turns to look through the night vision scope.

'I can't find anything,' said Delphine, her ears ringing. Hunting for a smouldering paper frock or a split branch's raw pale marrow, she found her gaze drawn past the trees, to the bright blob of her house beyond. She imagined she was looking through a submarine periscope. She imagined the strange silent shape with its odd windows glowing spectral green was an enemy battleship. She let the crosshairs centre on its heart.

A light flickered in an upstairs room. Delphine blinked. The house was still.

There it was again. Movement. Her bedroom.

Someone was in the house.

They parked the scooter a short way from the drive.

Delphine's heart was belting. The rosemary bushes smelt pungent and intoxicating.

'Right,' she whispered. 'You head in, start switching on lights. That ought to put the willies up 'em. I'll bring up the rear.'

She hugged the rifle to her stomach. The gravel was soaked in faint light from the house. Someone was in there, rifling through *her* memories. Mother's engagement ring. The little black poplar tortoise carved for her by Father.

Her heart was doing that funny fluttery thing again. She took a few slow breaths in and out through her nostrils.

Martha's eyes pulsed softly. She began to blur and fade.

'Be careful,' Delphine whispered.

Martha's red armoured carapace was a blotchy watercolour, an afterimage. She lifted a black fist away from her smudging body, bopped it twice. A fading shape moved away across the gravel.

Delphine gazed at the house. Her field of vision sparkled with queer, floating transparencies. She felt the weight of the rifle, the tremor in her knees. Maybe she had been mistaken.

But she could hit a five-inch target, unscoped, at thirty yards. At night. She knew what she had seen.

She rounded the mobility scooter and paused at the tangle of bramble bushes that marked the end of the drive. Wind rustled the bare aspens. The sound merged with the metallic warble of her tinnitus.

She kept close to the hedge, using the rifle as a walking stick. Gravel crackled under her brogues. A good defensive measure, gravel – though she had always assumed that, in a siege, she would be the defender.

A light was on in the kitchen, and one upstairs. She might have left them on – she usually did. The curtains were closed. She watched for movement, for shadows playing across the fabric. Nothing.

She heard a noise behind her and glanced back down the drive. All she saw was a flat, shifting blackness. A dark blob seemed to retreat, merging with the bushes. Was she imagining it? Her bad eye made judging distances difficult.

She reached the cottage's stone wall and pressed herself against it. Her gaze kept flitting to the clotted blackness of the lane. Oh, pull yourself together. Of course things were moving in the dark. This was the bloody countryside.

She edged towards the doorstep and peered round the corner.

The door was ajar. Naturally – Martha had opened it to get in. Through the frosted glass, the hallway was flooded with a sour yellow wash.

Delphine pressed a palm to her chest, waited for her heart to settle. Had she locked the War Room? Perspiration clung to her brow and top lip. She listened. The old drop-dial mahogany wall clock began striking midnight.

A dull bang from the kitchen.

She scrabbled to lift the rifle. Her chest swelled with indignation.

How bloody dare they. She clambered onto the doorstep and shoved the door so it swung and crashed against the wall.

'You have ten seconds to *get out* of my house!'

She chambered a round and fired down the corridor. The far wall exploded in a shower of brick dust and plaster. She chambered another and stepped into the house. She felt the doormat slip.

One leg slid out from under her. Her weight shifted onto her opposite leg and her knee gave out. The hallway swung. She threw an arm out. Her palm hit the oak parquet floor, her wrist bent back on itself and she landed on her stomach.

For a moment, it was not quite real. The floor was a vertical line bisecting her vision. Light seeped down the hall from the kitchen, a smear of greased gold.

I fell. I have had a fall.

She breathed in; her ribs pressed against hard oak. Her left arm was pinned beneath her. She could feel her right ankle, snagged on the lip of the door. The rifle lay a few feet away.

She burned with humiliation. You pathetic, stupid old thing. She tried using her free hand to push herself up, to roll over. A sharp pain flared in her hip.

She thumped the floor, hard. No self pity. Pain was just annoying, unsolicited advice. Her hip wasn't broken, just stiff and bruised. She would have time to feel sorry for herself tomorrow.

She groped for the rifle. A spasm racked her leg and she bit down, refusing to yield to it. She closed her fingers round the barrel.

A boot pinned the gun to the floor.

Footsteps clumped down the corridor. Strong arms dragged her to her feet.

'I've phoned the police!' She was yelling. She would bite them if she had to. 'They'll be here any second. There are cameras everywhere!'

A figure stood in the doorway, tall, whip-thin, dressed in black. A plastic mask obscured their face.

'Take her to the van,' they said.

CHAPTER 2
SWEET AND BITTER WATER
(One day before the inauguration)

Just before dawn, Hagar climbed into the cemetery. She was shaking with fatigue. Sea mist clung clammy and grey among the burial mounds and tomb slabs, moistening the brows of horned and cloven-footed smokestone idols. Beyond the cemetery walls, the city of Fat Maw slept, drugged by a jungle swelter, oblivious to its impending ruin.

She had contemplated the Grand-Duc's death for nearly 400 years, ever since he had dragged her, shuddering and maggoty, from beneath a heap of corpses and cursed her with endless youth. She did not remember the moment the parasite had entered her body – the moment she became permanently joined to Morgellon, dependent on him. He had not asked if she wanted to receive the honours. She had just been lying there, like an egg in a nest, and Morgellon had plucked her out. With the angel's guidance, she had taken steps to draw him out of his self-imposed exile. But now, the day before his royal clipper was due to arrive in Fat Maw, she was terrified she might fail to see it through.

Of course, there was the standard technical challenge of executing a peer. What she was attempting was officially impossible. Morgellon was a peer, and therefore immortal. Like any peer, he could regenerate injuries at a phenomenal rate. She had felt the tip of a parade sword scrape between his third and fourth ribs and puncture his heart during a boarding action near Cape Endurance, grapeshot perforate his gut when a cannon misfired at Namnetum, a ceremonial mace shatter his collarbone in some half-forgotten village during that long summer of burning. Each injury had slowed him down by mere minutes, so the standard prompt, humane methods of assassination were out. Even decapitation – which was rather more involved than the frigid autopsy tables of the Institute had led her to believe, particularly when the subject still lived – was insufficient in and of itself. Complete incineration, dissolution or dissection into fine particulates were the only known permanent measures. Mortifer Bechstein, the notorious ex-Lord Cambridge, had regrown from a severed calf left in a steel mantrap even as the rest of his body crumpled and carbonised atop a hastily constructed execution pyre.

Secondly, despite years of squalid self-neglect, Morgellon was not weak. The talents that came with his arising had combined with a regal, questing paranoia to make him spectacularly adept at self-preservation.

Within the perpetuum – a loose and often strained alliance of which all peers were members – he was one of the oldest and undoubtedly one of the best resourced, his territories encompassing the continents of Gallia and Albion as well as colonial possessions, of which this one, Avalonia, was undoubtedly the most valuable. He commanded armies and local garrisons, constabularies and networks of informants.

His innermost circle of bodyguards served fixed one-year terms, drafted from barracks across his empire via a clandestine lottery system of Hagar's devising. They were not told the nature of their posting until they arrived, kept isolated from the outside world throughout their service, and well-remunerated on discharge. The arrangement appealed not to their love of the Grand-Duc, but to their pragmatic self-interest, and in this, Morgellon was wise. He had many enemies, both beyond and within the perpetuum. Open conflict did not suit the peers' self-image as enlightened immortals, possessing, as it were, an unseemliness that belied their claims of divinity. On the other hand, proxy wars, assassinations, and all flavours of subterfuge were tacitly accepted (with the proviso that one must not get caught) as part of the natural order. After all, the best proof of one's right to power was the ability to retain it. Loyalty was the most contemptible of the virtues, and the most easily counterfeited.

Thirdly, any assassination attempt was complicated by her relationship to the Grand-Duc: Morgellon was a peer, and thus experienced no pain. She was his servant, and, like all handmaidens and valets, she felt pain on her master's behalf. If she drove a dagger between his shoulder blades, she, not he, would feel its point parting skin and muscle. If she shot him through the head, she would experience a blinding white agony and lose consciousness, and when he recovered, her treachery would be exposed. If he died permanently, so would she. That was the beauty of the honours system. The servant could not live without the master. Treason was suicide.

Still, formidable though these problems were, they were not the source of her fear. She had spent decades planning how to achieve the impossible. The Grand-Duc's arrival tomorrow was her best, last chance to kill him.

What gave her pause – what saw her trudging here now, amongst the stupas and bone-cluttered family vaults, reeling with doubt – was the thought that, in the critical moment, she might shrink from administering the decisive stroke. Even with so many lives at stake, she might blench, she might collapse, because in setting him free, she would lose him.

The realisation came in a creeping, freezing wave. For so long, Morgellon's death had driven her, but tomorrow, if all went to plan – if her nerve did not fail – it would be reality. She would have to live out the last days of the world without him.

Hagar walked past row upon row of graves. Here was her old anatomy teacher, here was the captain of the guard next to his first and second husbands, here was the quartermaster of the *Lady Vain* who had chewed riverroot and licked her black teeth while looking at seacharts. Incised into each smooth marble ledger was a name: CHARLOTTE ABRAXIA, BRISH KILVAIN II, DERLETH SKARROWMERE.

Real, vital people, reduced to a few scars in rock. *Truly, they shall be as the morning cloud, and as the early dew that passeth away, as the chaff that is driven with the whirlwind out of the floor, and as the smoke out of the chimney.* There was no crawling out from beneath the heap of corpses. Every day it grew deeper.

Hagar wiped a film of sweat off her top lip. So much of her life had been marked by corrigibility, impermanence – a sense that no action was irrevocable, no mistake final. Wounds healed. Massacred populations were gradually replaced. Pain and glory oscillated around a steady median. What she contemplated, what bore down on her, implacably, was a single, permanent act. If she failed, this living damnation might persist for millennia. Billions of fates balanced on the blade-edge of her courage.

No longer. A tiny, feckless aristocracy had fed off the world's life energy for too long. The secrets of this planet were meant for far greater things. The honours were just the beginning.

Delphine would not stop her. Not even Morgellon would stop her. She would win because she had to. She would use his powers to tame the beast. She would save everyone.

The city would be waking soon, hungover, ugly with remorse. Paranoia gnawing at its sinews. A rich, ripe cholera-corpse, bloated with contagion.

Ready to explode.

Hagar picked her way down the steep, twisting street, towards the low town and the stilt city. The cobbles were littered with spent firecrackers, incense sticks and the occasional pale slash of glutinous vomit. Bunting that, in the blazing torchlight of the previous night, had fluttered gay and magnificent, now sagged between shuttered windows like lank seaweed.

As she descended, the atmosphere grew more humid. The bay was southwest-facing, crescent-shaped. To the northeast, the Maw delta exploded out of the jungle, a mile-wide chain of islets and mudbanks, threaded together by wooden piers, pontoon docks and rope bridges. The stilt city curved south, a palimpsest of boardwalks and ad-hoc cabins scribbled over the sea. Windmills flashed in the early morning sun. Spiked heads of lightning rods shivered like strange thistles.

An ache had started in her stomach. She recognised the pain as

Morgellon's. He had not taken his medicine yet. Withdrawal symptoms were beginning to rack his body.

It was too late for drunks and too early for beggars. Most of the street was still in shadow, sunlight a strange, encroaching benediction upon the slates and chimney pots.

She heard footsteps and ducked into a doorway.

A member of the city peace came running down the hill – a short, human woman clad in a white cotton smock and green sash, her carbine on a shoulder sling.

'Miss Ingery? Miss Ingery!' She sounded out of breath.

As she was about to run past Hagar stepped out into her path and hailed her. 'Good morning, officer.'

The officer nearly barrelled into her. She took a step back, clasping her chest.

'Miss Ingery, Sheriff Kenner requests your presence at an incident on the Rue Viné immediately.'

'Hasn't he got better things to do, with the Grand-Duc arriving?'

The officer shrugged apologetically. 'That is the message.'

'How did you find me?'

'I was on my way to your lodgings.'

Hagar scrutinised the officer's close-set brown eyes. 'Can you tell me the nature of this incident?'

The officer shook her head. 'He requests you attend immediately.'

'What's the address?'

'I'm to lead you there myself.'

Hagar felt the gaze of a dozen shuttered windows overhead. Technically, she could refuse. Kenner was not arresting her. She outranked him. Technically.

A glazier's sign creaked in its brackets. What could be so important that he would send for her so early? And why her, of all people? He hated the palace interfering.

'All right.' Hagar straightened her leather gloves, surreptitiously checking the garrotte concealed in her cuff. She flattened down her jacket and flashed the officer her best compliant smile. 'Lead the way.'

The skeleton lay in pieces on the stone floor. Holding a handkerchief over her nose and mouth, Hagar took a rough inventory: here was the skull, lying on its side, yellow in the candlelight, then several inches away the separated mandible, missing most of its teeth, then the cervical vertebrae still connected with a pulp of white gristle, the clavicles and scapulae, the ribcage mostly intact, bedded in traces of a nondescript puce mush, both arms – one of which lay some distance off to the right but was held together by knots of connective tissue, the knuckle bones, metacarpals and short phalanges scattered like the oddments of some exotic children's game, the other arm flush with the ribcage and missing a hand – the massy pelvis, again glistening with grots of organic matter, then the thighbones splayed, the shinbones and fibulas pointing back towards each other in a bandy-legged parody of a dancer.

Hagar crouched. She surveyed the bones with a sense of anti-climax – she had expected a murder scene, not a relic. She could not see how this musty old skeleton was a matter requiring her expertise.

'Don't touch it,' said Sheriff Kenner, his voice deep, his inflection flat. The mountainous harka was watching solemnly, his candle smoking in the foul cellar air. His huge forearms were a striking oxblood against his white cotton smock. When he inhaled, a bulge rose in his throat, straining against the muscles of his jaw.

Beside the skeleton was a three-legged wooden stool and an old-fashioned pepperbox pistol with four rotating barrels. She glanced at Kenner.

'Has this been fired?'

Kenner hesitated. He had to stoop to keep from catching his huge horns on the ceiling beams. They were wide as his shoulders, his neck extending from a great hump of muscle in such a way that he appeared to be perpetually lunging. The candle fluttered as he exhaled heavily through the slits of his nostrils. He gestured with an upturned palm.

Hagar was unsure whether he was indicating she should stand, or that she should pick up the gun. She chose the latter.

The pistol's grip was smooth, coated in a matte lacquer. She held the candle close to the lock plate. It was dusted in grains of fine black powder.

'Fingerprints?' she said.

'Just the deceased's,' said Kenner. 'And now yours, of course.' He let the innuendo hang. 'The victim wasn't shot, as far as we can tell. The gun was not fired. All four barrels are loaded.'

Hagar stared at the pistol. She lifted it to her nostrils and sniffed. Under the cellar's pervasive, faecal stink she detected a sharper, acrid scent – something like urine. Perhaps it was the smell of the spent fulminate charge, or the metal. She sniffed again, then caught Kenner watching her and put the gun down.

She pressed a knuckle to her lips. 'What smells so bad?'

Kenner swung his candle to reveal a bucket in the corner. 'The victim had been in the room for some time.'

Hagar glanced at the skeleton. 'Decades, at a guess.'

'You misunderstand. He was alive last night.'

She regarded the bones with new interest. She had thought the address looked familiar, though she had never been here personally. Could this be Dr Noroc? Had he been right all along?

The ache was spreading through her midriff, a liquid bruise. She phrased her next question carefully.

'Did he . . . live here?'

Kenner stared. She wondered if he had heard, then he said:

'The victim believed someone – or some coalition of persons – was trying to kill him. He had accused several . . . prominent citizens.'

'Let me guess. They're all in the running for Prefect?'

Kenner nodded. Hagar had spent some time catching up with Fat Maw civic law. The Prefect was elected by the city aldermen from one of their number. To qualify as an alderman you had to own property and rent your annual seat on the council. In practice, the only people who could afford to do so were the clique leaders – the Doyens, Doyennes or Doyennos. They took contributions from their members to buy their place on the Spire Council and, in return, they represented their clique's interests. Whoever they chose would take on administrative duties for the continent and would be made into Lord Jejunus' valet or handmaiden, just like Hagar.

'We thought he was mad,' said Kenner, 'but talk like that could be seen as seditious. An incitement to revolt. We put him under house arrest, for his own safety. We planned to keep him here until tomorrow, when the election is over.'

'You're saying he died a few hours ago.'

'That's right.'

'Sheriff. This is a skeleton.' She tongued the gap left by her missing canine. 'How can it be him?'

Kenner tilted his head back. He peered at her over the collars of his eyes, his face judderingly underlit.

He took a couple of clumping steps forward, his hooves crunching on the gritty stone floor. He lowered his candle and pointed at the bones.

'Bronze bracelet on left wrist. Damage to the left eye socket consistent with a known existing injury.' He gestured towards the corner. Candlelight gleamed off something small and round. 'Glass eye.'

'All easily faked.'

He snorted. 'It troubles me that you consider procuring an entire human skeleton easy.'

'People die, Sheriff. Bones are in plentiful supply and low demand.'

Kenner inhaled, the candle flame fluttering. 'The victim did not leave this room. The door locks and bolts from the inside.' He held the candle towards the lone exit. Hagar saw that part of the jamb had split; the sturdy iron bolt housing lay on the floor in a mess of splinters. 'We had to break it down to get in. There's no other entrance.' The candle flickered as he swept it about the cellar. 'The floor is stone, the walls and ceiling are solid.' He reached up and thumped the heavy black joist bisecting the ceiling. 'We had an officer posted at the top of the stairs. The victim didn't trust us to keep him safe. He insisted on barricading himself in the cellar.'

'Is there a room above this?'

'Yes. The kitchen. The officer could see it at all times.'

'Is it possible your officer did this?'

Kenner looked down at the floor, breathing in deep, ruminating tides.

'Yes. And I'm aware of the implications, given the current political climate. I'm holding him at the poste de police – partly in case of reprisals.' Kenner sighed. 'I don't believe it was him. Even if he had wanted to commit murder, I don't see *how*. The victim refused to open the door to us. He was armed and paranoid.'

Hagar glanced at the fallen skull, the blind shock in its sockets. 'When was the victim last seen alive?'

'Yesterday. But we heard him when the shifts changed. An officer knocked on the door. The victim refused to open it but he answered her questions. There's no other way out. Eight hours later, when the shifts changed again, the officer reported concerns the victim was not responding. We broke in and found the body.'

'What was left of it,' said Hagar. Pain was intensifying, a hot ache in her bones and organs. She steadied herself on the wall, concentrating on the texture of rough plaster, the immediacy of the sensation. It was real. It was hers.

'You seem uninterested in who the victim was.'

Hagar gritted her teeth. 'On the contrary.'

'It's as if you know already.' Kenner's tone was low and affectless.

She clawed at the wall. 'Damn . . . Wait!' Her heart was bursting. She felt the arteries in her left arm open up.

Suffering left in a cool rush. She stifled a gasp of pleasure. Morgellon had taken his dose for the morning. God bless you, Uncle.

She opened her eyes. The room had tipped onto its side. She was looking up at Kenner from the floor from where she had fallen. His face was a mask of disapproval.

'What's wrong with you?' he said.

'I suffer from fits.' She picked up her candle, which was still lit, and straightened it in its holder.

'Brought on by awkward questions?'

'Brought on by my bond with our Lord Jejunus.' She left an appropriately reverent pause. 'I experience the Grand-Duc's pain on his behalf. Sometimes it overwhelms me.' Especially when he delayed taking the medicine he was addicted to.

Sheriff Kenner glowered, but invoking the palace had the desired effect. Whatever he thought of her, the reality of her position, and a reminder of her true age, carried weight.

The heavy red ridge of his brow sank over his eyes. 'He was a doctor.' His jaw worked in slow circles. 'Which means he was a member of the leech clique. They're one of the weaker cliques, but on a day like today, an attack against even the most junior member may be viewed as a declaration of war. You see my problem.'

A pleasant torpor was spreading through Hagar's limbs. She felt giddy with it. Ecstatic.

'Must you solve it?' She spread her arms, revelling in the movement. She giggled. It was horrible, how Morgellon's moods bled into hers. Kenner must think her quite mad. 'Dispose of these bones. Say the doctor left town. By the time the truth gets out the election will be over.'

'I thought nuns didn't lie.'

'My vows forbid my telling a lie. Not from acknowledging the utility of one.'

Kenner contemplated this. 'Perhaps. Still.'

'Someone in this city can enter a locked, windowless cellar, subdue an armed man and strip the flesh from his bones.'

'Just so.' He inhaled through a closed fist. 'Can it be a coincidence? The Grand-Duc leaves the protection of his palace in Athanasia for the first time in generations. The day before his arrival, an assassin appears who can . . .' He swallowed, leaving the implied blasphemy unspoken. The rulers of the perpetuum were, officially, unkillable. 'I need to make progress.'

She caught an edge to the sheriff's glance. 'You think it was me, don't you?'

'It's one of the more palatable scenarios. You have a reputation. At least the Grand-Duc would be safe.' He turned his eyes to the ceiling. 'Ado's Salts?'

A memory surfaced. She grimaced, closed her eyes. With the expertise of centuries, she pushed it back under.

'What about them?'

'They eat flesh, don't they? Mixed with water. Might someone have flooded the room? There's a mousehole just behind you.'

Hagar turned. In the bottom of the plaster was a hole. She went down on her hands and knees and held the candle to it. She could not fit her hand inside. It appeared to go back just a few inches.

'I've some experience of them,' she said, 'and the answer's no. We'd smell them. Ado's Salts stink. Also, they'd have stripped the varnish off the stool's legs.' She gestured at the wooden stool beside the skull. 'And where would all the water and dissolved flesh go?' She glanced around. 'The floor slopes away from the hole and there's no drain.'

'Poison, then?'

'I've never encountered a poison that eats flesh. A touch of necrosis here and there, yes. Withered extremities. But not this.' She walked to the open door. It was a single piece of solid wood. She slid her palm up and down it, feeling for hidden panels. 'The simplest explanation is collusion between several officers.'

'But why strip the flesh from the bone? Why not shoot him through the head and claim he attacked them?'

Kenner was right. It was a disturbing development, so close to the Grand-Duc's arrival. She had considered many impediments to her plan, but not a second assassin. If they killed Morgellon, they killed her. And she had so much still to do.

'Return to the poste,' she said. 'Keep news of this contained. Let me make enquiries.'

'Oh no.' Kenner shook his head. 'Don't interfere.'

'Too late. You asked me here. I have a mandate. If the city is unsafe, the Grand-Duc won't come ashore tomorrow and the inauguration won't take place.' And her chance to bring him down would be gone forever.

'I'll deal with it.'

'And I'll help.'

He rested a palm on the iron rosette of his dagger.

'Perhaps public order would be best served if I threw you in jail.'

'Is that why you allowed me down here? To see if I'd confess?'

'You've not yet denied involvement.'

She cast a glance over the scattered bones. 'It pays to choose one's words wisely.'

Kenner's wet, pink eyes narrowed.

'News of this will be out in a matter of hours,' she said. 'Your officers are implicated. If you kick down doors, the Doyens will lie to you, then they'll order reprisals against whoever they think violated the treaty. They—' she almost said 'trust', '—tolerate me. I'm bound by the vows of my order. I already have what they're competing for. I could be the last honest person in Fat Maw.'

Kenner lifted the candle so it burned an inch from his snout. 'I'll warn you one last time. Leave the city. Go and never return.'

'You know I can't do that.'

'Then there's nothing more to say.'

He snorted. The flame extinguished.

Hagar felt dozens of pairs of eyes fall upon her as she entered the slaughterhouse. Doyenne Lesang approached across the filthy stone floor, swinging a spiked hammer.

'Hello, Hagar!' She smeared her hands across her apron, took the cigarette from her mouth and leaned in to kiss Hagar's cheeks. 'Did you have a nice festival? So rare to see you here at the yard! I thought you hadn't the time, what with all your, ah . . . duties. Will you take some tea?'

'No, thank you.' Blood sluiced through a channel between them, bubbling into a grate. The huge, glass-roofed slaughter area stank of dung, coppery raw flesh and cigarette smoke. Terrified whinnies and bellows echoed off the bricks, underscored by the thin, whispering *thwip* of scolders striking rumps with willow switches, scrapes and thumps and the crack of butchers' spades cleaving skulls, and a constant locusless chorus of merry whistling.

Lesang rested the head of her hammer upon the ground and turned to the scruffy, freckled harka beside her. 'Fetch me a brew, would you, Jib?'

'Yes, Doyenne.'

Lesang had thin, keen eyes, lit up by a great splash of white that ran from her cranial ridge to her muzzle. She was short by harka standards, with small, straight horns bracketing a spray of vanilla hair. Her apron came down to her shins and was filthy with gore. When she smiled, she showed all her teeth.

She flicked her cigarette into the drain and beckoned to Hagar. 'Walk with me.'

Hagar breathed through her teeth, trying not to taste the warm, rank air. No one knew more about meat off the bone than the flesh shambles clique.

Lesang strode on ahead, swinging her hammer, nodding to butchers as she passed. Elaborate stone archways were set into the walls, the capstones so worn that the once-fearsome visages carved into them had softened to a smooth, babylike innocence. Over a century and a half ago, enemies of the state had been tried here, the hearings brief, the judges masked. Though each trial had lasted little more than an hour, they had run back-to-back for months.

Goats were tied in rows to low wooden racks, their slashed throats bleeding into buckets. Hagar watched a sweating butcher grasp a goat by its beard, tilt its head back and slice into its windpipe with a cellist's grace. On the racks behind him, headless limbless torsos bucked and kicked their stumps. A boy straddled one and slit it from breast to belly. His long knife came out snared in rubbery white strands of sinew that lengthened and snapped. A cigarette jounced in the corner of his mouth.

'So,' Lesang said brightly, 'what can I help you with?'

Hagar had not been concentrating and tripped on a channel in the floor. She staggered a few paces, her boots skidding in slush. She regained her balance just as Lesang glanced back. 'Hagar?' The Doyenne's tone sharpened, not quite impatient, but chivvying.

'Last night there was an incident.'

'Didn't someone's attic catch on fire up by the spire? I suppose it was inevitable with all those fireworks.'

Hagar held her face still, trying not to betray surprise or nervousness.

'No, not that.'

'Something *else*?' Lesang's eyes widened. 'What's happened?'

Hagar watched Lesang for signs of dissembling.

'I've just come from a villa in the high town. This morning a doctor was found dead.'

Lesang let her mouth fall open. 'Murder?'

'All they left was a skeleton.'

'Goodness. That *is* strange.' Lesang turned and began walking forwards again. A severed goat's head whirled at her in a high arc from amongst the racks. She swung her hammer in a double-fisted backhand, connecting with a wet thump. It went tumbling back towards the thrower, trailing gore. Her workers sent up cheers and applause. She glanced back at Hagar, a little short of breath.

'You don't think . . .' Lesang broke off, sighed. 'No, I shouldn't say anything.'

Hagar saw an old, crook-backed harka collect the fallen head and toss it into a heap with the others. She glanced back at Lesang.

'I'd appreciate it if you did.'

'Well . . .' Lesang slowed until Hagar was at her side, then leaned in, lowering her voice. 'I wonder whether the crucibles might know a thing or two.'

'Crucibles?'

'Oh yes. I forget you're not a local.' Lesang let out a hoarse cackle, which cut off. 'The crucible clique. Chemists. You must have seen their headquarters, down on the quay, near the edge of the stilt city. Big smokestacks and a rainbow of chemicals pouring into the ocean. No mistaking the smell. I'm no expert but this death sounds alchymic, you know?'

Hagar pinched her brow, disguising a frown. Quite the supposition. 'Perhaps.'

Lesang straightened up and shrugged. 'Just a thought.' Her voice returned to its usual hearty volume. 'What an upheaval, eh? You can see how busy we are here – what with the festival just gone and the Grand-Duc's arrival tomorrow. Everyone's eating like the world's about to end.' A little black teardrop of clotting blood hung under her eye. 'Who do you think will win the vote?'

'Honestly, I don't think it matters.'

Lesang said something that was lost beneath the din of slaughter. She turned and began to walk backwards, clutching her hammer just beneath its head, passing it from hand to hand.

Hagar was feeling wheezy. Someone rattled past with a barrow of legs, whistling. The sound of terrified bleating built and built, then cut off.

Up ahead, a blinkered white mare was being led out of one of the tunnels, nickering and stamping. *And behold a pale horse.*

Lesang raised her hammer and hailed the butcher leading the animal. 'Morning, Trem. Mind if I take this one?' Up close, the mare was a yellowish ivory, slathered in filth up to its hocks. Probably Stokeham stock.

The butcher Trem had a bad eye and distended prognathic jaw. He gave a little grunt of assent and, nodding, handed her the horse's grubby halter. Lesang led the horse to the beginning of a channel in the floor. She set down her hammer and patted the horse's withers and the horse settled. She turned to Hagar. 'How strong are you?'

Hagar regarded Lesang's lean brown forearms, the lustrous bulk of living muscle. She glanced down at her own scrawny limbs, locked in perpetual juvenility.

'I surprise people.'

Lesang held out the halter. 'Would you like to help?'

Hagar hesitated. The mare scuffed its hooves on the stone. Lesang was waiting expectantly.

Hagar took the rope. It was heavier than she had anticipated, slightly greasy.

Lesang picked up her hammer. One face was flat; the other tapered to a long cylinder. She took a knife from her apron and dug about in the cylinder's hollow end, teasing out a plug of grey meat. Hagar felt the mare tug on its halter. Its nostrils flared as it sniffed its strange pungent surroundings.

'Now, Hagar, if you'd be so kind as to step this way. Get a good firm grip on its head.'

With a lingering sense of unreality, Hagar came closer, reached up and snaked her fingers through the rope nosepiece. The mare resisted, shaking its head.

'Shh shh shh.' Lesang rubbed the horse's nose, brushed back its dirty blond forelock. She stepped aside, out of the creature's range of vision. 'The saltpetres have designed a contraption with a little recessed bolt.' Her voice became soft and lilting. 'Uses gunpowder. Blasts a hole through the skull. Pop – and there you go. Takes all the love out of it.' She lifted her hammer and gently, almost tenderly, lowered the long tip until it was just above the creature's brow. The horse strained and flinched. Hagar clung on, her feet slipping. 'That's it, that's it.' Lesang kept the hammer perfectly still. 'We'll make the change, of course. Can't fight progress. But for me . . .' The horse began to settle. Lesang met its gaze. '. . . the real craft comes in disguising your intentions so well, she doesn't recognise the instrument of her destruction – even when it's right in front of her eyes.'

Lesang raised the hammer.

Hagar felt the mare's hot damp breaths against her knuckles. *And they had tails like unto scorpions, and there were stings in their tails.*

The hammer fell.

She felt the impact through her arm. The horse's legs tucked and the beast dropped, dragging her with it. She landed on her shoulder. Her hand was trapped in the bridle. The horse thrashed and convulsed and she felt each kick. Through the high glass ceiling the sun was white-gold, blazing.

Strong hands gripped her wrist. They unhooked her fingers. Another grabbed her collar and hauled her to her feet. The butcher Trem gave her a glance, then stepped round the bucking horse. He carved a long slit in its top lip and used the loose skin as a handle, wrenching the head back and dragging his knife across the throat. Blood gushed from the ragged hole, blush red. The mare pedalled its forelegs in slow, ersatz circles. Already another butcher was dragging a meathook on a long chain and attaching it to the animal's rear.

'Looks like you caught the worst of it, there,' said Lesang. The boy from earlier returned and handed her a steaming mug. 'Ah. Cheers, Jib.' She blew on it. 'Is it right that your order forbids eating meat?'

Hagar tried to brush the straw and excrement from her breeches, but found she was mostly spreading it, grinding it in. She spat on her gloves and rubbed them against each other. The stench wafted from her palms, vinegary, nauseating.

'Death is sacred,' she said.

Lesang sipped her tea. 'Do you ever resent it? Being his servant, for all time?'

Hagar wiped her hands on her gilet, considering her answer. 'It's all I know.'

Lesang held Hagar's gaze. Then she smiled.

'Hmm. Just wondered.' She drained her tea in a single steaming gulp. 'Well, good day to you, Hagar. Thank you for your news. Do give the other Doyens my regards . . . if you happen to see them.'

Hagar touched the brim of her hat, allowing her expression to harden for just an instant.

'Good day to you, Doyenne.'

Hagar felt threat roiling off Lesang like bloodsteam. The Doyenne held herself with a conqueror's ease.

A chain tightened and the white horse began to slide backwards across the slaughterhouse floor, its lips dragging, limp jowls trailing a black-syruped smear.

As the short, pale, human girl left the slaughterhouse, two harka sat at a wooden table across the wharf, smoking pipes.

Watching.

The girl tilted her black hat against the mid-morning sun. Lank sandy hair dangled from beneath the wide brim, spilling in clumps down the back of her cloak. She wore a padded gilet and riding breeches, heavy boots and a thick belt from which hung various small lacquered boxes. She looked no older than ten.

The first harka blew smoke from his nostrils. When he spoke, it was in Low Thelusian, with its slow, throaty cadences and grinding vowels.

'*Chi vis va, fra?*' See yon girl, brother?

'*Ja, fra.*' Aye, brother.

'*Sin neco.*' Kill her.

'*Ja, fra.*' Aye, brother.

The second harka – flat-skulled, boxy – upended his pipe into the ashpot and moved to rise. Two of his fingers were splinted together, bound in yellow gauze.

The first harka glanced up, his eyes wet and pink beneath thick, flaking lids.

In Low Thelusian, he said: 'It must look like a kill.'

'Rope, then.'

The first harka lifted his clay cup, pressed it into the hollow of his broad grey chin. 'No. A maid might hang herself from sorrow.'

'Aye, she might.' The second harka was watching a fat, filthy gansa that had landed in the water. The bird paddled between smashed barrel staves and oil rainbows, gnashing at the bloated rinds of discarded market fruit, gobbling them, flesh and all. 'But this world has no sorrow as would make a maid skin herself first.'

He moved his knife back and forth, flensing the air, the blade flipping and flashing like a miraculous fish.

The wind was low and the skiff-taxi crept sluggishly across the bay, lurching in the wake of steam ships, waves clapping against its hull.

On opposite spits of land, the great lenses of Fat Maw's twin lighthouses caught the sun and flared, refracting shafts of emerald, cinnabar, magenta.

The sea was a chalky, turbid green. She remembered the days when you could toss a silver duke from the stern of a caravel, peer over the taffrail and see it shining at the bottom of the bay. Schools of black fish used to whip through weeds in diamond formations while flat, boneless bottom-feeders shuffled across the seabed, breathing clouds of silt. Now all that lay beneath the surface was run-off from the industrial district and the browning bones of the drowned.

A trio of islands stood in the calm waters of the bay. Locally they were known as Les Trois Soeurs. The skiff was crawling towards the middle sister – the old jail.

Hagar stared at the rat.

The rat stared back. It was brown and improbably fat. It had wedged itself under the skipper's seat in the bow and sat on its haunches, twitching, alert.

'Does he normally ride with you?' she said.

'Eh?' The human skipper was lounging over the gunwale, trailing a bare foot in the water and eating a peach sweetheart left from the Festival of Tides. He was bony and tanned and one of his calves was inked with a picture of a blue taldin, tucking its wings in a hunting dive. He wiped honey from the corner of his mouth.

Hagar wrinkled her nose and nodded at the seat.

He bent down and peered between his legs. 'Oh! Nah. He's a freeloader.' The skipper remained doubled-over, his voice taking on an increasingly strangulated quality as blood rushed to his head. 'Look at that. Staring straight at us.' He pursed his lips and made a squeaking noise. 'Cocky bastard.' He sat back up, crimson-faced. 'Rats in this city been acting strange lately – coming out in broad daylight, snatching food right off your plate.' He took another bite of his sweetheart, batter crackling, juice streaming down his chin. 'I saw one in the market, squaring up to a fox, trying to steal its lunch.'

'Perhaps they've found a champion to rally around.' Hagar tipped her hat forward and lay back against the prow. A ship's bell rang across the calm water.

'Dad told me it's a sickness.'

She ignored him, hoping he would take the hint.

'You know,' he said, apparently taking her lack of response as encouragement, 'like the roaches sent. Back in the . . . what do you call 'em. The old wars. When the insects made people sick.'

'Yes. I've heard those stories.'

'The rats get this disease – in the water or whatever – and they lose all their fear. They don't care if they die.'

'Sounds like a blessing.'

The skipper hissed. 'If you don't fear death, pretty soon, death comes for you.'

'Yes. That's the blessing.'

Hagar dozed off for a few moments and awoke to the skiff's prow knocking gently against a wooden pontoon. A human soldier stood on the bare planks in the dark green uniform of the Jejunus Palace Garde du Corps, her repeater carbine held loose at her hip. Behind her was a small cove, disguised by a crease in the cliffs. The soldier spoke to the skipper:

'Stay in the boat.' The soldier held out a palm; he tossed her the coiled-up painter. She crouched and secured it to a mooring post. 'Miss Ingery. Would you please step onto the platform.'

The old jail sat on a table of land rising from the bay in skirts of sheer grey rock. Even in the sunshine, the island had a character that steered the soul irresistibly towards thoughts of perdition. Its stark, aloof geography had suggested a jail long before tall watch-towers and grim buttresses emerged to formalise its duties. Gibbets had once hung from the western turrets, greeting ships with an edifying message about acceptable standards of conduct within the city limits. Morgellon had ended the practice after just a few decades, ostensibly on the grounds of public decency.

In truth, Hagar suspected it had offended his sense of spectacle. Birds had learned to associate the clang of the executioner's bell with the arrival of food, flocking round the gibbets in thick, squalling clouds. A corpse would have scarcely cleared the parapet before a liquid mass of gulls and taldins fell upon it, pecking, rending, shrieking. The weight of birds would snap the rope and send the body plunging into the sea. During the heyday of the Wind and Thunder Faction, executions had been so frequent that the walls and turrets of the western towers were blasted white with droppings. Corpses had mounted up on the ocean floor, attracting colonies of carnivorous seaworms. Fisherfolk shared stories of slicing open a giant eel's belly to find a human, vesperi or harka eye staring out. Some said certain priests of the Six-Ways prized them as delicacies.

To see, as one's ship entered the bay, a line of broken gibbets and a jailhouse crusted with excrement inspired neither fear nor respect. *We are capricious and incompetent*, the ragged black tassels had seemed to say. *Even in death, criminals escape us.* Morgellon had learned one of this fallen world's most important lessons: that public suffering, no matter how grotesque, bestowed upon its recipient a talismanic dignity.

Death was redemptive. In the moment the neck snapped or the executioner's axe bit through the spine, the debt was repaid – thus the crowd found themselves gazing at the shattered body of a sinless being.

Camps, mines, the labour fields – in denying criminals death, they denied them salvation. Fatalities were slow, incidental and distant. No one sang folksongs about corrupt aldermen succumbing to pneumonia after digging pit latrines in the snow. No one valorised the serial counterfeiters shovelling gravel to line long rural roads in northern Thelusia. No one noticed the convicts who, a year or two years into their terms, simply disappeared.

The skiff slewed deliciously as Hagar placed one foot on the pontoon. She wobbled, reached out to the soldier for support. The soldier frowned, kept both hands on her gun.

Hagar regained her balance, brought her second foot onto the pontoon.

'Please relinquish all weapons,' said the soldier.

Hagar took her silver pistol from her jacket pocket. She opened the breech, showed the soldier that both barrels were empty, then handed it to her, grip-first. She gave the soldier her jacket. The soldier rummaged through the inside and hip pockets and patted down the lining. She dropped the jacket on the deck beside her. She repeated the process with Hagar's hat, groping round the lining, checking the hat band, experimentally flexing the brim. Then she had Hagar take off her boots.

It was trivially easy to keep the soldier from finding her dagger, using sleight of hand to wedge it blade-down between the planks of the pontoon, hiding the exposed pommel under the ball of her foot, then retrieving it when she retied her boots.

'You have an hour,' said the soldier, stepping aside.

In the cove the air was shady and cool. Her boots scraped on pebbled mortar. There was a doorway cut into the rock, with empty crates stacked outside and a stairway leading up. Hagar glanced back over her shoulder, then began the climb.

The gatehouse was open. She walked beneath the portcullis. She glanced up and saw gull chicks sleeping in a nest of matted seaweed woven over the rafters.

In the courtyard, a young man – really a boy – glanced up from his digging. He was shirtless and had red hair. Hagar averted her eyes, but he seemed unashamed.

'All right,' he said.

The entire courtyard had been divided into plots of soil, from which various green shoots and knuckled buds were emerging. From somewhere deep inside the old jail came a steady purr.

Hagar spoke with a palm shielding her face. 'Is she—'

'Upstairs.' Through her fingers she could see the boy leaning on his spade. 'She's expecting you.'

He went back to his digging. Hagar could see the links of his spine through his pale freckled skin.

She stepped through a low doorway into the south wing. Since her last visit, more contraband paintings had appeared in the stairway, hanging from heavy steel pins driven into the stone. They were buckled and yellow with water damage, curling at the corners, held flat by their frames. Some were shockingly indecent. One showed a beaming woman with golden-brown hair in nothing but pink underwear, her arms raised towards the sun. There was writing on the picture: *LET YOUR BODY BREATHE. Achieve LISSOM GRACE and*

PERFECT HEALTH in AERTEX CORSETRY. The newest, heavily creased with a diagonal tear, was teal and red and navy blue. It showed the head and shoulders of a dour man with thick eyebrows, above a single word: *HOPE*.

Little indulgences from sympathisers were proper for a resident of this stature, decades of house arrest representing, in perpetuum terms, no more than a dignified sabbatical. She gazed upon the strange artefacts with their cryptic messages. She had visited England, years ago – many times, in fact. That particular threshold had been destroyed, of course. Where these tatty curios were coming from she did not much care. She could not understand the pull some felt towards the old world. It was a drab and fallen place.

Stairs wound up into the tower and down into the dungeons. Hagar headed up.

The purring grew louder.

Through corroded iron bars, she glimpsed fishing junks in the bay, the busy quayside, the northern lighthouse glinting on its narrow hook of land. From this height, the sea looked glassy, green and calm; she could imagine swimming back to shore. Such was the allure of the material world – a trap designed to look beautiful from Heaven.

With the final steps Hagar found herself leaning into each stride, huffing. Her legs quivered. She passed an oval looking-glass nailed to the bare stone wall and, for an instant, was sure someone was watching her.

She froze, her whole body tingling with the instinct she had cultivated over decades during her time with the order. Foolishness, of course. She had merely glimpsed her reflection. Her nostrils twitched at the familiar scent of incense.

At the top of the tower, she emerged in a round room. A woman was sitting in a wicker chair beside the window, looking out to sea.

Her blond hair flowed into a long Dutch braid, winding twice round her torso, hip to shoulder like a sash, before trailing over the back of the chair, almost to the floor. She wore a white cotton dress that came down to her ankles. The chair creaked as she turned.

'Back so soon?' she said. Her right arm was swaddled in linen.

'Hello, Patience.'

A circular blue rug edged with tassels covered most of the floor. Spilling from a set of oak bookshelves, volumes lay eccentrically catalogued in ones and pairs and stacks around the room. More were piled up on a writing desk, bookmarked with strips of paper or ribbons or string. In the centre of the desk was an intricate, insectile device comprised of metal and levers, fronted with tiers of black teeth, like tiny organ keys with letters on them. It was a sort of miniature printing press.

The purring had become a steady buzz reverberating through the ceiling.

Patience DeGroot stepped from the chair and padded, barefoot, onto the rug's thick pile. 'I don't suppose you brought me the newspapers?'

She meant contraband ones: the *New York Times*, *Le Monde*, the *Telegraph*. Dispatches from Patience's old home. Chronicles of strange, unhappy people in strange, unhappy clothes, who believed they were utterly alone in the universe, who thought their petty disputes the central business of existence. Hagar shook her head.

Patience's shoulders sank, but she kept her pinched smile. 'Well,' she said, 'you made it.' She stopped in the middle of the carpet, her covered arm swinging at her side. 'And that is something.'

Around the room, incense smoked in small bronze braziers. There were far more chairs than one person needed.

'So,' said Patience. 'Two visits in as many weeks.'

Hagar prodded the front of her palate with her tongue, tracing the ridged capillaries. There was something guarded in Patience's manner – a wariness she was trying her best to disguise.

'It's been three weeks.'

'Ah.' A book lay open, facedown, on the carpet: *A Brief History of Time*. Patience nudged it with her toe. 'Time flows a little differently here on Elba.'

Hagar did not correct her on the island's name. Patience always talked in these half-riddles, wandering in and out of lucidity. Probably the isolation. Or homesickness.

'Did you kill him?'

Patience flinched. 'Who?'

Hagar could not help but smile. That there might be more than one answer was telling.

'The doctor who died in the high town last night.'

Her human hand smoothed the white folds of her linen-bound angel-arm. 'You're very direct.'

'When expedient. Lying is a kind of violence to progress, don't you agree?'

'If we're going to joust can we at least do it in the sunshine?' Patience gestured towards a final flight of stone steps. 'After you.'

Hagar climbed, opened a hatch and emerged into the heat of the midday sun. Encircled by the rough-hewn battlements, two canvas-backed chairs sat on either side of a box covered with a sheet. The source of the snarling noise was an odd little engine, puttering inside a red metal frame on wheels. A dirty white cord snaked from its rear, leading to a glass cube lit from within. Hagar bristled with discomfort. More contraband from across the threshold.

Patience appeared beside her. She was about Hagar's height, and the sudden proximity of her face made Hagar's neck hair stand endwise.

'When I heard you were coming, I put the icebox on.' Patience had to raise her voice to be heard over the motor. 'Are you thirsty?'

'Mm.'

Patience walked to the engine and pressed something. The snarl dropped off and it stopped shuddering.

'It runs on corn oil. Powers our little heater come winter.' She patted the handle. 'Now, I was saving this for a special occasion.' She knelt at the icebox and opened the glass door with her human hand. The sides of the box were badly scuffed and faded, but Hagar could make out the remains of some heraldic design – two bulls' heads clashing against a yellow sun. She thought they might be supporters from the coat of arms of the defunct eastern harka dynasty, Haus Rinderpest. Patience took out a ribbed glass bottle full of black liquid.

Hagar started. Bottled godstuff? To drink the very *substance* of the thresholds was worse than a mere peccadillo. Then it caught the light and she saw how the liquid turned burnt copper, how thin it was.

Patience took two glass tumblers from the icebox and placed them on the box table. She held a bent piece of metal between her teeth and used it to uncap the bottle. The bottle hissed. She poured measures into each tumbler, the liquid foaming. A brown scum formed on the top of the drinks, then gradually evaporated. Patience added liquid to the tumblers until the bottle was empty. When she put it down, Hagar noticed it was crimped at the middle, like a godfly.

Patience picked up one of the tumblers and held it out for Hagar. 'Here. Don't worry – it's not booze. Sorry it's not as cold as I'd hoped.'

Hagar took the drink. It fizzled and spat in her hands. She followed Patience to the battlements and they looked through an embrasure, back towards Fat Maw. As you looked south, the buildings grew bigger and sturdier, until the stilt city merged with the industrial district and the low town. Behind smokeries, slaughterhouses and brickworks, the high town rose in a mazy snarl of white render and terracotta eaves, its summit capped with the thin silver stiletto of Mitta's Spire.

'I don't know any doctor,' said Patience, pausing to sip, 'and it wouldn't matter if I did, because I haven't murdered anyone.'

Hagar stared down into her drink. She lifted it towards her lips and a perfume of cold needling droplets ghosted her nose.

'That's a shame.'

'I'm telling you the truth.'

'That's what I mean. If you had killed this doctor to settle some personal score, or to stir up mischief on behalf of a clique, or out of sheer boredom, I'd consider his death just. Frankly, I'd be relieved.'

'Tell me more,' said Patience. 'Perhaps something will come back to me.'

Hagar took a sip of her drink. It burned. Stinging cascaded down her throat and pushed up through her sinuses like a mustard rush. She coughed and winced and her eyes watered.

'Villa in the high town. Man locked himself in a cellar. As far as the Sheriff knows he was no one of consequence, but any death of a clique member, this close to the vote . . . You understand, of course. We found him this morning, stripped to a skeleton. No way in or out.'

'Ah. This is why I'm a suspect.'

'Isn't it true you can reach through walls?'

Patience gave her wrapped angel-arm a squeeze. 'Theoretically, yes. But I can only reach for things I can see.'

'You can see the high town from this tower.'

Patience thinned her lips, as if she thought Hagar was being fatuous. 'Well, yes, in the broadest sense that's true. But I believe you said your murder took place in a cellar. I haven't got x-ray vision.'

Hagar tried another sip of the queer acidic drink. This time, the shock was less pronounced. Behind the prickling pangs, she tasted an intense, cloying sweetness. Her jaw clenched.

'What about your valet?'

'Reggie?'

'Can you reach for things he sees?'

Patience sighed. 'What difference would it make? Neither of us are allowed to leave the island. And I can't deposit things or people. Only retrieve them.'

Centuries of watching her speech for falsehoods had made Hagar unusually alert to them, and she fancied she sensed one now, or at least an evasion.

'Is he your only servant?'

'He's not my servant.' Patience rolled her eyes. 'And I didn't kill your doctor.'

There it was again.

'Perhaps you're not as limited as you would have me believe.'

Patience laughed, throwing her head back. 'Limited? *Limited?*' She raised her angel-arm and its linen bindings unravelled. The flesh beneath was rippling, expanding. Creamy-mauve filaments twisted from the pulsing mass, flowing upwards as if through invisible tubes. Hagar backed up against the battlements. Thickening strands helixed around a central column. The arm mushroomed ten feet, twenty. Taut webs of tendon-like matter anchored themselves to the floor and battlements. Blood vessels bulged and branched, burrowing fat blue counter patterns. White lymph wept from the mouths of yawning fistulae. An elaborate basketwork of cartilage was expanding, jawing open like a terrible flower.

It held there, swaying – a great thornbush of living flesh some thirty feet high, spinnakers of skin bellying in the breeze.

Hagar gripped her tumbler, white finger-links flattening and swelling against the glass. The meat tree hung over her, held in place by guy ropes of sinew, sweating. Patience looked at her sidelong.

With a snap, the flesh retracted. The tower was empty.

When Hagar looked, Patience stood with her right arm clenched into a perfectly human fist.

'I've had decades of solitude to explore just how limited I am.'

She let the arm drop. The fingers lost their shape and fused. The palm smoothed. In moments, it was a featureless fleshy club.

She picked up her black drink and drained the glass.

'I know why you and your master spared me, when I arrived in Avalonia, all those years ago,' she said. She steadied herself on the crate. 'It's the same reason the perpetuum has a taboo against female peers taking male helpers. Don't try to deny it. I've had plenty of time to study my history. Anwen was right. They're terrified of us. It's the antipeer, isn't it?' Hagar felt herself flinch at the forbidden word. 'If a peer and her valet conceive. That's who Anwen's daughter was. She had some kind of power you're all scared of.' Hagar tried to hide her shock. Anwen was the one who had given Patience her powers. Had she told Patience about Sarai's likely talents, too? Surely Patience was guessing.

'But Reggie and I aren't . . .' Patience took a moment to compose herself, straightening her hair. 'Tell him. Tell Morgellon. There's no chance of our producing what he seeks.' Her expression hardened. 'Why do you serve him, Hagar? After all this time? Why do you fawn when he despises you so much?'

Hagar closed her eyes. She knew the answer. It was the same one Mr Loosley had given her, not so far from here, a human lifetime ago.

She looked up. 'When you lived in England, did you know a girl called Delphine?'

A flinch. The reaction lasted a split-second – Patience was clearly accustomed to masking her feelings – then she recovered, and a moment later she was making a show of looking puzzled.

'I'm sorry?'

'Before you received the honours and came to Avalonia. Did you know anyone by the name of Delphine?'

Patience dipped her head. She sighed – a deliberate, theatrical sigh. An attempt to misdirect.

'That was a long, long time ago.'

'What can you tell me about her?'

Another micro-expression, the briefest hint of discomfort. 'I don't remember much. What do you want to know?'

'Everything.'

Patience looked up, perhaps judging how much she should disclose. She took a deep breath.

'She was the daughter of an artist called Gideon Venner. He came to us at Alderberen Hall in 1935.'

'Us?'

'Spim. The Society for the Perpetual Improvement of Man. He joined us because he was ill. Mentally, I mean. Used to spend all his time painting in the stables or sitting in our little meetings looking like this.' She pushed out her bottom jaw and pantomimed a glower. 'To be honest, I didn't see much of her. She was only a child. Always hanging around with the groundsman. Henry, I think his name was? She found out about the threshold, in the end. Stood up to Anwen. The last time I saw her, she shot me in the face.'

Hagar nodded. That was a detail she could believe.

'She didn't like you?'

Patience rolled her eyes. 'I don't think she meant it as a compliment. Anyway, she must be dead now. Guess that's true of everyone I knew on Earth.' She laughed unconvincingly. 'Anyway . . . where did you hear that name? In an old newspaper or something?' She was trying to make the question sound offhand, but her whole body language screamed avoidance, fear.

Hagar hesitated. There was something more here – not just uncomfortable memories. A thread to be pulled. Something hidden.

From the cliffs below came the faint, dissonant clang of a bell.

Patience held herself tight, alert. 'Oh. That's time, I guess.'

Hagar almost lingered. But she knew the consequences of violating the terms of Patience's house arrest. Even as a member of the palace, she could be locked up or ejected from the city. Shot, even. Kenner was itching for an excuse.

Besides, she had an appointment to make.

On her way back towards her lodging house, Hagar noticed three human men following her. She slipped into an alley. Two more were waiting for her.

They were big, with scarves pulled up over their faces. Hagar turned and the other three had cut off her exit.

The alley was cramped but she supposed she ought to give a convincing account of herself.

'Hello, gentlemen,' she said, reaching slowly for her blade. 'I take it you've heard stories of my cruelty?'

The men drew leather saps and billy clubs.

Hagar sprinted and launched herself off the wall, dropping her heel onto the bridge of the first man's nose. She felt the crunch. Blood splattered down his white tunic. He recoiled, hollering.

The man behind him swung with his sap. Hagar ducked, sidestepped the tediously inevitable backfist, then drove the point of her knife into his windpipe. A shadow fell over her from behind.

She threw herself flat against the wall. The first blow swished through air. A club thumped into her hip. She dropped into a simple but superficially impressive stance from the theodic kata: the fool's pact. The thug behind her pounded his sap into her shoulder.

They had adapted, abandoning attempts at a big, knockout blow in favour of quick strikes to her limbs that reduced her mobility. Clever. She shimmied from side to side, ripening bruises taking the edge off her form. She had not gone down easily. That was the main thing.

The next blow dropped her to her knees. Strong damp hands twisted her arms behind her back. A leather hood fell over her head. The drawstring pulled tight, cutting off her prayers at the throat.

CHAPTER 3

WHEN THE DEVIL DRIVES

Meshes of light scrolled across the mask, growing brighter, distorting.

For an instant, she saw it all: the high golden cheekbones; the leering, merry mouth; the semicircular eye sockets. The van rocked gently as the car passed, the interior falling into near-blackness.

Delphine listened to the car fade. Her heart was pounding. The back of the van smelt of mud and motor oil. Rain drummed the roof. The driver was doing a steady forty or fifty on winding country roads. Her shoulder blades compressed against the plywood panelling as the van took a corner.

'Sorry we had to meet like this.'

The voice was nasal and precise. If she detected a tremor, perhaps it was the rumble of the van. He was sitting opposite her, though she could only make out his silhouette and the tips of his long, slender fingers, steepled.

She tried to think. Adrenaline was surging through her system. The front seats were too high to climb over. Were the rear doors locked? Doubtful.

'You're not in any danger,' he said. 'I didn't want to be there if the police arrived. Perhaps you were bluffing.'

Delphine breathed through her nostrils, waiting for her eyes to adjust. The wipers squeaked.

'Who are you?'

'Call me Butler.'

'Mr Butler—'

'Not Mr Butler, or Butler something. It is just Butler.'

She dug her fingernails into her palms. The pain brought her round. Come on now. She wasn't some wide-eyed child.

'What do you want?' she said.

Behind the mask, the figure cleared his throat. 'That rather depends. What do *you* want, Mrs Venner?'

Delphine gripped the curved brass head of her cane, steadying herself as the van climbed a hill. He knew her name. Not a conventional burglary, then. Something worse.

'Ms.' She tried to disguise her fear with a sigh. 'And I'm a very old, very tired, very intolerant woman. My stroke medication is lying on the kitchen cabinet and I need to urinate. What I want is to go home.'

'Vesperi. Avalonia. The honours.'

He recited the words like an incantation. Ice water trickled down her heart.

'Where—'

'Your email.'

Her stomach cramped. She had forgotten sending it. This was some unhinged fellow from her mailing list. He had read her message and he was vulnerable and he had seen some kind of embedded command. Stupid, stupid, stupid.

'How many people did you send it to?' he said.

'I don't know.' Her mouth had gone dry. The truth might make him angry. 'A few.' She reckoned near a hundred.

'Harka. Threshold. The perpetuum.' The mask tilted forward in the darkness. 'Is that what you were hoping to hear?'

Tingles ran down the nape of her neck. This was no ordinary crank.

She nodded.

'Good,' he said. 'Now. If you can answer a few questions, I'm sure you've some you'd like to ask me.'

Her skin prickled. What if they were after Martha?

'Was your father Gideon Venner?' he said.

She took a deep breath. 'Yes.'

'And he was resident in Alderberen Hall from 1934 to 1935?'

'It must have been around then, yes.'

'Did you ever visit him at the Hall?'

'We lived there with him.'

'Who?'

'Me and Mother.'

The seat creaked as the figure shifted. 'You would have been a child at the time.'

'I was.'

'And what did you see while you were there?'

Flashes of black wings against a summer sky, her father burning. She had felt it all these years – the wrecking ball ending its long upswing, fat with potential energy; the gun on the mantelpiece; the debt in the heart. She had known it would come for her in the end.

'Horrific creatures from another world.'

His steepled fingers separated, balled into fists. 'Go on.'

'Bat-things – vesperi, they were called. They came through a gateway hidden on the estate – a pool of black water. The "threshold". Lord Alderberen's mother, Anwen, came through it. She had been given a power called the honours. You had to be stung by a special insect – a godfly. It meant she didn't age or die or feel pain. I shot her and blew her up with a grenade, but she survived and her wounds healed.' Delphine glanced up. 'You think I'm senile, don't you?'

The mask nodded with the motion of the van. 'I'm not a doctor, Ms Venner. Did Anwen say why she'd come to England?'

'She said they'd kidnapped her daughter.'

'"They" being?'

'Lord Alderberen and a man called Mr Propp. He was a sort of . . . guru. He ran things at the Hall.'

'And what happened then?'

'Well . . . I killed some people. And my dear friend Henry rigged the chamber containing the threshold with explosives. He disappeared. I got out just before the whole place went up. My father was in there with Anwen. I don't know what happened to them either. Either they died in the blast, or they escaped through the threshold to Avalonia.'

'Was the threshold destroyed?'

'Oh, utterly. I'm sure of it. We—' She caught herself. Don't mention Martha. 'I checked it, years later. The MOD took over the grounds during the war. No, it was the CID back then. Anyway, they didn't seem to realise it existed. Nothing there but a mound of dirt. Henry was very thorough. Said he'd set the charges so the lake flooded it.'

'I see.' The van slowed as it approached a junction. Delphine could feel the exhaust vibrating through the soles of her feet. 'And do you know of any other routes to the other world?'

She thought of Algernon and the other lanta, their disappearance. Her decades of work. Her leads.

'None whatsoever.'

The figure visibly sagged. He let out a sigh.

'Thank you.' He rolled his shoulders. 'You've been honest and to the point and that has made this whole process much easier.'

Delphine straightened up a little. 'Now, Butler, I've some questions for you.'

In the dark she could not quite see what he was doing. He was holding his right hand up and appeared to be pulling at each of his slender fingers in turn.

'Yes, yes,' he said distractedly. 'Fire away.'

'I've been searching all my life. You're the first person I've met who *knows* something. Just tell me – have you found a way through? A threshold?'

Something black fluttered in the air between them. He had whipped off a glove.

'If you wouldn't mind tilting your head back juuust . . . a . . . touch . . .' His hand was moving towards her face.

Delphine flinched. 'What are you doing?'

'You're one of very few people alive on this planet party to a colossal secret.' Up close, she saw that his ungloved fingers were freakishly long. 'A dangerous one, frankly. But you're no threat to us. I think it's best that you forget this meeting.'

'What's that supposed to—'

'My apologies for disrupting your evening. We'll make sure you're returned to your house safe and sound.'

As his hand closed in, a light seemed to coalesce round his fingertips.

She lifted her cane.

'Hit me if it makes you feel better,' he said, making no attempt to defend himself. 'I don't mind. I'm sorry I can't help you. Truly.'

'Fine.' She pulled the cane away a bit. 'But will you pass on a message?'

He paused. 'What?'

She swung and clubbed the driver.

The cane's heavy brass head connected with his temple. He cried out. She yanked, hooking his eye. He punched the horn, swerved. The tyres skidded. Delphine lurched forward into Butler.

She pressed her face into his mask. 'No . . . *surrender.*'

The van's back end swung out. She grabbed his collar and let herself fall with the momentum. Her head whacked the wooden floor. He was on top of her. The van clattered over ruts. He slipped and she rolled. They tumbled over and over till he boomed into the rear doors.

He grasped at her jaw with long, rough fingers. She drove her cane into the mask's eye socket. The plastic split. He clutched at the hole.

The crack and splinter of branches. The van fishtailed. They hit a rut side-on. The floor bucked. Delphine grabbed the door handle.

The whole vehicle tipped.

Gravity shifted. For a second, Butler rose weightless, then he faceplanted into the panelled wall with a sickening crunch. She landed heavily on top of him. The windscreen blew out. The van shuddered, clattered. Its body howled with the whale song of stressed metal. She slammed back-first into the bench seat. They were skidding, spinning. She clutched at the bench's steel frame but her fingers slipped; they were wet. A series of impacts shook them from beneath. The horrible scraping sound eased to a tidal hiss, the sucking, fading backwash of pebbles in spume. Then it stopped.

The van lay on its side, indicator ticking. She smelt undergrowth, diesel. They were still.

Delphine rolled onto her shoulder. A splintering pain filled her elbow. She breathed, waiting for it to pass. Booze was probably taking the edge off.

Strange lattices of moonlight webbed the van's interior. She could just make out Butler facedown against the panelled wall, his arms splayed. Under his jacket, his shoulder blades were bulging out at grotesque angles.

She eased herself onto all-fours. Her left wrist hurt terribly – she could not make a fist.

A rustle from the front seat.

'Sir?' It was the driver. He sounded drunk. He snorted wetly, spat. 'Sir? Are you . . . ugh.' More rustling. She glanced over her shoulder. He was engulfed by the fat white mushroom of the airbag. 'Wait. I'm coming back.' The click of his seatbelt unfastening.

Gingerly, she began crawling towards the back doors. She was shaking with adrenaline. She inched past Butler, taking care not to nudge him. The driver shifted in his seat, moaning at some blossoming injury as he struggled with the door.

A snuffling noise came from behind the mask. Delphine held her breath. The noise stopped.

At least he was alive. She reached the back doors. Wincing, she squeezed the door handle. She lifted the top door then eased the lower one down onto the wet grass.

The night was fragrant with rain. They were at the bottom of a hill. The tail lights picked out a shining path of gouged earth and flattened grass. Jesus. They must have skidded forty feet.

She plunged her cane into the damp earth and hauled herself onto her knees. Placing a palm against the van, she struggled to her feet. The snuffling noise came again, louder. She turned. Butler was dragging himself out of the van, panting.

'Well.' He stood, brushing dirt from his palms. 'That's a nuisance.'

'Don't move.'

Butler cocked his head. Cracks forked the mask's gold plastic.

'Now why on earth would I comply?'

Delphine licked her dry lips and tried to ignore the pain in her wrist. 'Because my friend is holding your driver at gunpoint.'

'You can't honestly think I'd—'

'It's true, sir.' The voice came from the grass behind him. The driver was on his hands and knees beside the upturned rear wheels. Blood dripped from his nose. A pistol was pressed to the side of his head.

Butler turned to look.

'I said *don't move*,' said Delphine.

The pistol muzzle twisted itself against the driver's temple.

He grimaced. 'Don't shoot! Don't shoot!' She couldn't place his accent.

Butler looked back at Delphine. He was lit from behind by the tail lights, a tall silhouette framed with vapour rising from the sodden grass.

'You wouldn't hurt him,' he said.

'Martha, give me the gun.' There was a swirling in the mist beside the driver; the pistol dipped then flew through the air. Delphine caught it. 'Thank you, darling.' She hefted it in her hand. Black steel with a chequered grip. She pressed the catch on the toe of the pistol butt and checked the magazine. Fully loaded. Martha was such a treasure. She slapped the magazine back into place with the heel of her palm and aimed at Butler's head. 'I'm not a reasonable woman, Mr Butler.'

'It's just B—'

She squeezed the trigger. The pistol kicked and put a hole in the back door. Butler flinched.

'Reckless, in many ways.' Blood ran hot in her veins. Something about the weight of the gun made her feel younger. 'Exceptionally petty.'

The rear lights lit rain falling diagonally.

Butler spoke in a low snarl: 'What do you want?'

'Take me to Avalonia.'

'All right,' he said.

For a moment, she thought she had misheard. She had expected resistance.

'Good,' she said.

Rain dripped from the mask. The cracks widened and shrank with his breathing.

'I'll have to call for a pick-up,' he said.

'Do whatever you have to.'

'The phone's in the front of the van.'

'Where precisely?'

'Glove compartment.'

'Would you, darling?' Delphine gestured with the pistol.

She waited. The clatter of glass crystals – Martha walking through the smashed windscreen. Moments later, a silver flip-phone drifted round the side of the van. It floated to Delphine's hip and stopped, a foot off the ground. She twisted her cane into the dirt so it stood upright when she let go. Keeping the gun trained on Butler's chest, Delphine reached with her free hand and took the phone.

Butler was staring at the space beside her. His arms went slack. 'Is that . . .'

From beneath the mask came a sound like the *pop-pop* of radio static, like someone blowing bubbles in milk with a straw, like ripping.

That noise. The blood seemed to flow away from her skin. Monsoon rumble filled her ears.

A dry, ratcheting *rik-ik-ik*. Martha was answering. A short exchange followed, clicks and chitters that dipped in and out of audible range. What on earth was she playing at? Delphine glanced at the pistol, checking it was still there. Her fingertips had gone numb.

At her hip, vapour bulged and twisted. Motion blur wafted away, starting at Martha's antennae, working down her armoured hull to her hooked feet.

'No!' Delphine hissed.

'My apologies,' said Butler, reaching for his mask. 'Had I known the company you kept.' He performed a curt half-bow and closed his fingers round the damaged portion of mask. It shattered like a poppadom. He straightened up, shards of plastic dropping away.

Red-lustred fur. Half a grin of intermeshed spiny fangs. Moist frills of cartilage fanning out from a nostril slit. A yellow eye with a black pit.

He pushed back his hood, revealing tall ears with coral-pink interiors.

She stared in cold horror. In disbelief. She understood what those deformities on his back were now. Wings.

'I expect you assumed I was human. Surprise.' He raised an arm, extending his slender fingers. 'Take all the time you need to adjust. In the meantime, pass me the phone and I'll have someone bring a car.' She saw now the short black fur, the unnatural length. 'Ms Rao will be keen to meet you.'

A vesperi.

She almost fired. She saw herself doing it, the bullet punching through his breastbone, his body hitting the van, the second, third shots, the way his corpse would buck, the fragments of skull and brain matter.

She felt a tug at her trouser pocket. When she glanced down, Martha was looking up, her eyes pulsing an aqueous green.

Martha raised a fist and bopped it twice for *yes*.

Delphine exhaled heavily. She looked at Butler.

'All right.' She tossed the phone underarm. Butler snatched it out of the air with shocking deftness. 'But if you try anything, I *will* shoot you.'

'I believe you wholeheartedly.' He flipped open the phone. 'I am, after all, a "horrific creature from another world".' He glanced at Martha. 'And you know what we're like.'

A car came within the hour. Butler drove.

They purred down empty B roads at a steady fifty-five, headlights on full beam, illuminating spectral winter oaks, lone telegraph poles, the slumped shell of a caravan. He wore his hood up over his ears, a red scarf covering the lower half of his face.

Delphine sat in the passenger seat, the pistol in her lap. It had a long black barrel like a Luger – you might mistake it for one, at a distance. Finnish-made, built for harsh winters. Reliable but heavy. A smart choice by Martha. She ran her thumb over the manufacturer's logo moulded into the grip, keeping the barrel tilted towards Butler's stomach.

'There's really no need to do that,' he said, out of the corner of his mouth.

So strange to hear the creature speak. She had fragmented memories of Mr . . . what was the name? Loxley? A gristly, brutish vesperi who had worked for Anwen as a bodyguard. All the others she had encountered had been children – short, lithe, still able to fly. Her eyes kept alighting on the twitch of his lozenge-shaped pupils as he scanned the road. Her brain resisted processing him as a person.

'I'll be the judge of that.' Shimmering transparencies swam at the corners of her vision. She kept fighting the urge to nod off.

She lowered the electric window, bringing herself round with a blast of cold air. Martha, who had been dozing in the back, started at the whirr as the pane dropped, her antennae blowing backwards. The dark fields smelt of moist earth, slurry. Soon it would be dawn.

'Where are you taking us?' she said.

'To our base of operations.'

'Where's that?'

Butler glanced across at her, his yellow eyes like uncut citrines. 'If I tell you that, you might shoot me before we arrive.'

'I shall try to restrain myself.'

'Not good enough. I'm sure you and Martha appreciate the need for discretion.'

Condensation streamed down the windows. Delphine rested her head against the wet, freezing glass. She felt herself dozing off, resisted without enthusiasm, but the desire was so seductive, closing her eyes so easy.

In her dream she was on an infinite boardwalk in mist. Grey headless creatures stalked her on the underside of the planks. Bare trees rolled past in the distance and the sky was a lurid, heartsick purple. There was something about getting across before something closed. Sometimes she was in the car, only it was on rails.

She came round with a jolt. The pistol had slipped into the footwell.

She sat up, blinking. One side of her face was freezing from pressing against the window, the other was prickly and hot. Tall hedgerows rose on either side of the car. The sky passed from dark navy in the west to bright bands of lavender and cyan on the eastern horizon. They headed towards that horizon at speed.

She looked round at Butler. 'How long have I been asleep?'

'A few hours. *There is no peace, saith my God, to the wicked.*' Again, that huffing sound through the scarf.

She checked the rearview mirror; Martha was still in the back, curled up asleep. Delphine sniffed, then bent over and groped for the gun. Something went in her lower back. She straightened up and the funny looseness became a knifing pain in her spine.

Butler glanced across. 'What's wrong?'

'Nothing!' She gritted her teeth and rode out the pain until it softened. All her medication was at home. Her pipe too. 'Where are we?'

Butler eased off the accelerator as he rounded a corner. 'Home.'

As she looked out the window, Delphine felt a creeping sense of familiarity. She pulled a handkerchief out of her coat pocket and wiped her clammy face. It was like she had seen this road in her dream.

The realisation came by stealth. These fields. This slow bleeding dawn. She had seen it all before.

They were heading to Alderberen Hall.

The granite monster was smaller than she remembered. Less threatening, too – from its plinth above the gatehouse, the vesperi looked less like it was bearing down, more that it was standing firm, wings spread in an attitude of defiant resistance. In the weak morning light the stone was strangely bright. Her memories from childhood were of an ancient thing, crusted with blond lichen, weathered, foreboding. This statue looked like it had been power-washed.

But it was there.

The car idled before the wrought-iron gates. The last time she had passed them she had been thirteen. Part of her had always known she would return. That the Hall would return for her.

Butler lowered the electric window. A rush of freezing air snapped her alert.

There was a box on the gatehouse wall. Above it, a brass plaque was screwed into the stone. In an arty, serif font it read: *SHaRD.* Butler's leather seat creaked as he leaned out of the window and pushed a square button beneath a speaker's black grille.

Delphine checked the pistol was still loaded, checked the safety was on. When she was out of sorts she liked to strip and clean guns and put them back together again. This one was probably the most challenging in her collection – lots of fiddly, irreplaceable parts. She hadn't attempted it in years, and then only in the workshop. She probably didn't have the coordination anymore, nor the grip strength, the eyesight, the steadiness of hand.

She gripped the barrel, felt the vibration of the engine through her palms. A horrible, weightless anticipation built in the pit of her stomach. What was taking so long?

'Should you press it ag—'

'*Hello?*'

Butler thrust his head towards the speaker. 'Butler here. Returning with two guests.'

A loud buzz from inside the walls. The gates hummed, shuddered and began to open.

Fingers of crushing arthritic cramp were questing out from her collarbone, spreading from an old break. She was back. Dear God, she was back.

Butler pushed back his hood, put the car into gear, and eased his foot up off the clutch.

They rolled into the estate.

This moment had played out in dreams – landscapes disfigured and rudely conjoined, various players from her life drafted in as *dramatis personae*. Sometimes she was in the car with Father or Algernon, sometimes her return was ever-deferred by mazy lanes or fog or towering walls. Mostly, she was already back, without noticing it: shelling peas in the library, floating supine across the burning lake. Walking from her bedroom back in the cottage to a room filled with stuffed hybrids and addressing her long-dead mother as if it were all very ordinary – as if the two rooms had always been connected, and she had never thought to step through.

Flat grassland spread all around them, studded with Scots pines. The light was peach and crisp; she saw every blade of grass – its stark, variegated wetness.

She felt the young Delphine riding in the car alongside her, bored, indignant. Unafraid of the rolling wilderness, laying claim to everything she saw with a colonial dispassion: *that shall be mine, and that shall be mine, and that, and that* . . . Utterly secure in the knowledge that the world was her birthright. Entitled. Combative. Strong.

Presently, open grassland became coppice, the trees close and bare and brown, smothered in thick coats of ivy. Ferns lay sallow and shrivelled amongst wet black logs.

The woods thinned out into two rows of pollarded beeches lining the road, their shocks of whip-thin branches casting long, raggedy shadows.

Her breath caught: here was the lake.

In the sharp dawn light it was a gobbet of mercury. Land flowed down to make a depression and the lake filled it with sky. A short wooden jetty had rotted on its pilings and collapsed into the water. Brown reeds scruffed the far bank. She let her gaze linger on the water's wrinkled skin, delaying the moment when she would glance up to the hill beyond, to the mound on which once stood the ice house.

She already knew the ice house was gone. Martha and the other lanta had done dozens of recces in the years after Delphine had lived here. During the war the government took over the estate and used the grounds for training. God knows what the army would have done if they'd found a working threshold. But they didn't seem to realise anything was there. Martha reported seeing secretaries hacking out memoranda on typewriters and soldiers doing manoeuvres in the woods, but the old ice house remained a buried, flooded wreck.

And now, as she looked, she saw the hill was not even really a hill. A grassy mound, near the treeline, a few draggled wildflowers sheltering in its indented crest.

It didn't look like a place that had once harboured a portal to another world. A place that had claimed her father, and dear Henry. The sinkhole into which spiral fates inevitably twisted. It was a drab hummock. Unremarkable.

She looked at Butler, just to see the bloom of his noseleaf, his teardrop eyes, the velveteen ears with their heart-shaped tragi. Here was weirdness, impossibility. Life grotesque and wondrous. Confirmation that she was not alone.

He noticed her staring. The corner of his mouth fishhooked downwards.

'What?'

She blinked, looked away.

The road trended gently downwards. They bore round to the right. She knew it; she felt the route in her sinews.

At the end of a long, snaking road was a country house of dirty gold brick. Dark mullioned windows. Classical columns. Boxy east and west wings mirroring each other.

Alderberen Hall.

She breathed, but the sensation budding and fruiting in her chest was not excitement – it was closer to grief. The Hall looked wrong – everything was smaller, blander. Between the beeches rose the short black stubs of electric lamps.

It was not *her* Hall.

The east wing, yes, that was as she remembered, though the frames of the mullioned windows had been repainted, but as her gaze travelled west she could see the exact point where the masonry turned from old to new – the faded mustard stones becoming brighter, cleaner – where substantial sections had been rebuilt and restored. Chunks of the old west wing still stood – darker blotches of stonework staining the new flesh like psoriasis – but they only served to throw the repairs into greater contrast. The Hall was no longer symmetrical – its left side looked bulked-out, shiny, and the whole edifice seemed to slump under the weight of its scars.

She really had believed they were going back. Back to the Alderberen Hall of her childhood. Back to crab sandwiches below stairs and cold cuts of goose and the smell of dried lavender in a pottery jug on the bedside table. Back to the rattle and scrape of foils on the lawn just after Thursday lunch (or in the music room if it was raining), to the odours of pipe smoke and floor wax, to the feel of bare feet passing from cold boards to plush Asian rugs. Back to long sleeps in thick eiderdown and fat white pillows, like being buried in a snowdrift, Mother and Daddy just a thin partition wall away, to dear Henry, impatient, slapping a powder of mud from his gamekeeper's jacket, never venturing upstairs, made uncomfortable even by his proximity to it, most at home underground.

She had believed she would finally reach it – the vast, textured realm she had been keeping alive in her head. As if it were a doorway that had always been there, and she had stepped through.

The Hall swelled. It bore down on her, a great wave.

Butler let the car coast as they approached the forecourt. Gravel scroffled under tyres. A white van like the one they had bundled her into was parked in front of the stables, beside a Land Rover, a black estate car polished to a liquid shine, and two golf carts. The car crunched to a stop.

Butler twisted the rearview mirror towards him. He produced a plastic comb from his pocket and began working it through the red-brown fur on his scalp and jowls with neat, vigorous little strokes. His ears trended from cherubic pink around the earhole to mushroom brown at the curving tips. She remembered her manners and looked away.

'You might want to conceal the gun,' he said. 'Not the best way to make a first impression.'

'You don't know what impression I want to make,' said Delphine. She looked into the back. 'Martha? We're here.'

The leather seat swirled with blur. Barely discernible in the shifting air, a faint cobalt glow – two eyes with blueflame hearts. The belt unclipped.

Delphine slipped the pistol into her jacket. *Tout jour prest.*

Her lower lumbar felt brittle as meringue. She planted her stick in the gravel, and by way of a see-sawing motion managed to prise herself out of her seat.

The air was crisp, her breath forming wisps. Beneath six classical columns, a concrete wheelchair ramp with metal handrails led to a pair of double doors.

A solid high note sang from an electric motor and the doors began to part.

A woman stepped from the house in a grey wool greatcoat, rubbing her palms. She looked around seventy, sinewy with a strong, prominent chin and long greying hair tied back in a plait. She was short, apparently of Indian extraction, with a wide brow, severe tortoiseshell eyes, quick, large hands and a senator's nose. She was puckish, dignified and handsome.

'Ah! Here she is!' She strode up to Delphine and held out a hand. 'Ms Rao.'

Automatically, Delphine met the handshake. 'Uh . . .' She struggled to think what to say. She talked so rarely these days. The woman's grip was clammy, burning. 'Delphine Venner.'

The woman pumped Delphine's arm. 'Delighted. Butler told me all about your exploits over the phone. Most impressive.'

Delphine leaned on her stick. 'I want to speak to whoever's in charge.'

Ms Rao clasped her hands behind her back. The greatcoat was a little large on her – with her big, red-trimmed lapels and twin rows of brass buttons, and gravel crunching under her boots, she made Delphine think of a Soviet general in the final days of the regime, inspecting the tatty remnants of his troops in a barracks on the Arctic Circle.

'That's me.' She slipped her hands into the pockets and began bopping up and down to keep warm.

'Who are you?'

'Ms Rao. I'm sorry – did I not say that already?'

'And you're . . . what? The estate manager?'

'Manager, caretaker. Owner.' She shrugged. 'Whatever you like.' She glanced about, frowning. 'Butler mentioned you had a, uh . . . friend?'

Delphine felt Martha close to her leg, blending with the car's front hubcap. 'Can you get me to Avalonia?'

Ms Rao flashed Butler a look, raising her eyebrows and pursing her lips. A second later, the professional smile was back.

'Let's go inside, shall we?' She swept her arm towards the double doors in a wide flourish. They whinnied open.

Delphine hesitated. She looked from Ms Rao to Butler. The Hall loomed.

She nodded.

'Let's.'

Everything was familiar but wrong.

The grand staircase had been fitted with stairlifts – one on either bannister. The chequerboard floor was gone, replaced with a smooth and intricate stone mosaic of an octagon with red roses at its points, encompassing an equilateral triangle, its summit pointing downwards, within which lay a large, glyphic impression of an eye.

She strained against the peculiar discomfort of two superimposed sets of impressions. Everywhere she looked, memories asserted themselves violently, incoherently – she thought she heard a dinner gong, or the harpsichord; black shapes fluttered at the edges of her vision; she smelt peppery smoke. But none of it fitted. The doorways had been widened. They all had panels next to them with big green plastic buttons. The paintings were gone – instead there were framed photographs lit by electric lamps mounted on a steel bar that ran under the mezzanine. They appeared to show stages in the Hall's restoration – a few were in black and white, and looked like they had been taken during the war. A feeling of smallness took hold. Woozy unease was flowing outwards from her belly, and her legs felt watery.

She stabbed the rubber tip of her cane against the floor mosaic, seeing if she could jemmy up one of the ceramic tiles.

Ms Rao's boots echoed as she crossed the room. 'I thought we could take breakfast in my office. That is, if you're hungry?'

'Coffee,' said Delphine, focusing on the stylised rose at her feet.

'That can be arranged.'

'Good.' Her guts griped. 'Now if it's all the same I need you to show me to the lavatory.'

Delphine sat on the toilet, nauseous and out of breath.

The room was big, white, clean and cold, with plastic handrails, an emergency pull-cord, and enough space to manoeuvre a wheelchair. She thought it might have been the old equipment room, for storing archery targets and foils and masks, and the plywood sawhorses Mr Propp made residents jump over during wakefulness drills.

An extractor fan whirred somewhere behind her head. On a corner shelf, a little battery-operated air freshener periodically spritzed a tangy, medicincy sandalwood mist. She slid her fingers into her hair, gazed down at her capillary-threaded, puckered knees, and exhaled.

She had expected to weep. That seemed like the sensible thing to do, given the circumstances. Bleed the radiators. Regain equilibrium.

She felt as if thumbs were digging into her temples. Her tummy would be griping for hours. Her ankles were swollen. Her collarbone throbbed. She could feel bruises all up her hip. Her wrist, at least, felt better. She could close her fingers.

She flushed the toilet, then turned both taps on.

'Right, you can turn around now. I'm done.'

The metal towel rail fluxed as a hidden Martha turned to face her. Delphine squirted her hands with slimy, purple liquid soap that smelt of cough medicine. The water was near-scalding, which was almost a relief. Steam condensed on the mirror.

'Listen,' she said, keeping her voice low beneath the roar of the taps, 'if anything happens to me I want you to make a run for it, understand? Don't wait.'

Martha rapped twice on the towel rail – *clunk clunk.*

No.

'Martha – I mean it.' Delphine took a comb from her back pocket and wetted it under the stream. 'It's my fault we're here.'

Mauve blotches were all up the left side of her face from where she had fallen. Her flesh hung sallow and mottled. She looked as if she were wearing a facepack made out of tapioca. She combed her hair flat. Stupid, self-indulgent girl. What was all this grumbling going to achieve? You wanted this, didn't you? Well? Didn't you? Now you've got it. So you'd better bloody lump it.

She adjusted her collar, smoothed down the creases in her waistcoat. Come on, now. Calm, assertive command. Works on dogs, works on people.

She stepped out into a corridor that smelt of gloss paint. Pale sunlight was bleeding through the southern windows onto potted yuccas and art prints behind glass. Ms Rao was waiting.

'Follow me,' she said.

A wood-burning stove sat in the fireplace, the gaps either side stacked with split ash logs. Small ginger flames licked at a glass panel smutted with soot. Ms Rao adjusted the vent and straightened up.

'There.' She wore a dark maroon suit jacket with a silk blouse and a skirt cut just above the knee. Without her bulky coat, it was apparent that one of her shoulders hung lower than the other. It lent her an arrogant cant, half surly prizefighter, half libertine.

Delphine sat in a plush velvet wingchair of curlicued mahogany. The room felt naggingly familiar, as though it rhymed with something in her memory, but she couldn't quite place it. She was tired. Things had been moved around. On a pine desk were two plasma screen monitors, a black plastic keyboard and a mouse. The opposite wall was taken up by tall, glass-fronted bookshelves that reached the ceiling, full of big leather tomes.

The east wing had mostly survived the fire. Wait. Could this be the room she once escaped by scrambling up the chimney? She remembered the fireplace as a grand, imposing thing. This one looked rather pokey. She couldn't have fitted up that, could she?

Behind a beige stitched-leather pouffe, she could just make out the swirling outline of Martha.

'Well?' said Delphine.

Ms Rao hiked up the sleeve of her blouse and checked her wristwatch, chunky silver with a brown leather strap.

'Rounds are just finishing,' she said. There was a knock at the door. 'It's open!'

A breakfast trolley jankled into the room, pushed by a bullman with tawny hair and splayed horns. Delphine gripped the arm of her chair. A harka.

Her brain immediately processed him as someone in costume. He was about her height, but very heavily built. He had big dark eyes with large lashes, and a white-pink snout. His nostrils expanded when he inhaled, exposing moist interiors lined with pale hairs. He wore a necklace of coloured wooden beads and a loose, long-sleeved T-shirt. From the legs of his cotton trousers, his hooves left indents in the pile rug. Ms Rao did not look up from her desk.

'Thank you,' she said.

If he minded Delphine's staring, he hid it well. He set down glass coffee cups with silver scalloped handles shaped like butterfly wings, two silver cafetières frosted with condensation, hot croissants in a wicker basket, a glass butter dish, a silver toast rack, a lazy susan laden with miniature apricot, raspberry and plum jams, a plate piled with some sort of flatbread, and stacks of sweet, square cakes she did not recognise.

The harka rolled his broad shoulders. His horns were marbled with swirls of pistachio. He reversed out of the room, dragging the trolley.

Ms Rao pushed down one of the cafetière plungers with the heel of her palm. 'Shall I be mother?'

Mother would have said the coffee grounds represented repressed sexual desire. Frank dissections of Delphine and Algernon's psyches had been one of her favourite breakfast table pastimes.

Ms Rao poured the coffee. 'Do you think your friend would like some?'

'What's that supposed to mean?'

'Butler told me you've got a lanta.'

'I haven't *got* anyone. She's not a pet. She's a person.'

'Sorry, sorry.' Ms Rao held up her palms. 'A bad choice of words. Look. I hope you can see we've plenty of secrets of our own, here. You're both quite safe.'

'You broke into my house in the middle of the night and had me kidnapped,' said Delphine, stirring cream into her coffee.

Ms Rao smiled. 'Things got a bit out of hand, didn't they? But you acquitted yourself *excellently*. Do you mind if I explain what we do here?' She gestured at the food. 'Please, eat. You must be ravenous.'

Delphine's stomach growled, clenching. Part of her wanted to hold out, as a show of displeasure. But Ms Rao was right. She was starving.

She tore open a croissant and slathered it with butter and raspberry jam. Flakes of pastry stuck to her fingers, her shirt cuffs. She bit into it and washed it down with smooth, nutty coffee.

'Speak,' she said, through a mouthful of pastry.

Ms Rao watched approvingly. This small concession visibly energised her. Delphine was minded of the old prohibitions against accepting the food and drink of the faery court if one were captured by the gentry below. Ms Rao popped one of the little cakes into her mouth, then turned in her swivel chair and shuffled the mouse. The two monitors blinked on. The left one was split into sixteen low-res CCTV images showing different parts of the estate – mostly corridors, but also the courtyard, and one which looked like the road leading up to the gatehouse. The other had an email inbox. Ms Rao clicked something and pulled up Delphine's email.

'So,' she said, wiping her lower lip, 'I've had some time to find out a little more about you. You haven't left much of an online footprint.'

'I don't have a MySpace, if that's what you mean.'

'Your family get mentioned occasionally. Mother and father, was it, who lived here?' She clicked through to a browser page with lots of green text against a black background. She squinted. 'Gideon and Anne Venner?'

'That's right.'

'Mostly absurd conspiracy theories. The most popular one seems to be that Lord Alderberen was killed by the Masons.'

'I killed him.'

Ms Rao chuckled lightly, then caught Delphine's expression. Her laughter cut off.

'Can you get me to Avalonia or can't you?' said Delphine.

Ms Rao returned her attention to the computer. She was clicking through various images of scanned documents.

'That entirely depends. What business do you have in such a dangerous, lawless, frightening place?'

'It took my father. And a man who was like a father to me. And a dear friend.'

'And now you want it to take you too, ah?'

Delphine set her cup down in the saucer. She took a moment to compose herself. It had been a long few days.

'What I want, Ms Rao, is to look for them.'

Ms Rao paused, an index finger hovering over the mouse. She turned to face Delphine.

'Avalonia is a land of many opportunities. But, with respect, it is not a place to seek closure.'

'All the same, I would go.'

'I'm keen to meet your lanta friend.'

'Her name's Martha.'

'Martha. Yes.' Ms Rao picked up a triangle of toast and began buttering it with brisk strokes. 'Here's the meat of it: we've a threshold here on the grounds.'

'But we checked!' Delphine punched the arm of the chair. 'We came back time and time again and it was gone and . . . and *buried*.'

'Good! That means our security measures are working as they should. Don't be too hard on yourself. We've only had it functioning ten years.' Ms Rao bit a crescent out of her toast and gestured at Delphine with the remainder. 'We need a portal lanta.'

Lanta like Martha had a strange affinity with the swirling black godstuff of thresholds. The fluid was like a wild animal they could tame and command. Without lanta actively guiding them, thresholds lay dead and inert. If there was a way to activate one without a lanta, Delphine had never heard of it.

'We lost ours a few months ago,' said Ms Rao. 'We haven't been able to make outward journeys since. If, uh . . . *Martha* is prepared to help us out, we can make a sortie to Fat Maw in the south before monsoon season starts in earnest.'

'A sortie?' Delphine refilled her coffee to the brim and took a second croissant. 'You make it sound like you're some kind of paramilitary group.'

Ms Rao spat out a mouthful of crumbs. 'Sorry!' She patted her lips with a paper napkin. 'No, that's not quite right. We're more of an . . . aid organisation. Look.' She checked her watch. 'In a quarter of an hour the residents will have finished breakfast. Let's pay them a visit, then I can show you what we do.'

The smoking room was unrecognisable – again Delphine had the sensation of being in a waking dream. She vaguely remembered heavy drapes, a sense of cloying damp. Instead, there were bright, expansive bay windows offering views of the lake.

As the latch-tongued longcase clock gonged ten o'clock, residents began to filter in – some dressed in normal clothes, some still in their pyjamas. One elderly man with rounded spine and cabbage ears wore a pinstripe shirt, cufflinks and navy-blue braces. Other residents were wheeled in by orderlies and parked at tables. Ms Rao greeted each by name as they entered; most responded with a nod or a quiet hello.

Ms Rao addressed the room: 'Good morning, everybody. We have a guest with us today at *SHaRD*. I know you'll all make Ms Venner feel very welcome.'

Some residents smiled in greeting, or murmured. A large black gentleman sitting by the window wearing a grey suit and wide-brimmed straw hat clapped his big hands.

'Shard?' said Delphine.

Ms Rao turned to her. 'Sheltered Housing and Retirement Dormitories.' She spoke in an undertone. 'We don't accept many visitors . . . for obvious reasons. Our residents are of varying capacities. Please don't be offended if you don't get much out of them. They're used to their routine. It helps with memory.'

The residents slumped in adjustable armchairs or complicated electric wheelchairs. There were about a dozen of them. Chins sagged into chests. A television blared. Delphine felt herself withdrawing, uncomfortable. The elderly still seemed a different species, even though most here were probably no more than a few years her senior. In a funny way, they were just as improbable to her as Butler. Monsters.

'We're part of an effort to establish peaceful relations with the other world,' said Ms Rao. 'The hidden nations, the new world. Bonmundi. Swargaloka. Gehenna. Naraku. I don't know what your preferred term is.'

'Avalonia?'

'Is but one small island in a whole world of powers and competing interests. It's a delicate business, obviously. Our teams make discreet diplomatic links and trade resources to fund our efforts.'

'This is your team?'

Ms Rao leaned in uncomfortably close, almost parking her chin on Delphine's shoulder. 'Don't be fooled. These are some of the most competent, self-reliant men and women in the country.'

She took Delphine by the elbow and led her to a wheelchair parked in front of the plasma screen TV. BBC News 24 was on, the picture cutting between clips of North Korean troops marching in formation and President Obama addressing a press conference, while a headline ticker crawled along the bottom of the screen. Delphine tugged her arm away, more petulantly than she would have liked, and turned to the figure in the chair.

He was a cadaver. Clear plastic tubing ran from swollen nostrils to an oxygen cylinder. Long rinds of ivory hair clung to a dappled scalp the colour of goat's cheese. The head was slumped forward.

It nodded and sank with each shallow breath. Rheumy eyes were underscored with thick sickles of red.

'Ms Venner,' said Ms Rao, 'this is Judge Easter.'

The figure in the chair did not stir.

'Hello,' said Delphine.

'He can't hear you. Deaf as the proverbial. Vision minimal. But he's my most valuable attaché.'

He made a soft gibbering noise. His lips parted just a fraction, clear strings of sputum hanging from his gums. He smelled faintly of talc and sour milk.

'You might get to meet him properly, once you're on the other side,' said Ms Rao, leading Delphine away. 'Once he's in the field we can't shut him up.'

Delphine took a moment to process what she'd said. 'You're going to let me through?'

'That's what you want, isn't it?'

Delphine's stick clipped the leg of a chair and she stumbled. Ms Rao caught her arm.

Delphine stared at the floor, her heart pounding. To be free of this fucking body. To escape this crumbling world.

'Yes.' She brushed Ms Rao's hand away, this time with a sort of dignified disdain. 'Yes, I'm ready.'

'Oh good,' said Ms Rao. 'Shall we go there now, then?'

The lift rattled as they descended through the floor of the house. Ms Rao leaned against the handrail. She was such a contrast to the residents – vigorous and full of appetite. Age had not demolished her features so much as vindicated them.

They stepped out into a limey, musty tunnel. It was split into a crossroads. Delphine scrunched her toes within her brogues. Now this, she did remember.

The western tunnel was sealed off with blast doors. She counted at least three security cameras. Industrial trolleys stood beside the wall. Plastic hazard signs were screwed into the rock, sandwiched between layers of Perspex – a black triangle against a yellow background, showing a lightning bolt arrow striking a prostrated human in the chest: *DANGER OF DEATH*. Another showed a skull and crossbones within a white diamond: *TOXIC GAS*. The sign next to it showed a man inside a red circle with a line through it: *UNAUTHORISED ACCESS PROHIBITED. GAS MONITORS MUST BE USED*. Finally, there was a yellow information sign depicting a faceless stickman in various states of discombobulation:

TOXIC GAS IN THIS AREA
EXPOSURE MAY CAUSE:
HEADACHES (the stickman clutching his full stop head)
NAUSEA (the stickman leaning over a bucket)
DIZZINESS (lines radiating from his head)
BREATHLESSNESS (hunched forward)
COLLAPSE (crawling)
LOSS OF CONSCIOUSNESS (on his back, head haloed with stars)

'Persuasive, isn't it?' said Ms Rao. 'Security theatre.' She tapped a PIN into a keypad. 'No one's ever got this far, but you never know, uh? Ah!' She pressed on a long metal handle and the blast door opened like a bank vault. She swung it back. It was a foot thick, studded with big rivets. She stepped through the hatch into the tunnel beyond. 'Come.'

Insulated cables and thick pipes ran along the roof, the passage lit by halogen lamps. Delphine's knees ached and her calves were weighed down with a cold deadness. Just stiffness from all that time in the car.

'I hope I'm not teaching my grandmother to suck eggs,' said Ms Rao, 'but do you know how a threshold works? For humans, I mean?'

'Of course.'

The truth was, despite a life devoted to studying all aspects of the channel, Delphine was realising how much of her knowledge was theoretical. Till meeting the residents in the smoking room, she had not truly appreciated the practical difficulties in finding humans who could make the journey. The explanations in the Prentice manual were characteristically fanciful and verbose.

'It's nothing to worry about.' Ms Rao patted her shoulder with an overfamiliar congeniality. 'You will be perfectly safe. But best I refresh you on the basics so there are no unpleasant surprises. When you travel from Earth to Avalonia, your body will undergo radical changes. On the other side, your physical age will have decreased by around seventy years.'

Delphine exhaled slowly. 'Martha said it makes people younger.'

'*Humans*. And only on the outbound trip. Vesperi, harka and lanta stay the same age.'

'And humans who've received the honours,' said Delphine.

Ms Rao raised an eyebrow. 'You're well-informed, Ms Venner.'

'Prentice says it's because humans are the only species with a soul.'

'Or perhaps somebody wanted to keep us out.' She laughed, although the way she said it did not sound like a joke.

'How did you arrive at seventy?' said Delphine. 'Seems a bit precise.'

'Because anyone younger than that disappears.'

'You've lost people?'

'People have been lost.' Ms Rao pursed her lips. 'Same problem coming back. Avalonia to England, a human gains about seventy years.'

Prentice offered a colourful account of a man 'in his middle years', born in the other world and foolish enough to attempt the journey to Earth. He had emerged 'a wreck upon the shore of decrepitude', before dying of heart failure.

They stopped at a second blast door. This time, the only sign was on the door itself – a blue circle containing a white image of a masked figure. Two round sockets and a white muzzle. Delphine felt her breathing quicken. Underneath were the words: *RESPIRATORS MUST BE WORN.*

Ms Rao stepped back and looked up at a security camera mounted in the corner. She waved.

The grey lens of the camera regarded her mutely. Nothing happened.

A clunk.

The bulky door swung outwards. It was held by a harka with lush, auburn hair spilling from between recurved horns. In her other hand lay a huge pump-action shotgun.

Again, that dizzying wash of unreality, her brain straining to make sense of the signals it was receiving. It tried to interpose safe interpretations on what she saw: *costume, electronic puppet, animal*. Anything but *person*.

The harka was wearing a black stab jacket with white iPod earbuds hanging over the collar. She tilted her head back, trapezoid muscles standing out against her red-brown neck.

'Ms Rao.' She was chewing something between round white molars.

Heat washed from the chamber, with a stench that turned Delphine's guts to water: beer, peat, bitumen.

Godstuff.

The guard slapped a hand on her shotgun's slide action. She moved aside.

The door had a high lip along the bottom. Delphine had to grip the jamb for balance while she stepped through. On the other side, the floor was tiled, a handrail running along a wall covered in abstract mosaics of interlocking circles or tessellating triangles. Delphine followed Ms Rao down a short corridor vaulted with steel buttresses. Her breaths came sharper, shorter. She was sweating. She paused to wipe hair from her brow.

They emerged in an expansive terracotta-tiled chamber – far larger than she remembered. The floor sank in a series of concentric circles like an open-cast mine. At the very bottom was a round pool with a raised edge – a well filled with inert black water.

She wobbled. The air was so humid she could barely draw breath.

The descending circular levels were linked on the near side by steps with a handrail, and on the far by a zig-zagging succession of gentle ramps. Gutters carved in the tilework sloped down towards a plastic grate at the foot of the well. Recessed lamps set into the walls lit shifting veils of vapour. There was no trace of the old chamber at all.

'It's like a leisure centre.'

'It's practical,' said Ms Rao. 'Easy to clean. A common artefact of the transportation process is temporary incontinence – especially with first-timers.'

Delphine watched currents of steam fold and warp. She blinked, trying to recall the stark stone effigies, white stripes of lime, dark and dripping rock.

Did she feel cheated? The heart of her trauma had been sanitised. Her feelings wafted through the atmosphere, inchoate, a thousand tiny particulates.

Ms Rao clapped and the sound rang flatly. 'I'll show you round.'

Wooden doors with portholes led off the main chamber. One opened onto a room with a gurney and medical equipment, a second onto a lavatory and shower. A third room had racks lined with robes of various sizes, shelves of wooden clogs and sandals, loose canvas slacks, white cotton shirts, and a selection of eyeglasses. A fourth room was lined with wooden cots and hammocks.

'Reception areas,' said Ms Rao. 'Takes a while to recover after transport.'

The final room contained radio equipment. There were microphones on anglepoise stands, headphones, PC monitors, and several large hutches. She saw no animals but smelt the foetid-sweet, sawdusty scent she associated with guinea pigs. In a corner, a white mini-fridge hummed quietly.

'Our broadcasting station,' said Ms Rao. She sat in the black swivel chair and slotted a pair of headphones round her neck. 'From here we can communicate with the base camp, the boats and our transponder in Fat Maw.'

'Fat Maw,' said Delphine. The name felt sticky in her mouth.

'It's a port city on the southwest coast of Avalonia. Biggest settlement on the continent – gateway to the entire world. Good staging post for operations.'

Outside, they sat on a tiled bench built out of the wall, looking down at the pool. Ms Rao went to a fountain set in a recess and returned with two paper cones. She handed one to Delphine. Delphine sipped. The water was silky, cold, delicious.

'How d'you get this place?' said Delphine.

'From my father.'

'Investor, was he?'

'Oh no.' Ms Rao chuckled to herself. 'He inherited it.'

'From who?'

'The old earl, Lazarus Stokeham. They were good pals back in Mysore. I think Dad was the closest thing he had to a brother.'

'And what are you after? Money?'

'Oh, constantly. Costs a lot to run an operation like this.' Ms Rao sat and propped her chin against her knuckles. She gazed into the descending circles. 'Little flies that make a person immortal. Imagine. If we could get one back to Britain, and learn how this . . . substance . . . repairs people . . .' She gestured at the pool of godstuff. 'We could change the world. Think of how many lives we could save.'

Delphine slurped her water. 'You can't save a life. Only prolong it.'

Ms Rao smiled. 'That is a proposition I am willing to challenge. Vaccines, antibiotics. Illnesses that not so long ago were fatal are now no more than an inconvenience. Do not mistake norms for inevitabilities.' She wagged her finger, as if re-enacting some historic reproach. 'With a little imagination, we could breed animals that could regrow flesh when you butcher them. Infinite food.'

'Sounds horrific.'

'More horrific than famine? Perhaps you would temper that disgust if you'd seen worse privation than an empty fridge.'

For the first time since she arrived, Delphine felt the tiniest, most grudging stirring of respect for Ms Rao. Charm was the redoubt of scoundrels. A rebuke was honest.

Delphine gazed down at the pool. Its black surface lay inert.

'You're an altruist, then?'

'Hardly. I'm just muddling along.' She looked across at Delphine. 'I'm sincerely sorry we didn't find you sooner. You seem like our sort of person.'

Delphine tried to think of a cutting retort.

'You don't know me,' she said.

Ms Rao squeezed her paper cone until it buckled with a soft pop. 'My team have sent me copies of some documents they found in your house.'

'What?'

'You didn't think I'd show you all this without checking you are who you say you are? You've accumulated quite the body of research.'

'It's my life's work.'

'There are sketches of a godfly.'

'From memory,' said Delphine.

'You've seen one?'

'Yes. It stung my father.'

Ms Rao tapped the crumpled cone against her knee, then stood decisively. 'Listen. If your friend Martha is prepared to open the threshold, I'll consider allowing you to make the trip. I want to send a team to Fat Maw, to follow up a lead. With seasonal rains it's probably the last trip we can mount for four months. It's quite a journey, but you could accompany them there and back, providing you're prepared to work.'

Delphine laughed – a convulsive, mirthless reflex. It spilled out of her, all high and damaged, and left her panting in the wet heat. 'I'm eighty-six.'

'Well, quite. You fit the age profile perfectly.'

She laughed again. How strange that now she found herself here, on the cusp of it all, offered the thing she'd hunted all her life, she was afraid. With the death of hope came a kind of peace. But she wanted this. What if it was a lie? What if . . .

She inhaled heavy, wet air. 'Let me take a walk.'

Prothero Wood was fragrant with wet bark and leaf mulch. Stout, forking boughs carved the light into continents. Delphine sat in an electric wheelchair, with Martha on her lap eating a napkin of sugar filched from breakfast. When the ground got too boggy they got out and pushed.

Once, she had dashed through these paths heedless. She remembered scoffing at Henry's slowness, his grunts of discomfort and the stink of the mustard poultices he would apply to his perpetually crocked back. A marvel now, it seemed, how he had kept going so long, with his early mornings and his damp, cramped cottage – no central heating, no NHS. Getting by on tea and beer and a sort of holy grumpiness, the grim calm of the ascetic mixed with the pragmatist's recognition that the hole in the thatch does not fix itself.

The trees thinned and the hard earth softened to marshland. She drove the wheelchair along a boardwalk, tyres bumping over planks of uneven, salt-smoothed cedar. Bronze rills trickled through gullies, draining back towards the horizon's narrow, shimmering blade of ocean. A sharp wind made her nose run.

She stopped the chair at the edge of a slow-flowing trench, set the foot brake. Stunted vegetation shuffled in the breeze: purple, grey-brown, verdigris. She had forgotten how the saltmarshes' colour palette felt wrong, uncanny – like an old television screen damaged by a magnet.

Martha climbed down from the wheelchair and walked to the edge of the trench, leaving hooked footprints in the soft mud. The comb-shaped heads of her antennae fluttered and sniffed at the loamy, freezing wind.

'Well?' said Delphine.

Martha faced the ocean. Her maroon armour was lustred with sea spray. From the east, a flock of redshanks called in high yipping voices.

Delphine felt a constriction in her chest. 'Martha?'

The wind surged in a big, woofing show of power, wrinkling the ponds.

A horrible dragging guilt pulled at her stomach. Martha was going to make Delphine ask. She would not simply offer her power. Even when the others had left, when it looked like nuclear war might destroy the world and Algernon and the other lanta set off to hunt for an escape, Martha had stayed to be with Delphine. She had never asked for anything, except to be able to live her life in peace.

Delphine had to go. To reclaim what was lost. She had learned to live with this pain in her heart, but seeing the threshold had turned the dull ache to burning agony.

'Martha.' Her voice was cracking. 'Darling I have to say something.'

Delphine closed her eyes and breathed. The air tasted brackish and good.

'You've always been . . .' She opened her eyes. 'Martha, I know you've probably made up your mind already but I just want to say. We can go home if you like. Back to the cottage. We can forget all this nonsense and go home because it's been a good life, with you. I know I'm an awful fuss but it's been a good life and I don't regret it. I can't. You mustn't . . .' She took a shuddering breath, concentrating on a patch of sea holly. 'I wouldn't want you to think because I spent all this time looking for a way through, that I was trying to get away from *you*. That I wasn't satisfied. That you weren't . . .

enough, or something.' She began pulling at each of her fingers in turn. 'Oh dear. I'm sorry. I'm not saying this very well. I just mean . . . You're important to me. More important than this other business. So. That's it, really.'

Martha turned. Clayey mud was splattered up her shin plates; it dripped in grey-brown gobbets from her bristly thighs. Her eyes waxed aurora green.

She raised her arms. Her back split open.

Two smooth leathery sheaths unhinged, separating down the middle and swinging up. Beneath was a pair of tatty, translucent wings. They rustled, then fizzed into motion.

Martha bounced lightly on her curved toes. She bent her knees, jumped and rose steadily into the air.

She hovered, her blurred wings sparking bright video-glitch colours. The pincers either side of her mouth flexed as she chatter-ticked in clickspeak.

She took off, towards the woods.

Hidden amongst wind-hunched oaks was a cottage. Delphine rode the wheelchair to the edge of the clearing. Waist-high grass and tall weeds grew in dense profusion. There were rosemary bushes laced with crystalline cobwebs; a tiny, pudding-shaped goldcrest was whiffling from branch to branch, calling in his bold bright voice: *See! See! See!*

She stood, unhooked her stick from the back of the chair and made her way into the undergrowth.

There was no sign that anyone had come this way in a long time. She tramped down grass and swatted weeds with her stick. Henry would have been horrified. Behind the thick windowpanes, the curtains were drawn. The thatch was mossy and worn.

Again, that shrinkage – that gap between her memory and the thing itself. Henry's old cottage was small and rain-wet and not at all grim and runic like the one in her dreams. But it was here – it was real.

Martha was standing at the doorstep, talking to the front door. Delphine stopped behind her. She let out a moan as the stick took her weight. The door was crusted with sunburst lichen.

Delphine bowed her head in prayer. She pressed a hand to the rough stone wall.

Oh Henry. You'd be probably be furious if you knew I was coming after you. Are you dead? Can you hear me, up in heaven? Or am I talking to myself, like Father used to? Am I doing the right thing?

She heard scraping and opened her eyes.

Martha had set something down on the doorstep. It was a fist-sized chunk of limestone, shiny with water. It left a little dark puddle on the step.

Martha turned and walked past Delphine, into the long grass. Delphine stooped and picked up the rock. On the underside was a smooth ammonite. As she moved to replace it, she realised there was something written on the doorstep – white letters scraped out in limestone:

WHITHER THOU GOEST.

Ms Rao was in the courtyard, overseeing the unloading of pallets from a van.

'Martha says she'll do it,' said Delphine.

Ms Rao turned. 'Good. Thank you.' She glanced around the gravel. 'Is she . . .'

'She'd prefer to remain incognito for a while.'

'Of course.' She slid a walkie-talkie from inside her greatcoat. 'I'll have Butler make arrangements for your journey. We'll need a couple of days to prepare. In the meantime, we have some preparatory materials for you to read. There are guest suites made up on the first floor. We need to give you a few shots,' Ms Rao patted herself on the tricep, 'and they can make you quite poorly so it's good to rest as much as you can. I'll radio for someone to escort you there. We'll provide supplies for the trip but let us know if there are belongings you need collecting from your home. You'll need new clothes, of course.' She looked Delphine up and down, smiled. 'We'll find something in your size.'

'Wait.'

Ms Rao lowered the walkie-talkie from her ear. 'Yes?'

'You didn't let me finish,' said Delphine. 'She says she'll do it – on one condition.'

*

Avalonia is a continent in the southern hemisphere.

Delphine sat up in bed, reading a primer that had been pushed under her door. It was printed on A4 sheets held together with a staple. The text was thoughtfully large, including the header at the top of each page: *PLEASE RETURN TO A MEMBER OF STAFF AFTER READING FOR SAFE DISPOSAL.*

It comprises a mix of tropical rainforests to the north and monsoon forests to the south. Hills and mountain ranges create large areas of sheltered lowland in which a wide variety of flora and fauna thrive. Though the majority of relationships within these ecosystems appear to be non-zero-sum, there are a number of significant apex predators for which you must remain vigilant.

Delphine adjusted her reading spectacles and flicked a few pages ahead. There was a rough sketch of the island, shaped rather like a jagged apostrophe or a croissant placed on its end. Oh gosh, she was getting peckish again. She relit her pipe and took a couple of contemplative puffs.

Remember that although many residents of Fat Maw speak versions of French or English, the language has undergone – and continues to undergo – marked semantic drift. A non-trivial portion of their contemporary vocabularies are loanwords from local tongues such as Low Thelusian, Sinpanian, and the various river dialects that travel southwards from settlements throughout the continent. Listen before you speak. New recruits are advised to spend at least one month in Fat Maw developing their ear before attempting to converse with residents who are not employed by our agency.

She flicked ahead again. There were drawings of vesperi, harka and lanta, with arrows explaining anatomy and secondary sexual characteristics. A vesperi's sex, it said, did not stabilise until after puberty, around the time they grew too heavy for flight. Gender was a looser, more malleable designation to vesperi than one's virtue name, a term which led to the footnote: *See* ***Primer 1B*** *– Onomastics.*

She could not see how she was supposed to absorb all this in a few days. It reminded her forcibly of the grim duties of school, the French verbs by rote and the succession of kings and queens. She knocked her pipe out into an empty mug and took a chocolate from the dish on her bedside table. Martha was sleeping in a cot under the window. Delphine yawned. Needs must.

*

to dreams of chimney stacks, oil and gripped wrists he sleeps he sleeps he slee

When she woke she was lost. Meshy, spiderweb shadows spread across an unfamiliar room with a high ceiling. She groped for the bedside table and found her spectacles. It was only as she sat up that she remembered where she was.

She glanced about, still vaguely suspicious she was in a dream. The primer lay splayed on the quilt where she had fallen asleep reading it. On the other side of the room, a pine wardrobe stood next to a commode with a metal frame, upholstered in grey, wipe-clean plastic. The commode's potty attachment clung to its underside, pale, accusing and vaguely parasitical.

She slid her bare feet down onto the rug and spent a few moments collecting her thoughts.

Her hip and shoulder were tender from where the van had flipped. This was real. She was back at Alderberen Hall.

She lowered her head, her tangled hair spilling forward, hanging over her brow and round her ears. A liquid weight sat in her belly, churning.

She found her wristwatch behind the bedside lamp and slipped it on. The time was almost four a.m. She flexed her fingers, watched a blue stirrup of veins tighten about the knuckles. Feeling rather light and outside herself, she raised her fist to her lips, and kissed it.

Delphine chose to walk the final few hundred yards from the lift to the ice house without assistance. Ms Rao had changed into autumnal reds, her shoulders draped in a loose-woven woollen shawl. Delphine had slept fitfully over the past few days. The injections had left her feverish, misremembered phrases from the primers dancing around her brain. As they walked, she hallucinated tinny music-box-like melodies tinkling from the ventilation system, modulated by fan whirr into queasy warbles. The walls of unworked stone seemed to close in. She felt like a death row inmate trudging towards the execution chamber.

They reached the final blast door; Ms Rao signalled to the camera and the door opened. She led Delphine into the thick, wet heat of the ice house. Delphine went into one of the side rooms, where a white bathrobe lay folded on one of the beds. She changed slowly, lingering as she removed her socks, focusing on the sensation of wool dragging over skin. She was not sure she felt fear any more. She was not sure she felt anything.

When she padded back out in the central chamber, Martha was there, arms by her sides, eyes fluxing a sombre metallic blue. Butler stood beside her, dressed in a white cotton toga that came down to his knees, his wings folded. Ms Rao was waiting too.

Martha climbed into a recess at the edge of the pool. Her hemispherical eyes waxed purple, cycling red, white, gold.

The waters of the pool began to turn.

Delphine peeled her tongue from the roof of her mouth, gluey strands stretching and snapping. A beery, hoppy stench wafted up from the pit.

Ms Rao walked down to the edge of the pool. She held out her hand. In her palm was an apple with a red ribbon tied round it.

'Test!' she said. She let go.

The apple punched into the viscous liquid, rolled onto its side, and sank. The small dent it left curled and stirred back into the whole.

Ms Rao looked towards the radio room, tapping her foot.

Delphine watched the steaming water. She imagined the apple, fizzing away to nothingness. Was it really the same apple that emerged on the other side? Or did the threshold take an impression of it and produce a copy? Was the first apple destroyed? Was she walking to her death?

A call from the radio room: 'Received!'

Ms Rao gave a thumbs up. She turned to Butler.

'Channel's open.'

Butler bent his knees. He leapt. His wings fanned, toga billowing. He dropped feet-first into the godstuff. It yielded cleanly and he was gone.

Delphine gripped her walking stick. Her depth perception was doing funny things. The descending circles around the pool seemed at once flat and infinitely deep. She took a step and her whole body swayed. Her ears were ringing.

Ms Rao looked at her. 'Ready?'

Delphine's stomach clenched. Oh pull yourself together, woman. She had made a bargain. This wasn't about what she wanted. She walked down the long, zigzagging ramp towards the well.

The atmosphere grew ever more humid. Sweat dripped into her eyes. The metal rail felt hot under her slick fingers.

At the edge of the pool, the stink was intense and complex, notes of bramble and soap rising then falling back into a hoppy, tarry stew. She thought she might vomit.

She hesitated. She folded her fingers round the collar of her robe, working her thumb over the soft cotton.

'Ready?' said Ms Rao. Her face was underlit, faintly cadaverous.

Delphine felt her cheeks prickle. 'Should I get undressed?'

'Not unless you want to.' She looked down into the waters. 'When you're ready, just lie back. It feels . . . unusual. But it doesn't hurt.'

Delphine exhaled. Right. Come on then. She rested her walking stick against the handrail and sat on the lip of the pool, next to Martha. A damp heat washed against her spine.

It was the old diving board trick. Jump before your conscious mind is ready to object. Before the lizard brain intervenes. Take your instincts by surprise. On the ceiling, the tiles formed a pattern. Very faintly, in shades of red and orange and peach, she saw the eight long petals of a lotus.

Delphine closed her eyes. '*And lo, I am with you alway, even unto the end of the world.*'

A heartbeat. She had meant to go then. She puffed and tensed. Why was it so hard, letting go? 3 . . . 2 . . .

She drove her heels into the floor, pitching herself backwards. She slapped into something hot and wet and thick.

Godstuff closed over her as she sank. The texture was like syrup. It surrounded her slowly, flowing up into her nostrils, pushing into her ear cavities, seeping between her lips and filling her mouth. Her skin tingled. Godstuff oozed over her tongue. It tasted of old lightning.

A high staticky crackling. Her bathrobe was breaking apart, fizzing away to nothing. Gravity released her. She hung, suspended in the endless medium. She had no sense of up or down. Was she supposed to be kicking, swimming towards a surface? Resisting somehow? Had she misread the manual? What about breathing?

Somewhere at the back of her mind, it occurred to her she was dying.

She opened her eyes to discover she no longer had any. A faint prickling pressure met the inside of her head. Then even that sensation dissolved, and she was fading

CHAPTER 4

THE GOOD DOCTOR

(Two days before the inauguration)

'Someone is trying to kill me.'

Dr Noroc timed his revelation to coincide with an outrageous hoof-to-groin foul down on the Bataille court; half the arena exploded in roars of disapproval, the other side hurling back whistles, jeers. The referee blew his horn. He called the offending player, a lithe ginger-brown harka with a flat head and oily eyes, down to the edge of the pool. The referee said something and the player cocked a torn ear towards him, cupping a palm round it. The referee waved his blue chevron flag: a dismissal. The crowd leapt to their feet.

The festival day match was always raucous. Amidst yells and whoops and shoves, Hagar watched Dr Noroc. He had shrunk back inside his headscarf, brown cotton rucking against his hunched shoulders. His clothes were hanging off him, his eyes sunken, his hollow cheeks tinged with a dolorous grey-yellow pallor. She felt an unexpected jag of pity. He was a ghost of the man she had known back at the Mill. He looked like a skeleton.

'Perhaps you should kill them first,' she said. She had only agreed to meet him because she was afraid he might do something foolish. He was paranoid, gripped by guilt – but what if someone knew his secret? She bit into a plum sweetheart. An unpalatable thought.

As the spectators settled back onto their long plank benches, she gazed down towards the court. The two teams gathered on their home lines at opposite ends of the lozenge-shaped pool. The brick clique against the flesh shambles clique – builders versus butchers. Tan bricks shone in the morning sun while sashboys adjusted the straps binding wrists behind backs. Players spat and muttered, waiting for the restart.

'I'm serious,' said Dr Noroc. His triangular chin was stippled with patchy silver whiskers. He kept massaging the scar crease beneath his glass eye.

The referee's horn blasted – a deep, martial reverberation. The crowd began stamping in time, waving their leaf umbrellas. Hagar noticed her heart rate rising. Players hopped from the poolside onto the low wooden posts by their home lines. The posts were spaced an average of four feet apart and grew gradually taller as they approached the centre of the pool. The middle posts – the ones where all the action happened – stood some ten feet above the water. The arena rang with the haphazard tattoo of cloven hooves on hickory.

'So am I.'

The brick clique team, in yellow sashes, broke down the left flank. The foul had reduced them to four players. Their guard, an immense snorting brute that Hagar had heard fans call L'Île Noire, shuffled from hoof to hoof on the post beside their home line.

Hagar felt a tug at her cloak and slapped Dr Noroc's hand away. Noroc stroked his sallow cheek, glaring reproachfully.

'So you're just going to turn your back on me, is that it?'

She felt her neck tightening with irritation. 'As a servant of the perpetuum I have a duty to protect all Avalonia's citizens.' She lowered her voice. 'Whatever they may have done.'

Dr Noroc kept his fists bunched in his lap. He spoke at a murmur. 'Somebody . . . I don't know who . . . some *maniac* . . . has got me confused with another doctor.' He was shaking so hard his wire-framed spectacles slipped down his nose. 'A doctor who . . . they believe . . . made certain *sacrifices* for the good of his country, many years ago.'

'Sacrifices, you say?'

'But that's not how they see it.'

Hagar tongued a plug of plum-flesh out of the hole in her upper gum. Beneath her show of nonchalance, she was deeply troubled. Few knew what had gone on at the Mill. He was plainly delusional. Wasn't he?

'Do you know how they arrived at this . . . theory?'

'Of course not! There's no way they could . . . they have a poisoned mind.'

The five-strong purple-sashed flesh shambles team were loitering around their end of the court, holding back, running down the clock. Brick supporters began to boo, joined by a few of the opposing fans.

'Can you describe this person?'

Dr Noroc's head shook within his scarf. 'I've not met them. But they've sent notes. Threats.'

At some clandestine signal the flesh shambles team surged forward, vying for the higher ground. The spectators began drumming their feet, a great anticipatory rumble.

'I understand your concern, friend doctor,' said Hagar, putting on a show of civility in case any of their neighbours were listening in. 'The run-up to this weekend's inauguration has seen a lot of bluster. Nasty letters, rocks thrown through windows. Not honourable, not pleasant. But a long way from murder.'

A roar shook the arena. Hagar glanced down in time to see a yellow-sashed brick player land a front kick square in an opposing harka's breastbone, the contact so perfect Hagar dug her nails into her thigh. If anything, the touch was a little *too* square – better to strike the collarbone or shoulder and knock them askew, leaving them open for the second, decisive blow. The kicked flesh shambles player leapt backwards and landed cleanly on the post behind, where he grimaced and coughed. She felt her blood quickening, touched a finger to her ribs.

'But how could they . . . *Why* would they think I had . . . been involved in such . . . pursuits?'

'You're reading into innuendo.' Purple sashes spread into an enveloping line as the flesh shambles players advanced. 'Exactly as your mystery correspondent intended. I expect identical letters have appeared all over the city, filled with vague allusions to dark pasts. Pricking consciences. They want to silence anyone associated with a rival clique. Some faction wishes to suppress the vote so their chosen candidate can be made Prefect.' She blew through pursed lips. 'I've seen these tactics a thousand times. They play on the vanity that one's sin is unique.'

Dr Noroc grunted and rocked forward. Hagar turned, thinking for a wild moment he had been stabbed, but he straightened up, shaking his head.

'No, no, no.' His voice dropped to a murmur. 'They call me by a . . . specific name. Not the name hanging outside my practice. Not the name I came to this city with. The name of another man.' He stole a glance at her, his good eye twitching. 'A man long dead.' He pushed his spectacles back up the bridge of his nose with a trembling finger.

He meant, of course, his own name, 'Noroc'. She had arranged a whole new identity for him when he arrived in Fat Maw, forged papers, a pleasant villa in the high town. He had promised to slip into his dotage in quiet obscurity.

'A name alone means little.'

'Not just a name! The threats are full of . . . *details*. Things that no one could . . .' He massaged his brow. 'Accusations so definite that a stranger might mistake them for truth.'

Hagar crunched down her final chunk of sweetheart, warm honey bleeding over her tongue. Poor Noroc had learned nothing from his suffering. He clung to life as a miser clings to pennies.

'In my experience,' she said, the last word making spit well in her mouth, 'assassins don't announce they're going to kill you.' The brick's three yellow sashes were retreating, the five purple sashes of the flesh shambles side exploiting the higher ground to drive them towards the side of the arena. She felt a pang, just above the heart. 'Not the successful ones.'

'Well, this one *has*.'

'Then their purpose is not death but intimidation. You are intimidated. Their job is done. Enjoy the rest of the match.' She rose to leave.

A cornered yellow player parried his opponent's strike with a hook kick, twisting the other harka to one side then dropping into a sweep and knocking his ankle from under him. The ankle whipped up in a wide arc and – for an instant – the player seemed weightless, then the equilibrium broke and she went sprawling backwards into the pool. The crowd sprang from their benches.

Dr Noroc stood and grabbed Hagar's wrist. 'I want passage on a ship to Thelusia. I want a new name and a house and a job.'

Hagar glanced down at the rough sinewy fingers digging in. 'Let go.'

His grip tightened.

'You have to help me.' His breath was damp and rancid, heavy with a lingering sour tang. 'The last note said they're going to kill me tonight. During the festival.'

All around them, spectators were dancing, yelling, pounding hooves on rough orange-brown boards. No one intervened. Even if they noticed, Noroc would look like a tired father reprimanding his eccentrically dressed child.

She stepped towards him so his wrist bent back on itself. His squeal merged with the shrieks of the crowd and she twisted easily out of his grasp, dealing him a backhanded slap across the forehead.

He dropped back into his seat, stunned. A little red crescent marked his pasty brow. Hagar adjusted her signet ring, rubbing her thumb over the engraved carnelian crest.

'I suggest you lock your door.' She sniffed, wrinkled her nose. She recognised the heady floral scent a perfume ward. 'Have you been visiting a shaman?'

He looked up at her, yellow teeth clenched. 'Who else can I turn to? You won't help. Even God has forsaken me.'

'Oh, doctor. You misunderstand. Perhaps your death is God's will.'

Around them, sweaty jostling bodies sang with ardour. A brick player had broken through the flesh shambles' siege and was bounding towards their undefended home line. He sprang from post to post in a series of bravura, mocking bounds.

'If you can't protect me, I'll find someone who can.' Noroc prodded his glasses back up his nose, pinned them there with a forefinger. 'I know things. I'll go to Lesang! She'll protect me. The palace isn't the only authority in Fat Maw.'

Hagar considered throttling him. She saw the hot, quick motion of it, the wire round the throat, his struggling lost in the tumult of the crowd. His bloodshot eye was full of rueful, petty terror. It would be an act of mercy, for both of them.

But his threat had no teeth. She had terminated the Mill decades ago. The last trace of Noroc's research was wrapped around her wrist – and only she knew that. He had nothing to offer her enemies except wild stories.

And she did not want to hurt him, not really. If she killed him while he remained in a state of ignorance and fear, he would only be reborn in a new body, to repeat the whole ugly cycle again. To escape rebirth, you had to go willingly. Without malice or fear. How rare it must be to achieve such a thing. There was always unfinished business.

She curled her fingers round the cuff of her jacket. 'The assassin might be working for Doyenne Lesang. Did you consider that?'

Noroc blanched. 'But what should I do? The letter said once I'm gone, they'll kill the Grand-Duc.'

She laughed. She could not help it.

'Many have tried.' Her mirth frothed away to a cold hate. 'I think you are dealing with a fantasist.'

Noroc held out his hand. It hung there, filthy, quivering. With a start, she recognised the gesture – he was begging.

She took a step back. Noroc closed his fingers on nothing. Around them citizens exploded from their benches, cheering, bellowing, shaking fists at the teal sky. Their bodies created a hollow, a strange, shaded grove in which Noroc dropped to his knees and bowed before Hagar – a last, ersatz display of submission.

Poor wretch. Power was all he understood. She turned and left him there, greasy silver hairs protruding from beneath his crumpled headscarf. His terror was genuine, of course. But he would never comprehend the real tragedy – that submission was not enough.

What saved you was remorse.

As Hagar walked down the quayside, she noticed a harka keeping pace with her in a sailor's rainskin. His heavy brown poncho was an odd choice for a clement day, the hood fastening over his horns, half-obscuring his face. Occasionally he paused to regard the bay. A small steamer had docked beside him and blue-capped hawser clique orderlies were busy humping packing cases down the gangplank. Perhaps his aimless, shuffling demeanour was genuine. Perhaps he was watching her for one of the cliques. She pretended not to see him, sneaking glances when she dared.

A biting salty stink wafted from the great wooden doors of the fish market. Hagar passed a fisherwoman sitting crosslegged on the boardwalk, gutting a bottle-green decapus. She made a slit across its scalp, thrust a hand into the gap between the creature's eyes and turned it inside out like a velvet purse. Clinging emerald skin peeled away, birthing a slick white ghost. She began sawing through the stretchy translucent cartilage, dropping sweetbreads into a bucket – the ink sac, the pancreas, the dual underhearts.

The encounter with Noroc had left Hagar unsettled. So much rested on the next two days. The angel had seen only a possible future. Not an inevitable one.

'Miss Ingery.'

A deep voice brought her up short. The sweating red bulk that was Sheriff Kenner stood glowering on the boardwalk, the gold threads in his sash scintillating with the motion of his chest. He placed one hand on his dagger; with the other, he wiped perspiration from his muzzle.

'I'm very busy,' said Hagar. She continued to walk.

'Then let's not waste time,' said Kenner. He fell into step alongside her. 'Leave the city.'

'I've work to do.'

'I can't guarantee your safety.' Beneath his white smock, the humps of muscle supporting his neck shifted restlessly.

'I don't ask you to.'

'Age has made you complacent.'

'I don't think I'm invulnerable, if that's what you mean. If someone wants to kill me – I presume one of the cliques over whom you hold theoretical jurisdiction has given you notice of such an intention – they're at liberty to try.' She pushed her hat back and squinted at him. 'Exactly how much esteem do they hold you in? Enough to use innuendo? Do they respect you enough to grant you the courtesy of euphemism when they announce which of the city's laws they're planning to flout?'

'Last warning. Your presence is a disruption. Leave.'

Hagar breathed in the Sheriff's musk of sweat and tobacco. 'Do you fear death?'

'Yes. And I find your obsession with it far less intimidating than you imagine.' His nostrils flared, tiny white filaments trembling as he breathed in, his chest swelling. 'The flesh shambles clique are petitioning to the Spire Council to have the inauguration postponed.'

'What? Why?'

'They plan to file a formal protest tomorrow morning regarding "the movement of improper financial inducements liable to prejudice the election". Bribes, Miss Ingery.'

'Yes, yes, I know what a bribe is.' She shot a glance over her shoulder. The harka sailor was still following, his arms hidden beneath his poncho, projecting a demeanour of studied disinterest. Possibly too far to eavesdrop. She supposed he might have shore leave for the festival. His presence might be coincidental. 'The Grand-Duc is already on his way. They can't.'

'Forgive me, but legally speaking, they can. Towards the end of his tenure Prefect Colstrid introduced several statutes for precisely this situation.'

'Statutes?'

'Apparently he thought it best that interested parties have some legal recourse, to discourage dealing with constitutional issues in, ah . . . the traditional manner.'

'Typical Tonti. Thinking he could stop murder with a bit of jurisprudence.'

'Well.' Kenner rolled his huge shoulders. 'It looks rather prescient – or ironic – given the manner in which Prefect Colstrid relinquished his position.'

Oh Tonti. Perhaps you were wilier than I gave you credit for.

'Didn't stop his dying like a stuck pig, did it? I lived through the War in Heaven. You can't legislate your way to consensus.'

As they walked, the quay was opening out into the more upmarket, less smelly marina, warehouses, fish guts and drooling sewage runnels giving way to restaurants and clubhouses. Carillon music rang from the balcony of a mustard bar. Sampan stalls passed under the board-walk, laden with fruit and leaf-pouches of pipe weed. A hunched, whiskery vesperi was working the boards with a decrepit yak-hair broom, sweeping bones, wrappers and rinds into the water below. The sound of the Bataille Des Mats crowd had faded to a subliminal sigh. Unlit torches hung ready in braziers for the evening's shunning.

'This is your fault,' said Kenner. 'Your arrival has the cliques nervous. They think you're here to rig the election. Anyone thought to be in your favour is immediately the object of suspicion.'

'I'm surprised they're so keen to court the dead hand of the palace.'

He scoffed. 'Many fear the Grand-Duc's emergence after so many years is an attempt to reclaim power. They'd prefer he didn't come at all.' He stopped, turned to face her. 'We're one outrage away from civil war. Mark me. I'll do whatever's necessary to preserve order.' He touched a hand to one of his horns and performed a curt salute. 'Fair tides, Miss Ingery.' And he stomped off into the stilt city.

Hagar stood in the middle of the boardwalk, people filtering round her. She pressed a palm to her breastbone. Were her hands shaking? If Lesang's butchers submitted their petition and the council approved it, the inauguration would be cancelled. Morgellon would not attend. She would lose her opportunity to confront him. Everything would be ruined.

Hagar tightened her hand into a fist. No.

She glanced back at the harka sailor, who was loitering beside the wooden veranda of a coffee bar. A vesperi pedlar was going table to table with a clutch of bamboo cages stuffed with sweetwings; the tiny birds were dyed garish festival-day colours. The pedlar grabbed a bright green bird from its cage and offered it to the sailor. It struggled and trilled in her grip.

A sampan loaded with lobster pots was passing under the boardwalk. Hagar saw her chance. While the sailor was distracted she walked to the edge of the boardwalk and stepped off. She dropped fifteen feet and landed in the bow of the boat.

The sampan rocked. She dropped to a crouch and tossed the startled pilot a comte. He caught it overarm, checked the denomination, then slipped it into the pouch on his belt and nodded, before going back to working the boat's single-oar.

They drifted away from the quayside, into the mazy boating lanes of the stilt city merchants' district. The petition had not been submitted yet. It would be simple enough to find out the name of the flesh shambles' legal representatives. Perhaps they could reach an accommodation. She would have to drop in on them.

Hagar picked her way across the steep roof of the vitrifacsimilist's shop, her black hood fastened tight about her ears, her garrotte wire coiled inside the stiffened cuff of her leather duster. The tiles were dry and grippy beneath her boots. She remembered the icy roof of Colstrid's lodge, and felt thankful for the balmy weather.

Her enquiries had given her an address – the Rue Infinie, right at the summit of the high town – and a name – Advocate Ashesh-Ro. To her right, the sun was low over the ocean, liquid and blood-lush.

She advanced in a slow, loping scramble, right hand clutching the scalloped ridge tiles. To her left, the roof terminated in a wide bronze gutter streaked with verdigris, guarding a drop to the tree-lined esplanade three storeys below. From across the street came pettish caws and the jangle of bell-harnesses. Trains of skroon would be lining up at the foot of Mitta's Spire while handlers daubed their beaks with fluorescent paint, ready to drive the spirits back downhill into the sea.

Hagar thought of Räum alone in his stall and her heart ached. These past weeks, she had rewarded his lifetimes of service with neglect. Would she have time to visit him, before the end?

She stopped to rest, hooking three fingers through one of the ridge tiles' cruciform holes and relaxing her legs. To her right, red light soaked the rooftops and parapets, spreading down towards the bay. Lotan Reef winked with rubies. Shadows flowed into sidestreets and alleys, branching and darkening. As the sun sank towards the sea, Fat Maw's high town resembled a great cracking scab.

She hung back when she reached the rooftop's gable end, so no one would see her from the alley below. On the wind she smelt barbecued wetpig, torch smoke. The jump onto the roof of the Advocate's chambers was about four feet horizontally, perhaps five down. The roof had a gentle pitch and a large skylight in its southern face.

Four feet was not enough to be chancy, but the centuries had taught her that feats on the upper end of easy were where most people came undone: carelessness while fording a river on skroon, a moment's distraction loading a cannon – straightforward tasks that encouraged complacency. Lord Cambridge's valet Kizo had lived over three hundred years and survived at least twenty assassination attempts – two of which had been ordered by the Grand-Duc himself – and then snapped his neck falling downstairs on the way to morning temple. Valets were, after all, just as killable as regular mortals – the tiny sliver of the honours they inherited prevented ageing, but no more. Officials whispered that he had been pushed, but Hagar knew such gossip was dust tossed to conceal a more disturbing truth – Kizo had been killed by routine.

She slotted two of her grapnel's flukes under the ten sinuous arms of the small stone decapus that capped the roof ridge, and ran the rope twice through her belt. Across the street, pale streamers fluttered from the silver minaret of Mitta's Spire in ugly rinds. Strings of firecrackers belted the narrow turret beneath, helixing down to where the spire sank into the cobblestones. She thought of everything that lay buried under the square. Such a betrayal, yet Morgellon still chose to honour him.

She understood perfectly. There was no reasoning with love.

The bricks had turned a swooning, drunken crimson. The shunning would start just after sundown. She had to hurry.

Hagar braced a sole against the lip of the roof and jumped. Smoky wind whipped over her eyes. She threw her palms out and landed, monkey-deft, on Advocate Ashesh-Ro's roof. She blinked away tears, staying crouched, feeling the slates' warmth through her gloved palms, enjoying the kick of her heart.

She rose. Her climbing rope dipped back over the alley up to the roof she had leapt from. Tonight, every street was spiderwebbed with festival bunting. An extra black line would not excite comment. She secured it to the modest ball finial at the end of the Advocate's roof with a half-hitch.

She walked to the skylight. It was stained glass, a stylised composite of blue and green teardrops edged with thin lead curlicues, depicting Okap̄ the God Fish eating the sun. The window was shut. Hagar had long ceased to be impressed by decadence, but there was something both affected and affecting about installing such a delicate and expensive pane so far from where common eyes could see it. If the Advocate had wanted to flaunt her lucre she could have set it on the ground floor, facing the street.

Hagar knelt and peered through the cobalt-tinted panels beside Okap's flowing whiskers, down into the office. Advocate Ashesh-Ro, Hagar had learned, had a reputation for long dinners, sexual profligacy and a matchless work ethic. Whether or not this reputation was deserved, only its final component mattered. If the butchers planned to submit their petition tomorrow morning, the Advocate would be working late to ensure the evidence was correctly catalogued and cross-referenced.

Through a greenblue wash, Hagar gazed down upon a pentagonal desk, with clockwork oil lamp, ink and blotting paper, and heavy lead legal seal. The lamp was lit – a harsh, diffuse glow wobbled within the mantle, like the sun through fog. The desk was surrounded by three low-backed captain's chairs of dark, polished leather. Beside the chair nearest the lamp was a silver stand holding a glass ashtray. One of the desk drawers was open.

She heard a thud and shrank back. When she eased her head forward she saw a figure rounding the table in crushed silk legal vestments, dark half-cape and long woollen shunning hood.

Already dressed for the festival. Hagar had got here just in time.

The hood obscured the figure's face but he or she appeared of medium build for a vesperi, and limber – wings presumably folded under the cape. The figure dumped a stack of documents on the desk, pulled up a low-backed chair and began rifling through them hurriedly with felt-gloved fingers.

This, surely, was Advocate Ashesh-Ro. Hunting down a final affidavit before she headed out to celebrate. Professional to a fault.

Hagar felt a warm rush of fellow-feeling. She had dabbled in jurisprudence for half-a-dozen decades back at the Institute. It was like plunging a knife into a river. Law changed so quickly, rippling and flowing round the expediencies of the age. She preferred the sure and timeless edicts of the body, a book that remained the same each time you opened it.

Hagar had not, in her discreet enquiries, managed to discern what the Advocate looked like, but she half-remembered the virtue-name, Ashesh, from the great vesperi families of the Thelusian diaspora: those lean, grey-furred clannish bureaucrats with their severe northern features and wolfish ears. She saw something flash on one of the gloved fingers. Above the middle knuckle sat a chunky signet ring – probably bearing the embossed insignia of the Noble Southern College of Pandecti.

It was almost too easy.

Hagar shuffled back out of view and examined the skylight itself. The stained glass appeared much older than the window frame, perhaps an heirloom, brought over with the families of the Second Diaspora. A symbol of continuity, survival. It could be raised via a brass screwjack. That meant a maximum gap of a few inches, and you could only turn the handle from the inside. There was no way to open it without kicking through the glass.

She kicked through the glass. The ornate panes gave like eggshell, lead struts twisting inwards. She dropped through the gap and landed on the pentagonal desk in a blue and green cascade.

The Advocate sprang to her feet, knocking her chair over.

Hagar flexed her fingers. 'Fair tides, Advocate.'

Advocate Ashesh-Ro stood flattened against the bookcase that covered the rear wall. She lifted her head, and the light from the oil lamp filled the interior of her cowl.

She had ruddy skin, a sharply defined jaw and dark, defiant eyes. A human.

'You're not the Advocate.'

The figure – the young girl – was breathing heavily beneath her hood.

Hagar took a step forward. A sliver of glass caught in the tread of her boot; she felt it score a scar in the desk's smooth finish.

'Where is she?' said Hagar.

The girl held Hagar's gaze, trembling, glowering. She looked too young for a junior barrister, too young for a clerk even. Since when had the Advocate started hiring humans?

Plastered to the girl's temples were twists of damp grey hair. She rolled her shoulders in what felt like a challenge.

'Who are you?' said Hagar.

The girl thinned her eyes and drew her lips into a tight, angry bud.

Hagar took another step, glass crunching under her heel. '*Qui êtes-vous?*' Her toecap nudged the stack of papers. More documents were heaped on a row of cabinets, beside a ceramic tithing bowl – presumably for six-ways clients – and brazier. She glanced at the stranger's gloves and hood. 'Are you a *thief*?' The term elicited a tiny but palpable flinch. 'You realise Advocates operate as agents of the perpetuum? That makes breaking and entering legal chambers a felony.' She began counting out offences on her fingers. 'Lèse-majesté, embracery, larceny . . .'

Hagar noticed the girl's attention straying and followed her gaze upwards to the smashed skylight. The rope hung slackly through a jagged hole fringed with twisted prongs of lead.

Hagar regarded the scratched desk. 'True, this is probably tortious malfeasance.' She knelt, sliding a hand down towards the misericord concealed in her boot. 'But as a representative of Maison Jejunus I have a prerogative when it comes to protecting interests of State and Crown. Which is to say . . .' She stood, gripping the thin blade by its tip. 'Why are you here and who sent you?'

The girl nodded past her. 'I hope you brought a second knife for him.'

Hagar turned to look. Behind her was a thick wooden door, treacle black, its upper panel a relief carving of vesperi soaring over a stormy ocean upon stylised wings. Above a discreet sliding latch, the door-knob was a polished oval of smoked blue glass. The door was ajar. A blow swept her legs out.

She twisted as she fell. A bluff! Impressive. Her palms thudded into the desk, skidding through glass splinters. She caught a flash of movement and rolled. The silver ashtray stand crashed into the spot where her skull had been. Hagar sprang to her feet. She punted the stack of documents into the air and danced back.

Through a shower of flapping papers she saw the girl, clutching the ashtray stand lengthways like a staff, glaring defiantly. This was no clerk.

Hagar snorted and widened her stance. Her palms stung. She had gone years without a proper fight. Her skin tingled, the old training kicking in. Good to test her skills. A warm-up before tomorrow.

She glanced around for her dropped misericord. The girl stepped forward and push-passed the ashtray stand at Hagar's head. Hagar caught it easily, pivoting to absorb the impact. She switched to a one-handed grip and swung the stand in a wide, chopping motion, aiming for the girl's skull. The girl dropped and the swing missed. She scrambled under the desk.

She was making for the door. Hagar let the ashtray stand drop and took two quick steps back, yielding to the muscle memory drilled into her by successive Canoness Umbra Primes at the Sciamachian Order, her knees relaxing so her torso dipped, then tensing with explosive force. Gravity shifted around her, her ankles whipping up over her while the glass-strewn hardwood floor glinted below like ice floe. Her right hand went to her opposite cuff; as the desk swung back into view, she spread her legs and landed in a wide stance, bending her knees and taking several quick steps backwards to distribute the momentum while pulling the garrotte from her sleeve.

Her shoulder blades kissed the door. She yanked the wire tight between her fists.

The girl was barely out from under the desk. She saw Hagar and stumbled back. Her hood slipped.

The clockwork lamp had fallen to the floor. The mantle had shattered and a puddle of leviathan oil burned with clear white flames. The girl's underlit face was carved with hard black lines. Her tangled hair shone gunmetal grey. In the shifting flames she looked young, then old, then young again.

'I don't want to kill you,' said Hagar. Her climbing rope ran from her belt to the skylight in a long black arc. 'I'm on a mission of peace.'

The girl breathed out of the corner of her mouth. She seemed to be weighing her options. The burning oil gave off a rank, fishy stink.

'You're working for one of the cliques, correct?' said Hagar. 'Who was it? The saltpetres? The pilcrows? No matter. They told you to come here, ransack the Advocate's offices – threaten her a bit, perhaps? Because of the flesh shambles' petition?'

The girl's arms lowered slightly, though she remained tensed, alert.

Hagar let the garrotte wire slacken, in a show of reciprocity. 'We may have a common goal.' She wondered how much to say. Negotiation was probably futile – the girl might not even be listening. Still, another corpse would be inconvenient. 'I want nothing to complicate the Grand-Duc's arrival.'

The muscles of the girl's face twitched.

'Who are you?' she said. Her accent was not Avalonian.

'Where are you from, child?'

The girl blinked. The look in her eyes was confusion or fear or both.

Hagar heard footsteps on the stairs. Whoever it was had almost reached the landing. Hagar sidestepped, moving an index finger to her lips. The girl's gaze flicked from Hagar to the door. Hagar shook her head.

The smoked glass doorknob clicked, then began to twist.

'Run!' yelled the girl.

Hagar slapped the latch home. The doorknob rattled. The voice on the other side said: 'Delphine?'

That name. Was that the one Arthur had mentioned? Hagar looked up just in time to see the girl draw a pistol – boxy, black, with two grips and a compact barrel. It did not look native. Hagar stared as the girl lined up a shot on her head.

'Wait,' said Hagar.

If the girl had meant to kill, she could have. Instead at the last moment she jinked the muzzle to the right and fired, blasting apart a fluted glass sculpture bracketed to the wall. The report was ear-splitting. Hagar staggered, clutching her temple. The girl tucked the gun inside her robes, jumped onto the desk and grabbed the rope.

Hagar ran at her. The girl hauled herself upwards with impressive speed. Hagar grabbed the end tied to her belt and shook it, but the girl clung on, gripping with her feet. The girl grasped a bent strut of lead, and, screaming with the effort, dragged herself up through the smashed skylight.

The doorknob turned back and forth. Someone rapped on the wood.

'Hello? Delphine? Are you all right?'

Silk vestments billowed as the girl disappeared through the skylight. Hagar cursed. She tilted her head and lights streaked, leaving little tails. Everything was overly bright. Her mouth had gone dry. Someone was at the door and the girl was getting away – a girl who had seen Hagar's face.

Hagar pressed her gloved palms together. Crushed glass ground against crushed glass. She closed her eyes and prayed.

Give us help from trouble: for vain is the help of man. Through God we shall do valiantly: for he it is that shall tread down our enemies.

She breathed out, breathed in, and opened her eyes. One problem at a time. First, the petition.

Hagar snatched her dagger from the table. She ran to the documents stacked on the cabinets and slit the strings holding them together. She hurled them into the pool of burning oil in great loose drifts.

The door crashed as someone barged it.

She ran along the polished bookshelves, tugging down heavy, gold-leafed tomes in ones and twos and hurling them into the spreading blaze. The cost of collections like this ensured law remained in the hands of the wealthy, or those who were prepared to accrue considerable debts to the wealthy. They were not books so much as bricks in a wall.

Sweat was threading down her brow and temples. She vaulted onto the table and grasped the rope. The floor was lush with fire. Any relevant papers were ashes. Advocate Ashesh-Ro had bigger problems now than countersigning a few affidavits.

Hagar gripped her misericord between her teeth and began to climb. The office door boomed with repeated blows. The bitter stink of bubbling varnish joined the leviathan oil's briny tang.

At the top, she used her knife to knock away slivers of glass. Heat beat against her calves. Her gloved fingers scrabbled for the ridge between the frame and the roof tiles.

She heard the latch bang loose from its housing and felt a great woof of air as the door opened.

Her cloak flapped in the sudden draft, the fire sucking thirstily. Sweat trickled down her neck and stung her eyes.

'Hey!'

With a last grunting effort she hoisted herself through the shattered skylight and onto the rooftop.

The girl had climbed across the alley to the opposite roof. She sat straddling the roof ridge, aiming the gun at Hagar.

She fired. Slates just shy of Hagar's toes exploded musically. The shot rang across the esplanade. Any other night, gunfire would have drawn armed peace officers, but citizens were walking around with aprons full of firecrackers, discharging miniature cannons. Hagar looked for cover, but on the Advocate's flat, featureless roof she was utterly exposed. The girl lined up a second shot, her signet ring winking ruby in the bloody sunset.

Hagar felt dizzy. She had been overconfident. The fatal mistake. Time slowed.

The girl held the gun two-handed. She closed one eye.

Hagar took a step forward. She took another, then a third, and walked off the edge of the building.

The alley surged towards her then the rope tied to her belt pulled taut and she swung into the opposing wall. Her boots connected hard, knees slamming up round her ears, teeth clacking in her skull. She was hanging a storey and a half from the ground. She looked up. A trickle of grit fell towards her. A jolt passed through the rope.

Hagar's soles skidded against the wall. The girl had unfastened the grappling hook.

Hagar released the rope, kicked. Cobbles, red sky. She hit the opposite wall, kicked off it, and crashed into the ground shoulder-first. She rolled, throwing her momentum sideways. Her belt-boxes chattered on the cobbles. She was still.

She lay on her back, panting. Her jacket had absorbed the brunt. She opened her eyes.

She twisted aside; the grappling hook clanged into the spot where her head had been, flukes gonging like a church bell.

Small mistakes.

She stumbled to her feet. She had skinned her palms and her shoulder ached, but she was alive.

Delphine. Was that the girl's name? *She helps you, though she may not mean to.* Hadn't the angel said something like that? It had been so long ago. Her accent was certainly peculiar. And that gun was definitely contraband.

And let it be, when these signs are come unto thee, that thou do as occasion serve thee; for God is with thee.

Hagar retrieved the grappling hook. Portentous or not, the girl was a potential witness. One way or another, she had to be dealt with.

Hagar watched a silhouette drop the last few feet from a pulley rope at the rear of the wine merchant's. She saw the smooth profile of the hood, then the robe melted, crumpling round the figure's ankles.

The street was steep, lined with slanting, semi-timbered houses. Oil lamps shone in large, ornate windows, some of which had been decorated with necklaces of taldin skulls or bloodwrack and other traditional wards. The sun had all but set. Hagar had trained in the darkness. *In Umbris Sorores.*

She crept to the western side of the street, where it was darkest, moving lightly on the balls of her feet. The girl walked a short distance, then stopped before an oriel window. Behind the glass leered an eyeless totem of sticks and woven grass, crowned with a diadem of sea briars. Her hair shone white in the lamplight, her expression consumed by shadow.

Hagar ducked beneath a windowsill, holding her breath. The girl was dressed for the festival – leather half-cape and a long woollen shunning hood. She pulled the hood down over her face, checking her reflection in the glass.

Hagar pressed herself into the recess beneath the low sill. If she stuck to the shadows, the girl would not spot her until they were feet apart. Bangs echoed over the roofs of the houses. Drumskins began to reverberate with fat, bass pounds, accompanied by the frightful jankling of bellfists. The shunning had begun.

Hagar waited. She had to know who this girl was, what she had come for. She had a part to play – Arthur had promised. Thudding came from the top of the street. The girl tightened the cord round her hood and turned from the window.

Demons came pouring down the hill.

Skull-masked and razor-beaked, lip-stitched, gnash-jawed, serpent-maned and pit-eyed, segmented prowling ones, skittering little ones, roaring, clicking, popping, jeering, jangle-stamping, swinging smoking torches, beating drums with clubs, rolling a barrel of flaming tar before them as they danced and swarmed and revelled.

Colour flooded the street. Shadows stretched, solid black blades, then retracted and shrank as more and more torches appeared. Ugh – light. Hagar recoiled, hiding her face.

A firecracker went off with an echoing bang. She suppressed the instinct to throw herself flat – her old war reflexes. When she looked up, the girl had already clattered past, shoes slapping the cobbles as she pelted downhill.

Hagar spat. She could not let her get away. She drew her collar up round her ears and gave chase.

Hagar stalked the girl for over an hour, from the cobbled streets of the high town down to the docks, towards the boardwalks of the stilt city. The moon was a slitted eye above the northern headland. A distant din of bells and drums carried on the breeze.

As they left behind the southern wharfs' vast coal-burning cargo ships and sleek clippers, the vessels grew smaller, more makeshift – turtleboats, rickety fishing junks and old river barges converted into homes. Tethered softshells slept in their giant pontoon-nests, their sonorous, creaking snores covering Hagar's footsteps as she crept low and furtive from crate to crab pot to capstan. On the landward side, cabins stood on multiple tiers, raised on wooden posts and connected by rigging and plank walkways. A heady musk hung so thickly that it coated her tongue – a mix of tar and brine and effluent.

Hagar slipped a cartridge into her little single-shot pistol and snapped the breech closed. She had acquired it from a gunsmith in Athanasia in part-exchange for an antique fowling piece some twenty years ago. She had just been turned away from the palace, yet again. She remembered the sting of rejection, how dust hung in the cramped shop, her cheeks still burning with humiliation. She remembered wondering if the Grand-Duc's allies – her rivals – would let her leave the capital alive. The gun had been her way of assisting providence.

It was nasty but inaccurate. Good for close quarters. Insurance, in case the girl was still feeling combative.

The girl stopped beside a black mountain of nets. Boats were moored with ropes and chains. Hagar dropped behind a stack of empty cages and peered through the corroded mesh. Silhouetted, the girl glanced up and down the boardwalk.

Hagar removed her boots and socks. She moved on the balls of her feet, stealing along the edge of the boardwalk, the sea lapping at thick christwood pilings some twenty feet below. In the faint moonlight, the girl's hair looked silver.

Hagar broke cover and tackled her.

The girl went down hard. Hagar heard the crack of her head hitting the boards. A leather book went skittering across the planks. Hagar pulled her knife and straddled her.

'Delphine?' she said, raising the blade. 'Is that your name?'

The girl scowled, reached for her belt.

Hagar drove the knife into her shoulder. It slipped in easy.

'Tell me!'

The girl grunted, grabbed Hagar's wrist. She swung her elbow into Hagar's windpipe, rolled. They clattered over one another; the dagger slipped a little deeper and the girl cried out. She shoved. Hagar skidded backwards across the boardwalk.

The girl staggered to her feet, ran. Without thinking, Hagar grabbed a length of chain and slung it after her. It struck the girl in the back of the skull and her legs crumpled. Hagar ran to catch her, but the girl's face thumped off a wooden mooring post and she tumbled off the boardwalk.

The body dropped twenty feet and hit the ocean with a flat slap. Hagar ran to the edge. She dropped to her hands and knees and looked down.

Wooziness swept over her and everything went dark. She blinked and found she had collapsed against the boardwalk. She must have gone down too fast.

Her back was wet. It was raining.

Below, the dark ocean slopped against the pilings, marbled with spume. She watched, waiting for the girl to surface. She could see all the way under the boardwalk. She waited. And waited.

And waited.

CHAPTER 5

THIS CHICKENSHIT OUTFIT

She sank. Meat in a soft black void. Then heat. Thirst. Skull ache.

Let me sleep, let me sleep.

She woke.

Delphine lay on a canvas bunk. Here were plank walls and a door. She was in a small room with a low rush roof. The air was muggy.

Her gut clenched. She sat up. The room swooned. A big clay bowl lay on the floor next to her bunk and she had just enough time to turn over before she threw up into it.

She vomited dark fluid, pints of it. It came up easily. Stomach acid burned her throat and nostrils. She spat out the last few drops and lay back in her bunk, sweaty, shuddering. A dirty white air conditioning unit oscillated softly.

She closed her eyes. The room lurched. She opened them again and it steadied.

Her bunk sat low on a floor covered in coarse rope matting. On a crate next to the bunk stood a pottery jug, covered with a piece of muslin. A slit in the rush-mat blind admitted a thin knife of light that sliced the crate in two.

She studied the jug. She had the oddest feeling it only existed because she was concentrating on it. She checked the room. Four walls of blond unvarnished wood.

She peeled back the muslin. The liquid inside was clear. She sniffed it. No odour. She dipped in two fingers and sucked them. It tasted like water. Was she imagining water? Had she created water?

She checked the room again. Still there.

Her tongue felt gummy against the roof of her mouth. She lifted the jug and drank. Cool fluid ran from the corners of her mouth, spilling down her chin and neck. Her belly was sore so she sipped rather than gulped. The water had a leafy aftertang.

She set the jug down. Where was she? The room looked just the same as it had when she had woken up. Was time repeating itself? Had she thought that before?

More nausea. She pinched the bridge of her nose until it passed.

She ran her thumb across the jug's glaze. Words were etched in a script she did not recognise. What was that? Cyrillic? She looked at the thumb rubbing them. She looked at the hand.

It was not hers. She tried to pull away and the fingers twitched and followed. A strange pale arm hung in the air. She tried to swat it and the phantom limb swiped at nothing, mocking her.

She dropped to the floor. The arm followed her. She covered her head and shut her eyes. She inhaled, felt alien lungs stretch beneath an expanding ribcage, foreign bones straining against a tent of foreign skin. She was full of other. This was not her body.

She tried to breathe but it was the alien body that was breathing. She was trapped inside. The heart was a kicking pain. Oh God. She was trapped, she was dead—

She bit the inside of her cheek. Calm down, you foolish thing. What would Mother think of all this?

Mother used to say panic was a form of regression. It was a mistaken application of tactics which had served one well as an infant. In grown-up life, there was no parent waiting to recognise your distress, to swoop in and rescue you. No adult at all – except you.

She opened her eyes and stared up at the rafters and the underside of the slanted rush roof. She inhaled, focusing on the smell of the rope-mat floor, musty and fibrous like an old library. She counted her breaths: one . . . two . . . three . . . four . . . five. Right. Shall we have a look, then?

She glanced down.

The arm lay beside her like a dead branch. Three moles dotted the bicep. The forearm was covered in short dark hairs. She could see the tendon where it met the wrist.

She imagined the index finger rising, thought about electrical impulses shooting out of a brain, activating tiny muscles.

The finger twitched.

She winced, looked away. Sick fear was swelling in her chest.

She concentrated on the planks in the wall. They were rough, shaded ivory to deep orange. Her focus seemed to lock them in place. Perhaps she had died, and this was the afterlife, and if she didn't keep imagining her surroundings and holding them together, they would dissolve and she would melt away into nothing.

She lifted the wrist. Faint arteries threaded over the tendons. She made a fist. The flesh on the back of her hand was firm, the knuckles the same light pink as the surrounding skin. She flourished the fingers in a little arpeggio. They obeyed.

She sat up and looked at the bare feet. *Her* feet. She wriggled her toes. Scrunched them. Released.

A shapeless white smock came down to her knees. Clothes lay folded beside the bunk in a neat square – a white cotton vest, white cotton knickers and a pair of blue canvas trousers. She picked them up, turned them over. The vest had a label in the collar: *FABRIQUÉ EN CHINE.*

She stood. The body stood. The two actions occupied the same space. Instinctively, she grasped for stick or bedpost. There was nothing to grab.

She shifted her weight from one heel to the other. Balance held her as the sea holds a fish. She rolled her foot heel to ball. She had arches. She raised her foot. Took a step. She went up on tiptoes.

She windmilled her arms. Her shoulders swivelled, loose, compliant. She strolled across the room, then marched, then sprinted. She dropped into a squat and monkey-scrambled across the matting on her hands and knees. She leapt off the bunk. She tried placing a palm on the floor, listening with her whole body for the muscle-memory of a cartwheel. Had it gone? She attempted one half-heartedly, ended up kicking her legs out in a wild, capering genuflection. Come on, Venner. You've got to commit. She took a run up, throwing herself into it. Her ankles swung high over her head and when she landed upright her hair flopped into her eyes.

She threw a few punches, though it was decades since she had shadow-boxed. Her heart was hammering. When she bit down, full sets of smooth molars sank into register.

'What are you doing?'

She swung round. A figure stood in the doorway, one hand on the rickety jamb.

Delphine spun on her heel, revelling in how thoughtless the motion felt, how it seemed to execute itself. He was silhouetted against blazing white sunlight. She swept hair out of her eyes, squinted.

'It's me, you idiot,' said Butler.

Delphine blinked. 'How long have I—' She flinched. Her voice was wrong. 'How . . .' It was high-pitched and smooth. 'Ah. Ah. Ah.' It was like a strange child kept anticipating her every word. She put a hand to her throat. 'Oh God.'

Butler sighed heavily. 'Any bleeding, severe internal pain, problems breathing?'

Delphine prodded her ribs through her smock. 'No, I don't think—'

'Right then. Put some clothes on. We've got work to do.'

In a rush, she remembered the deal she'd made. 'Wait. Is—'

He slammed the door.

Delphine wriggled out of the smock and pulled the T-shirt over her head, squeezing her wide skull through the hole. The fabric had that salty new clothes smell. She hopped round the room as she yanked the trousers up her legs.

She opened the door. Heat hit her in a drenching wave.

Reed-thatched huts stood on a red dirt plateau. To her right, a steep scree slope climbed up and up, till it broke into rust-dark cliffs. To her left, the ground fell away, dropping forty feet to black thorns and jagged glinting stones. Far, far below, under a lamina of pallid cloud, trees rose in a dark, clotting mass.

Her skull pulsed with a thrilling numbness. She was on a mountainside.

Butler was skulking in the shade beneath the hut's ragged eaves, useless wings drawn round him like a cloak. He glanced at Delphine sidelong.

'Put those on.'

Delphine looked down. In the stirred dirt outside the door lay a pair of wooden clogs.

'Wait.' Her new voice made her lose her thread. She closed her eyes. 'Butler. Please. Is she here?'

'Follow me.'

When he rose from the wall, she saw he was wearing a maroon silk shirt with the sleeves rolled up past his elbows, and a grey sarong with gold galloon trim. He began walking away, his clogs scuffing up little devils of red dust.

She stepped out of the shade. Her left foot sank into dry, powdery dirt.

Searing pain rushed. She leapt back, slamming into the hut. In the shade, she crouched and massaged her sole. The ground was scorching hot.

She picked up the clogs. They were flat rectangles balanced on a pair of four-inch wooden teeth. She sat against the hut and fastened the cloth thongs between her toes with thumb knots. She set off after Butler.

He was following a wide track of fine black gravel away from the huts, marching with purpose and stamina, at a pace that Delphine felt was spitefully fast.

'Hey!' she called. 'Wait!'

She pursued for a few lunging, treacherous yards, the clogs wobbling beneath her. She was going to turn her ankles. Christ's sweet tree, she loathed heels. She stopped to tighten the straps.

Liquid heat radiated up from the gritty track as she squatted, bathing her cheeks and brow. The air was sweet and thin. She rose. From the foot of the mountainside, an undulating canopy spread for miles, coating foothills and misty valleys in dense, verdant havoc. Purple-underbellied anvils of cloud pulsed on the distant horizon as they swapped lightning with the earth. The scale of it caught in her heart. Oh Algernon. We found it.

Butler was blurring with heatwarp. She stumbled after him. Her burnt soles felt tender against the flat paddle of the clogs. She began to get a feel for them, shifting her weight onto the balls of her feet, letting the wooden teeth bite into the dirt. She focused on the crunch of clog on grit. Her pace improved. Something lithe and silver flickered across the track, using her shadow for cover.

Though Butler appeared to be moving at a gentle trot, she was falling behind. She doubled her pace. The heat was punishing. Her vest was glued to her breastbone with sweat. Breaths came harder, thinner. She wished she had drunk more water before setting off.

She tried to speed up; one of her clogs went over on its side. She threw her arms out, so raddled with adrenaline, she squawked.

For Christ's sake, woman. Keep. Your. Head. She pumped her arms, accelerating for the final, steepest part of the climb.

She crested a rise and found herself on the red cusp of a crater pond. On the plateau beside it stood a long hut with shuttered windows and solar panels lining a wide, palm-thatched roof. A cauldron sat over a charcoal fire pit. Steam rose from its wide mouth; she smelt red meat, wine, spices. Flat grey stones lay round the pit edge, cooking papery blue fish that hissed and smoked.

Butler was already in the shade of the eaves, kicking his clogs off.

Delphine slowed as she passed the fire pit. Her stomach gurgled. The nausea was gone. She was ravenous.

'What are you waiting for?' said Butler. He held the door open.

Delphine wiped away sweat. Sunlight glinted on the crater lake. The sky was a delirious azure against the red of the mountain.

She peeled her vest away from her skin, raked her fingers through her hair. Her knees were trembling. She could not cower in this moment forever.

Delphine took a long, slow breath. She entered the hut.

Delphine's breath caught.

A woman on her side, one leg drawn up beneath her. White-gold hair was splashed over an angular skull. Her eyes were closed.

Delphine stared, disbelieving. 'Is she . . .'

Butler blew smoke out his nostril slits. 'She's sleeping.' He crushed his cigarette out on the lid of a box. 'Shut the door.'

The cabin was shady and sweetly cool, lit by electric bulbs and filled with the whine of a boxy plastic air-con unit. Cloth blinds hung across shuttered windows. Butler stood between stacks of ribbed military packing chests. There were boxes everywhere, filled with cartons of Marlboro Reds, generic paracetamol, shrink-wrapped designer shirts, single malt whiskies, newspapers. Behind him, planks on a pair of sawhorses formed a makeshift table. The table was covered with comms equipment – a black plastic tower case covered in dials, sliders and LEDs, headphones, a microphone on a desk stand and a single speaker. Dirty white cables snaked away to a dangerous-looking tangle of plugs in the corner.

Delphine knelt beside the bunk. What was this feeling? A tightness in the centre of her forehead. A strange, thick resistance in her chest.

'Alice?'

The young woman lying before her did not seem real. The old Alice, the one Delphine had visited and cared for all the years, was gone. How peculiar. Perhaps the thing she was feeling was grief.

She tried the name again. 'Alice.' Using it felt deeply odd. Not that the figure didn't look like the Alice she remembered – quite the reverse. She was so familiar it felt like a cruel trick. 'Alice?' Delphine reached for her.

'Let her sleep.' Butler sparked a fresh cigarette. He snapped his lighter shut. 'Eat and rest. Crossing the channel creates a big calorific deficit.' He began walking towards the door. 'I need to oversee bringing the last of our cargo from England. Oh – and don't wander off down the mountainside. Don't wander anywhere, in fact.' He held his cigarette between thumb and long, slender forefinger, inhaling till the pink cartilage of his noseleaf folded in on itself. 'Stay in the cabin. The mood down at the camp is . . .' He stropped his toes across the rope-mat floor. 'Just stay here.'

'And do what?'

Butler glanced round at the packing chests. 'Pick out a gun?'

Delphine flipped the catches on another moulded gun chest. Fully half of the containers in the hut were guns and ammo. Ms Rao had amassed a disturbing amount of firepower. She must have smuggled guns from all over the world.

Alice slept on her bunk. Occasionally she would shift in her sleep, and Delphine's heart would stop.

Delphine lifted the lid and took out a Ruger submachine gun. She unfolded the butt and braced it against the fleshy part of her shoulder. It reeked of cleaning oil and grease. She aimed at a dark brown knothole in the hut's far wall, imagined squeezing, emptying the magazine in under four seconds – the hot, angry rasp.

She folded the stock and put the gun back in its foam cut-out. Too much.

Another case had three black pistols, all chambered for 9mm – Russian military by the looks of them. Eh. A bit vanilla.

She opened a third crate. Inside a grey foam cut-out was a matte-black shotgun. Remington 870. Twelve-gauge. Pistol grip with removable butt stock. Magazine extension.

She tested the shotgun's pistol grip in either hand, squinted down the rib. Not a patch on the elegant side-by-side fowling pieces of her youth. She shucked the slide action and heard that vulgar, showy *ka-chuk*.

Delphine returned the shotgun to its crate. In adjacent cut-outs were black plastic sidesaddle and stock shell-holder mounts, still in their blister packs, and an aluminium mount for a mag light. She wondered if the weight of the torch would throw the aim off, or, if you mounted it on the cheek side, whether your supporting hand would naturally compensate. She could try it out – maybe strip the thing while she was at it and check all the parts. There was a work-bench in the corner.

A cough from the back of the room. Delphine turned.

Alice blinked, opened her eyes.

Delphine ran to her.

Alice looked around. She yawned. She closed her eyes.

'Alice? It's me.' Alice wrinkled her nose and murmured. 'Are you all right? It's Delphine. I know I sound different but it's me. Look.'

Alice grimaced, squirming against the bunk. She rubbed her eyes. Her skin was shiny with sweat. She half-opened her eyes and peered at Delphine.

Delphine felt the room dissolve around them. 'Hello, darling.'

Alice's pupils flicked about. Her left eye was pink and watering. She frowned.

'What's happened to the . . .' She winced, pinched the bridge of her nose. 'Ohhh . . .'

'It's all right. You're all right.' Words that would have sounded calm and authoritative in her old voice came out in an eerie singsong. 'I'm here. Don't worry. Everything's fine.' How much should she explain? How much was Alice capable of understanding? 'Darling? Do you remember who you are?'

'Mm?'

'Do you know who you are?'

Alice smeared a palm over her clammy face. She nodded.

'Of course. What time is it?' Her voice was scratchy with sleep.

'That's a bit of a complicated question. Just gone midday, I think.'

'Oh God.' Alice took a deep breath and glanced around again. 'Where . . .' Her look became one of bewilderment. 'Where am I?'

'Alice. You had dementia. You weren't yourself. We've brought you to the other world.'

'Oh.' Alice studied her surroundings with renewed curiosity. 'So this is all . . . We found it, then?'

'Well. It rather found us.'

Alice stared off to the side, her lips pressed into a slit. 'Have I been away a long time?'

Delphine's image of her began to blur and break up. 'Years and years.' She took Alice's hand. 'Such a long time.'

Alice yawned again – a big, toothy roar. She studied the fingers of her free hand. She peered through them at Delphine.

'Whatever's happened to your face?'

Delphine touched her cheek, alarmed. 'What?'

'You're all . . .' Alice touched her own face, pinched the skin. She looked at her hand again, then sat up sharply. 'Oh! Oh!'

It took some time to calm her down. Delphine explained what had happened, how the threshold had taken seventy years from their physical ages, and Alice appeared to understand, but moments later she noticed her hand and the cycle began again.

Eventually Alice wore herself out, and settled into a kind of stupor.

Delphine went outside and filled two bowls with stew from the cauldron. It was thick and brimming with onions and peas, and Delphine went back for seconds. Butler had been right – she felt hungrier than she ever had in her life. She found a coolbox, cracked open two Cokes and drank both.

As Alice ate, her alertness grew. She asked questions about where they were and seemed to retain the answers. She looked confused but oddly calm.

'But why am *I* here?' she said.

'That was Martha's price for cooperation. That we could bring you with us.'

'Hm.' Alice nibbled her stew. 'And what did I think of that?'

'I don't think you were well enough to understand.'

'Oh.' Her tongue poked out the corner of her mouth, the way it used to when she was concentrating very hard. She looked up. 'What now, then?'

Delphine gazed into her bowl. 'I thought we might go on a little cruise.'

A wide and bloody river flowed into the mouth of a cave. Thin, limpid things flickered through the russet water. Even in the shade, Delphine was perspiring. All around, the jungle loomed. There were more huts, and, incongruously, the ruin of a little stone church. A thick, cloying fecundity wafted over the river bank. Across the cave roof, the black volcanic rock was pocked with air bubbles and smeared in sheeny beards of moss. Tangle vines hung from the plateau above, some plaited together into spherical nests dripping with tiny fire-red birds. The river continued underground, fading into darkness.

'What is it?' said Alice, dazed, awestruck. She was wearing a wide-brimmed rush hat and a white blouse with flapping sleeves.

'The Underkills.'

Delphine turned to see Butler standing a little way up the bank, eating chunks of steaming meat off a skewer. Grease dripped onto the silty ground. 'Underground river network branching south and west,' he said. 'This was all in your primer.'

Vesperi orderlies were loading crates from a jetty onto a long sampan-style riverboat. Most of the boat was sheltered by a barrel-arch roof covered in rigging. The stern was a squared-off raised platform surrounded by a low railing like the aftcastle of a pirate ship. On the open bow was a big headlamp.

Butler let out a piercing trill. A pair of vesperi looked up from the deck of the rear boat. He tumbled his index fingers, and the orderlies flipped the plastic crate they had just dumped so it was lid-side up.

'They're a bit distracted today,' he said. 'Latest rumour is a settlement a hundred miles south has vanished. Might be nonsense. Anti-Jejunus guerrillas might have skinned them all. Still.' He thinned his eyes. 'Ominous.'

Delphine stood holding Alice's hand. 'So we're heading . . . in there?'

'Mm.' Butler dragged the skewer laterally through his fangs, shearing off the last of the meat. 'Camp's not happy. No one's been south for weeks. The orderlies have been begging me to block the tunnels off. Seal in the monsters.'

'Are there monsters?' said Alice.

Butler wiped his mouth. He tossed the skewer into the water.

'That's rather a question of perspective.' He began walking down to the jetty. 'Come. I want to show you something.' Delphine's clogs were remarkably stable in the soft silt – practical, rather than eccentric indulgences. She took them off when she reached the jetty. Her bare soles moved onto rough, swollen planks.

Butler stopped at the jetty's end. Without looking down, he stepped across a yard of water onto the bow. Delphine reached the same spot and hesitated.

He looked at her askance. 'You're not afraid of water, are you?'

'Don't be stupid.' But when she looked at the gap, there it was again – a jolt of vertigo. For years she had braced herself before tackling the drop from the front doorstep to the gravel. She had trained herself to be careful, fearful. A woman of her age no longer 'fell'. She 'had a fall'. It had passed from verb to noun. A fall was an object, something one acquired. It had permanence.

She looked down at her new body – this miraculous biddable flesh. Already today it had carried her up a mountain.

She backed up, ran and jumped.

She cleared the gunwale. She landed; the boat rocked. Her foot skidded on wet deck, momentum throwing her forwards. The river swung towards her.

Butler grabbed her wrist. She jerked back, found her balance. He slapped something into her palm.

'You'll need this.'

She looked. She was gripping a sickle. The blade's crescent interior had been whetted to moon-white sharpness.

Before she could ask what it was for, Butler leapt onto the roof, beating his wings for extra lift. Delphine doubted she could get that much height off a standing jump. The boat's roof was covered in a lattice of rope rigging. She tried grabbing the rope and pulling herself up using her arms. To her astonishment, she could do it. She was a little ungainly, but good Lord. How many decades had it been since she had enjoyed this kind of strength-to-weight ratio? It felt like flying.

Butler stopped amidships and stamped twice on the roof. 'Sleeping quarters here.'

He dropped from the roof onto the raised deck of the stern. He pushed the tiller aside, stooped, and flipped a latch in the floor. Delphine hopped down beside him. He lifted a hatch.

Beneath, dirty water lapped round the fin-shaped curve of something black and oily.

'It's for hacking weeds off the propeller,' said Butler, looking up. 'There's a catch in the handle.'

Delphine found the recessed button and pressed it with her thumb. It clicked. Nothing happened. She flicked her wrist and the sickle shot out towards Butler's face. The hooked tip stopped an inch from his eyes.

He frowned. 'Don't do that.'

Delphine held the sickle up. It was about three feet long, all told – natty-looking piece of kit. She thumbed the catch and the shaft slid back inside the handle.

Butler slammed the hatch. 'And don't *ever* open this while the engine's running.' He fastened the little steel twist-latch with a grunt. She passed him the sickle and he slotted it into a pair of brackets on the cabin's outside wall. 'Right. You can learn the rest on the move.' He stood. 'We set off at sunset.'

The interior of the little church was cool and dark. Gnarled black briars snaked across the floor, mostly dry and dead. Odd, cobweb-like structures hung between them, rainbowed like a soap bubble. The air had a sweet smell, like pine mixed with cinnamon.

A tingle spread across her scalp and down the nape of her neck. She heard whispers.

Delphine turned round. Martha stood in a pool of soft green light cast by her own eyes. She was writing in her notepad. She finished and tapped the paper with the end of her pencil – *bap*.

'Yes, all right, all right. No need for surliness.' Delphine took the notepad and began reflexively patting her pockets for her reading glasses before remembering. She read:

henry was here.

She stared at the words. 'What do you mean?' She handed back the pad. 'When?'

don't know. long time ago i think. but he was here.

Delphine gazed upon the damp stone walls with a queasy reverence. 'Are you *sure*, dear?'

Whisper, whisper went the pencil.

it's a feeling. like the one i got before thompson died.

Delphine glanced around the church, imagining hints of him everywhere. All at once, it had taken on the hallowed sadness of a tomb.

As dusk settled across the mountainside, giant moths began to surge from the cave in papery helixes, burning pages rising from a bonfire. The Underkills echoed with the whispering gossip of their wingbeats.

The boat burbled away from the bluing light of the settlement, its electric lamp cutting a wedge through the mist. The craft sat low in the water, fat and laden, engine purr translating into a soft chattering of cargo crates. Vesperi orderlies lined the jetty, watching. When Delphine glanced back a final time, they were just silhouettes.

Butler stood at the stern, scalp fur slicked back, one hand on the tiller. His high, jackal ears twitched and swivelled – every so often his noseleaf creased as he spat another cannonade of clickspeak into the void.

Delphine stood on the foredeck, straddling the steaming lamp. In her right hand, she held the Remington, six one-ounce slugs in the sidesaddle mount, another six buckshot shells clipped to the stock. In her left hand hung the sickle, edge glinting.

Martha flew a short way ahead, jinking right and left, her eyes leaving faint trails in the wet air. Delphine breathed through her nostrils. The vibrant jungle stink was turning to something dank. The temperature dropped.

How strange, not to know the exact weight and flavour of tomorrow. To stand on the edge of time.

'Well,' she said.

Mist rolled through the gleam of Martha's eyes. Alice's hair was wet with condensation.

At Delphine's feet, the river unzipped in a puzzle of froth. Wake reflected off the rock walls and struck the hull with glassy slaps. The engine's growl echoed, layering and doubling until it surrounded them. She let the shotgun muzzle rest on the foredeck. The vibrations passed up her arm, into her chest.

The tremor was calming. Familiar. It felt like being old.

CHAPTER 6

A TIME TO PLUCK UP THAT WHICH IS PLANTED

(Four weeks before the inauguration)

Räum trotted through the gate, stepping from dirt to cobbles. His roadshoes clack-clacked on the new surface. Hagar jerked his reins and he came to a standstill. She pulled off her goggles and let them hang around her neck.

Masillia had grown.

The plaza was bustling: skroon-drawn carriages nosed sluggishly through a contraflow of bodies. She cast about for the post office; in place of the familiar gabled roof and salt-warped timbers rose an imposing structure of pale stone, big as a temple. The old wooden veranda, with its slumped roof and flaking blue paint, was now a flight of stone steps leading to a grand portico supported by four caryatids – tall white statues sculpted with flowing belted gowns and expressions of defiant stoicism. She knew who they would be before she marked the roundness in the jaw, the steep cheekbones and the downturned eyes. Still, it was a jolt to see Mitta there – gigantic, multiplied, sealed in Gallian marble. His silence a rebuke.

Morgellon had doubled-down on his grief, baking it into the very architecture. His old valet's sainthood was all but formalised, Mitta's treachery forgotten. Or, rather, *denied*. Replaced by an icon of eternal loyalty. But even statuary was fleeting.

People were rushing up and down the steps clutching parcels and envelopes, or brandishing string-bound folders of documents. So it was still a post office? Huh. *Plus ça change.*

Hagar brought Räum about to face the city, smoothing his neck feathers to keep him calm. Sloping red-brown roofs spilled down the hillside, following the zigzag of mazy backstreets, punctuated by bursting fronds of green succulents. Down in the bay, single-jib fishing boats drifted alongside the new huge full-rigged steam ships. The stilt city had spread. Most of the water was still in shadow. Twin lighthouses glinted on the narrow mandibles of their respective headlands.

Hagar rubbed the crusts from her eyes and marvelled. She felt light and sad and mortally afraid. She had reached the vast silvered barrier of the ocean.

They could go no farther. This was where it ended.

Late that afternoon, her feet aching, she walked down to the harbour.

'I need to charter a ship,' she said. 'One of your steamers that visits the southern floe. With a hold full of ice. And a crew. And I need them to be ready to leave for the next four weeks.'

The fat skipper smiled indulgently. Behind him, greenish water slopped against the quay.

'Off on an adventure, are we, little one?'

Hagar was already growing weary of this city's aggressive avuncularity. She popped the top three buttons on her riding coat and flashed him the ducal seal within.

'I am deadly serious.'

He tugged at his beard. 'Mademoiselle, the Festival of Tides is in just a few weeks, and just after that it's—'

'Inauguration Day, yes, I know. When can you be ready?'

'Ah.' He wafted his cigarette. 'It is not this easy. We have commitments, the steward must acquire provisions – where should this ship prepare to go?'

'Anywhere in the world.'

The skipper spilt his mug of red wine all down his trousers. He leapt up, snatched a rag off a hook on the side of his hut and began slapping at his sodden thighs. He was chuckling.

'Mademoiselle, this is quite a story you are telling me, and for that, I thank you. I will tell my friends tonight and watch them debase themselves in the manner I just demonstrated. This will be most enjoyable. I am in your debt.'

'How much to charter the ship?'

He sniffed the rag and pulled a face. 'More than the moons and the stars, my child. More than the dewdrop wept by the fattening grape and more than the taldin's shadow that swims through the corn.'

He was misquoting the *Consolations*. It had never sounded good out of the original Sinpanian. Hagar felt a queer mix of irritation and longing. Her skin itched and she saw flashes of herself driving the pommel of her dagger into his temple, then perforating his paunch again and again as finally he took her seriously. She was a fool. She clutched at her fringe. Why had she ever believed Morgellon would change? That she might be able to reason with him? Why did she still care?

She took a breath.

'I am well resourced.'

'It would certainly be a costly suicide.'

'How costly?'

The skipper scratched his thick eyebrow with a cracked fingernail. 'Thirty dukes a day to be sea-ready, plus the cost of inventory.' He hung the rag back on its hook. 'Sixty a day once we're at sea. She is a vessel of great speed, but if someone tries to board us, neither my crew nor myself will resist, so I suggest you hire guards.' He turned to face her, squinting at the midday sun. 'Three hundred down.'

'I could book passage on steamers for the next fifty years for that sort of money.'

'You could, mademoiselle.' He stepped in close to her, and she could smell the hot sour wine soaking into his tattered trousers. 'So I anticipate there is a very compelling reason why you do not. Yes, I think this is most likely.'

'Fifteen a day while you prepare, forty a day if we cast off.'

'Ho ho.'

'I can get you your deposit by sundown.'

The skipper walked to the quayside and stood with his toecaps hanging over the water, rocking back upon his heels, looking out across the forest of masts. His hair was a salt-stiffened nest of brown and grey radiating out from a blotchy bald patch.

He rolled his hunched shoulders in their sockets. 'Twenty-five a day in dock, fifty at sea. I'll need at least a week to secure a suitable vessel. And I'll need proof you can honour your debts.'

'Done.'

He looked her up and down. 'Good. Deliver the money by sundown and I'll start preparations.'

'If anyone asks any questions—'

'We didn't speak. Yes, yes, this is implicit.'

'I doubt they'll believe you,' she said. 'We're watched even now.'

The skipper took a step back from the quayside. 'Ah. And if they ask?'

'Tell them I've chartered a boat for my lord and master. Tell them . . .' She flexed her fingers, then bunched them till the knuckles popped. 'Tell them I plan to make a little pilgrimage.'

Later that evening, Hagar took a mallet and short-handled pick, wrapped herself in the cowl and long brown robes of a murmurer, her tools hidden and the hood pulled low over her eyes, and slipped out onto an unpaved backstreet.

She walked barefoot, in keeping with her disguise. Shrubs with orange berries and sticky leaves had pushed up through the dirt. The earth was sticky underfoot. She heard rustling as rats ran parallel to her, freezing whenever she stopped. The humidity was high; moisture condensed on her cheeks, her upper lip. The pick swung heavy at her hip, clipping her knee – she had to hold it steady, and when she did she realised her whole body was trembling.

She turned onto the Rue Fulmar, where the air was laced with the fishy tang of leviathan oil. Lamps burned through open windows, lit not for light but because their stink deterred pinflies. Smooth cobblestones pressed into her arches. A harka girl walking a fox mongrel on a length of twine was coming down the hill, and Hagar dipped her head, as if in penitent humility. The fox strained on its leash as she passed, dirty blond tail lashing the dust, fangs standing out in a snarl.

'*Coucher Dagobert! Ici!*' The girl yanked on its string. '*Désolé, bonne sœur.*'

Hagar did not look up.

The street led towards the oldest part of Fat Maw's high town, the holy quarter. She passed tall box-framed houses built in the Sinpanian style from a mess of imported materials, their upper storeys leaning precariously over the street on timber jetties. Many of the big family room windows had been modified with wrought-iron balconies, from which hung drying housedresses, lotus creepers, sumptuously embroidered blankets and birdcages pulsing with sweetwings. The tiny pink and orange birds sang in cacophonous trilling arpeggios. Most houses had a block and tackle hanging from a bracket on the top storey, sometimes with a rush basket attached to the hook. One pulley had a wooden slat attached via a loop of rope, perhaps so residents could sit on it and lower themselves down to the street.

As the road dipped back down towards the jungle, the cobbles gave way to a muddy track. Sharp stones knifed her feet. The houses became squatter and simpler: wooden frames with bark walls and threshed reed roofs. Hagar had the queer sensation she was drifting into the past. This felt more like the Fat Maw she had known. Faint at first, then rising in waves, came the sound of bells and singing.

Tides of perfumed incense wafted from the smokelore compound, and as she drew nearer Hagar realised the occupants were celebrating a funeral. The smokers had moved into the old naval school, patching the roof with poles and canvas. Rising crookedly from one of the holes was a tin chimney. Paper lanterns lit the entrance arch. From over the grey brick wall she heard the crackle of a fire pit.

It was odd, hearing Low Thelusian so far from the old country, the chants and the percussive jangle of bellfists, the sour floral aroma of the petty miasma. The smokemaster's coarsened voice resonated beneath the other mourners in a sonorous baritone, rich and griefy with the tongue of their lost homeland. He sang, and others followed, some simply moaning in time, vesperi voices adding a high contrapuntal melody that keened and sliced. The street was hazy with pyre-waft. Hagar found her lips mouthing the death chant, the life chant, the sad–ecstatic creed of the smokers, along with the master's song:

Vo yag, di maundi merto	Look thus upon this dying world
Den heforo, den flori sun zefoir	A star at dawn, a petal in the breeze
Den vot ardo sun foco	A lone prayer burning in a sacred fire
Den flati petto, den flucti com achoir	A puff of smoke, a ripple and a sneeze

Such half-truths! How perverse, to recognise life's treasures as hollow, melting illusions, yet not to search for the treasure beyond life. How base, to accept endless cycling death and misery as one's lot – and to call this wisdom! She longed to march into the courtyard and remonstrate with them. They were so close to waking up!

Angry, she hurried along the street. The music faded behind her – first the words, then the bells, and finally the thump of drums. She felt dizzy from the thunder of it. They were drunk on tragedy, resigned to oblivion. Surrender was all very well – an essential step in the journey to restoration – but what of love? If all was meaningless, whence sacrifice? The fatal mistake: they believed they were just another product of the great fraud, instead of the celestial beings upon which the fraud was being perpetrated. Half-truths!

The road sank in a twisting zigzag, edged by narrow leafed palms and ferns with sprays of club-shaped fronds. A green-gold civet emerged from the foliage to drink from a wheel rut. The steady din of the jungle's night chorus rose and merged with the shush of the ocean. The breeze was warm. A few stars quivered in the night sky. A tepid perfume of rain tickled her nose.

She stopped before a set of iron gates. In the moonlight, she could still make out the words on the faded wooden sign: *Jardin Des Anges De Couchage*. Her memory restored the curlicued letters to their former grave majesty. She remembered when the paint was still wet. For an instant, she could smell it.

A sentry box stood beside the gate, one side coated in climbing vines with brindled leaves and bright orange bellflowers. She knocked on the wooden shutter. From inside came shuffling. Someone yanked a cord and the wooden slats shucked up.

A vesperi sat on a fold-down seat bracketed to the wall. Like her, they wore a cowl. All she could make out beneath the grey hood were two yellow eyes, regarding her impassively. A wire bell-pull hung from an aperture in the slanted bark roof. On the floor lay a candle in a tin holder (unlit), a large knife and a gun.

Hagar reached into her robes. She placed her ducal seal on the counter.

'I'm here to see the Ambassador.'

The vesperi did not look up. Their hand went to the bell-pull and they yanked it in some quick, slow, quick-quick, slow code. The shutters dropped with a crack.

Hagar waited before the gates. The rain brought a freshness. She closed her eyes and breathed in the scent of moist soil. It smelt intimate, faintly indecent. She prayed for resolve.

With a dry scraping, the gates began to part inwards.

There was no path, just damp black earth, cool on her feet. She walked amongst looming, swollen fungi. Rain pooled in the purple-white trumpets of manna funnels and plashed from the scaly green caps of stocky, fat false jacks. Giant white puffballs shone like fallen moons. The old stone priory lay ahead, weathered, inert.

Behind her, she heard the gates grinding shut, the squeak of some mechanism evidently better at pulling than pushing. As she advanced, the soil became thicker, more textured, her toes sinking into a mulch of leaf litter and decaying bark. Gnarled saddle fungi stood at chest height, their moonlit folds the colour of old parchment. She passed the wrinkled, fleshy caps of godheads, hunched on puce stems like huge, dripping brains. Her robe was heavy with moisture, clinging to her skin like slimy vellum. With every step, the earth wheezed.

The priory was a single-storey building of grey stone, its corners reinforced with trachyte quoins. Steps led to a sturdy door with iron strap hinges. The lancet windows were unlit.

A death blusher mushroom rose from the dirt on a thick, fibrous white trunk. It was tall as a hay wagon, its cap pocked with ivory warts, its gills thickly bunched. The ground around the steps was carpeted in translucent yellow lobes.

She stopped at the edge of the fungus patch. Her mouth was dry, her stomach a tight knot. Had the Mucorians kept their promise? Was a promise a meaningful concept to them? Voluntary obligation with implicit penalties for non-compliance. Surely they comprehended the *utility* of a mutually binding social contract, even if it seemed arbitrary or eccentric.

She lowered her bare sole onto the alarm fungus. Leathery, tumorous sacs popped under her heel, sneezing a fine mist. She tensed, waiting for the death blusher to hiss, for its gills to slough apart, sighing spores.

Rain fell, undisturbed.

She exhaled. The glistening fruit bodies of the alarm fungus lived on the death blusher as a parasite, leeching nutrients from its bulbous stem base via a submerged threadwork of hairy ganglions. They could be cultivated to distinguish between species, even races within species – if she had been a lanta, she might have been prostrate by now, her eyes burning and filming over, her lungs filling with fluid. Or perhaps it was set for harka. Or high-caste vesperi. Perhaps the alarm nodes weren't grafted to the death blusher at all. Perhaps they activated something deeper in the complex.

Her feet moved from soil to stone. She climbed the steps. She grasped the door's heavy brass drop handle, and pounded the stirrup once, twice against the scuffed backplate.

Rain pattered against the death blusher's scabbed crown. Trickles of water pelted the mulch with a sound like moist, open-mouthed chewing. Cold water drooled between Hagar's shoulder blades. She shivered. The embassy ran to its own schedule.

She heard the *clack* of a spring-latch. The door drew back.

A young woman stood barefoot on the stone flagging. She wore a one-piece dark brown skeleton suit made of hide, with a row of shell buttons up the left side. Behind her, the darkness was heaped so thick that the wedge of light on which she stood seemed to hang over a chasm. Long fawn hair, twisted into loose plaits, spilled down her shoulder. Her head was lolling forward and she regarded Hagar with upturned eyes.

Hagar did not recognise the body. A new recruit from the under-city, perhaps. People went missing all the time. She had heard rumours of floating slave markets serving villages and plantations upriver. It was easy to exploit people who did not officially exist. Unless this was a volunteer. Hagar was not sure which possibility she found more disturbing.

'I've come for my girl,' said Hagar.

The woman's skin was pale to the point of translucency, under-snaked with thin blue arteries. As she tilted her head, the hair sloughing from her shoulder resolved into a filigreed mat of fungal strands, branching from a split at the crown of her skull. Hagar held out a hand, palm up, and pushed it into the mass of fine hyphae. She felt tiny fibres brush her skin, absorbing sweat and rainwater, tasting the minute grooves.

The woman stepped aside. The mycelium web slid from Hagar's fingers, slopping back over the woman's bare shoulder. A muscle below the woman's eye ticked.

'Miss Ingery.' She spoke in a husky monotone. 'The Mucorian delegation recognises you.'

'Ambassador.' Hagar bowed out of habit, and immediately felt absurd. She might as well salute a rosebush. Even the title 'Ambassador' was a misnomer, a foreign concept imported to make communicating with the Mucorians' linked protominds via a single body less disconcerting. If she noticed Hagar's embarrassment, she gave no sign.

Hagar moved to enter the compound, hesitated. 'Ah . . . Ambassador, would it be possible to have some form of . . . light?'

The Ambassador's pigmentless eyes were underscored with angry red crescents. She blinked.

She stepped away from the door and padded into the darkness. Hagar listened to the slap of feet on stone, a metallic rattling in a far corner, then the footsteps returning.

She had expected a stub of candle in a rude holder, and was surprised when the Ambassador handed her a modern oil lamp of lacquered steel.

Hagar shook it, checking there was oil in the reservoir. She reached under her robes and fumbled amongst the leather pouches and cedar wood boxes hanging from her belt until she found a packet of matches. The glass mantel was smutted with soot, so she removed it and wiped the interior with a damp cuff. She trimmed the wick with the little key at the base so it would not smoke when she lit it.

As Hagar performed these ministrations, an ache started in her gut – the old ache, the yearning cramps, the mewl of the Grand-Duc's body craving the black medicine. It would get much worse if he chose to delay taking his next dose, but still she did not rush. She had waited this long. She wanted to see clearly for the work ahead.

For the commandment is a lamp; and the law is light.

The wick flared – an impossible, piercing white star. The Ambassador closed her eyes. Hagar lowered the mantle and lifted the lamp.

The priory's interior comprised a long, windowless stone hall. Thick oak trusses spanned a vaulted roof. Small recesses in the walls held oil lamps identical to Hagar's – the one nearest the door was vacant. There was no furniture, nor tapestries, nor icons. Footprints led across the dusty flagstones to a flight of steps, heading down.

Hagar descended.

The old Calvarian catacombs had acquired a dry, bitter scent since the Mucorians' arrival just over seventy years ago. Poor Tonti had approved the embassy's location – an overgrown ruin on the edge of town, away from any houses but high enough up the hill to be safe from seasonal flooding. It had been one of his first acts as Prefect after Morgellon brought him in to replace Anwen. In a pattern that would come to feel emblematic of his tenure, what he had intended as cautious pragmatism served only to distribute resentment amongst the broadest possible audience. The protests had been violent, their suppression heavyhanded and bungling.

Ultimately, the only salve to the populace's ill-feeling was several decades of the embassy's presence having no effect whatsoever. Some vintners to the north had muttered darkly of wind-borne contamination during years when bitter rot or ash blight crippled the harvest, but for the most part the Mucorians had remained shrewdly obscure. Avalonian society was already replete with scapegoats – murmurers, the vesperi, the lanta – and as the wars passed out of living memory, so the few Mucorian embassies around the perpetuum – one in Fat

Maw, one in Cambridge, one off in Luminix, and one in the capital, Athanasia – were regarded less as beachheads in a sinister occupation, more as quaint historical courtesies commemorating the alliance that had turned the tide against the Hilantian menace. It was hard to feel threatened by something that had always been there.

Hagar navigated the warren of tunnels by means of the rough map she had sketched on her last visit. Long ago, the Calvarian monks had stored their dead with their produce, boiling the cadavers in wine to remove the flesh, and stacking the bones amongst the casks. They had believed their souls would seep into the maturing vintages, imbuing the wine with a rich, melancholy character while granting its drinkers wisdom and piety. Since the Mucorians had moved in, many of the casks had bloated and split, oozing mould studded with slender, black-capped mushrooms. Skulls of the three prime species gazed from beneath gossamer sheets of white fungus.

The route was longer than Hagar remembered. Her water flask was empty. She stopped to study her scratchy directions, the map brittle along its folds. Had she gone wrong at the last junction? The map appeared to indicate she should continue straight ahead. She might have made a mistake when she drew it. She had not been here for decades.

She rounded a corner and found a dead end. The tunnel wall was ridged with shelves of plate fungus. Hagar dropped to her knees and began clawing at the fungus with both hands. It came up in brittle, stinking clumps. A dust of tiny spores drifted from the broken gills. She imagined them filling her lungs with every breath, finding warm, damp nooks to land in. She burrowed at the dirt like a dog.

Her filthy nails scraped stone. She scooped more dirt away. There it was: a long groove, filled in with mortar. Sealed.

Hagar grasped her pick and started hacking.

The chamber reeked of earth and time.

A low granite ceiling, narrow walls and a dirty stone floor, markedly older than the tunnels above. The lamplight guttered, smoking blackly. She held her breath. The flame recovered.

Hagar pushed back her hood. Most of the floor was taken up by a single slate slab coated in fine grey dust. She knelt and blew, slapping at the carved letters until they became clear:

So quod the wyght who marke thes stowne
The welle be depe, I dorst not drowne
So quod the wyght who nappe withyn
I dorst not drowne, and thus I swym

She remembered the brief fad for epigraphs in faux-archaic English, many years back – she supposed the succession of wars had left the middle classes craving roots, however ahistorical or ersatz. A quaint pastiche of the old world, before the perpetuum declared it off-limits and closed several major thresholds permanently. The slab seemed undisturbed. She felt faint, perhaps from the foul thin air, perhaps from anticipation.

She set the lamp on the floor, then wedged the pick into the seam surrounding the slab. She started levering it up. The slab's underside was greasy. It slipped, nearly crushing her fingers. She braced a foot against the wall and heaved. The slab rose, resisting, then tipped. It hit the floor with a bang.

A waft of vinegar mixed with stale pomander gusted from the gravemouth. The coffin lay just as she remembered it. It sat in a rectangular pit about half as wide again as the coffin's widest point. An eight-pointed star was carved into the walnut lid. Either side bore two sets of brass handles with pommels shaped like sea-peonies. Hagar climbed into the hole and used the lower handles to lift the bottom half of the coffin out. It was deceptively light. It contained the only surviving parts of the harka six-ways martyr Godbless Potto: his jawbone and a disc of black meat, pickled in a clay jar – supposedly his tongue.

There was not enough room in the chamber for the coffin to lie flat, so, grunting and trembling, she hauled it up endwise and propped it against the wall.

She jumped back into the hole. She was sweating now, hot with work. At some point she had slit her palm; blood filled out the creases in her skin.

Beneath her, the ground was hard-packed sandy dirt. The coffin had left a mark like a giant squared-off footprint, with evenly spaced divots made by screwheads. She twisted the candle into the ground. Gingerly, tenderly almost, she began raking at the dirt with her fingernails.

She clawed shallow trenches. Beneath the dry surface, the earth had the consistency of putty, coming up in brown glossy rinds.

Shouldn't she have found something by now? Grace gave way to panic. What if she had been betrayed? What if the martyr's coffin had already been moved and replaced? She glanced over her shoulder, expecting the Ambassador to drop into the chamber clutching a pistol.

No. Triumphant confrontations weren't the Mucorians' style. Lamp oil and a match, perhaps. Or just the scrape of a heavy granite slab sliding over the opening. No explanation.

She tore at the gluey mud. Where was her faith? Why was she so weak? Or was she destined to fail as punishment for her weakness? Had she not been punished enough?

Her fingers snagged in a filthy webbing of lace.

She pulled at it. Fissures forked through hidden faults in the dirt. Hagar scooped up great chunks of mud, tossing them out of the pit. More lace. Fingernails. A tarnished ring. A torso. Pale skin. Blond hair.

Hagar heard herself crying, laughing. She blinked and her tears fell upon the bridge of a nose, white cheeks. Crumbs of dirt dropped away as the lips parted. Eyelids twitched.

Half-buried beneath Hagar, the sleeper opened her eyes.

She was beautiful.

CHAPTER 7

AN ARCH WHERE THROUGH GLEAMS THAT UNTRAVELLED WORLD

Delphine sat between heaps of packing crates, making herself a coffee on the portable gas burner. Martha was curled up in a cubby-hole under the boat's gun locker, her legs and arms tucked in, her eyes pulsing with rainbows as she slept. Condensation dripped off everything. It brought the smells out of fabrics and left skin puckered and sheeny.

Delphine took her coffee up to the open bow. Slick tunnel walls rolled through the lamp beam, wet, intestinal. Without sunlight, her circadian rhythms were in bits. She smothered a yawn with her fist. She reckoned they had been navigating the Underkills for four days. She had been sleeping in feverish snaps, waking fat headed in the humid, lamp-fogged darkness.

She sat and sipped her coffee, which burned her mouth, and ate a packet of peanuts. Her limbs ached from days of bending, squatting and lifting, but it was a satisfying pain, not the radiating, arthritic cramps she was used to – the soreness had a heat to it, a vitality. She was getting stronger.

Alice stood at the stern, one hand on the tiller, overlit by a swaying lantern. She had her sleeves rolled up. She waved. Inches above her head, the tunnel ceiling was covered in giant albino molluscs with translucent spiral shells big as crash helmets.

Delphine lit a cigarette. She puffed and took a long drag and held it. When she exhaled she felt lightheaded and sick. She had never really enjoyed smoking, not the way other people seemed to, but she liked the ritual of it. It made her feel sly and self-destructive, like a private detective. She especially liked the end – the final tug, then the grinding out or the insouciant flick. Finishing a cigarette felt decisive – a little accomplishment.

The boat shuddered as Alice accelerated into a straight. She was a good helmsman. Delphine took a last hit and flicked her cigarette into the river, an orange firefly arcing through the darkness. A wet mouth snapped it up and disappeared.

She found Butler in the cabin with a lapful of electrical components.

'What's the matter?' she said.

'The radio isn't working.'

'Perhaps if you fitted all those little pieces together.'

He made a snarling noise at the back of his throat. An oil lamp hung from a crossbeam and he worked by its swaying light.

'Maybe it's because we're underground,' said Delphine.

Butler stripped a length of wire with his fangs and sighed. 'Radio is a misnomer. It doesn't rely on radiowaves.' He held up a little glass valve filled with godstuff. 'It communicates between worlds. Location doesn't matter.'

'How long has it been broken?'

'I found out shortly after we set off.'

'When were you planning to tell us?'

He tweaked one of the leads of a capacitor and attached it to a battery. 'When I got it working.'

'So we've no way of checking in with base camp or contacting England?'

'Not at present.' He began picking through the mess in his lap.

'Why didn't you check it before we left?'

'Ah eh.'

'What?'

Butler took the crosshead screwdriver out of his mouth. 'I *did*.'

'What are you implying?'

Butler set the pieces down. He rubbed his eyes.

'Look, I feel there's been a misunderstanding. You're here because Ms Rao needed a portal lanta after our previous one absconded. I don't value your input and I don't require your company.'

'Well, I don't value your comfort and I don't require your approval. And you're outnumbered. So that's a bloody pickle we're in, isn't it?'

Butler closed his eyes. He touched two fingertips to his brow.

'This will take longer to fix if I'm forced to break it over your head.' His noseleaf scrunched as he inhaled.

'Fine.' She marched out of the cabin, hissing *arsehole* under her breath. Her face felt hot. She went and sat and smoked another cigarette. Then she filled a pipe and smoked that as well.

About a day later, she woke to silence. The engine had cut out. After almost a week of constant gruzzling, its absence felt like falling.

She scrambled onto the foredeck. Butler stood on a bank of silt and pebbles, his arms folded. The mooring rope was knotted round a stalagmite.

'What's going on?' she said.

He stepped back. Behind him, in the wall of the tunnel, was the mouth of a passageway.

'We need fresh water,' he said. He tossed a bowie knife into the air and caught it, blade down. 'Grab some gallon jugs from under the bunks.'

She fetched three plastic jugs and her sickle. When she stepped off the boat, she had a strange, nauseous moment of transitioning to solid ground; the tunnel seemed to scroll on without her, dragging at her essence.

She followed Butler into the passageway. He carried an electric torch, but after a few turns and a flight of steps cut into the rock, it was no longer necessary. Sunlight was leaking down towards them.

It felt eerie, painful even. She had to shield her eyes as they neared the top. The air grew rapidly warmer. Scents wafted thickly: wet earth and heady, cloying perfume.

Butler pushed through great serrated fronds blocking the entrance. The leaves slid back together with a slicing sound. They emerged on a steep hillside.

Alice was standing by a stream that frothed over pink rocks. Huge ferns trailed in the water. Sunbeams punctured the canopy, lifting mist from the understorey and highlighting clouds of butterflies. Here and there lay lumps of mortar, covered in moss. Screeches echoed from the treetops, answered by croaks, knocks, rasping stridulations.

'Is Martha here?'

Alice pointed up. Martha was hovering near the canopy, beneath a cat's cradle of thick creepers. Tangled in the centre of them was what looked like a big, rusted gate. Delphine walked underneath to get a better look. The gate had an embossed metal plaque on one edge. She could make out letters:

esse
t
fice

Butler's ears were pricked. He nodded downhill, into the jungle.

'Wine fruit grove.'

'You can *hear* fruit?'

He shot her a look, lips peeling back from his fangs contemptuously. 'The dogmoths they attract have a distinctive ultrasonic call.' He lit a cigarette. 'If we load up while we're here you're more or less guaranteed fresh food all the way to Fat Maw.' He began tramping down the hill, pumping his wings to disperse pinflies. Martha flew after him.

'Well?'

Delphine whirled round. Alice stood in the sunshine, damp white-gold hair swept down one side of her head. She was coated in sweat; her hair had corrugated in the wet heat. She wiped her palms on her vest, leaving red smears of mud. She wore a little polyester satchel at her hip, and carried a big machete. Sunlight caught the blade's whetted edge, painted a sheen across her wet clavicles. They lifted and sank as she breathed.

Delphine found she could not remember how to speak. Somehow she knew this person and did not know her at all. Alice threw her head back and smiled, her eyes gleaming.

'Fancy a walk in the woods?'

Even in the shade, the heat was punishing.

Butler stopped at a cluster of trees. He click-chirruped at Martha, who took a knife and flew up into the branches. He told Delphine and Alice that he thought there would be more fruit, farther downstream.

Delphine shadowed Alice as they stomped through mulchy leaf litter. She thumbed the catch on her sickle and hacked at lianas, the whetted blade slicing cleanly.

They came to a deep, circular pool, surrounded by overhanging trees and crested by a low waterfall of speckled pink rock. Soft apricot light filtered down through steaming vegetation. Creepers dabbled the water, covered in orange and cyan blooms.

Alice stopped and placed her fists on her hips. 'This must be the place.'

Delphine looked up at the nearest tree. A swollen trunk covered in glossy yellowy-white scales climbed unsteadily towards a rosette of huge, tongue-shaped leaves sheltering lush clusters of purple and blush-pink gourds. Sure enough, moths with curious cream-coloured segmented wings fluttered around the treetop, heat-drugged.

'Right!' Alice clapped her hands together. 'You get ready to catch.' She kicked off her shoes and planted a foot against the scaly bark.

'Alice, don't you dare.'

Alice glanced back over her shoulder and stuck her tongue out. With that she was off, climbing like a cat, gripping the bark with splayed fingers. Her light cotton skirt let her move freely, sliding her soles up the bole's smooth abdomen, pressing her arches into footholds.

'Alice!' Delphine's chest tightened. 'Come on now. You might fall!'

Alice laughed. From somewhere far off to their right, some creature up in the canopy replied with a cannonade of yips.

'I really might!'

Alice clasped a rounded knot of bark. She gripped the thick of the trunk with her thighs. The slick ridge of her tricep stood out as she tensed her arm, hauled herself higher.

She was just under the tree's spreading crown. Beneath huge, lolling leaves, old dead leaf bases hung like lengths of dried flax. She braided several together and gripped them like a rope. With her other hand, she reached into her satchel and retrieved the cleaver.

'Get ready!' She leaned back, allowing her body to hang out over the jungle floor. Delphine felt a cold, watery vertigo. Her scalp tingled and her legs felt weak.

'Alice. I'm asking for your own good. Come down.' God, she sounded like Mother.

Fuzzy pink wine fruit hung about Alice in plump clusters. 'But then I won't get to taste these amazing fruits!'

'Please. I don't want you getting hurt.'

Alice tipped her head back and looked down, her hair dangling in wet lengths. 'Then why did you bring me here?'

She swung the machete. The blade made a noise like spitting. A wine fruit dropped. Delphine's old cricketing reflexes kicked in; she stepped back and cupped her palms. It was a sitter. She caught it with a pleasing slap.

The fruit in her hands was pink with red splashes, shaped like a cannonball and coated in downy fuzz. She hefted it. At least two pounds.

'More!' yelled Alice.

Delphine looked up and two more fell at her. She caught one with her free hand and sidestepped as the second thumped into the leaf litter.

'Oi!' She tossed the others down beside it. Already Alice was brandishing the machete for another swing.

'Look out below!'

Chop. Thump. The blade bit through stalks. The long, dry fronds rustled. Fruit dropped. Delphine pivoted and skipped, catching them in ones and twos, falling into steady rhythm. Her body responded just as she wanted. She stacked wine fruits in a bright heap. Her heart drummed keenly and her face glowed. Every time she looked up, there was Alice.

Rain began to fall – a light, refreshing haze that trickled down the ribs of leaves and made boughs shiver. Delphine and Alice sheltered under a waxy green frond the size of a grocer's awning. The leaf litter was soft. Delphine slipped off her bag and set it down, heavy with spoils.

Alice took a wine fruit from the heap. She worked her flat, curved blade into the flesh, flensing it free with a twitching of the wrist. Gummy strands of red-pink pap elongated and snapped.

The rain made a sound like ripping or frying. The pool shattered and danced. Delphine breathed in the sweet aroma of chlorophyll.

'Oughtn't we to be heading back?' she said.

Alice shrugged. 'Probably.' She carved the fruit against the flat of her thigh, using the rind as a chopping board. Juice ran down her legs. She speared a chunk with the tip of the blade and held it out for Delphine.

Delphine took the pulpy, dripping flesh between her fingertips. She sniffed. It smelt sour, zesty.

Alice sank her teeth into a wedge. One of her eyelids pinched; juice squirted down her chin.

'Ugh.' She put her hand to her mouth. Delphine thought she was going to spit it out, but she chewed, her eyes widening. 'Ohhhh. Oh *wow.*'

Delphine bit into the fruit. The first flavour was a fizzy, tingling bitterness. She turned the pulp on her tongue – sharp, metallic notes rose, then . . .

'Mmm.' Resolution into subtle, unexpected sweetness – oranges, plums, persimmons. She chewed the flesh down to a stringy pith, then spat the remainder into the soil.

'Worth waiting for, isn't it?' said Alice.

Delphine closed her eyes and listened to the soft crackle of the rain. 'More.'

They shared the remainder, cleansing their palates with swigs from the canteen. Alice sat with one leg hugged to her chest, the other stretched out in front of her. Rain struck her exposed foot and ankle, sending up a shimmering corona.

They sat, not saying anything. Delphine pressed her palms into crunchy, textured soil. Her skin was tingling. She did not move.

'What was I like?' said Alice, at last. 'At the end?'

'You don't remember?'

Alice shrugged.

Delphine sighed. Thin palm fronds trembled with droplets.

'Surly. Opinionated. Impossible. Easily bribed with chocolate.'

'Sounds like me.' She smiled, and Delphine realised that Alice was a stranger to herself. All those hours together were lost now. She felt an ache in her heart.

'I tried to keep you home. I couldn't cope. You kept getting confused. You'd tell me off for moving things.'

Alice gazed at the dancing leaves. 'I don't remember any of it.'

'Good.' Delphine screwed her eyes shut. 'One day, I heard you howling. I found you on the bathroom floor. You'd run a bath and forgotten to put any cold in. Oh God. Alice, it was horrible. I'm so sorry. I hurt you.'

Delphine felt a hand on her shoulder. 'You did your best.'

'My best was shit. That's the thing, isn't it? Some people do their best and their best is shit. I don't want you to absolve me. I want you to promise to look after yourself.'

'I was dying, wasn't I? In the end, I mean.'

'Yes.'

'So there's nothing to lose, is there? None of this is real. It's just a lovely dream.'

Delphine's belly was a surging mix of hot and cold. 'What does that mean?'

'It means it would be silly to waste it.' Alice's voice became low, even though there was no one around to hear. 'I remember life before I got ill.'

The nape of Delphine's neck tingled. She felt a kiss thickening in the air between them, waiting to be born.

She was afraid. She wanted it so much.

Delphine closed her fingers round a fistful of earth.

She turned and kissed Alice. Alice's tongue was cool from drinking water. Delphine pushed forward greedily; Alice yielded, tilting her head back. Rain struck the pool with a sound like a thousand birds taking flight. Delphine stroked the nape of Alice's neck with her fingertips. Alice lay back a little farther. Clumsily, Delphine tried to shuffle closer.

Alice snatched Delphine's hand from under her and rolled on top of her, shoving her down into the soft leaf litter. Delphine landed on her back with a whump. Alice straddled her and pinned her wrists against the ground, grinning triumphantly, panting. Her damp hair spilled down and brushed Delphine's cheeks. Delphine felt a knee sliding up between her thighs.

Alice leaned in. Delphine thought she was going for a kiss, but she twisted her head and bit Delphine's neck. It was a gentle bite, a reprimand, and the sensation spread through Delphine's body in a warm analgesic rush.

Delphine kicked off her trousers; Alice slipped out of her skirt. Words had left them. Delphine lay pinioned on soft soil, listening to rain crackle against the leaf canopy. She could feel her flesh tingling under Alice's tongue, the hot press of their ribcages as they breathed, the pull of the tides, the turn of the planet, everything.

After, they bathed in the pool. Delphine washed dirt out of her hair, then she swam under the waterfall and let it pummel her shoulder blades. Silky weeds stroked her ankles. Her whole body was fizzing.

They put the wine fruits into two string sacks and walked back side by side. The rain had stopped. Steam rose from tree roots. Little gem-blue crustaceans scuttled across the sucking mud, digging with spade-shaped pincers. Delphine concentrated on the sensation of fruits against her back. As she breathed, she thought of the blood cycling through her system, feeding oxygen to her muscles – the improbability of it, the stunning preposterousness of life.

When they reached the hillside entrance Butler was waiting.

'Where the hell have you been?'

Alice held up one of the string sacks. 'Fruit picking.'

Martha was a short distance away, standing on top of a rock. Her antennae were twitching and her eyes had gone a pale mauve.

'You all right, dear?' said Delphine, feeling chewy and light-headed from the climb up the hill.

Martha hopped down from the rock. She took a twig, cleared away some leaves and wrote in the mud.

he was here

The words seemed to pulse with static as Delphine read them. They had depth and texture.

'Henry?'

Martha bopped her fist twice for *yes*.

As they descended into the earth, everything was buzzing. The dropping temperature made her arms prickle with gooseflesh. Torchlight swept across tallowy rivers of flowstone, picked out the vapour-dance of each breath. When she stepped onto the foredeck, the grain in the wood of each plank seemed variegated and rich with nuance. Her skull tickled. She had a feeling in her belly like she had swallowed the sun.

Alice brushed her fingers down the back of Delphine's hair, climbed aboard and went to her bunk. The wine fruits rumbled out of their sack, bright cannonballs.

Butler called from the tiller. 'You all right, Venner?'

Delphine picked one of the fuzzy pink things, hefting it in her palm, a grenade. 'Hmm?'

'Are you coming or aren't you?'

Delphine looked down and saw she had only put one leg in the boat. It took her a moment to judge the height of the gunwale and lift her other foot over it. Butler cranked the throttle forward. She stumbled as they lurched away from the shore.

'Right,' called Butler. 'Cut up a couple into cubes about an inch square and stick 'em on fishhooks.'

'What?' She had to shout over the roar of the engine. The boat turned, fruits rolling in the opposite direction. 'Hooks?'

'What in my instructions was even remotely ambiguous? Cut. Them. Up. Small.' He indicated with pinched thumb and forefinger. 'Stick. Them. On. Hooks.'

'Aren't we going to eat them?'

'Ha!' Butler threw his head back; for a moment it looked like his skull had split. 'No, they're for bait. You can't eat them. They're toxic.'

'What?'

Butler rotated a forefinger beside his temple. '*Psychotropic!*'

But Delphine barely heard him above the way the boat's wake smashed lantern light into a thousand golden fishes, above the hot ripe smell of red algae, above the taste of the memory of Alice on top of her, above the blood currents irrigating the branching grikes of her brain.

It was not her first experience with hallucinogens and by the fourth hour she remembered why she generally avoided them. Florid visions surged across the canvas of the water; sometimes she was God, watching the surge of armies from high overhead, choosing who would live or die. Sometimes the boat was a motorbike sidecar, watery tarmac rushing past inches from her nose.

With horrid abruptness, they emerged from the Underkills into greasy amber daylight. On the riverbank, vegetation formed a dense, strangling mat. Sun flared through slatted leaves, hurting her eyes. She thought maybe the jungle was on fire.

The rich, rotten stench of climbing orchids. The slow shifting parallax of the mangroves. Chitter-shrieking birds and insect choruses rose in unison then dropped away with the clinical precision of someone sliding a fader.

At some point, Martha was beside her with a coffee. She held it out for Delphine to take, gnashing her mandibular palps in encouragement. Her segmented red armour shone with condensation. Delphine felt odd, as if she had not seen her for years. Her heart was pierced by a needle of sadness. Sweet Martha. Her pupils were cobalt blue marbles in lakes of cream. She was so beautifully normal.

'Would you mind if I held your hand for a bit?' said Delphine.

Martha slipped her smooth fingers between Delphine's. Winged lizards swooped over the water's skin, their circuit boards glinting like black scales. The trees were whispering. Delphine listened for clues about Henry. Had they seen him? Was Martha right, or just yearning? And Algernon? Had he ever found this place? She put her cup down on the foredeck and rotated it clockwise and counter-clockwise, turning the jungle sounds up and down. Messages licked tantalisingly at the edges of her hearing. Gouts of flame leapt from the river.

She looked round and Martha was gone. The mangroves cast long shadows. How much time had passed?

A storm approached from the south – a yellow-grey wall eating the horizon. She braced and felt energy flowing from her clenched fingers into the boat, reinforcing its timbers, sealing its hull. She would protect everyone through force of will. Then the storm was upon them.

The brown river went from sleek muscular curves to spikes. Everywhere a chaos of explosions. Butler spread his wings over his head as an umbrella. Water streamed from the edges. Someone had brought Delphine a plastic poncho. They must have, because she was wearing one, rain rattling against the crackly plastic covering her head. Maybe she had grown it. Maybe she was repelling the rain with her strength of character. She knew she wasn't, but the thought had a cosiness. Who knew what was possible, really?

Rain hissed on leaves, made a cacophonous drumming on the cabin roof. The din mellowed her thoughts. Warm droplets massaged her skull. She was soaked through. She felt she had been reborn, somehow.

The rain eased, passed. Night fell, and tremendous anvil-shaped clouds appeared in the distance, lightning bolts arcing between them as the sky purpled and congealed. The air took on a coppery flavour. Gangs of iridescent moths flurried low over the river in heart-shaped formations, attracted by the glow of big, papery lotuses with orange and pink petals. The flowers parted in the sampan's wake, and when she looked back the river was a corridor of lights.

Why had she spent so long hiding? Tainted fruit or not, the world was glorious. Her chest swelled with thanks, a deep aching love for all this fickle transience. Perhaps she finally understood. It made no sense to prefer parts, to pick favourites like Alice or Martha or the warmth of the sun. No single thing could exist without the world that sustained it. Every part was dependent on the parts it touched – the trees recycling the air Alice needed to breathe, rain and dirt sustaining the trees, an intricate conspiracy of ancestors, loves and trysts and accidents funnelling down into her genetic legacy. Food became energy became muscle and skin. Shit and corpses became fertile soil. Everything was constantly arising out of things it was not, and each of those things arose from not-themselves, a cat's cradle of dependent geneses, cloaked in breathable gases, hurtling through the emptiness of space. I am the boat and also the water. To love one was to love the whole. And goodness, how that knowing hurt.

She laid her head on the foredeck and let the engine's vibrations penetrate her brain, her teeth. A figure was watching from the bank, bathed in blue light. Ice crystals formed on the gunwale. She closed her eyes and listened as the jungle whispered her name.

CHAPTER 8

THE GREAT WHITE LODGE

(Ten years and two months before inauguration)

It should have been simple. Hagar hid on a narrow plateau overlooking the Prefect's lodge. Her path was clear.

She did not feel the ice-axe go – her fingers were so numb she only saw the haft slip from her gloved hand, then heard the bang as it struck the slanted slate roof below.

A guard was slouching on the terrace, the heavy hooked iron head of his mammoth goad resting against the flagstones while he smoked a cheroot. He spun round in time to see the ice-axe fall from the lodge's wide eaves in a dusting of snow. It hit the stone slabs with a clank. He looked up.

Hagar's plan had been to lower herself onto the roof. She would have shuffled along the slippery ridge tiles to the gambrel end, tied a line round the chimney pot, and descended onto the Prefect's first-floor balcony. The key to surprise was not speed. It was patience.

Now, she would have to improvise. She tossed her staff aside, pulled off her goggles and leapt the ten feet down onto the roof, her crampons clattering against the tiles. She let herself slide down the roof until her boots hit the steel mesh of the snow guard.

With freezing mountain air scalding her nostrils, she slipped out of her thick musk ox coat, and began scooping snow onto the quilted lining.

'*Qui vive?*' The guard's challenge had a hesitant note. Perhaps he thought the bang was a mountain civet, or snowmelt from the cliff above, the ice-axe a tool left on the roof by a forgetful worker. All more plausible than the truth.

Hagar unhooked the grapnel from her belt, slotted two of its flukes into the snow guard's mesh, then paid out about six feet of line. Gripping her stiletto between her teeth, she shoved the coat off the roof and slid after it.

She dropped. Her stomach went up in her throat. She snatched at the rope; high-tensile line skidded through her gloves fast and hot. Her wrists and shoulders jarred.

She was swinging fifteen feet above the terrace. Directly below, the guard was staring down at the coat, a great brown-black splat of fur and exploded snow.

She slid her stiletto from her teeth and dropped.

The guard stepped back.

She stabbed at the space where he'd been standing. The flagstones surged up and she landed hard on the coat, snow blasting out the sleeves.

Her legs buckled. She rolled. The guard backed away, switching the goad to his left hand, drawing a pistol. Behind him, the terrace fell away into a gorge lined with steep, grey-blue cliffs floating in mist. He was taller than he'd looked from above. His greatcoat strained to contain his broad chest, his chestnut-red beard glinting with crystals of frozen breath.

'*Qui vive!*' Definitely a challenge.

Hagar rose slowly, turning her left ankle in on itself, pretending to put weight on it then grimacing as if in pain. She held up her left palm, hoping to distract him from the dagger hidden in her right.

'*Monsieur! Ne tirez pas sur une petite fille! Je suis tombé.*' Which was true. She clutched her breastbone, panting. '*Ma vie pour le Grand-Duc!*'

The guard's full, fiery brows beetled. Then he spotted the rope.

She thrust the knife into his chest.

With cold hands it was hard to drive the thin blade through the padded layers of his greatcoat, jacket and shirt. He grunted, looked down in dumb wonder. Hagar put the heel of her palm behind the pommel and pushed. She felt the tip grind against a rib.

She saw white flashes, the ground tipped and her cheek hit stone. Her head throbbed. He had clubbed her with the pistol muzzle.

A clatter – her stiletto striking the flagstones. The guard grunted, swore. She tried to rise but the courtyard was turning huge undulating circles. Through watering eyes, she saw him stagger towards her, one hand pressed to the wound, the other lifting the iron goad over his head. Against the cobalt mountain sky, its hooked tip loomed like a question mark, a straight blade rising out of it, an answer.

Her vision straightened. She clambered onto all fours, her head still swimming.

'*S'il vous plaît, monsieur!*' she gasped. '*Vous avez fait une erreur!*' Who hadn't? She remembered the words of her second Canoness: *Remember, sister – you may not lie, but if your enemies fool themselves through their own ignorance, this is their sin, not yours. Let them presume. Introduce doubt, confusion. One day ambiguity will save your life.* '*Votre père m'a envoyé!*' Which was correct, theologically.

He hesitated, the goad hanging in the air. Hagar barrel-rolled into his shins. He swore, tried to step back. She grabbed a fistful of greatcoat hem, sprang from the ground into a handstand, and mule-kicked him hard in the face with her spiked metal crampons.

She felt her heel connect with his chin, kicked again and again. The goad clanged to the ground. He grabbed at her knapsack. She kicked and kicked. He cried for her to stop. It sounded as if he had bitten his tongue. The blood was flowing to her head. Wooziness rushed through her. His fingers clutched at her legs. She straightened her back and kicked.

He crumpled; she let herself fall with him. He landed with a great 'ammph!' She rolled clear. His arms slapped either side of him.

The lower half of his face was a porridge of maroon and purple. She might have shattered his jaw.

He was groping for his pistol at his hip. During avalanche season it was probably a last resort.

But his shaking fingers were clutching at the leather sling holster and finding it empty, and Hagar was retrieving her faithful musk ox coat which she had bought from a one-eared vesperi trader down in the valley, its insides now wet with snow, shameful really after the fine service it had done her over the past two days, and he was trying to call out but finding his mouth broken and flooded, and she was walking towards him across the courtyard, dragging the damp musk ox pelt like a fresh kill, his one-shot pistol in her fist.

Hagar glanced back at the grand windows of the lodge, then over at the stone archway. The guard was trying to lift himself up, slobbering blood into his beard, steam rising with each shuddering breath.

She raised the pistol, slid her finger through the freezing ring-trigger. Hagar had no martial spirit – she could not fetishise a gun as some instrument of calcified valour – but she appreciated sensible design. The butt was ivory, incised with deep, curving grooves for better grip during cold weather. The ring-trigger was enlarged to accommodate a gloved digit, the breech lever chunky enough to manipulate with numb fingers. The guard was moaning something, over and over. He had pulled himself up onto his elbows and was crawling backwards, towards the low balustrade overlooking the gorge.

She raised the pistol. He shook his head, rolling his eyes back like a martyr. The pitch of his voice rose. She saw the strength draining from his limbs. He could have fought back, even now, but fear was making him drunk. He was anaesthetised by the sublime magnitude of death, had, at some level, chosen it. She could hear the softening in his tone, could hear him growing far away. Their meeting had been providential, thus – as with all God's intercessions – it was a kindness. Poor boy. Tenderly, she wrapped the thick coat round the pistol.

As the wind dropped, she heard his mushy, chanted words.

'*Ma sœur, ma sœur, ma sœur . . .*'

She knelt and smiled and wept. '*Oui. Nous sommes tous frères et sœurs dans le Christ.*'

She pressed the coat to his brow, like a kiss. Inside its damp, furry warmth, her finger found the ring-trigger. An end to suffering. One life closer to the Father. Deny my death, deny my salvation. Wind seared her cheeks and eyes. The man breathed fast and hard. He wanted this.

A muffled thump echoed off the flagstones, like snow sliding from a roof. The coat bucked. A scatter pattern of red droplets flurried into the wild white air beyond the balustrade, then hung, as if repenting, before whipping back towards the terrace and spattering it in soft rain. Warm kisses struck her eyelids.

Without the coat, cold was gnawing at her bones. She lifted his legs and hoisted them over the parapet. His body was lighter than she had expected – unburdened, perhaps, by death. No person remained, just the shattered trap. She rolled it over the smooth lip of the balustrade. The body bounced once on the black mountainside, then drifted, twisting into mists.

She tossed the empty pistol after him, and, a little ruefully, her ruined musk ox coat. She felt a weight in her heart as the coat left her hand. It had served her well the last two days. Still, better not to get attached to worldly things.

There was a small dark stain on the balustrade. Hagar looked at her rope, swaying from the eaves, too high to reach. The lodge was virtually soundproof, built to withstand the harshest mountain winters. There might not be any more guards inside – they were all concentrated down at the gatehouse, protecting the only road up the mountain – but if someone spotted that rope, they would raise the alarm.

She glanced up at the overhanging plateau from which she had jumped. It was capped with a firm crust of snow. She could not get back up there without getting onto the rooftop, and she couldn't reach the roof without retrieving her line and grapnel . . . which were stuck on the roof.

She slotted her stiletto into its scabbard. Her hands trembled with the afterglow of combat. She was not getting out the way she had got in. At the far end of the house, a wooden balcony hung above a swirling white void. She could not reach it from outside.

Hagar tightened the straps on her knapsack. Plans were a form of attachment – they made one cling to certain outcomes, blinded one to new possibilities. The conditions had changed. So must her strategy.

Hagar rang the bell at the servant's entrance and when a maid answered, Hagar garrotted her. The girl was perhaps sixteen – although after almost four centuries Hagar found it difficult to judge age – with large ears that managed to be rather fetching in their scooped, creamy flamboyance, like Easter lilies, her cinnamon hair tucked behind them, the capillaries in her wide eyes bursting as her face turned the colour of blood sausage.

It was an unpleasant business, especially the finish, when the girl was no longer fighting but Hagar had to make sure the job was done, gripping the wire while the girl hung limp. Hagar shot glances into the corridor to check no one was coming. At last, the body slumped. Hagar felt a terrible sadness in her belly and she bent and kissed the girl's clammy temple and pressed the lolling head to her breastbone.

There was a closet for coats and shoes that stank of leather and boot blacking. Hagar folded the body up behind the coats, upon its side with the knees tucked up to the beautiful pale ears. She covered it with a fur-lined oilskin. She envied it that comfort, that final rest. Hagar closed the closet and was about to step out into the snow when she remembered why she had come.

Be sober, be vigilant; because your adversary the devil, as a roaring lion, walketh about, seeking whom he may devour.

She crept into the lodge.

The inner walls were all smooth-planed golden timber, the ceiling lined with sturdy beams. She heard muffled clanks and bangs a short distance ahead. From beneath a door at the end of the corridor wafted a rich, gamey aroma.

'Adoleta?' The voice came from the other side – female, vesperi, harassed.

Hagar backed away, holding her breath, and followed a fork in the corridor, until she reached wooden stairs leading up.

Now she was out of the scything wind, sensation was returning to her extremities, and with it, pain. Her feet throbbed as she climbed towards a door padded with studded blue leather. The staircase seemed incredibly long. A burrowing, penetrating ache had started in her skull. Crossing the mountain, she had travelled light. Since making camp just below the treeline the previous night – where the fire had allowed her to turn snow and the last of her barley into a tepid porridge, to which she had added her final sliver of goat's butter – she had eaten nothing but nencha, the local sugar biscuits: fatty, sweet and, in these temperatures, hard as slate. Her stomach gurgled, her lips cracking when she clenched her teeth. Within her gloves, her fingers burned.

She had made a misjudgement, coming the long route. At the inn, the guide had warned her in his lilting highland dialect that the harsh winter was not yet over.

But he had worn that condescending smile, that look that said: *and of course you are just a little girl.*

Yet she had plied him with wide-eyed questions, and he had continued to drink his port-wine, and he had confirmed, hypothetically, the route one might take up the east face, marking the path on her map. She did not ask for the route to the Prefect's lodge – never reveal your true destination – but the last portion of the climb had looked easy enough.

And now her eyes were streaming, not out of remorse, but from partial snow blindness. She felt faint. The guard must have hit her harder than she had realised.

The best plans are the most unwise. That is why no one sees them coming.

Hagar decided that this plan had been very, very unwise. That was why it was so brilliant. That was why her larger plan would work. It was so audacious, no one would see it coming. Not Morgellon. Not even Arthur, silly boy. She clutched at the stair-rail and missed. Down in the corridor, she heard the kitchen door open: 'Adoleta!' Then her legs gave out, and there was weightlessness, sleep.

The first thing she felt was the press of the flames.

Her body was burning.

She tried to move and hot scourges mortified her flesh. Her arms were pinned by her sides. She opened her eyes. They were raw and weeping and she was blind.

She opened her mouth to cry out. Her tongue was dry and swollen. She inhaled. The air was hot, smoky. She blinked; blinking hurt. Light stung her eyes. Crushing pincers pressed into her temples.

She moaned. Her voice sounded weak and bleating. The squalor of her self-pity brought her round. She was alive. She still had a chance to make things right. The acrid-sweet smell of gopherwood hung in the air. As she blinked and squinted she saw the joists of a high timber ceiling. She was in the lodge.

She tried to rise and again pain flared across her skin. She was headsick; her legs ached as if they had been clubbed. A heavy gorilla fur blanket lay on top of her, pinning her down. She slipped a hand over her belly.

She was naked. The flesh felt clammy-cold.

Panic lanced through her. She tilted her head to hunt for her clothes and the room lurched; she thought she was going to vomit.

'Hagar?'

A male voice. She recognised the nasal vowels and breezy intonation – the stress landing on the second syllable instead of the first, so her name sounded exotic, vaguely lewd. She writhed, trying to burrow under the covers so he could not see her.

'No, no,' he said, coming nearer, 'please – don't move.' The scrape of a stool. 'I bring you some soup.'

Hagar dragged an arm up from under the blanket and with great effort rubbed her watery, stinging eyes. The room was oppressively bright. She squirmed down beneath the covers, her limbs protesting, until the gorilla pelt came up to her nose.

A middle-aged vesperi servant with teak fur and a white cloth cap set down a tray at the bedside. Hagar tried to bring her into focus and the ache behind her left eye intensified into a migraine. She closed her eyes. The pain receded.

Footsteps led away over rug, bare boards, then stairs. The servant had gone.

Prefect Colstrid grunted, his stool creaking.

'It is you, eh? Not some trick?'

She allowed her eyelids to part ever so slightly, peering out through slits. Colstrid had put on weight; his jaw and neck had melded into a contiguous bulge of tallowy flesh, and his loose-knit blue sweater swelled around a statesmanlike paunch.

'My cook finds you below stairs, unconscious, bleeding. You have no coat. You are wet, freezing. How is this possible, strange sister? Were you attacked?'

Hagar groaned.

'Ah, forgive me. I ask too many questions. Here – eat soup.' He leaned across to the tray and with fat, gold-ringed fingers took a white porcelain spoon, dipping it into a bowl of yellowish broth. He began conveying the spoon towards her concealed lips, one hand cupped beneath it. She gritted her teeth and shook her head vigorously.

'You must warm up,' he said. 'It's good. Look.' He lifted the spoon to his full, rosebud lips and tilted it, slurping. 'See? Not poisoned.' He winked.

Beneath the blanket Hagar shuddered.

'*Clothes*,' she whispered. He throat felt itchy and raw.

Colstrid frowned, then his eyes widened. 'Oh! Of *course*.' He turned and indicated a point in the room which Hagar's blurry vision could not yet discern. 'If you'd remained in your wet things you would have most certainly died. They're drying in the laundry room. In the meantime, you may borrow these from my maid.' He placed his palms on his knees and stood with a snort. 'She seems to have sneaked away for some private time with Mr Garn yet again, so it is only fair.' He sighed, then the sigh became a chuckle and the chuckle became a cough. 'Oh dear. I think soon he comes to me to ask my permission to marry. Her family has worked for me three generations, you know?' He took some folded clothes from the back of a chair and padded to the bed. He chuckled. 'I remember when her grandmother was just a little girl, scrubbing pots in the scullery.' He placed the clothes next to Hagar's pillow. 'Does time ever slow down again?'

Hagar was thinking about her belt, with her stiletto knife, and her tunic, with her garrotte wire threaded through the sleeve, and her knapsack, with its precious cargo – all down in the laundry room. Bracing against the pain, she spoke:

'Go . . . away.'

'Hmm?' He glanced up while lowering his backside onto the stool.

'Go . . . away . . . so I . . . can . . . dress.' The effort of talking left her breathless.

'Ah!' He began shuffling round on the stool, exposing his wide back. Providence was offering her an opportunity. She checked the tray for a fruit knife.

But even leaning forward made her head swim. She was too weak.

'Go . . . out.' She coughed, and it felt like a kick to the chest. 'Please.'

Colstrid slapped his thigh and rose, shrugging. 'Very well. Make yourself at home.' Some of the conviviality had left his voice. 'When I return, perhaps you answer my questions, eh?' And he stomped away in his heavy house slippers, the stairs groaning as he descended to the ground floor.

Hagar grabbed the clothes – white cotton underwear, long johns, a cotton slip, a blue woollen housedress and a pair of long blue socks. Garments passably warm enough for a well-heated house. Outdoors, she might survive fifteen minutes.

She felt as if she had been drugged. Perhaps sweet Tonti was at long last growing canny. Dragging each piece of clothing under the covers, pulling the scratchy long johns over her tender legs – these actions felt complex as teasing frayed thread through the eye of a needle, or stitching shut a wound. Her swollen joints ached. She found bruises on her shoulder, where she must have fallen, and another on her face, where the guard had struck her.

As she dressed, moving grew easier. Little by little, the sick, whirling sensations subsided. She heaved herself up onto her elbows. The bed was next to a huge open fireplace, heaped with blazing logs. A large black iron poker stood against the jamb, blunt but heavy-looking, and beside that an iron toasting fork, with three prongs that tapered to narrow points. Above the fireplace was an oil painting of Colstrid as she remembered him, at his inauguration over sixty years before, leaner, his lush dark hair swept back, clad in the ceremonial white robe, kneeling before Lord Jejunus, his chin raised, the sword point at his throat. A valet's oaths of fealty were to the perpetuum, but Morgellon's rather direct interpretation of the rites left onlookers in no doubt as to whom he considered the ultimate authority. The artist had filled the Spire chamber with long austere shadows, which Hagar thought fanciful given the river of candles surrounding them. She spotted herself, off to the right, also in her whites, but standing, her head lowered, identifiable only by her shortness and her ragged bald strip which the artist had taken great pains to capture, a lurid pink against the drab mustard of her long hair.

Vanity! How foolish that, even now, her ugliness made her heart hurt a little. Why did she care? The only one whose opinion she had ever cared about was dead. She had watched the beautiful grow old many, many times over. She would never experience their slow, hollow agony. She had always been wretched.

And there, at the back of the picture, was Mitta. His black marble effigy gazing down upon the ceremony. Deathless. Her breath caught. God damn him.

On the tray at her bedside was a teapot in the shape of a mammoth, all shaggy and indomitable with its exaggerated snout-spout leaking braids of steam. She shuffled to the edge of the bed, her legs aching as she swung them floorwards. She picked up the pot with both hands and, trembling, poured herself a cup. Her thoughts were churning, folding back on themselves. She needed heat.

She spooned clear honey from a clay jar into the tea and swirled it until it dissolved. The cup scalded her palms but still she clutched it tight, willing strength back into her limbs.

Through big glass screen doors she saw the balcony, and snow glowing against the black night beyond. Sudden flurries galed from the abyss; every so often, a chunk would pad softly against the pane, sticking.

Any moment they would find the body. Armed guards would rush up the stairs. Perhaps Colstrid would have her tortured. If he were wise he would have her hurled into the valley.

She sipped her tea, scalding her tongue. She was growing feverish, irrational. Little Tonti suspected nothing.

Her mission had not yet failed. She must remain calm. All she had to do was get warm, deal with him and escape.

Her heel knocked an object beneath the bed. She fished for it with her foot, her calf aching, and her toes found the edge of a small black box.

She picked it up. It was light and smooth, with a round lens on the front and a rectangular glass window set in one corner. She had seen cameras before, but this one had a suspect compactness, an alien sparseness of design that smacked of contraband. Probably either Colstrid or one of his servants had hidden it when they laid her in the bed. Theoretically, possession of a single object from the old world was grounds for a reprimand, a humiliating self-criticism session, and a loss of face before the Grand-Duc's assembly, but in practice it was the kind of peccadillo everyone with connections to the Albion threshold security indulged in – an unspoken perk of seniority.

Hagar hefted the device thoughtfully. From the little she had gleaned from smuggled newspapers, lately the old world had become a carnival of diabolic wonders. Vast electrical brains connected every home, consulted daily by patient, trusting families. Bombs could turn cities to ash in a finger snap. Fist-high fur-coated automata muttered arcane gibberish. Resplendent miracles jostled with unfathomable gewgaws.

Of course, these trinkets could not be allowed to reach the masses. They would turn indifference and disdain towards rumours of the closed-off barbarian world into fascination, perhaps worship. Most ordinary citizens were sceptical that another world existed.

She held the camera against her chest, its lens pointing towards the sliding glass doors, the wooden balcony, the falling snow. A box that captured time. *Hast thou entered into the treasures of the snow? Or hast thou seen the treasures of the hail, which I have reserved against the time of trouble, against the day of battle and war?* How could these queer riches not set a yearning in their owners' hearts? They were whispers of ingenuity and defiance, haughty little Babels that seemed to thrum with an inner fire. She pictured lost people all round that strange cousin planet, sitting on beds just as she was, surrounded by their glowing, nickering treasures, blank and heart-hollow, lonely, trapped.

Outside, spots of white swirled against black. She felt on the box for a switch. Oh Mitta, that you would come back to me. That I could have rescued those moments. Her finger found a sunken button. She pressed. A click. A bright flash. The camera whinnied; a slot at its base spewed a glossy tongue of card.

'Hagar!' Colstrid's voice boomed up the stairs. 'Are you decent, my dear? Cry out if not!' But already his house slippers were thudding up into the room.

Startled, she bent over, set the camera on the floor and backheeled it under the bed. She came back up too fast – her head swam and the room dimmed. She grasped at the bedside table, jolting the tray so the cutlery clattered. Scalding soup slopped over her fingers.

She winced and wiped her hand on the gorilla skin.

'Aha!' said Colstrid. 'She is risen.'

He leaned one palm upon the newel post, a slight sheen on his brow and jowls, his other arm trailing behind his back. 'There's someone who wishes to meet our surprise visitor.' He glanced over his shoulder. 'Come on then, my darling.' He stepped aside to reveal a female child of perhaps six years with odd, bulbous eyes and wide cheeks, clad in a one-piece garment of blond llama wool with attached bootees, a hood hanging down the nape and a glass clamp jar dangling by a loop of wire from her curled fingers. In the jar floated dozens of tiny polychromatic transparencies.

Hagar felt her blood turn cold.

'This is Agatha,' said Colstrid. He placed a big paw on the child's back and eased her into the room, her shuffling woollen bootees making a *shh shh* noise against the waxed hardwood. 'Agatha – this is Papa's friend, Miss Hagar Ingery. I know her from a long, long time ago – years and years before you were born.'

Agatha stared at Hagar, the largeness of her eyes accentuated by mauve crescents under the sockets. She had thin, tangled black hair, rather like a skein of fishing line.

Hagar had known nothing about a child. There were now at least three people alive in the household who had seen her. She could abandon the plan – invent a pretext for her unexpected arrival, sneak away as soon as the opportunity presented itself. But when Colstrid discovered two of his staff had been murdered, she would be the obvious culprit. Even if he did not publicly accuse her, he would never grant her the opportunity to get this close to him again.

Tonti Colstrid had to make way. Hagar had spent years considering her options. Her conclusion had been inescapable: the only way to draw Morgellon out of the safety of his palace was to force an election. It was no cruelty – as Prefect, Colstrid had enjoyed over six decades of sumptuous, circumscribed living. He had lived longer than any normal human. And now, there was a pattern to manifest.

But the cook and the child had seen her. For Colstrid's death to do its work, his killer had to remain anonymous.

And so they would have to make way also.

Colstrid rubbed his daughter's shoulder. 'Will you show Hagar what's in your jar?'

Agatha padded to the bed and dunked the large jar in Hagar's lap. Magnified by the thick glass lid, water rippled with pea-sized iridescent blobs. Hagar squinted. Her eyes still ached from the snow-glare.

'Baby dumpling squid,' said Agatha, with breathless gravity.

Hagar peered closer. The glass was cold beneath her palms. Should she strike now? She could throw a forearm round the child's throat, order Colstrid to lie facedown. Then she could shove the child aside, grab the poker, sprint across the room – no, wait, she should make sure she had the poker *before* she released Agatha – and as Colstrid rose she could bludgeon him to death. Then she could kill Agatha, head downstairs to retrieve her clothes – and find a new coat – and kill the cook. Perhaps it would be better to snap the child's neck first – witnessing her death might leave Colstrid incapacitated with shock. But then, snapping a neck was so much harder than one was led to believe – trapped in this withered, immature body, Hagar had never possessed much arm strength. Despite all her training she might only administer a sprain.

As her sight adjusted, the little creatures slowly sharpened – tiny rainbow squid with silver feline eyes and little arms like the cilia of an anemone, their freckled mantles warping as they swam through the lid's fisheye curve. Some spat streams of bubbles, jetting round the jar's circumference. Others drifted listlessly.

Keeping them in focus was making her nauseous. The clamp jar felt like a granite block pinning her thighs to the bed. She could compose elaborate assassination strategies all she liked – for now, anything that required more than a couple of slow, shambling steps was a fantasy.

'Some scholars think clouds carry their eggs to the mountaintops,' said Colstrid. 'Others think it's the wind. Some say they are the blood of the mountain spirit. Certain isolated Yotzean sects consider them harbingers of the great unmaking – signs that the barrier between earth and hell is disintegrating.' He laughed quietly. 'They appear in streams and pools and ride the snowmelt all the way down to the sea.'

‘They like to swim,’ said Agatha.

Hagar looked up at the child. A precocious intelligence shone in those amber eyes. She had been told Hagar’s full name. She was old enough to remember, to supply a description, an account. Colstrid had other children, by other mothers – more than a dozen, in fact, many of whom had grown up, had children of their own, and died.

‘Agatha,’ said Hagar. Her scratchy, derelict voice sounded strange in the snug and solid lodge. ‘She was a saint.’

‘Do you hear that, Agatha?’ Colstrid folded his arms across his belly. ‘It means you share a name with a very important woman from a distant land, long, long ago. Tell us, Hagar – what were the achievements of this saint?’

‘She had her breasts cut off and they tried to burn her alive because she refused to become a whore. She died in prison.’

Agatha watched the baby squid, their bright motion reflected in her pupils. She picked at the blond wool on her cuff. Colstrid’s stomach swelled and receded, his smile slowly collapsing. The fire lapped and crackled.

‘Agatha, it’s time you went to bed now.’

Agatha grasped the wire attached to the jar and lifted it from Hagar’s lap. The water inside sloshed violently, shimmering squid zipping in all directions. She shuffled back towards her father.

‘Go and find Jai and ask her to help you with your toilet,’ he said.

‘Where’s Adoleta?’ said Agatha.

‘She’s gone for a stroll with Mr Garn.’

‘Are they looking for pudding squid?’

Colstrid guided his daughter down the staircase. ‘Something like that. Off you go now. You walk the rest of the way on your own. Find Jai and perhaps if you ask her very nicely she’ll sing you one of the rain ghost songs.’

And there was no more protest.

Hagar massaged her thighs, trying to work feeling back into them. Her head was clearing. She felt shivery and feeble, but an ember of vigour had begun to glow in her limbs. She took her teacup from the tray, drank deeply. It was just as Canoness Umbra Prime had always counselled: *Wait. No one can parry time.*

'Have some soup!' cried Colstrid, returning to the room. 'You must repair yourself! It's mountain hare, caught fresh this morning.'

Hagar glanced at the viscous yellow-grey broth. It clung to the sides of the bowl like mucus.

'Forgive me. I don't eat meat.'

He shook his head. 'Ah, Hagar. You always were too kind for this world. Born to be a martyr.'

'Thank you.'

'We have bread left over from breakfast. I'll ask the cook to bring you some rolls.'

'No, no.' Hagar held up a hand. 'I'm fine for now.' She gestured with her cup and took a second swig. She placed it on the tray and refilled it. 'Is your cook the only other person in the house?'

Colstrid sighed. 'Yes. It seems Adoleta has gone courting and my bootboy is down in the village at his great-uncle's funeral until Stolasday. And now you pop up in my lodge like a little cave mushroom! Come now. How did you get in? Is there no one at the gatehouse?'

She spooned honey into her tea. 'You haven't told them I'm here?'

'You mean they don't *know*? They are supposed to be keeping me safe from black profiteers and Hilantian assassins. Any number of bandits want to reach me, to take me hostage, to hurt my child – and they let you, a little girl, walk through the gates unchallenged?'

'People underestimate me.'

'Is that all it takes?' He was marching up and down, swinging his arms. 'This most simple of ruses? Are they such fools that they see no danger in a child? You.' He thrust a finger at her, brow shiny with sweat. 'You remember how it was. Soldiers posing as beggars. Old vesperi with firebombs under their gowns. Acid everywhere.'

'I remember.'

'Why would they not stop you? Who has trained them thus? Which master do they really serve?' Colstrid rubbed his palms. He held them to his lips and kissed the Jejunus crest on his signet ring. 'People have no idea of the burden we carry, you and I. We have the souls of angels, yet we bleed like men. They call us servants. We are the keepers of the flame.'

She sipped her hot, sweet tea. 'You sound weary, dear brother.'

'I am tired of the world's foolishness.' Colstrid's waxy chin slumped over his sweater's thick collar. 'People forget so fast.'

'They die, Tonti.'

'The Hilanta will come again. This time, I think they will kill us all.' He dragged a stool to the window's edge and sat, gazing out into the night. 'So. Why do you come? Your messages are never good. Some new disaster, no doubt.'

'Yes. Some new disaster.'

His shoulders sank. 'Always, always more.'

'It is the way of the world, Tonti.'

Colstrid let out a noise halfway between a laugh and a sob. But he did not laugh, and he did not sob. He stared at the falling snow, his palms on his knees.

'I wish it were otherwise.'

Hagar set down her teacup and attempted to stand. She placed her feet flat on the floor, braced her palms against the hard mattress and pushed. Her knees buckled. She fell forwards onto her splayed hands. Her vision streamed with tiny white comets. No matter. She had caught herself by surprise, that was all. She rose again, using the bedside table for support. Her legs wobbled. She ground her teeth and took a step.

Colstrid glanced round. 'Ah. You see? Tea is good for chills.'

'I will put another log on the fire, if I may.'

He flapped an arm towards the hearth.

Hagar limped round the foot of the bed, approaching the large open fireplace. With every step, walking grew a little easier. The heat of the flames seemed to soak into her stiff muscles. She clenched and unclenched her fingers like the pudding squid's pulsing arms, imagining she were swimming through the crisp, fragrant air.

Split logs were stacked side-on with artful care, blushing ginger at their hearts, fading through a rich custard yellow to pale vanilla just beneath the bark. Hagar slid one from the top and trudged to the fireplace, halting just in front of the poker. Two wrought-iron firedogs held the burning logs, either one a Celtic cross with a fat point-cut ruby at its centre, sharp red eyes that flared in the dying light of the flames. Words were carved in stone beneath the mantle: *DEN VOT ARDO SUN FOCO.*

She bent, tossed the log onto the others, felt the glow on her cheeks. As she straightened up, she closed her fingers around the square shaft of the toasting fork.

'God loves you, you know.'

Colstrid laughed – a throaty, wolfish growl. 'You can take the girl out of the convent.'

'I mean it.' She tested the central prong with her thumb, winced. 'Do you think He would choose this for you? Decades of suffering? You feel alone. You see the world, forever melting. Everyone you love grows old and dies.' She began limping towards him. 'But we're not alone. We're loved, Tonti. And God is calling us home.'

'Did you feel it – when he hurt his wrist, yesterday?'

For a moment, she thought he meant God. Then she realised he was talking about Morgellon.

'Of course,' said Hagar, though she had been so ravaged by cold and fatigue that at first she had mistaken the dull, persistent ache for her own. As she rounded the foot of the bed, she picked up a brocaded cushion by its silk tassels.

'I wonder if Morgellon notices when he hurts himself. When he hurts us. Does he recall what pain is?'

To speak of the Grand-Duc in such familiar terms, even with a fellow servant, was a huge impropriety. Hagar allowed her shoulders to relax. Colstrid trusted her.

'There are pains and there are pains,' she said. 'You're young. You weren't here in the days of the Ordo Interminatis.' For a time, a small group of peers, including Morgellon, had indulged in debauches where they sought out experiences that would kill a mortal – flinging themselves off minarets, mutilating one another with archaic torture equipment, crushing their bodies to paste beneath millstones. Perhaps it woke them, briefly, from their stupors. Morgellon had called it a holy duty. For Hagar, it had meant only agony. 'We're fortunate.'

'Oh ho!' Colstrid nodded and threaded his fingers and rested his brow upon his knuckles. 'So we're told. So the people believe.'

Hagar did not reply, treading with light, slow steps, feeling the thick cotton of her borrowed socks compress between the ball of her foot and the wooden floor. The cushion brushed her calf. She breathed softly, through clenched teeth.

'The cliques have grown powerful,' he said. 'We waited too long. They have learned to cooperate.'

And now nothing will be restrained from them, which they have imagined to do. Hagar stood with the flames at her back, the three-pronged fork in her fist.

'They've grown strong in the Grand-Duc's absence. They run Fat Maw. If I try to suppress them now, it will be civil war. They'll burn the city to the ground sooner than relinquish control. Thousands of innocents will die.'

Even if Colstrid did move against the cliques, after the purge Morgellon would probably have him stripped of his title, in penance. A public trial, an admission of guilt from Colstrid – *I was too bloodthirsty, I was driven by careerism* – in return for his descendants' safety and a seemly state execution. Both sides appeased, ambitions pruned. That was what Colstrid feared. The deaths of citizens only mattered inasmuch as they would provide a convenient pretext for his denunciation.

What he did not know was that no pretext was needed. What he did not know was that the truly powerful acted without justification. The paraministers, the aldermen, the doyens and the priests – they would scramble to defend any act of capricious cruelty on the part of Morgellon and the perpetuum. They would invent moral imperatives and legal precedents that supported whatever outrage he set in motion.

Once, she might have attributed such behaviour to fear. But now she understood.

People would support almost any depravity sooner than admit they were powerless.

As she approached his stool, her shadow compressed, shrinking into her. Poor Tonti. His worries were unfounded. He would never live to break up the cliques, thus Morgellon would never offer him up as a scapegoat.

The nape of his neck was milky white, edged with fair, downy hairs. She doubted he had seen real sunshine for months, holed up in his winter retreat. His sweater's cable-knit collar hung loosely, away from the flesh. Muscle shifted under fluid, buttery skin. She remembered the subtle routes of arteries from her time at the École

De La Sagesse Immortels, how they had looked, blue pipes ensconced in a slit trench of fat, how each vein had opened beneath the whetted nib of a lancet. She remembered the sour tang of preservative. The whistle of escaping air.

Patience begets wisdom. Wisdom begets conviction. Conviction begets victory.

'Hagar.' As he lowered his head, the nub of his vertebra prominens pushed up from the surrounding meat. 'I think someone is trying to kill me.'

The central prong of the toasting fork entered his neck cleanly. She drove it deep into the right of his throat and kicked out the legs of his stool. He fell sideways. The handle of the fork hit the floor and he dropped on it with his full weight. The prongs pierced his windpipe, punching out of the left side of his neck.

Hagar kicked him onto his back and pressed the embroidered cushion over his face. She wanted to stop him crying out. She sat on the cushion and his slippers danced against the hardwood. He was already gone – the flapping of his fat hands was all reflex. Ruby-black blood dilated from his throat, a widening circle that made her feel as if the two of them were falling from the sky towards a dark island. She thought perhaps one of the fork tines had severed his spinal cord. A warm wetness soaked into her socks. She could hear blood draining between the floorboards. It made a noise like rain on a carriage roof. Soon a stain would begin materialising on the ceiling below.

Colstrid had stopped moving. Hagar stood, dismounted. Her sopping socks slapped on the boards.

The body lay with the arms splayed, palms turned upwards, and the ankles crossed. Where his shirt and sweater had ridden up there was a band of sweaty pale flesh.

She set the stool upright, sat down and peeled off her socks. They looked like the flattened pelts of freshly skinned winter martens. She walked to the fireplace. She enjoyed the damp tackiness of her bare soles against the floor. She tossed the socks into the flames. They smoked and frothed. She took the heavy iron poker from beside the hearth, hefted its flat head in her palm.

Her heart was beating with a steady intensity and she could hear the tiniest sounds: the crickle of bark combusting in the fire; a lock of hair rustling in the hollow of her ear; breath hissing from her nostrils. She plucked a droplet of blood from her eyelash.

She looked at the glass doors and the balcony and the swirling snow. She could drag the body outside and slide him through a gap in the wooden balustrade. The drifts were very deep this time of year. Brief confusion over whether the Prefect was dead or simply missing might confuse attempts to hunt for his assassin – it might give her anything between an extra hour and an extra day to get away.

But if the body were lost in the valley below, the – already tortuous – process of succession would be delayed. The protocol for declaring a functionally immortal person dead was understandably complicated. Without a corpse, a locum Prefect would be appointed, until the necessary time had elapsed – she thought it might be anything up to fifty years – before the perpetuum declared Tonti officially deceased and began seeking his replacement. The locum would not be granted the full powers of a Prefect (and thus would continue to age), so no official ceremony would be necessary, and Morgellon would remain hidden in his palace.

Meanwhile, Anwen's daughter Sarai grew steadily older. Hagar had hunted her down in the Avalonian jungle just as Arthur had foreseen, and had taken great pains to keep her survival a secret. Since then, Hagar had done everything she could to protect the child, but for all Sarai's power, she was no peer. She was subject to ageing, sickness and death. A delay of decades would mean her certain demise, and with it, the demise of hope itself.

No need to hide Tonti's fate. Besides, there would be other bodies.

She went out onto the balcony and washed her hands in snow. She scooped up more and scrubbed her face. When she stepped back into the attic the skin across her cheeks and brow felt tight and glowing.

Hagar poured the last of the tea. It was lukewarm and sour, enough to make her lips purse. The cup shook as it left her lips. Black leaves swirled in the bottom of the cup.

She draped a pillowcase loosely round the poker and dipped the end in the soup. Cradling it, she walked towards the stairs.

Creeping barefoot through the narrow lodge corridor, Hagar could hear Tonti's cook Jai singing both halves of a two-part piece: a low, slow harmony under quavering noseleaf trills. There were gaps – short periods of silence – where doubtless the song continued in a range only skyfolk could hear. That was the fatal problem with the vesperi – they dipped in and out of groundfolk's perception. Some part of their world would remain forever unknowable, and that which we do not know, we fear.

Hagar thought she recognised the refrain, maybe from the Siege of Atmanloka. Could it really be that old? Of course, back then many tens of thousands of voices would have joined in chorus. But which side had sung it? The defenders? Or the victors? Her memories were so elusive.

She smiled sadly at the irony. Jai was lulling the human child to sleep with a battle hymn.

As she neared the door Hagar did not bother to soften her steps. There was no sense in trying to sneak up on a vesperi. One could not disguise one's presence. Only one's intentions.

Hagar placed her palm against the oak-panelled door. The lullaby faded and stopped.

She entered. Jai sat at little Agatha's bedside. She had high, hunched shoulders and a grey woollen dress that came down to her bootcaps. Her furled wings were bound with a sash. In her cotton-gloved hands she held a bowl of milk, a wooden spoon resting in a groove on its lip. A taper burned on a small cupboard covered with lace. The walls of the room were decorated with framed cases of crickets, locusts and moths under glass, each creature pinned and identified with a handwritten name card. Agatha lay with her head sunken in a stack of three pillows, the purple and red damask quilt drawn up to her chin. On her bedside table, a pastille smouldered in a blue china dish, giving off a sharp whiff of gunpowder, pennyroyal and loam – the type doctors prescribed for feeble lungs.

Jai swivelled her head, candlelight picking out her stern projecting jaw, the ears that hung above her scalp like a black hood. She was unafraid.

Hagar held out the soiled pillowcase.

'I got soup on my pillow,' she said. Concealed by folds of cotton, the iron poker lay cool and weighty across her two palms.

Jai's yellow eyes narrowed. 'Where's Master Colstrid?'

It was strange, how similar the dry, faintly lisping Athanasian vesperi voice was to her own. It gave Hagar pause, long enough that Jai frowned, and Hagar had to twitch herself alert.

'Upstairs. Will you fetch me a new cover? It was my fault. I wanted to ask you myself.'

Jai glanced from the pillowcase to Hagar. She was on her guard. The smooth ridges around her nostrils expanded as she inhaled.

Hagar waited for a moment of distraction.

'If it pleases you, Miss Ingery, I'll bring fresh bed linen once I've put Mistress Agatha to sleep.'

Hagar took a step forward, smiling. 'I can put her to sleep.'

Jai hooked her thumbs over the rim of the bowl. Did she suspect? Or was she just resentful at the intrusion?

'No, thank you.' She spoke in a firm monotone. 'The master requested I tend to her.'

Hagar cast a slow glance back towards the stairs. 'I'm quite sure he won't object.'

Jai set the bowl down. She glanced at Agatha.

'Aggie?' she said. The child gazed in wonder.

Jai blew out the candle.

The room went black. Hagar blinked, as if the problem were her eyes. At the sound of movement, she recovered her wits and lunged, swinging the poker in a broad backhand.

It swished through space. The tip banged into the wall, scratching the timber with an ugly rasp.

A breeze kissed the nape of her neck. Behind her, the door slammed.

It might be a bluff. In the darkness, Hagar visualised the spot where the child's head had lain, stepped towards it and brought the poker down hard. Iron thumped pillow.

Jai had fled with Agatha. Hagar staggered – dizzy, impressed. She had not expected such decisiveness. Her plans were unravelling.

Jai might hesitate to assault a handmaiden, but if she reached the gatehouse Colstrid's guards would protect her and the child. Hagar could not kill them all. She was not even sure she could kill Jai in a fair fight.

But witnesses meant failure.

She groped for the door handle, finding it on her second attempt. As she stepped out into the dimly lit corridor she heard footsteps echoing towards the lodge's grand hall. She ran.

When Hagar reached the landing, Jai was halfway down a flight of green-carpeted stairs, clutching little Agatha to her chest. Below, candle stumps shone in clay candelabra on circular glass tables. The stairs descended into a grand hall decorated with yak rugs and leather divans and a stuffed snow gorilla posed in a fearsome attitude, its raised arms casting a long, antlered shadow up the wall.

Hagar flung the poker overarm.

Agatha cried out: 'Jai!'

The poker flew in a tight arc, spinning. Jai turned and it scythed through the space where she had been. It struck the snow gorilla's head with a whump. The gorilla rocked on its marble plinth; Jai spun to face it.

Hagar was on the stairs. Her joints ached and a liquid fatigue dragged at her limbs. She had overreached herself – she had not counted on a pursuit. Without turning round, Jai tugged at the knot securing her wings. The sash fell away, her wings spread like huge black sails and she leapt over the bannister, leathery envelopes filling as she spiral-glided to the floor.

Hagar leant over the waxed wooden rail. Jai landed heavily, weighed down by the child. She hobbled towards a corridor. Perhaps the front doors were locked.

It was too far to jump. Hagar almost called out: *I only want to talk to you!* But that would have been a lie.

Besides, the cook was too smart.

Hagar ran. Her feet were sacks of wet sand. How foolish she had been! Of course Jai had checked Hagar's clothes and found the misericord. Of course she had suspected Hagar's intentions. Jai knew the lodge. She was fit. She was energised by fear.

A yak rug rucked under Hagar's feet as she rounded the newel post. She grabbed a clay candelabra as she passed, hot wax splattering her forearm. The pain focused her.

Jai shouldered through a service door and it swung shut behind her. Hagar ran down the hallway. She kicked the door aside and found herself on the staircase leading down to the servants' quarters – the one she had been climbing when she passed out.

Jai and Agatha had vanished.

Shadows stretched and see-sawed in the guttering candlelight. Hagar descended, listening. At the foot of the stairs, she was about to turn right, towards the servants' entrance, when she heard the faintest noise from the opposite direction – a short high note that cut off.

A child's muffled sob. It was coming from the kitchen. Hagar followed it.

The lodge was built into the cliffside. If Hagar remembered rightly, any kitchen windows would open onto a sheer drop. Jai and the child were trapped.

Jai would hear her coming – Hagar pictured the vesperi flattened against the back wall beside the range, cowering, or perhaps standing tall, defiant – and so, wishing to calm the poor wretch, she called:

'*Pour la vie sois en paix, et que la paix soit avec ta maison et tout ce qui t'appartient!* I have no desire to cause you suffering!'

Which was true.

She had no weapon. She tested the candelabra in her fist. It felt light and brittle.

She put a hand to the kitchen door and pushed. It moved an inch and stopped. Something heavy was wedged against the base.

Hagar shoved. She turned her shoulder and barged. The door rattled but did not budge.

'Sister!' she cried. 'I bear you no ill-will.'

'I've rung the bell that summons the guards!' Jai's cry came from deep within the kitchen. 'They'll be here in minutes!'

Hagar's neck hairs prickled. An alarm? The plans she had read mentioned nothing about an alarm in Colstrid's lodge. Was Jai bluffing?

Perhaps it had been recently installed. It made sense to have some means of alerting the gatehouse – and Colstrid had certainly been paranoid. If Jai spoke the truth, Hagar guessed it would take five minutes for armed guards to run up the long, curving mountain road and reach the lodge.

Hagar barged the door harder.

'Let me in!' She barged it again, pain blasting her shoulder. 'You don't understand! I'm trying to save you!'

Hagar stopped, out of breath. The door was thin – made for swinging aside easily when a maid emerged with platters of hot food – but sturdy enough that someone as small as her would never break it down before the guards arrived.

She stepped back, her shoulder smarting. Could she start a fire? Ridiculous. Even if she found fuel, it would take too long. Besides, fires were unpredictable – good for destroying evidence, less reliable for killing. If either Jai or Agatha survived, she was undone.

She glanced about the corridor. To her left was a door with a small steamed-up porthole. She opened it and went in.

Cotton undergarments hung from great clotheshorses suspended on pulleys. An iron stove burned in the corner. Several brown felt bodices had been fastened – rather immodestly – around its thick black chimney, moisture beading on their surfaces as they dried. Next to the stove was a basket of split logs and an axe.

She spotted her clothes, hanging from a rack. She had nearly forgotten them. Aside from anything else, they were evidence placing her at the lodge.

She slipped off the borrowed housedress and donned her socks, boots and her trousers with their belt of boxes and holsters. The misericord was still in its sheath, and as she fastened the belt buckle – listening all the while for movement out in the corridor – the dagger settled at her right hip. Already she felt the old faith returning, the surety of purpose.

She found her goggles hanging from a peg and put on her blouse and tunic. She fastened crampons to her boots – though they were cumbersome indoors, she would have no time to attach them once she left the lodge. On the floor, most vital of all, was her little knapsack. She checked the smooth bundle inside. Her gut clenched at the thought of using it. But perhaps she would be forced to.

She felt her cuff for the stiff loop of garrotte wire. Still there. She inhaled hot, damp, scented air. It was time.

She picked up the axe and walked back to the kitchen door, cleats clacking on the boards.

The blade bit into the wood beside the hinges with a resonant bang. It was hefty and sharp and the door panel was flimsy. Hagar swung the axe with her whole body. On the second stroke, the axe head punched through and she had to brace her boot against the lower part of the door to tug it out. Splinters fell with the soft whisper of ash.

She felt dizzy and had to steady herself against the wall. The floor seemed to flex and tilt. When she tried to lift the axe, her arms did not want to obey. Feebleness spread through her limbs.

He giveth power to the faint; and to them that have no might he increaseth strength. Hagar squeezed the axe handle until the tremors rose up her arms. She bit down on the inside of her cheek. She would not fail. She was an instrument of salvation.

She hacked two ragged slits into the upper panel of the door, then pounded a hole between them with the flat of the blade. Behind, the kitchen was solid black.

She pushed the candelabra through the gap. Two of its flames extinguished. The dimensions of the room shifted, lit gold and red and purple. Long shadows stretched towards a far wall. A piercing breeze carried the salty, sweet scent of snuffed tapers.

'Sister Jai?' she said.

A plaited brown loaf, half sawn into rounds, sat in the centre of the kitchen table. A pair of plump, silvery fish lay nose-to tail in an earthen dish, strewn with white crescents of shallot, soaking in a marinade up to their sumptuous iridescent lips. Beside these were a chopping board, a bottle of dark rum and an empty mug.

Hagar's eyes were watering from the cold. She could hear the faint, mournful lowing of the wind in the valley.

A window was open.

She hoisted herself through the hole in the door. A coal scuttle was wedged between the door and a cupboard.

Another of the candelabra's flames went out. A single, trembling light remained.

She eased the candle's flame left and right, taking care not to snuff it by moving too fast. Bronze pots and pans lined shelves like skulls in an ossuary. There were glass jars of pickled fish, racks of boning knives and shucking knives and fruit knives, deep ceramic pudding bowls decorated with images of leviathans, and a cast-iron meat grinder bracketed to the wall, candlelight picking out the fluted profile of its funnel, the dark honeycomb mesh, the hand-crank hanging like a withered limb.

Hagar reached for the sheath at her hip and closed her free hand round the hilt of her stiletto.

Gingerly, she stepped round the table. A tub of sugar had been upset at the foot of a pie cupboard. Perforations in the cupboard's tin panels formed the eight-pointed star of the perpetuum. She advanced, the sugar crystals sparkling like snow.

A gust ruffled her hair. The flame snuffed.

Blackness.

Dropping the candelabra, she ducked and rolled. A grunt, a clatter, then a *BOOM* inches above her head. She was under the table. Something had struck the upper side, hard.

Obviously Jai no longer felt constrained by the laws against assaulting a handmaiden. In the dark, a vesperi had an overwhelming advantage.

Hagar scuttled backwards under the table. She listened for movement. Jai would be listening too, could hear a hundred times more clearly. With every passing second, the guards neared the house. The quieter the room became, the easier it was for Jai to discern Hagar's precise position.

Aha.

Hagar sprang onto her haunches, pressed her palms and shoulders to the table's underside and shoved. The table resisted, then rose. Objects slid down it. A bread board clattered to the tiles, then wooden spoons, shattering crockery, the jangle of knives and spoons. She charged forward on her hands and knees.

She could perceive vague outlines – a few faint angles where moonlight caught the edge of a cupboard, the scalloped rim of a salver. She stabbed at the darkness with her stiletto. She had studied blindfighting back at the Sciamachian Order, but it assumed both combatants were equally disadvantaged.

A hand yanked her tunic collar. Jai slung her round in a tight arc. Hagar slammed into a cupboard door face-first, the brass handle socking her in the eye. She pulled the door open – a blade thocked into the opposite side. Milky light frosted the thick edge of a cleaver wedged in the wood between her middle and ring fingers.

She thrust in the direction it had come from, found nothing but air. A fist pistoned into her cheek. She twisted with the blow, spun and jabbed her knife back towards her assailant.

Again, the blade met air. Another punch caught her square in the forehead. She crashed back into the cupboards. Cutlery clattered in its drawers. Pans toppled in a gonging shower. This cook was a mean fighter – but then, bare-knuckle boxing was to northern Gallian vesperi what dice games were to south-coast Thelusians.

Still. Jai couldn't punch what she couldn't see.

Hagar groped for the cutlery drawer, found it, and dragged the whole thing out, upending it in a cacophonous cascade.

Hagar charged, swinging. She sensed movement, jabbed at a shadow and felt resistance, as if the blade doubted its purpose, so she stepped behind it and drove it home.

Jai let out a tight wheeze. The knife returned slick.

A crash. Jai fell amongst the scattered forks and spoons. She was clutching at the wound in her side but Hagar stamped on her wrist then dropped a knee on her chest and wound the garrotte wire round her thin, downy throat. As Hagar's eyes adjusted, she could see Jai's tapered tongue lapping at the backs of her teeth, her crushed wings scratching and slapping the tiles. She was thumping Hagar with her free hand but the stab wound had drained the strength from her. Each punch was little more than a tap – almost sporting, like the touch of a fencer's foil.

Hagar pulled the two ends of the wire tight and smashed Jai's head against the tiles until she stopped moving.

Hagar stood, feeling giddy and outside of herself. A steady glow spread through her belly as she retrieved the candelabra, struck her pocket flint and relit two of the candles.

Her left eye would not open properly. Her teeth tasted of blood. The guards were surely almost here.

'Agatha?' said Hagar. 'Don't be afraid.' She glanced at the open window. Surely Jai would not have fought with such ferocity if the child had already leapt to her death. 'Won't you come out and talk to me?' She paused, listening. 'I know where your father has gone. *Je vais te conduire à lui!*'

The two fat fish sprawled open-mouthed amongst pottery shards in a stinking pool of alcohol.

Hagar began walking down the line of cupboards, creaking their doors ajar. Inside were white plates with gold trim, crystal dessert boats, nested sieves, cooling racks for scones and griddle cakes, porcelain taldin vinegar pots, pressed glass salt and chilli cellars sculpted to look like naval clippers, lined up beside a huge silver master cellar modelled after the royal galleon, with banks of enamelled cannon and an intricate – fanciful – effigy of Morgellon himself posing upon the prow, clad in braided epaulettes, sabre at his hip, his hair swept back, facing the future with a single outstretched finger and blank, pupil-less eyes.

Hagar fancied she heard shouts on the wind. She began marching down the line of cupboards, throwing doors open with a succession of smart bangs.

'Agatha!' Candle wax dripped onto the tiles. 'You have a part to play! You are a very important little girl!'

At the far end of the room, by the big, black iron range, a wooden flap hung at the foot of the wall. There was a lever set into a panel above it. Hagar cranked the lever and the flap swung upwards, revealing the round mouth of a rubbish chute. An icy blast made her eyes water. Hagar peered into the hole.

Surely the child had not escaped? It was a stark drop to an opening in the cliff. Might Agatha have tried to hide, clinging to the rim by her fingertips, then lost her grip? Hagar checked for a rope or line, in case the child was dangling by a harness, just out of sight.

A sharp, freezing pain in her lower back. Damn Morgellon. What had he done to himself this time? *Not mine.* An ache bloomed beneath her knapsack. She reached with her free hand to massage the intensifying phantom wound. Her fingers brushed something smooth and hard.

The handle of a knife.

Someone shoved her knapsack. She toppled into the open rubbish chute. She threw her hands out, clutching the wall. The candelabra dropped and clattered into the abyss. With a heave she pushed herself back into the room. She groaned as she tugged the blade from her back.

It was a bone-handled fruit knife with a short sharp blade. She turned.

Agatha stood an inch from her nose, staring.

Hagar breathed through clenched teeth, wet knife juddering in her fist. The wound hurt ferociously. Warm blood was soaking Hagar's undershirt and trousers. She dropped to one knee, holding a palm to the cut.

'Oh child,' said Hagar, between gasps. 'Oh child.'

In the faint moonlight from the open window, Agatha's eyes glowed. 'Are you here to kill me?'

'Yes.'

Agatha inhaled through her nostrils, lifting her chin. Her black hair was stuck to her face. She still wore her llama-wool pyjamas.

'He said you would.'

'Who?'

'The angel.'

The room fell away. The sound of the wind fell away. The pain remained, and it took on a hard, bright purity.

'Arthur visited you, too?'

Agatha nodded. She was shivering.

Hagar licked her lips. So Arthur had seen. That she would be tested like this. He had chosen not to warn her.

Hagar said: 'Did he tell you why?'

'He said death is an area.'

'Death is an *error*,' said Hagar. Her back spasmed and she felt her attempt at a reassuring smile tighten. 'He told you death is an error.'

Agatha dropped her gaze, abashed. Hagar reached up and touched two fingers to the soft fleecy wool covering Agatha's shoulder. Agatha flinched, clenching her fists.

'Shh shh shh.' Hagar drew back her hand. 'What else did he say?'

Agatha chewed at the collar of her pyjamas. Hagar pictured Arthur coalescing in twists of blue vapour, heard him murmuring revelations. What was this strange, nauseous plunging she felt in her gut? Was it envy?

'He said you're going to make it so that nothing hurts, and nobody dies.'

'Don't you think that would be nice?'

Agatha shrugged.

'This is not the real world, my darling.' Hagar ran her knuckles down the child's arm. 'We are angels, but long ago, we were tricked. These bodies are just prisons. You . . . the real you . . . is a spark trapped inside.'

'Like the pudding squid.'

Hagar thought for a moment. 'Yes. Yes . . . exactly like that. We've been captured in jars. And the only way we can be free, to flow down to the great ocean, is if the jars break.'

Agatha glanced at the hand stroking her elbow. 'How are you going to kill me?'

A great heaviness came upon Hagar's heart, and it was hard to speak. 'I think I shall just ask you to close your eyes.'

'And then?'

Hagar hung her head. 'And then . . . I shall bless you. If you give up this world willingly, when you open your eyes, you will be with the Father in the Kingdom.'

Agatha's eyes narrowed. Water shimmered in her bulging lower lids.

'What if I don't want to go?'

'Then you will be reborn into a new body, and you will remain trapped in this world for another life. You'll suffer all over again.'

Agatha blinked out tears. She wiped her eyes and nose on her sleeve, then stared at Hagar with a sudden indignant intensity.

'Why don't you go to the Kingdom?' she said.

Hagar's throat constricted; the roof of her mouth had gone gummy.

'Because I want to help everyone get there. Even people who've been wicked. I want to help everyone in the whole world so no one has to suffer ever aga—'

The click-scrabble of a far-off door unlocking. Footsteps.

Guards.

Agatha's eyes widened. She sucked in her little chin. She sniffed. Hagar lifted an index finger to her own lips.

Doors were banging open.

'Close your eyes,' said Hagar.

Agatha took a step back.

'Please.'

Agatha hugged herself. Moonlight bisected her throat horizontally. Her dark skin seemed luminous.

Hagar had the little fruit knife in her fist, still bloody. She had the cold pain of the wound in her back. She had her purpose – her terrible, burning love for all sentient beings.

Why don't you go to the Kingdom? Oh, dear Father. Oh, Uncle.

The crash of doors and boots drew closer.

'*Préfet?* Excellence?' They were just down the corridor.

Agatha took another step back. Her fingers raked at the fibres of her pyjamas.

She gripped Agatha's arm. 'It's time.'

Agatha screamed.

Hagar slapped a palm across the child's mouth. Agatha tried to bite into the webbing between Hagar's thumb and forefinger but Hagar slipped behind her and twisted Agatha's arm into the small of her back, and Agatha could not get her jaw wide enough. Hagar's palm was warm and moist against the child's contorting lips.

'Don't fight! Don't fight!' whispered Hagar, pressing her mouth to Agatha's ear, urging the child towards the open rubbish chute even as she heard the guards shouting to one another, even as their bootsteps stopped outside the kitchen door. 'God is waiting for you.'

Agatha's legs went limp and Hagar stumbled under the sudden weight, grunting as she felt the wound in her back yawn open. The floor lurched and the edges of the chute blurred. Blood ran down her left buttock in a warm trickle. The only thing sharpening her wits was the freezing draft coming in off the mountain.

'Excellence!' A voice through the broken door – female, human.

'*And the light shineth in darkness*,' said Hagar, '*and the darkness comprehended it not.*'

Agatha thrashed her head from side to side and bucked and

wriggled. She was weak but Hagar was tired and her hands were slippery with blood.

'Excellence! *Êtes-vous là-dedans?*' Boots pounded the jammed door.

Hagar shoved Agatha to the cusp of the chute. 'You can't enter paradise unless you go willingly.' Agatha's bootees skidded on the slick tiles. 'Please be brave. This is a happy time. You're going home.' A guard began clambering through the shattered door.

Agatha yanked free. Hagar tackled her. Agatha's head cracked off the roof of the chute and they tumbled in together.

Hagar kicked outwards and caught Agatha's woollen hood. Her crampons skidded on rock. She jerked to a stop. Pain lanced up her wrist. The child dangled limply, hanging over a fathomless drop.

'Wake up! Say you go willingly.' Hagar's grip was weakening. 'Agatha!'

The girl would die in ignorance. She would suffer all over again.

Guards were clanking and cursing through the kitchen. One shouted in dismay – they had discovered Jai's body.

Hagar whispered through clenched teeth: 'May the Lord make a good Christian of you, and lead you to your rightful end.' Futile, futile. The wool felt coarse against her sweaty fingers, the unconscious child unbearably heavy. '*Dormir, mon agneau ensanglanté.*'

She let go.

There was empty air. Pain pulsed in her back and wrist. A vague clamminess lingered on her fingertips.

With both hands pressed to the rock, she glanced over her shoulder. The wooden flap had dropped back down. The voices and footsteps were inches away.

Hagar edged down to the base of the chute, where it opened onto the cliff. The snow had stopped. The night was crisp and quiet, the air so cold it stung. She fastened her goggles over her eyes. The cliff was sheer, crusted with rime.

She hooked her cleats over the lip of the chute. Her fingers slipped as she struggled to open her knapsack. She pulled out a parcel of silk.

E vec vos que eu so com vos per totz dias entro a l'acabament del segle.

And lo, I am with you alway, even unto the end of the world.

She jumped.

Icy air rushed up her shirt sleeves. Her lank hair rattled. She was a tiny loose body in a void of crushing cold.

She spread her arms. The spider silk unfolded and flowed past her in a stream, then she felt a shock and she lurched upwards towards the perfect whole moon, a great glowing completeness in the liquid black.

She swung back. Her feet dangled. Above, a canopy billowed and filled.

Sleepy, freezing, she drifted into the valley.

CHAPTER 9
OTHER SHORE REACHED

Delphine woke on her bunk, dry-mouthed and groggy. Her head was pounding. She clambered out onto the foredeck and found Alice crosslegged, gutting an eel. Its green-gold skin lay puddled beside a saucepan of steaming water.

'The kraken awakes,' said Alice. Her hair was held back with a pastel-blue headband. Half a mug of ramen noodles sat on the deck beside her.

'How long have I been asleep?'

'See for yourself.' She gestured with the knife, her hand smeared with eel guts.

Delphine looked. The river had widened to a busy delta, maybe 200 yards across, full of narrow silty islands. Boat traffic was travelling both ways.

A wave of dizziness forced her to her knees. 'Oh my God.'

'Busy busy busy.'

Red-furred vesperi poled and sculled boats through channels between islands. Vesperi children flew in tight, helical dances, trailing paper kites. Birds followed in their slipstreams. A child banked and dived and when a bird with long, iridescent green and blue tail feathers mimicked the manoeuvre, skimming low across the water, the child tossed up a nut and the bird flared and snapped it out of the air.

Her hands tightened round the lip of the gunwale. She was a

child back at Alderberen Hall, watching a hundred black shadows rising over the woods. She heard the smashing of glass, talons clattering on hardwood, pops and clicks and the *luff luff* of wingbeats. The pink bootlace tongues. The stoved-in skulls. The stink of burning fur.

Christ's sweet tree. They had come for her.

'You all right, love?' said Alice.

Delphine pressed her brow to the cold wet wood and breathed. Every sinew in her body screamed *run, run.* Oh Jesus God. What had she been thinking, coming here? She was a stupid, cowardly old woman. A watery dread sloshed about in her guts. She genuinely feared she might lose control of her bowels.

No. Her fingers tightened round the gunwale. No, no, no. She stamped her foot against the deck. She would not stand down. Whatever would Mother think?

She met Alice's gaze. 'Very well, thank you.'

There were boats with canvas roofs and boats with roofs of bark and some with roofs of huge dark, waxy leaves. Several had smoking braziers at the stern and were serving up skewers of dripping white meat or folded leaves heaped with what looked like chunks of batter. Lines hung between masts, shrivelled rainbow jellyfish drying on pegs.

Here and there were humans too – lean and nimble in wide-brimmed rush hats, some with baskets strapped to their backs. There was a variety of skin tones; deep reddish-brown, white, black. Most were stripped to the waist; a prodigiously pregnant woman sat in the shade, making a fishing net with a pair of wooden shuttles while an odd boneless creature oozed round the bottom of her boat, occasionally nuzzling her thigh so she could muss its wet fur.

Delphine felt vulgar for staring. She flinched at unexpected movements. One very small vesperi child gazed at her with round orange-yellow eyes from the stern of a boat cutting upriver. They flicked the back of their ear with two fingers, repeating the gesture several times. She was not sure if she was supposed to reciprocate. In the end, she gave a sort of sheepish half-wave, touching her earlobe noncommittally.

Butler stood at the tiller, watching the river. He had changed into a kaftan-like garment with a grey sawtooth pattern round the collar and long loose sleeves. His wings were spread, pitched forward slightly to cut drag; in the bright morning sunshine, the semi-translucent membranes went from mahogany to rich royal purple beneath the pinions.

'Martha's in the cabin,' said Alice. 'Butler told her it was best to keep out of sight.'

The wet jungle smell was giving way to something fresher, more brackish. Delphine leaned back against the roof, her stomach cramping.

'How you feeling?' Alice ran the hooked tip of the blade along the eel's backbone and its guts flopped out into a bucket.

'Euphoric,' said Delphine. She leant over the side and vomited.

There was not much to come up. She lay, gut convulsing, retching strings of caustic bile. Milky residue folded into the boat's wake.

'Ugh,' she said, spitting out the last of it.

'Better out than in.'

Delphine wiped her mouth. 'How come you're so bloody chirpy?'

'Why wouldn't I be?' She looked down at the chopped-up eel. 'I'm having the loveliest dream.'

Delphine's chest was heavy with a washed-out, hollow feeling. She flexed and clenched her fingers. The skin round her cuticles had receded and cracked.

Prickles ran down her neck. Whose body was this? Everything was new and fluid. The cottage and broad beans in the garden and emptying the dishwasher felt impossibly distant, figments. She scarcely remembered who she was, what she was supposed to like. The expansiveness terrified her.

She hacked and spat into the river. Alice passed her a canteen and she swilled her mouth out. The tepid water stung her tonsils.

'Making room for breakfast?' Butler strode to the edge of the roof and tossed another eel down onto the deck. It landed with a thump and writhed against itself, juicy and oozing.

She looked up at him. He had the sun behind him and she had to shield her eyes.

'We're nearly there,' he said. 'Sober up. You can't afford to be half-cut your first time in the stilt city. They'll eat you alive.'

Delphine wanted to make some barbed retort but as she opened her mouth her skull seemed to tighten round her brain. She felt as if she had been awake and restless for days.

In the end, she managed a snarl. 'Your concern is touching.'

'I mean it, Venner. Grab a gun. Something you can carry easily.' He looked at Alice. 'Both of you.'

Islets and overhanging branches began filtering the river into a series of narrow straits. Butler went back to the stern and unlocked the tiller. He eased them portward, bringing them round for a slow pass between thick reeds and a long trading sampan with a bark shingle roof. Their boat creamed under a canopy of dense foliage: thick lianas twining up trunks, knotting boughs together and choking out light. Unearthly creatures brachiated across the latticework at speed – each had two gangling arms extending from a furry, pear-shaped torso with a pulsing aperture on its underside. Occasionally they would dangle for a moment, then drop twenty feet into the river.

The boat passed through a curtain of slender branches with glossy umber leaves. Delphine ducked; when she looked up, the river ahead was spanned by a colossal arch of wood and tarnished iron. Huge stone pilings supported it on either bank. Boats passed beneath a skeleton of black struts and long support cables draped in browning stranglevines. Birds roosted all along its length, and lacquered wooden decorations hung beneath like giant hanging baskets, spilling over with creepers. The apex of the arch bore a legend in twisting wrought-iron letters:

FORCE SANS RIVAL *HONNEUR SANS CESSE*

It was only as they drew closer that she saw the decorations were cages. There were corpses, partly smothered by creepers. Cheeks picked clean of meat. Remnants of legs dangling through bars. Each gibbet held at least half a dozen bodies. The boat passed under the arch and she winced.

As the delta widened they moved through a patchwork of low islands linked by piers. Thatched cabins stood in the mud on stilts. Two vesperi were stripping the bark off logs with machetes, exposing bright blond tranches of sapwood. Punts, rowboats, skiffs, dinghies and sampans were moored two or three deep.

The wet jungle smell was giving way to burning charcoal and rancid, frying fat, the hum of fish guts spoiling in the heated piss and excrement rainbowing the water's surface, the coppery smell of claret algae clotting in the shallows, the perspiration of massed and busy life threading amongst itself.

Delphine smoked while she wiped the machine pistol down with a rag. She pulled back the winged cocking piece, checked the chamber was empty through the ejection port, then pulled the trigger so the cocking piece snapped back into place. There was a little safety catch just behind the trigger. She pushed from auto to single shot to on, feeling its hard ridges dig into the pad of her thumb.

After a day of gnarly psychedelia it was good to focus on lines and buttons and edges clicking together. Every time dread frothed up in her belly, she would turn her attention to the feel of the gun. She reckoned it was about three pounds with the magazine – the weight of it kept her hands from shaking.

The rain started again, light, lifting the perfume of things up into the breeze. She tipped her head back and let it kiss her closed eyelids, trickle down her throat, pool in her clavicles.

The city emerged from a heat-haze – piers, floating docks and boardwalks standing above the water on thick wooden posts, linked by rope bridges, gangplanks and baskets on pulleys. They were too far away to get a proper sense of scale, but it looked vast.

An islet rolled past on their starboard side, covered in three burnt-out shells of huts. A banner hung over the ruins, black paint on a white background, but she did not recognise the alphabet, let alone the words. A symbol had been daubed onto the canvas: an image of a hand in an inverted triangle.

Delphine caught movement from the corner of her eye. A small, sleek cutter was closing astern, its bone-white headsails luffing in the heightening wind. A squat, flat-headed vesperi in a blue sash and long sleeveless blue tunic hailed Butler in clickspeak. Three other vesperi sat in the boat, dressed in blue and carrying guns.

Butler kept his gaze fixed on the stilt city ahead. Delphine wasn't sure if he'd noticed them.

The cutter pulled nearer until the two craft were almost touching. Very slowly, Delphine slid her hand to her machine pistol. She kept it just below the gunwale, out of sight.

The flat-headed vesperi leaned over and rapped the side of the cabin with a quarterstaff. Delphine flinched.

Butler pumped his wings. He kept one hand on the tiller and did not look down. His lips and noseleaf flexed; she caught snatches of clickspeak as it dipped into audible register. The flat-headed vesperi rapped the cabin again. Butler said something short and made a sweeping gesture with his free hand.

A film of sweat was forming between Delphine's palm and the pistol grip. What the hell was he playing at? The three vesperi sitting in the boat seemed eerily at ease, one gazing out across the river, another picking at his fangs. The guns in their laps looked crude, but at this range it hardly mattered.

The flat-headed vesperi stepped back. The cutter trimmed its sails and fell abaft, jibbing back upriver. Delphine exhaled heavily, slumping forward.

She took a minute to get her breath back, then walked across the roof to join Butler at the stern.

'What was that about?' she said, trying to hide the tremor in her voice.

Butler rolled his eyes and tutted. 'Money. They were shaking us down for port taxes.'

'Why didn't you pay them?'

He looked at her like she was mad. 'They're not real tax collectors, you imbecile. Just thugs. Hawser clique. There. Your first bit of local knowledge. Hawsers run the docks. Usually more civil than that. Must be new recruits.'

'How did you make them go away?'

'I told them we'd already paid our taxes, and if they wanted to check our papers they were welcome to accompany us to Middle Sister Island.'

'What's on Middle Sister Island?'

'Patience,' he said, and smiled at some private joke. 'Strange, though. Never been that brazen before. Something's brewing.'

As the rain grew heavier he spread his wings, sheltering them both. The few children still flying over the river alighted and sought cover. Smaller trees began bowing their heads.

He eased off on the throttle. Ahead, a shifting carpet of boats bumped and knocked. The river was choppy with rain, traffic-clogged. Plank piers stretched out across the dancing water, funnelling boats into lanes. Punts, rowboats, junks and sampans were moored together three deep. Vesperi in blue smocks strode from craft to craft as easily as if they were walking across flagstones, yelling and click-chirruping, halting some boats while beckoning others into nooks. Each carried a telescopic wooden pole with an attachment like a shepherd's crook at the end, which they used to pull boats in to dock.

Delphine watched in a kind of daze, noting how their taloned toes gripped rowlocks, their ears swivelling in different directions. Somehow the otherness of Butler she had assimilated and repressed returned now she saw them in number, just as she had as a girl on that window ledge in Alderberen Hall. But – and the realisation came with such clarity that for a moment, she wondered if the wine fruit was not finished with her – it was not their otherness which disturbed her.

It was their sameness.

The little tics – the pulling tight of rainskins, the yawns, the scowls. Ordinariness. Empathy rose in her like a kind of nausea. These creatures. These people.

Butler slowed the boat to a crawl. To starboard, the muddy shore of an islet held a pod of six giant, boat-sized turtles, all moored by big iron staples riveted to their soft shells.

Rain drummed on thousands of planks and roofs. Reed-thatched huts stood twenty, thirty feet above the river on stilts. The boat passed beneath a rope bridge on which a huge bearded lizard with orange scales lay basking, rain streaming from its cranial frills and segmented tail.

The growl of the engine echoed off seaweed-smothered pilings. Rigging, canvas and boardwalks were clotting together into a canopy that blotted out light. Ahead, lapping brown water vanished into darkness. Rain was filling the bottom of their boat with bilge water. The pilings grew closer, bigger. Milky lights flared out of the darkness before vanishing. The scent of the undercity was a brackish stew of loam, algae and piss.

A shadow rolled over the boat. The rain cut off. They continued into darkness.

Somewhere under the stilt city, they cut the engine. Delphine could not see her hands. She felt the boat drifting.

She listened. She heard herself breathing, the gentle slap of water against pilings.

A *tick-tick-tick* rang through the hollow blackness. Butler was echolocating.

The boat struck something with a dull boom. The deck rocked; Delphine clutched the side to stop herself falling in. She heard footsteps on the cabin roof.

Indistinct shuffling. Sounds tickling the edge of her hearing.

A rectangle of light expanded above. Iron hooks dropped on stout ropes. A trio of teenaged human girls with short-cropped hair and cut-off trousers rappelled down and dived into what Delphine now saw was thick and oily water. They swam under the keel, then surfaced on the opposite side and scrambled aboard, passing the ropes round the boat in a big loop. They slotted the hooks into metal rings woven into the ropes then, rat-wet and dripping, shinned back up the lines.

Butler locked the tiller. He lit a cigarette, scratched behind his ear and blew smoke up towards the hatch.

'Everyone hold onto something.'

Delphine gripped the taffrail. From above she heard the *rak-a-clack* of gear teeth and pinions. The ropes tightened. Wet fibres creaked.

The boat jerked, resisting. Her foot skidded. The boat tipped. She dropped to her knees, locked her arms under the rail. The boat rose, water drooling from the hull. Below, she saw her silhouette reflected in a square of dirty light. Her gut lurched. Alice was on the foredeck, peering over the side of the boat, eyes wide.

The rattle of labouring gears grew louder. They passed through a hatchway into a low-raftered boathouse lit by oil burners in long, fluted glass mantles. Boats sat in rows on wooden chocks, draped with tarpaulins. Three massive winches hung over the hatchway.

Butler stepped off the stern onto the boathouse floor. His tall ears twitched.

'Wait,' he hissed. He held up a palm, took a step forward.

'Hello?' he called. His hand slid to the shoulder holster beneath his kaftan. 'You can come out. I hear you. It's Butler.'

A figure emerged from the shadow of a carved wooden pillar. She was a little shorter than Delphine, with long sable hair tending to curls. She wore a fleece-lined waistcoat over a suit of thin crimson fabric, fastened to the trousers with a row of brass buttons. Lamplight picked out gold teeth and a red glass eye in the left socket. Her left arm terminated in a steel tomahawk head. Her left foot clacked as she set it down, sprung black iron cleats cushioning a skeletal prosthesis.

'Oh, it's you.' Butler glanced about. 'Where's Tammuz?'

She reached up with her axe-hand and swept a twist of hair out of her eye. She looked all of sixteen.

'You lied to me.'

Butler pulled on his cigarette and looked askance. 'Probably.'

The girl took a step with her metal leg. 'Are you afraid of death, Mr Bechstein?'

Butler was still for a very long time. Delphine could hear him breathing. He narrowed his eyes.

'I don't know what you *think* you know . . .'

The girl snapped her fingers. Tarpaulins flipped back from the parked junks and barges and a dozen human and vesperi guards rose, aiming carbines. The three teenaged boathands drew blunderbuss pistols.

The girl raised her axe-hand. 'Anything you want to say?'

Delphine shot a glance down the boat at Alice, who had dropped to a crouch.

Butler regarded the girl with a look of weary boredom. 'Not to you, Ms Colstrid.'

The axe-hand dropped. Twelve carbines fired. The force of the shots threw him back against the boat. He bounced off the hull and hit the floor.

Gunsmoke hung in the air. Carbine levers *cha-chucked* as guards chambered fresh rounds.

Delphine stared. Butler's body lay in a widening pool of blood.

The girl's prosthetic leg *clack-clack-clack*ed as she walked to the body. She nudged the head with a cleat; it slid limply. She wrinkled her nose.

'Please. Call me Agatha.'

CHAPTER 10

THE DEEP AND SECRET THINGS

(Twenty-three years before the inauguration)

The trail to Dr Noroc's Mill was poorly maintained, a dirt track smothered by roots and lianas, swallowed by sinkholes, and hinted at by flooded wheelruts boiling with silverflies. Hagar tried to ignore a growing tightness in her chest. Räum jounced and thundered beneath her, saddlebags slapping against his flanks, his muscular, double-jointed legs driving him forward through deepening mud. A translucent canopy of leaves stained the sun orange. Low branches snatched at her hat and lashed at her face.

The stream she usually navigated by had swollen in the unseasonably late rains, changing its course and draining into the Underkills below. Hagar feared they were lost. The whole point of placing Dr Noroc's facility at such a remove was isolation – for almost half the year it was cut off from the wider world, just like her old abbey in winter – but as Räum followed the trail north Hagar wondered whether she had been too covetous of her treasure hidden in a field.

The stream flowed fast and clay-brown, creaming over the top of a rotten trunk that had collapsed across its banks. She chose a spot farther upstream where the bank gently sloped and jade butterflies flitted amongst flowers with sagging red mouths. Hagar urged Räum into the water, stropping her fingers through his neck plumage to soothe him. He could run across a battlefield without hesitation – in each of his lives his training had featured weeks of running trenches at the Académie, flanked by students banging pots and blowing horns – but he hated rivers and pools where the water was too turbid to judge depth. A brave bird he was – had always been – but not foolish.

Hagar felt the current pushing round her ankles, shoving at Räum's flank, cool and insidious. Insects rasped against her cheeks. Then he was up onto the opposite bank, his scimitar foretalons slapping in the mud, her saddlebags jankling with kit. She patted his withers, digging into the stirrups as the ground steepened. Räum began taking the hill in a zigzag, clambering over the spreading roots of giant christwoods. She could tell he enjoyed the challenge of it, and she nickered little nonsenses to encourage him.

Only when they crested the hill and saw the iron gates, wedged between stone walls choked with vines, did the weight in her heart finally ease. In the ten years since her last visit, the forest had reclaimed the facility as its own, twining lianas through cracks in the stonework, deepening the drifts of wild ferns and orchids so the place looked more like an ancient temple than a house of science. That was good – it served her purpose, having the facility fuse with its surroundings, no longer appearing alien or noteworthy. The only hint to its true nature capped the very tops of the walls: spikes of dirty glass.

Räum was lagging as they approached the gates. She had ridden him hard, and he had worked without complaint. He embraced suffering with a holy eagerness.

She tugged his leather reins and he came to a halt before the chained gates. There were neither wheelruts nor footprints. Around the entrance, the ground was overgrown with clumps of purple doomlilies. Idly, she wondered whether an aboveground entrance was strictly necessary. She supposed it had been useful, before the nature of the work changed.

There was no bell to ring, no sentry in evidence. She eased Räum down into a squat and hopped onto the crumbly damp earth.

The air was humid, fragrant with a heady perfume. Her boots wheezed as she approached the gates. Through the black bars she saw the courtyard, the doors and shuttered windows of Unit One.

Shrubs had pushed up between the paving slabs, with plump,

bristled, tuber-like bodies and spreading carnelian blooms. Where was Noroc?

She gave the gate a shove. It did not budge – gave no indication it had ever budged. Two halves of an embossed plaque came together at the centre to form the legend: *Sagesse et Sacrifice.*

She let go, scabs of rust crumbling under her fingers. She unfastened her belt, with all its clattering boxes and holsters, tossed it through, then squeezed after it. For all the disadvantages of her perpetually juvenile body, it was at least easy to manoeuvre.

Unit One was a two-storey barn of black brick and dark timbers, flanked on the extreme edges of the courtyard by long huts: Units Two, Three and Four. She squinted at the shutters for signs of movement. The main doors opened and a guard stepped out in blue overalls and black boots with steel toecaps. He pointed a carbine at her head.

'How did you get in?' He spoke through the grille of a gas mask. His eyes were hidden behind smoked lenses.

Hagar liked the masks. They lent the staff a certain familiarity when she returned, even as she knew that all but the most senior researchers had rotated out since her last visit. No one lasted here long.

The masks were pure safety theatre. The mesh over the mouth kept out most large particulates, and the goggles offered limited protection, but given the nature of the work, they were largely irrelevant. Their main function, aside from offering the menials a sort of talismanic reassurance, was to separate staff from test subjects.

And perhaps, she thought, as she observed the inebriated sway in the guard's stance, to separate the person from their actions. Uniforms were a kind of exemption.

'Hagar Ingery,' she said, deciding that provoking this individual was unwise. 'I'm here to see Dr Noroc.'

The guard did not move.

'How did you get in?' he said, voice muffled.

'The gate was locked. I squeezed through.' She spread her arms, showcasing her slight physique. 'Would you fetch the doctor, please?'

The leather mask wore its permanently blank, faintly quizzical expression. His carbine muzzle loomed broad and black.

'Wait there.' The guard turned.

He walked into the building and slammed the door. She heard him locking it behind him. She glanced back at Räum, who had tucked his short wings and dipped his head. He was watching her, waiting for permission to sleep.

She tickled a sweet acorn out of her belt pouch and tossed it underarm, through the bars of the gate. Her throw went wide. Räum traipsed over to where the treat had landed. He drilled into the leaves with his sharp straight beak, tilted his bald head back, and swallowed.

'Ah, the good sister returns.'

She turned to find Dr Noroc descending the facility steps, smearing his palms down his overalls and wearing that wry crease of a smile that always sat low on his face. His circular spectacles caught light flashing through the high branches, turning to pieces of silver.

He took them off and wiped them on his overalls – a futile gesture in the sweltering autumnal humidity. His eyes were pink and his flesh was pallid; since she had last seen him, grey threads had appeared in his combed-flat hair. Still, he did not appear burdened, nor troubled to see her. Indeed, there was something childlike in the way he reached for her hand, held it in his palm and studied it, running his thumb over the backs of her knuckles, gently, inquisitively applying pressure to each before leading her towards the door.

'Come,' he said. 'Let me show you what you've missed.'

The doctor's assistant, a slight, wan girl with forearms wrapped in smokelorist bracelets, brought sweet tea into a cramped, windowless office on the first floor. Hagar noticed a tremor in the girl's hands, the wooden beads chattering as she set two glasses and a jug down on the table. The jug had chunks of ice floating in it – produced, Hagar supposed, by the hugely expensive equipment necessary to keep the facility running.

The office stank of smoke and unwashed bodies. A glazed clay ashtray shaped like a riverboat stood on the table corner, heaped with crushed-out cigarettes from the old world. The softwood panels of the wall were scarred with dents and long gouges.

Dr Noroc sat with his fingers spliced, one ankle resting on the opposite knee. The arms of his chair had the stuffing pulled out and the fabric lay limp and ragged. He tapped his thumbs together, gazing into a corner, then looked up slyly.

'You know, while you're here, I'd like to take an impression of your teeth.' He leaned over and began to pour himself a tea. 'It'll take barely a minute. We've a wonderful new medium for making casts.'

As she opened her mouth to speak, he tilted his head, peering inside. His eyes brightened.

Hagar smeared a palm over her lips. 'They're the same as they've always been.'

'Exactly.' He nodded vigorously, sitting back in his chair. '*Exactly*.'

Hagar did not quite understand what the doctor was insinuating. She poured herself a glass from the heavy, cool jug. She felt Dr Noroc watching her as he sipped his tea, examining, quantifying. The flesh on the back of her neck prickled.

'Your letter implied you've made progress,' she said, trying to move the conversation away from her physical appearance.

His smiled, and his eye ticked. 'We're always making progress, Hagar. Always. If an outcome cannot be replicated, this is information that refines our understanding. If a sample does not perform as we expect, it is not the sample which is at fault, but our expectations. Ours is a slow, slow practice – a fealty to clearsightedness, a constant realigning of our beliefs with reality.'

'You've certainly refined your rhetoric.'

'A decade of isolation brings challenges.' He stared past her, gaslight picking out fine blades of stubble along his upper lip. 'This isn't easy work. You start questioning whether it serves a greater purpose.' He tilted the glass to his mouth, swilled tea over his molars. 'The children look to me for leadership.'

'Children?'

Noroc's eyes creased as he smiled. 'I think of the staff as my family.'

'And what does your family have to show me, Doctor?'

'Ah. So you're slitting open the mother's belly to check on the baby.'

Hagar blenched, remembering Anwen. She sipped her tea, which was sharply frigid and cloying. Its unpleasantness brought her back to the room.

'Sometimes such a measure is necessary.' She looked at him over her glass. 'It's been an unusually long pregnancy. You understand my concern.'

'This is delicate work. So you understand mine.'

'I'm not here to shut you down. If I were, the palace garde du corps would already be heaping kindling against the walls. I come to check that my faith in you is not misplaced. Your "family" costs a great deal to feed.'

'Have you told the Grand-Duc what goes on here?'

She glared into her drink. Its surface was ringed with a fine ochre scum.

'I don't report to Lord Jejunus directly.' Morgellon had not permitted her within the palace grounds for over fifty years. Since he had not left in that time, she had not seen him.

'Forgive me,' said Noroc. 'I'd forgotten you're still in disgrace.' She could not tell if his apology was sincere. Certainly she detected no relish in his tone. 'I suppose citizens won't catch a glimpse of him again till he appoints a new servant. Not in my lifetime. How is Prefect Colstrid, by the way? Still in the Grand-Duc's favour, I take it?'

Hagar banged her glass down on the table. She wearied of indulging this man. He knew his work was important to her – but he did not know *how* important, could not guess that it represented her last hope. That she might contemplate closing him down was a useful fiction. She sensed the doctor responded better to threats than flattery. He had forgotten his place.

'What passes between a peer and his servant is none of your concern.'

Dr Noroc looked up with a sudden seriousness.

'On the contrary,' he said. 'It's my life's work.'

Unit Two was divided into small rooms accessible from a long corridor. In each room, a railed balcony looked down on an iron cage.

Beneath the tart scent of carbolic acid, Hagar smelt sweat, urine, excrement.

'Everything you see here is an answer to a question I have asked,' said Noroc, his diction stifled by his surgical mask.

Below, a naked human male was spread-eagled across a table, held in place by iron cuffs and a stout iron band over the sternum. His left arm had been amputated at the shoulder and positioned several feet away, manacled at the wrist and elbow. Pencil marks split the distance into inches.

'Here, the question is: will the parasite attempt to reconnect with the severed arm, or simply grow a new one? How far from the body must a limb be before the body rejects it? Where is the threshold for reintegration versus regeneration?'

Even as she watched, capillaries were extending from the shoulder stump, crawling over the flat surface of the wood, splitting and spreading like floodwater irrigating a system of ditches. To Hagar's left, a researcher in white overalls and full-face respirator mask stood with pocketwatch and notebook, occasionally leaning against the rail to scribble an observation. By the light of four gas mantles, a fine lacework of new arteries glistened. Flesh settled in fatty puddles.

The man's head had been shaved. His eyes were closed. He gnawed gently at a leather gag.

Hagar flicked the tip of her tongue over the gap left by her missing eye tooth. She watched the man writhing in his restraints, and her gut twisted.

'How does this advance our cause?'

Noroc sighed through his mask. 'By increasing our knowledge. Come.'

He moved to place a palm on her shoulder and she pulled away. His eyes narrowed; his mouth was hidden. He gestured towards the door.

In the next room, the subject was a human female. The head had been severed and placed some six feet from the supine body. Braids of meat were snaking downwards from the throat like potato roots.

'Does the head regrow the body or the body regrow the head?' said Noroc. 'Where does the core of the parasite lie? Where, if you will, is its soul?'

'So you're a philosopher.'

He raised his eyebrows. 'You don't think it an important question?'

Hagar pressed her tongue to the roof of her mouth. She could not honestly say she did not.

'And the answer?'

The doctor held up a finger. 'Well, of course, no two presentations of godfly infestation are identical. The sample host inflects the parasite's talents to a significant degree.'

'The honours manifest in different ways.'

'Ah. No, no, no.' She heard him laugh beneath his mask. 'The honours are a sacred duty bestowed upon the wisest and most virtuous. The sting of the godfly consecrates and formalises a promise to defend and nurture the terrestrial world and its inhabitants. Only a unanimous consensus at a perpetuum ganzplenum can authorise the creation of a new peer.'

'I know the rules.'

'Then you know why we don't speak of honours. We have no peers here. Only parasites and samples.'

He showed her a room in which two dog-sized snarls of cartilage and soft tissue lay pulsing at opposite ends of the sunken cage, separated by wooden dividers. 'We're isolating precisely where the parasite inheres.'

Hagar leaned over the rail, holding her hat in place, and realised that the two lumps of ochre flesh were halves of a human head, bisected laterally, trying to grow back to one another. She could make out the moth-wing twist of an ear, a hard seam of molars.

'The parasite will always prefer to reabsorb key parts over growing new ones,' said Noroc. 'In the dark, underwater as long as they're close enough, it senses them and attempts to make them reattach.'

'You speak as if there's an intelligence at work.'

Noroc did not say anything, but she thought she saw his lips move beneath the mask.

In the next room, a masked researcher was down in the cage, standing over a naked human female subject strapped to a gurney. The researcher held a lancet in a reverse pencil grip, calmly making crosswise incisions in the subject's eyeballs, then stepping back to observe their healing. The subject's head was held in place with straps and clamps, a gag filling their mouth. Stifled whimpering escaped through the wadded gauze.

As the wet blade punctured the cornea, Hagar winced, involuntarily closing her own eye. When she glanced up she saw Noroc watching her.

'Feel anything?' he said. A small damp patch had appeared in the white fabric of his mask, tracing the slit of his mouth.

She resisted the urge to rub the collar of her eye, to check the surface was still intact.

'This is very basic work,' she said.

'Not basic. Fundamental.' He led her back into the corridor. 'Contrary to folk belief and certain mythmaking efforts by various houses over the centuries, the godfly parasite is not magic. It follows rules, obeys certain economies. The more clearly we understand those rules, the greater our ability to . . .' He cleared his throat. When he continued, he spoke in an undertone. 'You know, much of this work is due to the, ah . . . broadness of my instructions. We could make much faster progress if you told me your final goal. What *do* you want, Hagar?'

Ah. So he was trying to blame her for all this. She glanced over her shoulder, down the corridor with its low, slanted ceiling. They were alone. She turned back to Noroc, looked at him squarely.

'I want what I believe is best for Lord Jejunus and all sentient beings.'

'Is the Grand-Duc aware of the work we do in his name?'

'That's twice you've asked me.'

'The first time, you declined to answer.'

'He directs his attention where he sees fit.'

Noroc let his gaze drift to the side. He nodded.

'I think I take your meaning.' He passed his cotton-gloved hands over one another in a washing motion.

In the next room, below the viewing balcony, a young human sat manacled to a sturdy wooden chair, his head fixed in place by straps. The sample was perhaps in his mid-twenties, though his shaven scalp, glossy scars and limbs tanned and coarsened from field labour gave him the wretched pseudo-age she had witnessed in soldiers. His thick fingers clenched the arms of the chair as a masked researcher harvested sticky white grubs from the cysts in his throat, tweezing them one at a time into a glass flask. Behind the researcher was a mesh cage containing several large brown rats.

Hagar felt for the young man, who was clearly uncomfortable and frightened – though presumably not in pain. She had procured samples for the mill from Fat Maw's criminal class – drug smugglers, violent indigents and political enemies: separatists, pro-Hilantian radicals, foreign agents – people facing execution or a life on the labour farms. Still, she felt a grinding sadness at his predicament, almost a solidarity. She wished he would open his eyes and glance up, so she might smile, offer some momentary consolation.

Of course he was not truly like her. He had been given the honours, however Noroc's legalistic weasel language might disguise it. He was a peer. He no longer felt pain. The maundygrubs gestating in his throat were a part of the process usually kept secret. Most peers hid the lump with high collars, silk scarves. It hardly seemed godly, appointing servants by allowing a supple white worm to burrow under their skin. Hagar had been unconscious when Morgellon did it to her. She was glad.

Noroc appeared beside her on the rail. He leaned in and whispered:

'This is a study I think you'll find particularly compelling.'

The researcher stoppered the flask and picked up a thin steel rod. They heated the rod over a gas flame. Blue fire flared in their mask's lenses. After about a minute, the researcher pushed the rod into the sample's shoulder with a twist. The sample shuddered and inhaled sharply, but did not cry out.

Hagar tensed. She pictured a valet somewhere in the facility, strapped to a cot, bucking with agony as he felt searing steel chew into phantom muscle. She had made a terrible misjudgement. This was grotesque, inhumane. Noroc's isolation had sent him insane. He was torturing people for sport.

'Watch the rats.' Noroc's voice was soft, mollifying.

Increasingly nauseous, she made herself concentrate on the mud-coloured rats in the cage below. There were three, each perhaps two feet long including the tail. She watched them rake at the mesh of their cage. They were shrieking.

The researcher withdrew the rod from the sample's shoulder, bringing with it a little corkscrew of red flesh, which dropped to the floor, smoking. The cauterised wound began folding in on itself, a tiny puckered mouth. The rats were writhing over one another, thrashing and squealing.

Hagar shoved herself back from the rail. She rattled the door handle – yanked the door, but it would not give. She pushed; it opened and she stumbled out into the corridor. She slapped her back to the wall, gasping.

Could she have made a mistake? Was she deluded? Why would God show her such suffering, if not to chastise her, if not to demand: repent, repent?

Dr Noroc was coming. She wiped her eyes and fastened her riding goggles.

Everything was smaller through the goggles. Distant. Manageable.

Noroc stepped into the corridor. His skull flattened where it met the curvature of her lenses.

'Naked flames irritate my eyes,' she said, relieved at how bland the words came out. The statement was technically true.

Noroc performed a shallow bow. 'I should have warned you. My apologies. You see now why our researchers take precautions.'

'Those rats . . .'

Noroc straightened. 'Please, ask whatever you wish.'

'Are they . . . Have you . . .'

'Yes.' His pleasure was audible. 'They bear pain on the sample's behalf, experiencing it as their own. We've mastered creating the first sample-to-animal bonds.'

'His servants are *rats*?'

Noroc's eyes narrowed. 'Let's go outside.'

As they walked the weed-tangled rear courtyard, Hagar wondered – not for the first time – if Arthur had been mistaken. Perhaps Noroc had been brilliant, once, but granted the scientific freedoms he had craved, he had become a butcher, sacrificing progress to satisfy his lavish, bestial appetites. She could not see the value in these intricate, vaudevillian cruelties, except as validations of Noroc's escalating megalomania.

She stopped, turned to him. 'Why don't you give yourself the honours?'

'It's forbidden.'

'This whole facility is forbidden, Doctor. You're torturing and slaying peers, whatever taxonomy you care to hide behind. Why not become one?' She studied the oily grey filaments in his black hair. 'Who else could do this work? Don't you want to live to see its completion?'

He pulled the surgical mask from his face. His top lip was moist. 'Do you consider your three and a half centuries a gift?'

She kicked at a dark green clump of urchinbane. 'I believe they have purpose.'

'And do you believe you are the same person you were before you received your . . . infection?'

'Of course not.'

Noroc nodded, turning away from her. His steel toecap clipped a loose slab and he stumbled. He was drunk. Of course he was. So was everyone here. That was how they survived.

He steadied himself, smeared a palm across his glistening brow.

'I wonder how much of a person the parasite leaves intact,' he said. 'I wonder whether the person who wakes up a peer is the same one who bowed their head to receive the anointing sting. Whether they are . . . *directed*. I see signs of an additional intelligence.'

'I feel no presence. I'm not a Mucorian.'

'Certainly the godfly parasite is more *subtle* than a Mucorian.' He smiled. 'In a Mucorian the host consciousness is completely and permanently supplanted. All traces of the host personality disappear within twelve hours. It's impossible to say whether they're still *aware* in any meaningful way – all attempts at removing the fungus once its fibres have penetrated the brain stem have resulted in the death of the sample. Yet Mucorians have fine motor control. They can understand commands. They can speak. They retain the sample's known languages. *Something* must remain. Unfortunately thus far we've been able to learn little from the Mucorians themselves. They seem . . .' he circled his palm, '. . . unresponsive to questions of a reflexive existential nature.'

'You're holding them captive and torturing them.'

Noroc flashed her a look of boredom. 'Without my intervention they wouldn't have hosts at all. I'm giving them life.'

Mucorians had been created by the Hilanta as biological weapons. The art's crowning glory, really. By the last of the wars, Hilantia had revived dozens of the old technologies – mycocraft in particular. They had cultivated paralysing moulds, boulder-sized puffballs that could be launched from siege weapons, and windborne spores that caused madness. Vesperi had been routed from their homeland – the great aerie-cities of Lepakkoma were completely destroyed. The perpetuum had lost northern Albion. With Lord Bechstein preoccupied by domestic purges and Lord Jejunus holed up in his throne room in Athanasia, the remaining perpetuum forces had been in disarray. It was then the Hilanta had introduced the Mucorian parasite, presumably intending to strike a knockout blow.

The parasite was a fungus that could be ingested or introduced through open wounds. Once spores took root in the brain, the parasite took control, suppressing pain, assisting with healing, sharpening perception and linking with other Mucorian-controlled minds in a crude network. Compared to the honours, their powers were limited – indeed, Hagar was unsure whether the parasite suppressed pain or simply had no capacity for understanding it – but crucially, the parasite was sovereign over its host – as the Hilanta discovered to their cost. They had meant to raise an army of soldier-slaves from their prisoners of war. Instead, the Mucorians rose up against their masters. Being largely impervious to the fungal weapons from which they were developed, they turned the tide of war decisively.

Despite their contribution, it was hard for Mucorians to find a place in society when they inhabited the bodies of that nation's war dead. Still, their continuing existence was a powerful disincentive to Hilantian dreams of conquest, so the perpetuum officially recognised the Mucorians, and granted them a tiny island off the remote Dellamore Atolls, as well as several unassuming embassies. It would always be an uneasy alliance. The bodies they used aged normally. To survive as a species, Mucorians needed hosts.

'We've three live samples in Unit Four which we've infected with the Mucorian fungus. If you wish to view them you're very welcome.'

'Perhaps later.'

'But your comparison is suggestive, Hagar. Yes, the Mucorian parasite dominates the host, but as you know, there are less wasteful, resource-intensive ways to overthrow an empire than total conquest. The godfly parasite's influence may be more insidious.' He licked a corner of handkerchief and dabbed his lips. 'The power behind the throne.'

Hagar watched him gravely, trying to ignore her quickening breaths. 'That doesn't sound like science, Doctor.'

'All disciplines intersect eventually.' He looked at her. 'Haven't you ever wondered what the parasite derives from this relationship? What it gets in return for its lavish gifts?'

'I'm not a naturalist.'

'You know the insects worship it? The godstuff.'

'Some lanta consider it sacred,' she corrected.

'Sacred.' He weighed the word on his tongue. 'Something precious, which is to be feared.' He dropped his gaze to the twisted plants at his feet. 'You probably think I do this for a feeling of power.'

'Yes.'

He shook his head. 'When you study the world – *really* study it – you don't feel powerful. You realise how tiny you are. How impossible it all is.' He bent down and ripped up a weed. 'But I'm still young. I have time. Already we've improved upon the godfly parasite's work. Rats are just the beginning. We'll unpick age. We'll unpick sickness. We'll save the world from the error of death.'

Hagar felt a crawling sensation on the nape of her neck. The doctor's phrasing was suspiciously particular. Had Arthur visited him too? Was that the source of his zeal?

Noroc raised his chin as he spoke. Some of the old poise was returning to him. 'Come on, then. We both know who you're really here to see.'

'Where is she?'

'Where she always is.' He pointed downwards. 'The ice house.'

Noroc waited until the guard had locked the steel-panelled door behind them. He bolted it from the inside and turned to face Hagar. In the cramped stone antechamber, she had to crane her neck to meet his gaze.

'Remember: don't look at them. You'll be perfectly safe.'

She detected no malice in his warning, but no concern either. His face was underlit by his lantern, sweat greasing the line of his jawbone, windpipe curving from the soft palate beneath. He spent an abnormal amount of time adjusting his shirt cuff.

'Thank you, Doctor.'

Droplets sweated from milky fissures in the ceiling, dripping onto the brim of Hagar's hat. The room was little more than a box cut out of the rock, big enough for two harka to stand abreast. There were holes bored in the wall that had once held a torch bracket, from back when House Dellapeste still used this place as a prison.

Noroc unlocked the second door with a large key hanging from a leather cord round his neck. The door opened onto a long stone corridor with a series of roughly hewn archways in either wall and a metal gate at the far end.

Someone was singing.

'Stay close,' Noroc said.

He began walking down the corridor, lamplight gliding over the slick, pitted rock like chalky fish ghosting a riverbed. Hagar followed, keeping her eyes on the seam running down the spine of his overalls – it made her think of the elytral suture on the wingcases of portal lanta. The air was stale and she felt lightheaded.

'Hagar.'

The voice was delicate, male, lilting. It came from one of the old cells. She kept walking.

'Hagar. Hagar Ingery.' It was neither urgent nor mocking. It sounded tantalisingly like someone she ought to know. But that was all their guile. She could feel them digging around in her head for scraps of biography. 'The bay looked beautiful, didn't it?'

Dizziness washed downwards from her scalp. She stopped, shut her eyes.

'Ah. Almost,' said the voice. 'Almost.' The walls seemed to buzz. She could not tell if the voice was real, or inside her head. Or both. 'Oh. But you took me into yourself. You *understood*, Hagar! Oh. I'm so proud of you.' She pinched the bridge of her nose. The burrowing sensation intensified. She was losing herself. No. 'Why do you grieve so, Hagar? I went willingly. It was you who wouldn't let go. Speak to me. Speak to me.' She took a step forward. 'You cannot hide. *For his eyes are upon the ways of man, and he seeth all his goings.*' The voice groaned, beatifically, almost obscenely. 'Not an error. A *gift*. When will you tell the truth to Arthur?'

She whirled round. Through rusted iron bars, sitting on a cot made from crates covered by a tatty hide, was a man with jutting shoulders, angular elbows and knees, sleek black hair and a soft, sentimental face that fell as her eyes met his. Vapour rose from the back of his skull. She could smell soap and burning.

'Won't you dance with me, sister?'

'Mitta,' she said.

An arm locked round her throat and she was rising. She tried to cry no, she wanted to stay, she needed to hear his gentle, mirthful voice. The crackling and churning in her skull expanded into a white, ablative rush.

'Hagar.'

She opened her eyes. Dr Noroc was standing over her.

She was sitting upright. She raised a palm to shield her eyes from the lantern.

'I told you not to look,' said Noroc. 'They can make you see things.'

She was in a small stone chamber lit by gaslights.

'Was that . . .' Hagar closed her eyes and massaged her eyeballs. Of course not. He was long dead. 'I was unprepared.'

'Being a handmaiden grants you no immunity – we've conducted tests, naturally.'

'So you must run a gauntlet of, ah . . . samples with mind-altering powers, every time you want to come down here?'

'We've developed countermeasures.' He rucked up his sleeve. On the underside of his wrist was a glossy, shrivelled thing, like a date or prune. The flesh around it was mildly inflamed, and it took her a moment to understand she was looking at a giant, bloated tick. A brown stylus extended from its engorged body, puncturing the skin just below his palm. 'A little breeding programme inspired by studying the resistances of our guest.'

A device for neutralising the talents of a peer? He had been holding back. Testing her, perhaps.

'Does it work?' she said, trying to hide her eagerness.

Dr Noroc pulled his cuff back up and used it to clean his spectacles. 'Against these samples, yes. It suppresses any attempt at remote mental influence. But their powers are modest: mild hallucinogenic phenomena, changes in perception, mood alteration – small beer compared to the talents of our Grand-Duc.' The innuendo was clear: he understood she planned high treason. He seemed untroubled by the prospect. He placed his glasses back onto his nose. 'We can't keep them in the main facility. Too disruptive. We lost some staff to . . . emotional disturbances. At least here they deter intruders.'

Hagar stood, adjusted her hat. 'I'm convinced of their efficacy.'

Noroc led her through a low tunnel and down a flight of stone steps cut into the rock, moving with officious urgency. Hagar wondered if passing through the mind-readers affected him more than he let on, even with his device. She wondered what their effective range was – whether they sinuated into researchers' dreams.

The temperature dropped. Noroc's lamp filled the air around him with rippling vapour rainbows. Moisture streamed down the walls and dripped from the galvanised-iron handrail. Hagar became aware of a low vibration, an almost subsonic thrum, permeating the rock, the rail, her teeth.

At the foot of the stairs was another antechamber and a steel-panelled door. Noroc approached a wall of speckled grey-black igneous rock, lit by a single gas jet. He stooped, pressed his palm to the wall. A disguised cylinder of stone swivelled beneath his fingers. He slid it out, then took a thin metal rod from under his jacket. The rod had a complicated claw-head lined with gear teeth. He inserted the rod into the recess and gave it a quarter turn.

Hagar watched as the steel door began rolling aside. It was a perfunctory bit of subterfuge – the seam round the hidden lock was clearly visible – but Noroc was making use of systems left over from the old jail.

Noroc glanced back. His spectacles were milky with condensation. 'Tread carefully.'

On the other side of the door was a wide chamber of polished green marble. Hagar entered, leaving Noroc behind. Black, helical trees twisted up through the floor, wrapping round glass pillars. A stream ran through the centre of the room, crossed by a little wooden bridge. Banks of gas jets blazed in glass wall sconces. The air was rank with the stink of clotting algae, sour ferrous notes and a faint undertang of sulphur.

Intricate bas-relief friezes decorated the walls, depicting towns and villages populated by hundreds of little people, all engaged in different tasks: a woman sowing seeds, an old man in a rooftop aviary tending to an owl, a young woman rising into the air, children walking into a lake. There were dogs the size of houses and lots of complicated waterways and waterfalls. To her right was an unfinished room, marble melting into bare rock and mounds of earth where the roof had collapsed.

To the north was a perfectly circular tunnel. The temperature dropped as she followed it. Gooseflesh prickled her forearms. She passed a huge library protected by glass doors, a double bed on the white sand shore of an underground lake full of tiny luminous jellyfish, and a room with a table, chairs and a large stone fireplace.

The tunnel opened out into a massive cavern. Below spread a valley of hunched, stark trees lit by hundreds of paper lanterns. On either side rose sheer walls of red quartzite. She followed a winding grit track downwards, past branches heavy with icicles. She could hear water bubbling over rocks. Here and there were squat statues in obsidian or pink marble, odd, expressionless figures with torch sconces set into their skulls and lumps of cinnabar for eyes.

Her breath emerged in wisps. Her hair and underclothes were damp with sweat. As she approached the grove, she shivered. She pushed through a wall of black briars. Her boots crunched on frost.

Four partially frozen streams flowed at compass points into an oval pool, surrounded by a dozen or more lanterns. Vapour coiled off the sweating ice. In the centre of the pool, a man floated naked, submerged up to his neck in turbid, steaming water.

He was lean with bony shoulders. Steel-grey hair hung across his face in ratty tangles. Even with his eyes closed and his flesh intact, she could sense the fire within.

'Gideon.' She took a step towards the pool.

A familiar *crunch crunch crunch.*

She turned. From the mist stomped a huge armoured golem, as wide as it was tall – brass-coloured cuirass, domed helm sunken into the breastplate, stocky legs protected by inch-thick greaves, and disproportionately long arms that ended in jointed metal gauntlets. Its riveted shoulder pauldrons were edged with black metal trim. Sprung metal cleats left clawed hoofprints in the frosty earth. From its visor slit emanated a blue glow.

It charged.

Hagar took a step back; her boot skidded in a sludge of lichen. The golem clenched its armoured fist and wound up a right hook.

'That's enough, Judith.'

The golem halted and slid, its chestplate stopping inches from Hagar's face. It let its fist clank to the floor. For a moment, it was still, then it swung itself round and clumped back to the woman who had spoken.

Sarai sat on a curved wicker chair at the pool's edge. She wore a necklace of red beryl and an olive dress that sagged in the wet air. Her long hair was tied back with a ribbon. She closed the book in her lap and took off her spectacles.

'Hullo, Hagar.'

'Hello, Sarai.'

She had aged. Odd how it was still a surprise. Since Hagar's last visit, the last of Sarai's hair had greyed, her features continuing their slow collapse. Hagar tried to recall the face as she had first seen it, on the day of Sarai's birth. A heartbeat ago. There was so little time left.

'Calix said you'd be visiting,' she said. Hagar never heard anyone else refer to Dr Noroc by his first name. It unsettled her in ways she did not understand.

'What are you doing all the way down here, languishing in the dark? It's not healthy.'

Sarai ran her fingertips over the raised letters on the book's cover. 'I was reading to Gideon.'

'You need sunlight. What happened to the beautiful atrium you built?'

'I undid it. Besides, I like it here. And I think Gideon's calmer when I'm around.'

Hagar caught the petulant edge to Sarai's voice and decided not to argue. The girl seemed safe enough. That was the main thing.

Hagar turned to Gideon. 'Good afternoon.'

He lifted a hand and scraped strands from his eyes. Each time his fingers brushed a hair, it curled and blackened.

He peered at her. His gaze flicked to Sarai.

'Is she real?'

For all his dishevelment, his voice was soft as smoke. He reminded her of Nebuchadnezzar, lost in animal squalor yet sustained and protected by a strange inner majesty. *And his body was wet with the dew of heaven, till his hairs were grown like eagles' feathers.* God held his honour and brightness in trust. He would return to the Kingdom after his time among the beasts. Back in the old world, he and Arthur had fought side by side in a great war. Gideon had believed Arthur slain. When Arthur appeared to him, the reunion had cost Gideon his reason.

As Arthur, with all his foresight, must have known it would.

Sarai stood and set the book on the chair. She walked over to Hagar. Up close, it was easy to see Sarai's resemblance to her father in her high cheekbones and tucked jaw, blended with her mother's subtle poise and large, appraising eyes. She raised a hand; her fingertips stroked the air an inch from Hagar's cheek.

The hairs on the back of Hagar's neck stood on end. Sarai let her hand drop, wrinkled her nose.

'As you or I.'

Gideon sighed and lay back in the pool, water fizzing and boiling off him as he let himself sink.

Hagar and Sarai began walking down a little trail in the woods.

'How have you been?' she said.

'Well.'

'No aches and pains? Fevers? Tiredness?'

The path was edged with clumps of black-lobed, semi-translucent shrubs. Sarai trod carefully, following her old footprints, affirming, deepening.

'All of those things. I'm not as young as you. Not any more.'

They passed a water feature – limestone shelves, shaped to look like natural formations, that channelled the stream through a series of cataracts. Icicles fringed twisting grottos. Red algae clung to the rocks.

'Your skills have improved,' said Hagar.

'Gideon helps. It's all from him – the heart of it. I just . . . give his feelings shape.' She made slow horizontal passes with her hand and the rock tumoured, oozing open, ice shattering. A silver spire punched out of the summit, rising six or seven feet to a lancet tip.

'Sarai.' Hagar had to hurry to catch up with her.

'Yes?'

'I have something to tell you.'

'I know.' Sarai's shoulders slumped a little. 'You never come here unless you have to.'

'In life there are few true obligations. I may come for selfish reasons, but they're wants, not needs.' Hagar sensed her evenhanded philosophising was coming off as indifference. She struggled to express affection – her few experiences of it had always been mixed with cruelty. 'It pleases me to see you. I wish visiting was easier.'

'Hmmph.'

'I said one day, the time would come for you to leave this place.'

Sarai stopped. 'This is my home.'

'It's a prison, Sarai.'

'To you, perhaps. To me, it's paradise.' She walked on, back towards the pool. The trail reshaped itself in front of her, straightening and widening, trees gnarling over it to form a tunnel of tangled black bowers. Paper lanterns scabbed over into smoking iron censers.

'I don't mean today. But soon. Very soon. It's not safe for you here anymore.'

'Judith will look after me.'

Hagar could no longer see her hands in front of her face. She faltered after Sarai's silhouette, towards the glow of the pool.

'Judith can't save you from sickness or old age.'

'I don't want to be saved. I know I can't live forever.'

Hagar's toecap caught on a root and she stumbled. Her heart was pounding.

'This isn't the limit of your power. You can do so much more. It's staying here that holds you back.'

'I have all I need!' Sarai threw her arms out and turned a slow circle, the branches above her braiding into a thick black knot. 'Anyway, I don't like it out there. It's too noisy. All those moods all . . . stirred together.'

'Exactly! They *need* you, Sarai. You could give their feelings form.'

'Their form would be hunger. Chaos.'

'True. Even their suffering is tainted. But imagine if they felt as purely as Gideon. The world you could build. The transformations.'

Sarai stopped on the edge of the pool. A column of steam rose from Gideon as he stood in the shallows, scooping up water and watching it boil away in his palms, over and over.

'I could help them,' said Sarai.

'You could take them to paradise.'

CHAPTER 11

WARS AND RUMOURS OF WARS

Butler sat up, coughing. His kaftan had holes in the chest, purple and sodden, with tacky dark scar tissue showing through.

He spat tooth fragments and a stringy gobbet of blood.

Delphine stared, her head spinning. Butler's wounds were healing. He had the honours. He was a peer.

He retched, hacking black sputum into his palm. He wiped it off with a handkerchief and held up something between thumb and forefinger: a bullet.

'Oh, how unpleasant,' he said.

'So the rumours are true,' said the girl who had called herself Agatha.

'You shot me based on *rumours*?'

'*She shot you based on my orders*,' came a crackly voice. '*Consider yourself relieved of duty*.'

'Ah.' Butler laughed and scratched his neck. 'I should've guessed. So nice to hear your voice again, dear leader!'

A delay, then: '*You're a coward, Butler*.' Ms Rao's words were coming from a speaker somewhere in the shadows. '*Agatha – search the boat*.'

'Wait, wait, wait,' said Butler. 'What exactly am I accused of here?'

Another delay. '*Defecting*.'

'What?!' He rose, flicking blood from his clothes. A dozen carbines swung to point at his head. Slowly, he raised both hands. 'Steady now. I heard you the first time.'

'If he moves from that spot, fire,' said Agatha.

'Look.' Butler made a show of holding his arms frozen in the air. 'I don't deny I've concealed my identity from some of our newer team members.' He glanced down at his chest, where already tufts of wet fur grew through the holes in his kaftan. 'Obviously. I am . . . *was* a member of the perpetuum. I'm sure you appreciate why I might want to keep information like that a secret.'

Delphine felt chills. Adrenaline blurred the edges of her vision. She remembered the crunch as his face had struck the van door. Something had broken, yet in all the fuss she had not questioned it. Come to think of it, she had never seen him eating.

'But you've always known what I am.' A rise in volume indicated he was addressing Ms Rao over the radio. 'And I've not defected from *SHaRD*. Not . . . knowingly.'

Agatha shook her head and gave him a pitying smile. 'The camp told us what happened.'

He squinted. 'What . . . happened at the camp?'

'*You killed half the guards and escaped with all the weapons you could fit in one boat.*'

'No, we didn't,' said Delphine.

Several carbines swung to target her.

'*Delphine. I thought he might have killed you all.*'

'As if I'd give him the chance! And there wasn't this . . . *massacre*. We left under perfectly ordinary circumstances.' She pointed at Butler. 'And I did *not* know he was one of those, those . . .' She thought of Father, burning. 'He lied to me, too. But we didn't kill anyone.'

'I didn't *lie*,' said Butler out of the corner of his mouth. 'You never asked me.'

Agatha studied Delphine for a few moments. She turned to Alice. 'What's your story?'

Alice pressed her lips together. 'Well . . . I didn't ask to come, but I'm not a hostage or anything. And I didn't see anybody get shot.' She glanced at the glassy pool of blood. 'Except Butler, just now. Your waistcoat is very nice, by the way.'

Agatha looked momentarily confused. She blinked and turned back to Butler.

'*You haven't responded to radio hails for weeks.*'

'It's broken!' said Delphine.

'Someone sabotaged it,' said Alice.

'Go. See for yourselves.' Butler gestured towards the stern. 'If you can fix it I'd be most grateful.' A long pause. Delphine could feel the carbineers' gazes burning into her.

'*Search the boat,*' said Ms Rao.

Agatha took a deep breath through her nostrils. She signalled to Delphine and Alice.

'Step off, please.'

Delphine gave the carbineers a wary glance, then stepped down onto the plank floor. Alice did the same, the boat groaning in its harness. Agatha nodded to the three female deckhands with the blunderbuss pistols. They holstered their weapons on their belts and boarded the vessel at the foredeck.

'*Wait.*'

They froze.

'*Is the lanta there?*'

Agatha glanced around. 'No sign.'

Another pause. '*Be careful.*'

'Ms Rao, if I may,' began Butler loudly, 'what exactly are you hoping to find?' He hooked a finger into one of the holes in his kaftan. 'A large cache of guns and ammo, presumably?'

During the lag, Delphine thought she could hear a faint, whispering hiss, but it might have been the sea.

'*Please be quiet, Butler,*' said Ms Rao. '*Let them do their jobs.*'

'I just . . .' He winced, touching a fist to his lips. 'Do you really think I'd bring it all straight to our boathouse, knowing you could radio ahead to warn them? Doesn't my being here at all strike you as a little . . . tactically suboptimal?'

This time the delay went on for a clear fifteen seconds.

'*Your objection has been noted.*'

The three deckhands began rummaging through cargo crates inside the boat.

'I mean, forgive me, ma'am . . . I know brazen stupidity and I are on nodding terms, but don't you think, given my track record, I might at least, oh, stash the weapons in the jungle before we made port, and take moorings that belonged to someone other than allies of the people I'd just betrayed?' He swept his arms out. 'For example?'

As he turned, all twelve carbines zeroed in on his head again. He rolled his eyes. 'And, by the way, you can point those guns at me all you like. I heal all wounds and I can't feel pain. All you'll achieve is making my robe slightly more tattered. Sooner or later you'll run out of bullets.' He took a step forward. No one fired. He glanced at Agatha. 'Did she tell you *all* the stories about me?'

Agatha looked him up and down. She licked her gold molars.

'I heard the one where they burned you on a pyre. I always thought it deserved a better ending.'

She spun on her heel and strode towards Delphine. Delphine took a step back and nearly fell through the gap between the boat and the floor. Sprung cleats bit into the boards. Agatha stopped, lifting her axe-hand till the cool flat of the blade came to rest under Delphine's chin.

Agatha narrowed her eye. 'And how many bullets can this one take?'

Delphine saw herself reflected in the girl's glass eye – her distended, toothy grimace an unconvincing attempt to mask her fear. Memories of shame and powerlessness burned like acid in her belly. She felt old, but also very young.

'Don't hurt her,' said Butler.

Agatha turned towards him, the axe pressed to Delphine's jaw. 'You're not in a position to make demands.'

Delphine dropped to one knee. She shoved Agatha's axe-hand, grabbed her by the shoulder and twisted her round, tripping her. As she stumbled Delphine locked an arm round her throat and pressed the tip of the sickle to her jugular. She gave the blade a push, felt Agatha twitch.

'Weapons down, please,' she said.

Several carbineers swung their aim from Butler to Delphine. She planted her knee in the base of Agatha's spine and forced her to kneel. Delphine's heart was thundering. She could barely hold her hand steady. She cleared her throat. 'Sorry, just to be clear, I'm implying I'll kill her if you don't *put your guns down this bloody instant.*'

'*Agatha? What's going on?*'

Butler looked at Agatha. 'I think they're waiting for a cue.'

Delphine felt the weight of multiple guns pointing at her head. She gritted her teeth, waiting for the muzzle flash.

'*Agatha. What's happening?*'

Agatha took a long in-breath.

'Guns down,' she said.

Hesitantly, the carbineers began lowering their weapons.

'Tell them to line up in front of the boats,' said Butler. 'Hands flat on their heads.'

'You heard him,' said Agatha.

The guards started clambering out of the boats. They were human, harka and vesperi, all clad in simple one-piece overalls. Delphine was no good at judging vesperi or harka ages, but the humans looked no older than Agatha – sixteen at most. As they stepped into the light, they winced, dropping their gazes; unarmed and flushed from cover they looked grimy, callow and sheepish.

A thump came from the boat behind her. She glanced over; the three deckhands were filing onto the foredeck, hands above their heads. Behind them, floating in the air, was a matt-black pistol.

God bless Martha.

Delphine stood. Slowly, she removed her hand from Agatha's throat. Agatha staggered away, tugging at her collar, scowling. Butler watched approvingly.

'There,' he said. 'That's a bit more civil, isn't it?'

Butler and Ms Rao talked for over an hour. He allowed Agatha's crew to transfer the boat onto wooden chocks and perform a thorough search of its contents. Agatha herself muttered a couple of orders to her deckhands and retreated through a hatch. Delphine, Alice and Martha sat together on a stack of planks, Delphine smoking, Martha brewing a round of sugary coffees on their little gas burner.

As the adrenaline left her body, Delphine felt exhausted. She kept replaying Butler's wounds healing. Somewhere under his clothes was that tumorous growth, packed with writhing white grubs – the promise of eternal youth, in return for bearing his pain. How old was he really?

'*Well,*' Ms Rao was saying, '*this is troubling. Very troubling indeed.*'

'The idea that I'd turned traitor must have seemed appealing by comparison.'

'*It would certainly have been neater.*' Some clattering. A long delay. '*Look. I'm not sure how secure this line is.*'

'Understood.'

'*In light of recent developments, I've urgent housekeeping to attend to. If our organisation has been compromised, it stands to reason that I may face infiltrators on this side of the threshold. Continue as planned. Meet our contact in Fat Maw. You're authorised to offer whatever is necessary in return for good intel leading to our acquisition of a live, viable godfly. We'll formulate a plan for your return in due course.*'

'Yes ma'am.'

'*You should know I told all staff everything. About your past as Lord Cambridge, and your abilities. They needed to know in case they had to capture you.*'

'Well, that is . . . inconvenient.'

'*Yes. Yes, it is. So be discreet when you move through the city. Word may spread.*'

'I'll be all right.' He glanced at Delphine. 'I have backup.'

The sun heated the wet city to a steaming swelter. Butler led Delphine and Alice out through a hatch into a mass of cabins.

He had swapped his bloodied kaftan for a simple hooded tunic with slits in the back for his wings, and he moved with the grace of a local, picking his way over half-finished ropes, heaps of netting, stacked driftwood, small spreading fruit trees planted in the hollow clay heads of idols, and tethered lizards basking in the thick heat. Delphine could barely keep up. All available ground had been built on, porches and awnings conjoining like the jungle canopy. Roofing materials ranged from rush thatch and sheet metal through to glossy dark leaves or stuff cannibalised from boats – a sampan sawed into sections, or sail canvas stretched over the ribs of a keel to form a huge tent. Windmills turned upon masts, vanes churning as sunlight flashed off their wet blades.

Here and there walls had slogans daubed on them, or symbols.

Gradually, the cramped huts opened out and the boardwalks grew busier. Boulevards ran between rows of cabins, rumbling with handcarts, foot traffic and the occasional fox or lizard on a leash. Butler crossed a narrow rope bridge over a canal, sampaneers ducking as they sculled their single-oared craft underneath. The bridge yawed sickeningly as Delphine edged after him, exaggerating her missteps into swings.

The press of bodies was overwhelming. She had never liked cities – the rush and impatience. To be honest, the presence of people.

The street grew increasingly crowded. Delphine dug her nails into her palms. Someone clipped her arm and she nearly swung for them. She took a deep breath, squeezed through a clench of bodies . . .

. . . and found herself standing on a wide, half-empty wharf. Ahead spread a flat, bottle-green bay dotted with sails and steamships. A cool breeze bathed her damp skin, ruffled her hair.

Half a mile out, a reef of chunky bruise-black rock created a breakwater. The bay was enclosed by the pincers of two narrow headlands, sheltered across its mouth by three small islands. To her left, the stilt city curved for miles, its maze of wharves and piers eventually becoming a solid stone quay with warehouses and chalk white jetties. Behind it, Fat Maw rose in a sprawl of winding streets and mismatched architectural styles, red roofs and white render, grey turrets and black timbers, towards a summit capped with a long silver spire that caught the midday sun, burning like a star.

She exhaled. Her shoulders sagged.

Butler stopped to get water from a standpipe fed by big rooftop rainwater tanks. Next door was what appeared to be a temple: a small square building, surrounded by a low stone wall, open to the ocean. Carved timber pillars supported a steeply pitched roof covered in bark shingle. The sides of the pillars facing the sea had worn down to smooth curves, but the leeward sides depicted vesperi, humans, lanta and harka clad in gowns and feathers and jewels and wreathes, dancing and embracing. Delphine ran her fingers over the grooves. Some of the images looked quite saucy.

Inside the temple, upon a plinth, was a stone statue of a harka sitting crosslegged, hands joined in his lap, clad in robes and wearing a crown. Some people were placing offerings in depressions at the statue's feet: garlands of flowers, fruit and what looked like dead animals.

Delphine felt as if she ought to pray. She rested her brow against the pillar, gazing down at her boots. She did not believe in any god, not really, though she sometimes caught herself wishing. She had always admired Martha and her fellow lanta's fondness for Christian ritual – how they had absorbed Bible stories and scripture, how they had risen each morning, like little monks and nuns, to gather in the living room and pray silently. Yet she was not sure they believed in it, not in a literal way. She had asked Martha once or twice, and had received vague, circular answers, as if Martha did not understand the question. The lanta – which is to say *her* lanta, the ones who had lived in England with her and Mother and Algernon – seemed to crave that point of communion, that shared observance, but she suspected the attendant doctrine was irrelevant. Their prayers and contemplation and evenings of listening to Algernon read from the Bible were more in praise of their old friend Henry than God – a practice sustained because they knew it would have pleased him. In a sense, it had been their way – and Delphine's too – of keeping Henry alive.

But here she was, in a vital, obedient body, feeling the wind prickle the nape of her neck on the shore of a world she had almost stopped believing in. Alice standing a few yards away. Impossibility upon impossibility. That counted for something, didn't it?

'You all right?' said Alice, shielding her eyes from the sun.

'Yes, thank you, love.' And, for that moment (what a queer, miraculous thing!), she was.

Perhaps it was healthy to set aside a corner of one's mind for the irrational. Such small acts of defiance kept reality supple. But such danger, too. A dance on the edge of a volcano. All life's sweetest gifts – love, imagination, wonder, hope – lay adjacent to madness.

In the end, she closed her eyes and said thank you.

Butler bought them lunch from a vesperi trader in a long rush cloak. Gondolas were moored up and down a pontoon dock, colourful produce laid out in heaps on mats. The air was a din of trilling song and clicks and cries – she caught snatches of French and English, and other languages she did not recognise. A great living stink rose from the water, its surface confettied with fruit peels, fragments of wood and fish bones floating on a scum of oil. Birds like fat, filthy geese fought over scraps, each waggling the stumps of crooked vestigial wings beneath their larger flight wings.

The trader handed Butler several big leaves fastened with dried grass, and a vine covered in closed green buds, which he wound round a stick before passing over.

They sat in the shade of the boardwalk, on a plank bench between piers. Delphine opened her leaf. Inside was a tepid porridge of brown grains with nuts and chunks of fish. She ate with her fingers. It was oddly sweet, but she was almost shaking with hunger. Butler lit a cigarette and stared out into the bay.

After a while he said: 'I have to visit someone in the high town. It's probably best I go alone.'

'You lied to us,' said Delphine.

'No. There were just things I didn't mention.'

'Because you knew if you told me we'd never come.'

'My past is none of your business.' He looked away. 'Listen. If base camp sabotaged our radio and gave a false story to England that means the threshold is under hostile control. We can't go home. So you'd better decide whether you're prepared to work with me or whether you want us to go our separate ways.'

Delphine snapped off one of the green buds. 'Why are you afraid of her?'

'Who?'

'Ms Rao.' The bud crunched under her molars. It had a buttery, hazelnutty flavour. 'She says jump, you say how high. You're a peer, aren't you? What are you scared of?'

'Nothing. What you perceive as fear is simply an unwillingness to play the usual games of dominance and submission. My alliance with Ms Rao gives me access to resources and communication networks. I cooperate because she's useful to me.'

'She's got something on you. More than just your secret.'

He glanced at her, and, to her surprise, smiled. 'You genuinely can't imagine working with someone unless they were threatening you, can you?'

She snapped off another bud, her cheeks burning. 'Fine. Who's this contact we have to go see?'

'A person of influence. But I think it would be best if—'

'I'm coming.'

'Delphine,' said Alice.

'He said I have to work with him. Here I am. I'm no use unless I learn how things work.'

'Just hear him out.'

'No,' said Butler. 'It's fine. She's right. Can't learn it all from bloody primers. And . . .' He grimaced as if tasting something sour. 'You've proven you're at least borderline competent in a pinch. Both of you have.' He stood. 'Let's head back to the boat and change into something more appropriate.'

The restaurant spilled out across the cobbles, tables and chairs arranged close together and shaded by palm leaf awnings decked with paper lanterns and poppets made of twigs and twists of seagrass. The clientele was largely human and harka. Teapots sat on every table, beside ashtrays and dishes of coloured ice. People smoked and chattered and ate with their hands, passing plates in a kind of bucket-chain system that seemed to obviate the need for waiters.

'Remember,' said Butler out the corner of his mouth, 'do. Not. Speak.'

He wore sleek royal purple trousers that tapered at the knee, a silver belt buckle and a single-breasted waistcoat of deep caramel.

Delphine stuck close behind him, dressed in a vest and shorts, and a loose, light, poppy-blue cloak that hid the machine pistol strapped to her hip. Alice and Martha were back at the boathouse, unloading.

She was finding it hard to concentrate. The smell of seared, smoked cuts of meat made her mouth water.

She could not deny that Butler had natural presence. He carried himself with understated authority; customers were compelled both to look up and to drop their gazes as he passed. A little of it rubbed off on her. She felt herself standing taller, letting her gaze rove around the tables. It felt good.

Perhaps it was unwise to be drawing attention to themselves. Most patrons avoided eye contact, but a couple of gazes lingered, coolly appraising.

Inside, she squeezed between the backs of chairs as she followed Butler through a noisy, smoky room towards a doorway covered with a felt curtain. On a stool beside the doorway sat a harka orderly with deep cherry-brown hair, a mealy patch about his muzzle, and horns carved in the shape of stone towers. He was laying square cards in a double cross formation on a tray table set on his knees, either playing solitaire or performing some sort of divination.

He glanced up as Butler approached. One of his eyes had flecks of white in the iris.

'There's nothing for you back here, friend.'

'I'm here to meet Doyenne Lesang,' said Butler.

The guard looked him up and down. 'Name.'

'Butler.'

'Butler . . . ?'

'Just "Butler".'

The guard sniffed, tapping the edge of a card against the tray table. He cocked his head and looked past Butler at Delphine.

'Who's this?'

Delphine returned the guard's gaze with what she fancied was an insouciant swagger, dropping a shoulder and sweeping hair out of her eyes.

'His bodyguard,' she said. Butler flashed her a look but she pretended not to notice.

The guard licked his fat thumb and slid a card from the top of the deck. He set it down with a snap on the extreme left of the two-cross layout. The card bore an image of a tree in flames.

'And your business with the Doyenne?' he said, without looking up.

Butler peeled off his glove, revealing a chunky silver signet ring. Embossed into the ring was an image of eight tentacles linking to form a circle. He held his hand over the guard's tray table.

The guard nodded at the doorway. 'Fair tides.'

Behind the curtain, a flight of stairs led down, turning at right angles once, twice, until it opened out into a homely basement room with a single large table laid with candles, at the head of which sat a short harka, clay red with a tuft of vanilla hair hanging down over her cranial ridge. She looked up and smiled.

'Ah, hello! Thank you for your message. Take a seat.' She slid a ribbon into the book she had been reading and slapped it shut. She turned to a human female orderly sitting at the opposite end of the table, the only other person in the room. 'Ask the kitchen to send down more tea, would you?' The orderly nodded, rose, and clumped off up the stairs.

Delphine took a seat next to Butler, a little uneasily. All around the room stood glass cases containing coil upon coil of monstrous taxidermied snakes. On the walls were stylised images of knives, hatchets, hooks and saws made with wire stretched across pins. On the end wall was a small hatch.

Doyenne Lesang placed both palms on the table and leaned forward, keen-eyed, beaming. She had small, straight horns and a splash of milk-white fur highlighting her face.

'So. Now. To business.'

Butler performed a small bow. 'Doyenne.'

Lesang smiled blankly. It was impossible to tell whether Butler's show of deference pleased or annoyed her. There was something searching in her gaze – something rather sharper than her amiable demeanour implied.

'I understand you're interested in godflies,' she said.

'Acquiring one, specifically.'

Her smile tightened. 'Ah. Good. I'm so fond of directness.'

'Best to get to the meat of it.'

A rattling came from behind the hatch. Lesang stood.

'Did you know murdering Lord Jejunus isn't technically a crime?' she said brightly. 'There's no legislation, on account of the fact that perpetuum law doesn't recognise that killing a peer is possible.'

Butler cleared his throat. 'I rather think the lack of legal impediment would prove moot.'

Lesang lifted the hatch and took out a tray with a pottery jug and cups. 'And who would want to do such a thing in any case, eh?' She set the tray down and began pouring tea.

'Who indeed.'

'So.' She sat back down. 'You realise what you're asking is both treasonous and involves seeking out one of the most sought-after and highly prized commodities in the world?'

Butler spooned red spice from a kidney-shaped dish into his tea. 'Not everyone values them. Some long to see godflies eradicated forever.'

'Which makes sourcing one still harder.'

'But I understand you are very well-connected.'

'Hmm. Yes.' Lesang cradled her cup. 'You hear all sorts, don't you?'

Butler picked up his tea with both hands, fingers extended. Delphine wondered how he managed to hold the cup like that without burning his fingers, then she remembered. After a clear ten seconds of silence, she caught him looking at her out the corner of his eye. He cleared his throat. Delphine wasn't sure why no one was saying anything. He glanced at her cup. Then back at her. Then at her tea, his eyes widening.

Delphine picked up her cup.

Lesang nodded. 'Fair tides.' She waited until Delphine and Butler had taken a sip, then drank herself.

Butler set his cup back on the table. 'Can you help us, Doyenne?'

Lesang squinted at the ceiling. She made funny shapes with her mouth.

'You have my shipment?'

'Yes,' he said. 'All at the boathouse, ready for collection.' His signet ring *tink*ed against the rim of his cup as he lifted it to his lips. 'My employer wishes me to make it plain that it is merely a demonstration of good faith. It by no means represents the limit nor even the majority of our resources.'

Lesang relaxed back in her seat, grinning broadly. 'Well, recently we started hearing rumours.' She licked her thumb with her wide purple tongue and flattened down a lock of hair that had fallen across her eye. 'Someone has been claiming they have inside knowledge of a secret programme that went on years ago. Illegal cultivation of godflies. Anointing of peers without authority from the perpetuum. Experiments on live subjects. Technology from the War in Heaven.'

Delphine paused mid-sip. For an instant, Butler's eyes widened. He reset his features in an expression of professional disinterest.

'Rather light on specifics.'

'Eh. There were a few spicy details. Mind-readers. A man who burned. Technology that suppresses a peer's—'

'Wait – what did you say?' Delphine lurched forward, nearly spilling her tea.

Lesang glanced at Butler. Butler shot Delphine a glare. She returned it, harder. He dipped his head, and his demeanour appeared to undergo a soft reset. When he looked up, the coolly indifferent sophisticate was back.

He exhaled. 'Sounds . . . enticing.'

'That's what we thought. And with the Grand-Duc's arrival in two days' time. Too good to be true, right? A honey trap to lure out traitors.'

'An exceptionally sloppy one.'

Lesang refilled her cup. 'Wasn't asking much either. Safe passage out of the city. Fake papers. Enough to make a new start somewhere else. Claimed his notes were with a legal representative who'd been instructed to burn them if he turned up dead.'

'Sensible.'

'Well. Here's the thing. I think I've tracked him down.'

'Ah. Not so sensible.'

'There's a doctor holed up in a villa in the high town.' She slid a slip of paper across the table, which Butler took without looking. 'He went to the city peace only this morning saying he's been getting death threats. Didn't say why, of course.'

'How do you know it's the same man?' said Butler.

Lesang sipped her tea. 'I have my channels. I expect I'm not the only one who's heard about it, either. Only now, no one can get to him to do the deal because Sheriff Kenner's put him under guard "for his own safety".'

'How might one secure an audience?'

She chuckled. 'I'm not sure you can without breaking the law.' She rose from her chair. 'It's the festival tomorrow. Why not join the revelry? Masks and costumes. Lots of noise. I expect Kenner's staff will be stretched thinly.' She worried at a spot on the table with one of her short, red fingers. 'Very thinly indeed.'

Butler pushed his seat back and stood. Delphine did the same.

'Thank you, Doyenne.' He produced a small wooden box from

his waistcoat, popped the lid, and sprinkled a pinch of what looked like dried herbs on his and Delphine's chairs. 'Fair tides.'

'She's hiding something,' muttered Butler as they walked back along the quay. Here, buildings were far grander than in the stilt city – bunting hung between unlit gas lamps, ready for the morrow's festivities. They stopped beside a fountain where the bronze figure of a vigorous young man held one arm aloft, water jetting from the mouth of an eel clutched in his fist. A plaque underneath simply read: *JEJUNUS*.

Butler squinted at his reflection in the rippling water. He took out a pocket-comb and began working it through the clumped fur on his scalp.

'How d'you know?' said Delphine. She had felt it too, but could not separate her churning gut from a greater malaise, a premonition that time was running out.

Butler grimaced as the comb snagged. 'Centuries of lying, of being lied to. None of the information was *false*, necessarily, just . . . incomplete.'

'So she has her own agenda,' said Delphine. 'So what? You heard what she said. A man that burns. That's Da—, that's my father.'

Butler dropped his voice to a whisper. 'This isn't breaking into the cottage of some cantankerous old lady. These are trained armed guards.'

'I can handle it.' Even as she said it, she knew she was lying. But what choice did she have? They had to go. She was so close.

'Ugh!' Butler dropped his face into his palm. 'Didn't you listen to her? The man is paranoid. If you charge in and,' Butler glanced about and lowered his voice still further, 'try to *murder all his guards*, do you honestly think he's likely to come willingly? What are you going to do? Knock him out and drag him?'

'If necessary.'

'And how many miles can you drag a body, eh?'

'Do you want to find out?' She felt all rushy. 'What's the point of all this if we're just going to give up? My father might be alive. I don't care if it's hard. Waiting is hard, Butler. Hiding is hard. I'll do whatever I have to.'

Butler turned away, glaring out across the bay. His gaze was fixed on the middle island, where weathered grey towers rose above high cliffs. Vesperi children were jumping off the quay, thumping their wings and swooping low over the water.

He turned back to face her.

'All right.' He smoothed down the front of his waistcoat, tugged at his cuff.

'What's the matter?'

Butler hooked his toe under a loose cobble. He spent a clear five seconds prising it up.

'Butler?'

'Well,' he said at last, 'if you're serious, there's someone who can help us.'

'I'm serious.'

He looked up and met her gaze. 'I hope so. Because you're not going to like this.'

Delphine stood at the end of a jetty, gazing into the bay, breathing hard. Seaweed slopped on stone steps. White light on the dirty water looked like a city seen from a bomber at night. A hot wind washed over her face. She felt utterly vulnerable and furious.

She heard footsteps and instinctively reached for her gun. She let go. What was she doing? Her heart rate quickened. Anger, every time. It was the only home she knew.

She couldn't face Alice now. She couldn't stand the thought of being seen.

A slim figure stopped ten feet away.

'Fuck off, Butler.'

He glanced around. They were alone on the jetty, save for big puncheons of rum stacked in a pyramid and stamped with a marque that looked like a wheatsheaf and weasel. He took a step forwards.

'She's one of us.'

'She's a monster.'

'I understand the two of you have history.'

'She's the reason I lost my father.' Delphine breathed against a tightness in her chest. 'She betrayed us. What else haven't you told me?'

Butler looked at the ground. Sunlight picked out red capillaries in his ears, like little cracks.

'I'm sorry,' he said.

Delphine blinked. She braced for the sarcastic addendum.

He ran a fingertip down the edge of his noseleaf, exhaling so the inner gills flared. He looked up.

'What they say about me is true, you know,' he said. 'Whatever Patience did, I was a thousand times worse. Murderer. Tyrant. Centuries of it.'

'Then you're a monster, too.'

'Probably.'

The breeze was stinging Delphine's eyes. She dipped her head and rubbed them.

'How do you live with yourself?' she said.

'I haven't made peace with my actions, if that's what you're asking. I've no right to absolution. But I don't believe hating myself is a moral good either. Not on its own.' He broke open a fresh packet of cigarettes, took one and offered it to her. 'I do what I can and it will never be enough. That's my punishment.'

She peered at him as she took a cigarette. 'Am I supposed to be moved? The lonely plight of the tragic ancient. I mean really, Butler. I would've thought with all this time you could have come up with something more original than self-pity.'

He glanced at her sidelong. 'I might say the same to you.'

Delphine glared at him. 'What's that supposed to mean?'

He blew a long trail of smoke, dabbled his fingers in it until it broke apart.

'People you love are still alive. You're wasting time.'

They smoked in silence. In the lee of the black reef, gulls wheeled and darted above a flotilla of giant turtles pulling a barge.

Delphine flicked the butt into the water.

'All right,' she said. Something had shifted inside her. 'All right. Let's go.'

In the undercity, a rowboat carried them through a black, stinking shanty town of tarp and timber. Butler navigated by speechsight. Delphine could hear the slop of oars cutting through the water, rowlocks squealing in their mounts. Behind her sat Alice and, semi-invisible on the bow, Martha.

Dwellings were made of rafts lashed together, fitted with outriggers and moored to their neighbours. Rushlights lit the shape of sleeping bodies.

They reached a place where free-standing braziers lit the thick stone pilings. She heard the hubbub of raised voices, arguing, laughter. Gondolas were moored in rows, rough jute blankets hanging on ropes between them to create partitions. At one end, a barge was loaded with kegs and bottles and several rough drawstring sacks.

Butler brought the boat up to one of the stone pilings, and fastened the painter to a thick iron ring. From an adjacent gondola, a vesperi slouching in a rope hammock cast them an idle look, a sawn-off carbine resting on her belly. Butler hailed her in clickspeak. He flashed his signet ring.

She waved them through.

A human serving boy met them, a rag tossed over his shoulder. He was bald except for a few greasy wisps of hair. Coral-white welts blotched his neck and forearms. He led them down a long thoroughfare between blanket rooms, ducking under ropes. Distended silhouettes moved against the translucent walls. Gondolas rocked beneath Delphine's feet, but weeks on the water had improved her balance.

She glanced back at Alice. 'You okay?'

Alice kept her eyes on the shifting floor. She looked nervous, but she nodded.

At the last-but-one room on the right the boy peeled back a curtain and bowed. Butler dropped a few coins into his waiting palm and stepped through.

The room was made up of three gondolas covered in bits of rug, a board laid over the centre to form a table, and candles burning on clay dishes. In one corner, a figure was half-sitting, half-sprawled, drinking directly from a bottle. He wore a black half-cape that fastened over his shoulders with studs, and a loose hood.

Butler took out a handkerchief and set it down over the thwart of one of the boats. He sat, nodded towards the figure.

'Mr Gillow. We're ready for transport.'

The figure set down the bottle. He picked up a heavy knife. With the tip he pushed back his hood. Underneath was a spray of dirty red hair. Pale skin.

Reggie Gillow. Delphine had known this was coming, but still her chest cramped. She glanced at Alice. She was watching him, her expression mild, tricky to read. She was blinking rather more than usual. What was going through her mind? Delphine looked back at Reggie. He seemed so young. Just a boy, really.

He wiped his lips with the back of a gloved hand. He looked Alice up and down, a cursory appraisal, then turned to the group.

'Who's first?' His voice was almost too quiet to hear.

'Me.' Delphine stepped forward. He squinted at her, as if he were not quite convinced she was real.

'Well then.'

Her hands were shaking. A smell hit her nostrils: peaty, hoppy, tarry.

She glanced down – black liquid was seeping through the deck, puddling round her feet, smoking. She stepped back in horror. Something snagged her ankle. She staggered – a tendril wrapped round her left arm. It was a raw, wet pink. She felt a jolt of panic, tried to wrench free.

'Easy now,' said Butler.

Delphine grasped for him but another tendril snapped round her wrist. She felt the deck dissolving beneath her, her feet sinking into a swamp of godstuff.

'Please!' she gasped. 'No!'

And then – it was as if the floor simply collapsed. She dropped.

At first she thought she had landed in the ocean, then she felt the godstuff close around her, thick, warm, enveloping.

Tendrils dragged her through a void of viscous blackness. She lost her sense of down. The tendril round her wrist slipped. The other tendrils immediately lashed tighter, yanked harder. Suddenly, she had the sense that if she broke free, she would be lost forever. They were guiding her, pulling her through. Her lungs were bursting. Colours fluxed across her closed eyelids, fluorescent chequerboards, starfields, auroras. She opened her mouth—

—and surfaced in a rush of noise and cold, the pressure around her dropping instantly.

She surged backwards into the air; tendrils whipped her rightside up and deposited her, staggering, back on her feet.

She was in a musty chamber of granite blocks, lit by oil lamps. A generator hummed in a corner. Radio equipment stood heaped on a wooden crate against one wall. The air was cool and tasted of cement.

Standing in front of her was a short woman in a white cotton dress hitched up to her knees. A long blond Dutch braid snaked several times around her body. One of her arms branched into a thicket of fleshy, threshing limbs. Their eyes met.

'Good afternoon,' said Patience.

Delphine stepped forward and punched her.

CHAPTER 12

THE BEGINNING OF SORROWS

(Seventy-five years before the inauguration)

Hagar pressed the scalpel to the middle of Anwen's belly and slit downwards. She cut from the navel to the pubic bone, maintaining a firm, even pressure. The skin yielded easily under the nib, yellow fat blooming through the incision. The body wanted to undo itself, to give up its secrets.

Anwen's valet, Mr Cox, howled through his gag. His screams were growing hoarse; the muffled blasphemy had turned to pleading. Anwen, meanwhile, watched the process with detached fascination. Her bed had been specially lowered so Hagar could reach across it.

Hagar wiped the scalpel then returned to the top of the incision, this time slicing through the subcutaneous fat. She licked her lips. Her throat burned with a fierce thirst. The ship's cabin was roasting, lamps and candles burning everywhere to give her light to work.

She set the scalpel down on a silver tray, then pushed two fingers of each hand into the wound and drew the layer of yellow fat aside. Mr Cox roared, straining against the bonds securing him to his bed. He had asked to stay awake during the procedure. Well, he had got his wish.

'Retractors.'

A vesperi assistant clad in headscarf, gloves and butcher's apron swivelled a horizontal steel arm over Anwen's abdomen. Two curved metal paddles, like coal tongs, were fixed to the bar via wingnuts. Hagar loosened the nuts, then with the assistant's help spent a few moments tucking the paddles over the peeled-back fat, holding it in place. Already the top of the cut was beginning to heal, skin and fat oozing together, crusting, repairing. She was moving too slowly.

'Scissors.'

The assistant ran round to Hagar's side of the bed, jogging the table and making the surgical implements clatter. Hagar suppressed the impulse to slap the girl round the head. It was not her fault – Cox and Anwen had refused Hagar the three trained assistants she had asked for. They were obsessed with secrecy, even if it cost their child's life.

Hagar picked up her scalpel and recut the mending tissue. Beneath the opened fat was a shiny, fibrous white membrane. She put a nick in it with the tip of the blade, then held out her palm for the scissors. It took a second or so for the assistant to comply, and Hagar felt another flash of irritation. She had honed her abilities in stinking battlefield tents, working on soldier after soldier in an environment where a moment's delay could mean the difference between recovery and agonising death.

Working as fast as she could, she cut up and down the membrane, exposing the red curve of the abdominal muscles. When she pressed her fingertips into the midline to separate them, Cox bucked and thrashed. One of his restraints snapped with a bang. Even through his padded gag, which Hagar had insisted on to stop him biting through his tongue, she could clearly hear him telling her to stop, threatening, begging, delirious with pain.

As she clamped the abdominal muscles aside, the fascia above was repairing itself, sealing up. An exposed roll of bowel began retreating under a shrivelled white caul resembling damp muslin.

Normally, from this point on, Hagar would have worked cautiously, taking care not to perforate the bowel or bladder, but Anwen's waters had broken, and still the child had not come. If it was not dead already, it was certainly in grave peril.

Hagar hooked the scissors into the stretchy pink membrane beneath the abdominal muscle and began snipping. A simple incision was not enough; she chopped a wide oval out of it, so it would take time to close.

And there was the womb, bulging through the layers of skin and fat and muscle, a lurid fuchsia. Hagar began cutting through a final membrane. The metal retractors shuddered; Anwen's stomach muscles were pulling together, trying to reconnect. Hagar raked aside flesh with her fingertips. Cox was gurgling, thrashing.

'Scalpel.'

She gritted her teeth as she cut into the uterine wall. Too shallow, and it would heal before she got through. Too deep, and she risked cutting into the child's soft, pliable head, slicing the fontanelle. Anwen felt no pain and could rapidly heal wounds, but the child – for all her notional talents – was as vulnerable to injury as any human.

The retractor blades were bending. Hagar tried to keep the scalpel steady, remembering her work dissecting corpses – the satisfaction of a tidy incision, of preserving delicate blood vessels and nerves through skill and patience. As the wall of the womb separated, a wet, pale-pink sphere became visible. The baby's head.

The right rectus abdominus muscle slipped loose. It jogged her hand; the blade nicked the child's scalp. Hagar cursed. A second later the other retractor gave with a clang; muscles closed around her wrist.

Instantly tissue layers were regenerating, spreading like frost on a window. Hagar yanked but her wrist was stuck. She reached out with her free hand.

'Scissors!'

She drove them point-first into Anwen's abdominal wall. The finesse of the mortuary slab was forgotten; Hagar tore and slashed, ripping out chunks of muscle and tossing them aside, digging for the baby. Cox screamed and screamed. Even Anwen wrinkled her nose, observing with distaste.

Flecks of blood stung Hagar's eyes. She recalled the words of Moses: *Thou shalt beget sons and daughters, but thou shalt not enjoy them . . . The stranger that is within thee shall get up above thee very high; and thou shalt come down very low.*

Her fingers found the smooth roundness of the head, the soft curve of the jawbone. She pulled. For the first time since the operation had begun, Anwen let out a moan. The weight she had carried in her belly for months was finally shifting. Hagar's fingers slipped. Anwen's body clung to its prize.

Hagar resisted the urge to fight, adjusted her grip, and pulled gently. The suction broke; the baby's head crested easily from the long, ragged slit. The rest came like a snake shedding its skin. Anwen let out a sigh.

The child was bluish and limp, smeared with blood and white grease. A girl. Hagar held her, shaking. She had encountered many newborns over the years. Some she had delivered, some she had dissected.

Cox was murmuring something, over and over. Hagar could make out his words: *Is she alive?*

The baby convulsed. Her toothless mouth dilated and she started crying – a thin, abrasive keening. Hagar held her under the armpits. The umbilical cord trailed down into an incision which was already closing.

She handed the baby to her assistant and clamped off the cord. The child needed warmth, sustenance – things which, until a few seconds ago, it had never been without. No wonder we forget our true nature when we enter this world. Life is the beginning of lack. It is a machine for producing pain.

Later, Hagar sat on a palm-rope hammock in a guest cabin, reading Deuteronomy.

'Grandpapa's a good man.'

She looked up with a start.

Arthur was standing beside the table, dabbling his slender fingers through the spout of a jug. He looked as he always had – as he always would: a slim young man, full brown hair swept into a side-parting, his eyes slightly too small perhaps, his ears slightly too large, features just peculiar enough to be distinctive, a gaze just sullen enough to be handsome. He wore a light cotton shirt with the sleeves rolled up to the elbows.

'He bore all the pain just for her.' Arthur smiled. 'Thoughtful of him.'

Hagar felt the room closing in. Arthur was back. The angel had come.

'Why are you here?' she said.

'No need to whisper. They won't hear you. They're busy with Auntie.'

Behind him, through the wide diamond-shaped porthole, lay Fat Maw Bay. Afternoon sun scattered gleaming flakes amongst cutters, junks and low-roofed houseboats. A colony of heavily pregnant sea serpents had crawled up onto the curving breakwater of Lotan Reef, sunning their fat, scaled bellies. When gulls flew too close, the sea serpents lifted their broad, wedge-shaped heads and spat gouts of hot venom. Poison clouds hung in the sunshine, sparkling ruby, emerald.

Hagar closed her Bible and wrapped it in a cloth. 'I thought you'd abandoned me.'

Arthur's smile softened with cloying, proprietary pity. 'Of course you did. You always do.'

Hagar looked away, trying to hide her disgust. He was several centuries younger than her, yet already he carried himself with overfamiliar, smug avuncularity. But he was her only hope.

Slyly she looked him up and down, noting the clothes he had selected, the age he had chosen to present himself as. She pictured him as he truly was. He claimed to be at peace, but the figure she saw was a masquerade. He was ashamed of his true form. And no marvel.

'What will happen?' she said.

'Either they give the child away, or someone takes her. Maybe that someone is you. I only see glimpses, like light shining through holes in a tapestry.'

'Do her powers work?'

Arthur closed his fist around the jug's narrow throat. 'Yes. Not yet. But they will do.' He squeezed; his fingers passed through. 'They name her Sarai.'

Hagar gave a short, mirthless laugh. 'Of course. So you want me to . . .' Hagar glanced at the wall, lowered her voice. 'Should I take her into my custody?'

Arthur glanced at his palm. He looked round at her.

'I'm not your sergeant. I'm not here to give you orders. Do as you wish.'

Her tolerance reached its limit. 'Don't pander to me, boy. My wish is for guidance, instruction. Without that, you're no use at all.'

Arthur seemed unperturbed by her outburst. Indeed, he seemed to enjoy how it threw his exaggerated serenity into greater relief.

'I'm sorry.' He beamed beatifically. 'I must seem capricious, materialising and vanishing, dropping little half-clues and leaving you to do all the work. If I could control my gifts, I would.' His smooth brow creased with affected worry. 'I so *wish* I could hurry things along. The paths to victory are very narrow indeed. But I *see* them. They gleam like golden threads in the darkness. I don't think anything can stop us.'

'I could slit my wrists.'

He laughed.

'You could. But you don't.' His gaze shifted to the Bible in her lap. 'You have free will, of course. You're always choosing. Every action you take alters the course of history. Each decision ripples out through the system – it affects more people than you'd ever believe. We have incredible power, but we deny it. We're terrified. It makes us complicit. The knowledge was too much for poor Gideon. He's not yet ready. He didn't understand.' Arthur looked melancholy again. 'How could he? How can you?'

Teardrops gemmed in his eyes. Hagar did not know if he was really crying, deep in the pit where his true body lay, or if they were a staging choice. Perhaps he was sad. Certainly, he wanted her to think of him as sad.

'I'm not a child,' she said. 'You of all people should know that appearances deceive.'

'Of course.' His eye pinched a little. 'It's just a shell, isn't it?' He hung his head. 'I must seem very gauche to you. A very callow angel indeed.'

'Just tell me what to do.'

'Right.' Arthur turned towards the cabin door. 'I'm afraid Grandmama doesn't trust you – quite wisely, as it will turn out. She knows how rare this birth is.'

'It's not rare. It's unprecedented.' Hagar touched her bottom lip.

'That's why she has no intention of letting you leave this ship alive.'

Hagar felt a sick, spreading comprehension. She glanced at her belt and jacket, hanging above her boots from a varnished christwood peg.

'How long have I got?'

On the table sat a wooden breakfast trencher, covered in seeds and fruit rinds. Arthur held his fore and middle fingers above the scalloped edge and administered a sharp tap. The trencher shivered gently. He gave a little sigh of pleasure.

'Oh, maybe five minutes. The guards in the corridor break your legs if you try to run.'

'Help me escape.'

'How? I'm barely here.' He wafted his hands through a wooden support pillar. 'And I don't want Grandmama finding out I'm still alive. Not yet. You'll find a way. You always do. You must. How else could you be there at the end?' He was fading, the curve of his cheek turning to vapour. 'Already? Oh blast.'

'Wait.'

'I can't.' Where sunlight struck his legs, they turned see-through, glistering with ice crystals. 'I'm too weak. This is why I need you. Unshackle yourself from Morgellon. Use Sarai once she grows into her gifts. Find Gideon and Grandmama and bring them to me. She can use their suffering to end death.'

'But what do I do *now*?'

He swatted at the air, his palm sloughing apart. 'Grandpapa loves his daughter. Truly loves her. That's his weak spot, if you've the stomach for it.' She could hear Arthur's grin, even as his features faded. 'Don't turn your back on Loosley. And take a deep breath.'

'What's that supposed to—'

'Back soon, lovely. Ta-ta.'

Even as she leapt from the hammock she knew it was useless. A faint wisp winked out and he was gone.

Standing alone in the cabin, Hagar felt a churning heat in her belly. She had waited so long for him to guide her, countless nights when she had felt lost and lonely and hollow. Seeing him now hardened a conviction that had been building for a long time.

She did not like the angel. She did not trust him.

And when the time came, she would kill him too.

Anwen Stokeham, Lady Dellapeste, sat on a high-backed bamboo chair, a blue silk blanket draped over her legs. Golden hair, combed straight, came down to the embroidered shoulders of an otherwise simple cream gown. A velvet mask obscured the upper part of her face. That was new.

'I've named her Sarai.'

Hagar shivered. It was Mr Cox who spoke. The valet sat on a padded seat to his mistress's right, holding the swaddled baby, gazing at its scrunched, putty-coloured face. He was a wan, round-shouldered fellow who appeared to be in his late twenties physically, his chocolate-coloured hair uncombed and his jaw shaded with stubble. They had sent for her about five minutes after Arthur had disappeared, just as promised.

Hagar glanced from Cox to his mistress, confused by his breach of etiquette. Lady Dellapeste smiled thinly. Again, it was Cox who spoke, in a hoarse, quavering voice:

'Mr Cox is my herald. He now speaks on my behalf. Or perhaps it is more proper to say, I speak through him.'

Hagar frowned. This was new too.

She remembered the fraught young woman she first encountered in England decades ago, in secret meetings at Alderberen Hall. The trauma of her arising. How, upon receiving the honours, the young woman's thoughts had blurred with her valet's, driving both to the brink of madness.

She seemed saner now. But it was always like this with the young ones. Pantomime vanity. A sudden obsession with etiquette. Anwen's delusions had not disappeared – they had simply become less original. The molten lunacy of her first few weeks had cooled into the sanctified folly of tradition.

Hagar made eye contact with the figure behind the mask. As she bowed, she pictured the roll of puce bowel inside Anwen's stomach. Flesh-thing. Even you.

'As you wish, Endlessness.'

This seemed to please Lady Dellapeste greatly. Anwen made a show of sitting back in her chair, the lacquered bamboo creaking as she stroked her fingertips along the armrest. Nothing about her demeanour suggested she had given birth less than three hours ago – her relatively trivial injuries would have healed fully by now. Birth was just another kind of suffering to which peers were impervious.

'Thank you for your assistance,' she said, through Cox. 'You understand why I was unable to divulge the precise nature of the work before you arrived.'

'I was . . . surprised you entrusted me with such a responsibility, Endlessness.' She had almost said 'flattered', but that would have been a lie.

'You're the most experienced surgeon in the world. Perhaps in history. I would have settled for no less.'

Mindful of Arthur's words, Hagar kept her eyes on the baby as she bowed. 'I understand, Endlessness.'

Cox adjusted his grip on little Sarai, softly dandling her. She was an improbable, goblinoid thing with catfish lips, her temples still smeared with waxy white traces of vernix. Hagar wondered where the wet nurse was – why Cox bothered touching the child at all.

As she studied Cox's expression, she realised Arthur was right. Perhaps Anwen and Cox had attempted the impossible – a child born to a peer and a servant – in the hope of harnessing her powers and expanding their empire. But all thoughts of conquest had gone from Cox's face. He gazed down on his daughter with a look of meek incomprehension. The poor fool had fallen in love.

He flexed his lips. Hagar wondered whether he interpreted broad sentiments, whether he heard Anwen's voice in his head, or if she simply puppeted him.

'Will you pass on news of the birth to your master?' he said.

'Lord Jejunus prefers to stay within the safety of his palace, these days,' said Hagar, frankly. 'I've not been welcome in Athanasia for some time.'

Lady Dellapeste's lips curled into a smile below her mask.

'What do you think my daughter's powers will be?'

Hagar glanced at the two diamond-shaped portholes. The glass was thick and braced with lead crosspieces. Impossible to escape through without tools.

'I couldn't say for sure.'

'But in your best estimation. You've lived so very long, after all.' Lady Dellapeste rose easily from her chair, the blanket dropping round her boots. 'You must have your suspicions.'

Hagar glanced across at Cox. On the table beside him was a

bottle of Avalonian nectar – putrid, viscous stuff made from heavily spiced fermented berries – and a blue glass bottle of Cambridge rum, almost empty, a sunbeam lighting up a cut crystal tumbler beside it.

'A peer has not given birth within my lifetime. But there are rumours that it happened once before.'

Lady Dellapeste's head shifted beneath her hood as she turned to look at the baby. 'Go on,' she said through Cox.

'I have offered my opinion, Endlessness.'

'What powers did her predecessor have?'

'You don't know?'

Within the mask, her eyes narrowed. 'I am asking that you *tell* me.'

Hagar tried to appear blandly oblivious to the danger she was in. 'It's said he ate pain. He could use it to shape reality into whatever he desired. Nothing was impossible to him. He raised palaces from bare rock. Crossed the globe in a blink. Flattened cities with a snap of his fingers. Undid death.'

Anwen brought her palm down on the arm of the chair. 'Enough!'

Sarai started whimpering softly. Cox stood, shakily, and began to pace back and forth, rocking the baby. He kept his gaze on his daughter as he channelled his mistress, intoning words as if dictating to a secretary: 'Thank you, Miss Ingery, for confirming what I have long suspected. The great houses of the perpetuum know how powerful she is likely to be and consequently will make plans to deal with the existential threat she poses to them.'

'Endlessness . . . forgive my presumption, but it sounds as if you fear my master might wish your daughter harm.' Her mouth had gone dry. 'Upon my soul, I will tell him nothing of our meeting if you wish it.' She would tell him nothing of the meeting regardless.

'Upon your soul?' Cox's voice rang with mocking wonder. 'Didn't you already sell it to the Butcher of Atmanloka?'

Hagar flinched. They would not speak of Morgellon with such candour if they had any intention of letting her live.

She straightened her spine. 'He grieves, Endlessness. You'd want to carve your sorrow into the world if you'd lost all he has.' The impropriety of making such personal remarks had a delicious electric edge.

Lady Dellapeste rose from her chair. 'And you, Mistress Ingery. You of the three centuries. What have you lost?'

A strange ache clutched at the pit of Hagar's stomach. Her nostrils burned with a phantom smell. These people were just children. They had not the slightest conception of true suffering. They would learn in time, of course. The honours guaranteed that.

Hagar looked Anwen in the eyes. '*Where wast thou when I laid the foundations of the earth? Have the gates of death been opened unto thee?*'

Lady Dellapeste's lower lip curled with disdain. 'Three hundred years,' said Cox, 'and you still parrot the drab axioms of Scripture. How very ordinary you are, little girl.'

Hagar allowed her head to sag under the rebuke. *Behold, I am vile.* Perhaps Anwen would underestimate her if she seemed contrite.

'Endlessness, I perceive that I have offended you and beg your leave to retire.'

'Your master is a coward.'

Hagar laughed – a husky, ruined bark from the back of her throat. 'So are we all, in time.' It had not always been so.

Cox hugged the swaddled child to his chest. 'Mr Loosley will escort you back to your quarters.'

Hagar heard the click of the door unlatching. She spun round as he entered: a lean, broad-shouldered vesperi in a blue cassock edged with oval buttons and silver trim. His mouth was a snarl of mismatching teeth; a cudgel hung from one side of his belt, a flint-lock pistol from the other.

Hagar had heard rumours Lady Dellapeste had taken a second valet. Not just male, but a vesperi – another childish attempt to scandalise the ganzplenum.

Arthur's warning rang through her head. Loosley looked canny enough – calm, brutishly decisive – but did he expect her to submit without a struggle? Did he think it would be as easy as restraining a child?

'Thank you for your hospitality, Endlessness.'

'Before you go.' Lady Dellapeste gestured towards Cox with an open palm. 'Take a look at the child your master wants dead.'

Hagar hesitated, glancing between Anwen and Loosley. It was true that Morgellon would want Sarai dead. In this, he was not especially cruel – it was just sound politics.

Sarai's scalp was coated in a slick of downy black hair. A constellation of deep red bruises showed where Hagar's fingertips had dug into her skull. That such a fragile thing could end the world—

Hagar came round on the floor. A tone rang in her ears. Her temple pounded.

Someone had struck her. *Don't turn your back on Loosley.* A pressure in the base of her spine. Someone was kneeling on her, binding her hands. Cord bit into her wrists.

She struggled, but it was too late. A wave of nausea washed through her.

And from somewhere off to the left, came the sound of a father crooning to his child, laughing.

Loosley waited till the sun had set, then lowered her, bound in chains and sailcloth, into the pinnace moored on the galleon *Ceffyl Dŵr*'s starboard side. The oars creaked in their mounts as he rowed out into open sea, his boots planted against the thwart, briar pipe hanging from the corner of his mouth.

The black ocean rose and slumped beneath them. Her tongue was folded against the stiff dry rag in her mouth. By the light of the moon she watched Loosley's noseleaf flex in rhythm with his strokes. Once they were a good distance out, he slung the anchor over the side, sat and finished his pipe.

He had a purposeful composure that Hagar respected. She sensed no cruelty in him, and that was unfortunate, because it meant he was unlikely to linger over his task. He would not relish hurting her, would experience no pleasure except the brief satisfaction of a command successfully executed.

She watched thick, silver-edged clouds advancing in a slow avalanche, blotting out the stars. Why couldn't Arthur appear now, in a blast of lucent vapour, and scare Loosley into the sea?

Impossible, of course. His brief appearance – and that idiotic trick with the trencher – would have left him exhausted. She would not see him again for weeks – perhaps months. Besides, Loosley did not strike her as the sort to startle easily.

She wondered if she was to die by drowning, like St Florian, or by stabbing, like St Cassian. She had experienced the latter many times by proxy – punctures and slashes from daggers, swords, pikes, javelins and polearms, and once when Morgellon had drunkenly slipped from the balcony of his summer palace in Fat Maw and spitted himself three storeys below on the glass minaret of an ornamental fountain. Drowning she had felt only once, when the royal fleet was lost to a storm off the Makashalam Peninsula; from what she remembered it was like being stabbed in both lungs simultaneously – the sucking, flooding throb, the horrible catch when the breath would not come.

Loosley tapped his pipe out into the water. He folded his arms and rested them across his bony knees. He was gazing towards the coast, where fires were burning under salt cauldrons, lighting the wet mouths of inlets that mazed inland towards seamilk paddies and jellyfish farms. A breeze ghosted the long whiskers around his mouth.

He sat like that for some time, watching the land. He lit another pipe and smoked it. Hagar wondered what he was waiting for.

He glanced at her. She could not see his eyes. In the darkness, with his ears protruding, his head had the profile of a vast black moth. He reached towards her eyes with fingers that had fused into a claw.

His hand closed over the rag in her mouth. He tugged it out. Hagar coughed and gasped; the rag had absorbed all the moisture from her mouth and her tongue was covered in itchy fibres.

Loosley retrieved something from the bow and brought it towards her face. Metal glinted in the moonlight; she braced. Her lips felt the cold nozzle of a waterskin.

She had drunk nothing since breakfast. Water dribbled over her lips, lukewarm and chalky. Perhaps it was poisoned. More likely, this was his way of saying no hard feelings. She had encountered this type of senior henchman before – they eased their guilt through small acts of clemency, solidarity almost.

He let her drink till she turned her head away, water spilling down her lips. He set the waterskin down beside him and returned his gaze to the coast.

Hagar flexed her stiff jaw, running her tongue over her gums.

'What's your name?' Her voice came out in a rasping whisper, even more desiccated than usual. Her throat felt raw and cracked.

His ear twitched.

'The one they gave you at jatironi, I mean,' she said. She was taking a gamble. Perhaps vesperi no longer sent their children away to complete their transitions. Traditions changed, and she did not always keep up.

Loosley rolled his shoulders back and yawned. He turned his head towards her, eyes gleaming with the faint lustre of fire opals.

'She killed my sister.'

The voice that emerged from the scarred, broken-fanged face was soft and measured – hints of Low Thelusian's glottal purr smoothed by the precise consonants of southern Sinpanian aristocracy. He glanced down, brushed something from the silver galloon trim of his cuffs.

Hagar was momentarily wrongfooted. 'Lady Dellapeste?'

Loosley threaded his fingers and stared out across the water. He nodded.

'My sister was murdered by her soldiers during the Wind and Thunder uprising.' He breathed through the sharp prongs of his fangs. 'They went town to town staging public executions.'

Hagar half-remembered reading reports of a merchants' blockade over war duties. Her time in the abbey had distanced her from worldly affairs.

'I ambushed her riverboat. Killed her guards. Broke into her cabin and shot her through the head.'

'Alone?'

'Of course. Relying on others would have risked betrayal.'

'Of course.'

'I never believed in the stories of peers regenerating. Thought this whole mess was folklore.' Loosley grinned bitterly. 'She sat up, soaked in blood. Mistook me for a common robber. Smiled. Offered me employment.'

'Can she hear your thoughts?'

'Not like Rutherford's.' Hagar recognised the subtle shift in his intonation all too clearly – revulsion, masking shameful, perverse jealousy. He wanted Anwen to need him, despite himself. He cleared his throat. 'Perhaps it's the species barrier. But I don't think there's a him or her any more. Their minds have bled into one. They can sense my mood. My rough location.' He tapped the side of his skull. 'They're not here now. They sleep.'

The dock chains jankled as Hagar twisted in her constraints. The sailcloth was wrapped tightly around her, pinning her arms to her back. Her left leg had gone numb.

Loosley took a leather pouch from his coat and began refilling his pipe. 'I hear you're in disgrace.'

'My master refuses to see me.'

'Is it true you murdered his valet?'

'It's complicated,' said Hagar.

Loosley struck a match and lit his pipe. He closed his eyes. His tattered, useless wings expanded as he inhaled. He blew a ball of smoke then drew in it with his index finger: a vertical stroke, two quick lateral slashes and a loop. It smeared apart on the wind.

A smokelorist's prayer – a contract written on the air itself. How odd that Loosley should follow a religion that taught that change, decay and loss were unavoidable – he of the perpetual youth, he who feared death.

'She's planning to invade England.'

Hagar laughed sharply. 'Impossible.'

'We'll see.' He looked down at her. 'She'd rather die than let anyone intimidate her.'

Hagar felt sick and strange. The motion of the boat seemed to amplify, growing stormy. Why was he telling her? A confession? A token show of rebellion? Or was it simply that, in a few moments, she would be dead?

Loosley's silhouetted ears pricked. He straightened up, rotating his head left to right, then right to left, in slow, patrolling sweeps. He fixed her with a piercing stare.

'If you had the chance to kill the Grand-Duc, would you?'

Hagar shut her eyes. She saw Morgellon in the throne room. Gold fixtures. She examined her heart and discovered a knotty pain.

‘I don’t know,’ she said honestly.

Loosley stood, looking landward.

‘Someone’s coming.’ He walked to Hagar and grasped the sailcloth binding her. With a grunt, he lifted her.

The chains hung heavy. She struggled to pull her arms free but she was tightly swaddled.

‘Wait,’ she said, panic rising.

Loosley flashed her a look of boredom. ‘Our time is up.’

He swung her out over the portside gunwale, the pinnace listing under the weight. She kicked and thrashed, but the sailcloth held fast. A breeze drifted from the shore, heavy with the scent of vassago bushes. In the distance, a lean yawl, its mainsail trimmed, was cutting through the milky water.

She looked back at Loosley. He inhaled, and the soft, fanning gills of his scarred-up noseleaf closed in on one another. She tried to think of something to delay him, some sly thrust. But she knew all too well the bluster of the condemned. Any pledge would look like a lie.

‘If you kill me, I can’t finish my work.’

Loosley hesitated. ‘Yes,’ he said. ‘That’s precisely why I’m doing this.’

She felt his grip relax. She gasped. Her back slapped into the skin of the ocean. Cool water rushed over her ears, her face. Her vision blurred. A stream of silver bubbles rose from her trailing hair as she sank. Binding iron chains dragged her down, down. She relaxed her muscles. Better to conserve air until she touched the seabed, where the chains might slacken. The underside of the pinnace faded as light disappeared, a shrinking silhouette that merged with the night sky, as if Loosley’s little boat were rising to Heaven.

At last, her spine settled into silt. She kicked downwards with both feet, trying to squirm from her wrappings. He had bound her so tightly she could barely bend her knees. If she could pull an arm free from behind her back, the sail would loosen and she could escape.

Pinpricks of light sparked in a blue-black murk. The surface looked terrifyingly far away. She wanted to struggle, thrash, but she forced herself to think, strategise. The slightest unnecessary movement would consume air. Her head pounded, filling with a black fog.

She could feel death's hunger. She had denied it all these years. Finally, it had come to claim her.

Her thoughts were melting into one another. This was it – the starvation of the brain, experienced from the inside. It had been vanity to follow Arthur, to believe he could lead her to salvation. Perhaps this was God's will.

If she used her last moments to curse and fight, to feel fear and regret, to cling to life, she would perpetuate the cycle all over again. Who was she to deny providence?

Her heart drummed in her ears. She stopped resisting, let the heavy iron links pin her to the ocean floor. A fluttering glow spread across the darks of her closed eyelids. Her lungs filled with bursting, swelling pain.

They that are in the flesh cannot please God. She must submit.

In the darkness, golden flowers bloomed.

Submit.

Her head had gone numb. She tensed against the ache in her chest.

Submit.

She would never see Morgellon again.

The thought cut through her pain. Morgellon, trapped in his wretched body, wracked by grief and greed and bitterness. How many countless centuries would he remain now, caught in delusion, sucking others into the threshing cyclone of his misery?

Submit.

He needed her. She was selfish to leave.

Submit.

She did not want to die. Not yet.

Submit.

She strained against her chains. *Oh dear Lord, please save me. I am weak.*

She had to breathe. Seawater licked her eyelids, her closed lips.

I am useless. I am nothing without your grace.

The whole seabed tilted around her skull. Her heels rose towards Heaven. She was passing out.

The bare flesh of her scalp dragged through silt. Her air-starved brain was hallucinating as it shut down. Back at the École De La

Sagesse Immortels, she had read a fascinating book on the many anomalous artefacts generated by the mind in extremis, but oddly she could not recall any of them, hair brushing her face as she ascended, the ringing in her ears drowning out thought, merging with the sharp white light, with the ache in her chest, so sound and colour became one, she was returning to the vanishing point where all things merge, was remembering herself, was rising towards it rising rising—

She was actually rising. The shock almost made her inhale. She was upside-down and ascending, feet first, seawater flowing over her throat, around her jaw, pushing into her nostrils. Why was she rising? Oh God, she had to breathe. She bit her lip, fighting the craving for air.

She inhaled. Fluid hit her throat, her lungs. She coughed. Her chest knifed with cramps. She inhaled more water; the cramps turned to crushing pain. Sound returned: thumps and clanking iron. Wind whipped across her wet cheeks. She hacked; her chest stung. She was out of the water, hanging upside-down in mid-air.

Strong hands swung her up and round and dumped her onto the floor of a boat. Her breath snagged with each gasp; she rolled onto her side and hacked up sputum. Her eyes were raw from saltwater. She barely perceived the figure standing over her.

Hagar spluttered and spat. She hurt inside and out. It began to rain. Bullet-sized droplets drummed the deck. The figure spread their wings as an umbrella.

Loosley? No – this was a different boat. A single mast stretched up, impaling the clouded full moon. The silhouette looming over her was leaner, taller, the ears positioned higher up the head.

Thunder crumped in the purpling middle distance. The figure hauled in a small driftwood buoy on the end of a frayed rope. Already the mainsail was luffing fractiously, snapping moisture from its surface as the wind picked up. A storm was coming – lashing, punitive, righteous.

The figure moved with calm efficiency, raising the anchor and taking their place at the stern. As the boat drifted starboard, the mainsail began to fill. The figure brought the boat round in a slow, smooth curve; the boom swept over Hagar's head with a creak as they jibbed, then they were creaming west through the ocean, back towards Fat Maw.

It hurt to swallow. The chains had left tender bruises across her arms and back. She opened her mouth and let the rain strike her tongue in refreshing gobbets that tasted of sweet pollen.

'I rather think this makes us even,' said the figure at the stern, tacking into the wind as they approached the reef.

Hagar tilted her head back. She squinted through the rain.

'Bechstein?'

A flash of lightning lit a tableau of familiar features – the long nostril slits sunken within the subtly fleur-de-lis-shaped noseleaf, the regal, almost impertinent underbite, the thin, knifing eyes. It was the deposed Lord Cambridge. A waxed leather half-cloak hung about his shoulders, finished at the front with a brass buckle shaped like a stylised sun with eight spokes radiating from it. She blinked, studying his ghost-bright afterimage.

'I no longer use that name.' Though his face was shadowed, she could hear his scowl.

'I thought you were dead.'

'Apparently our respective Makers believe we have work to finish.'

Hagar snorted. Her sinuses stung with brine. She spat.

'We have the same creator. And He loves you, Mortifer.'

The ex-Lord Cambridge let out a mirthless snort. 'Hmm. I heard you'd spent time with the shadow order.'

Rain raked the skin of the ocean in crackling sheets. Waves began striking them abeam, slapping over their port side in bright blasts of spume.

'What do you plan to do with me?' she called over the rising wind.

'Release you, of course.'

'What?'

'Some of us see Maison Jejunus as a . . . necessary counterbalance.' The yawl crested a peak and became briefly weightless, before the keel thudded into the next wave. Bechstein strained to keep control of the tiller. Lightning flashed again, closer this time, and she saw mahogany fur slicked down the sharp contours of his cheekbones, the white fangs beneath set in a determined grimace.

Thunder boomed an instant later. 'Without you, Morgellon would be . . . ugh!' The wind ripped his wings back, exposing his head to the rain. He turned into the wind, using his body as a windbreak until he could ruck them shut. 'Your little protégée Anwen must be stopped.'

Hagar lay there, feeling her heart beat against her chains – *pum pum pum*. Rain struck her face. She was alive.

'And even Loosley believes this?'

'*Especially* Loosley. Why do you think he serves her so loyally?'

'It's his best chance of killing her.'

Bechstein flashed her a look. She had answered too quickly, with far too much venom – had revealed that she understood Loosley all too well.

The bottom of the yawl was filling with water. She shuffled and writhed like a caterpillar until she had propped her back against the mainmast. The first thing she saw was the black carcass of Lotan Reef bearing down on their port side.

Bechstein tacked hard to starboard. The boom swished overhead and the mainsail bellied with a woof. The reef rushed towards them, growing bigger, bigger. She felt the tide beneath the hull, sucking them towards the mass of coral-scabbed bone.

As if accepting the inevitable, Bechstein steered into the current, pointing their bow at the reef. The yawl accelerated. Her arms still bound behind her back, Hagar awaited the impact with a strange, tingling awe.

Just as they were about to hit, Bechstein threw his shoulder against the tiller. With the extra momentum of the tide, the boat turned cleanly, shearing through the swell. Their portside swung to within an inch of the great, petrified megacadaver, so close that Hagar could make out the polychromatic sheen of moonlit microorganisms coating its titanic ribs. She braced. The collision never came; the yawl glided past, as if sliding on greased rails.

As they passed the breakwater, the wind dropped. In the snug of the bay, the waves eased to a steady, undulating pulse. The jungle gasped under the rain. Bechstein's shoulders slumped.

'She thinks she can conquer the old world,' he said.

Hagar tried to disguise her fierce interest with a look of disdain.

'Mm. Loosley said. I wonder. It was her home, after all. She's young. She wants to impress us. It's probably bluster.'

'Perhaps.' Bechstein locked the tiller and stood. He pulled a sickle from his belt. 'And perhaps not.' He knelt before Hagar and raised the whetted edge to her throat. 'Now her daughter is born, we may have good reason to be impressed.' He hooked the crescent tip inside the sailcloth and dragged it downwards until it met chain. The material slit easily as skin. He made a second incision behind her and her arms flopped free. Her chains sagged. Bright starbursts of pain erupted from her joints.

'There,' said Bechstein.

Hagar rolled her shoulders, wincing. He stood over her, sickle in hand, rain dripping from his wings.

'You won't let me remember this conversation, will you?' she said.

'It's safest if you don't.' His face was completely in shadow. 'I work best in darkness.'

Hagar nodded with what she hoped looked like weary resignation. '*In umbres sorores*. It's the wisest path.'

'And the loneliest.' He hesitated. 'Shame, really. There are so few of us left.' He wiped rain from his eyes. 'You'll be a little disoriented, but I'll only take these last few minutes. You'll probably think the tide washed you back to shore. That'll be nice for you, won't it? Another confirmation of the hand of providence.'

She glanced across the bay, towards the few faint lights of the stilt city, the junks and coracles and sampans knocking together in the shelter of piers and jetties and launches. A lantern burned outside the harbourmistress's hut, swaying at the top of its long pole. She slapped wet hair from her face.

'What would you have me do with my new freedom?'

Bechstein lowered his sickle. Already she saw him focusing energy in the other hand, vapour rising from his fingers as he prepared to scrub their encounter from her memory. Many were the stories of Lord Cambridge's nepenthean touch. Of all the losses he was accused of inflicting upon his foes, it was at once the most merciful and the cruellest. Her nostrils tingled with a smell like ozone and old coins.

'*Lo, then would I wander far off, and remain in the wilderness. I would hasten my escape from the windy storm and tempest.*'

The words made her scalp prickle. She felt awake to the squalls, the thunder, the cool water pooling round her tingling wrists and ankles.

'Well.' She dipped her head and chuckled in her broken, ruined fashion. 'Mortifer Bechstein is quoting me Scripture.'

'Decades of exile offer a little reading time. There's a tragic poetry in the lives of the saints.' He focused power in his hand, his spindly fingers performing slow arpeggios. 'And Mortifer Bechstein is dead. I'm just a shadow.'

Gently, she slid her feet from her boots. 'That sounded like regret. Sins can't be cast off so easily – I've tried.'

He spread his leathery wings. There were rents in the membrane where the moon shone through. Vapour steamed from his fist.

'*Oh, that I had wings like a dove. For then I would fly away, and be at rest.*'

She rose placidly, offering her brow. He moved to place his palm and administer the memory-cleanse.

Hagar smiled. '*There is no peace, saith my God, to the wicked.*'

She sidestepped, twisted, and dropped backwards over the gunwale.

She stretched her arms cruciform and let the ocean hold her as she sank. Saltwater bathed her bruises. Many were the tortures this world inflicted, but she would not suffer it to rob her of her past. No memory, no remorse. No remorse, no salvation.

She turned underwater and began swimming for shore with fast, purposeful strokes.

CHAPTER 13
PATIENCE

Delphine stood, panting.

Patience DeGroot rubbed her jaw with her human hand. Ropes of maroon flesh trailed from her shoulder and lay on the floor in slack, juicewet coils.

'You disgusting, pathetic little monster,' said Delphine.

Patience inhaled, pursing her lips together as she held the breath, then let out a long sigh.

She smiled. 'It really is you.'

Delphine had imagined this moment many times, inventing various scenarios where they might meet again, investing each with the vivid detail of an erotic fantasy – what they would be wearing, the look on Patience's face, the utter submission, the violence – never once believing that it might come to pass.

She struggled to reconcile the figure in front of her with the one from her memories. Patience wore a white cotton dress, ankle-length, split up to the knee. Her cheeks were pink and strands of hair not pulled back into her snaking blond braid hung across her face in a messy fringe.

The reality was all wrong. Patience seemed like a replica of herself. Her hair had changed. Delphine hung her head. Talking with Butler had spoilt all her rage. It was tainted with awareness.

'You might want a sit-down,' said Patience. With a dragging noise, her tendrils slid back into her shoulder, plaiting and melding into a shapeless, fleshy club.

Rusted iron rings and brackets hung from the walls. The stonework bore several dark stains. Radio equipment lay stacked on a table. To the left was a doorway with a heavy stone lintel, and steps leading up.

Delphine touched her machine pistol through her shirt.

'I'll be upstairs.'

'It's a trap,' said Patience, her angel arm wrapped in white muslin fastened with a silver pin. 'Hundred per cent.'

They were in a large chamber in the old jail's northwestern turret. Butler stood with his wings folded, beside the window, smoking a cigarette and blowing the smoke through the narrow slit.

'You sound very sure.'

'Would you prefer I hedged? Hmm. Who can say? Maybe the Doyenne just wants what's best for you.'

Delphine sat in a cushioned chair, her machine pistol and loose ammunition laid out on a rattan side-table. Distributed across several tables was a substantial spread – bowls of steamed grains mixed with vegetables, baked spiced tubers, soft cheeses, flatbreads studded with dried cherries, clear jellies, soup, dumplings and ramekins of chutneys and pickles. Patience had told them to help themselves – the mailboat brought food every morning but she threw most of it away. Alice and Martha sat next to each other, working through a bowl of fruits.

Butler looked back over his shoulder. 'Maybe she wants what's worst for the perpetuum. The enemy of my enemy.'

'Darling, you really are an optimist. Doyenne Lesang has been consolidating power for years. The brick clique are hers in all but name. North of the river is all hers.'

'You get on well enough, don't you?'

'Oh, she won't pick fights unnecessarily. She'll be perfectly friendly until she decides it no longer suits her. She's been moving small arms into the undercity for months. Not isolated batches. Big numbers. Doyenno Becquel has the saltpetre gunsmiths working day and night.'

'Sounds like someone's preparing for war,' said Butler.

'Or perhaps a coup d'état. It may very well suit Lesang's purposes to have you start a firefight with the city peace. Draw resources on their second-busiest night of the year. I suspect she wants Sheriff Kenner's people out of the way.'

'You haven't answered my question. Can you help us?'

'Of course I can,' said Patience, looking irritated. 'The question isn't *can*. It's *will*. As it happens, our goals are in concordance. If this doctor fellow's claims are even half-true, he must be sitting on a great deal of very dangerous research. There are many people I want to ensure don't get their hands on it. Lesang gave you an address, didn't she?'

Butler waved the slip of paper.

'Good. In that case, Reggie can help you brute-force your way in, and I can pull you and the doctor out with my angel-arm.'

'By "brute-force" you mean "kill".'

'Unless you can charm the officers into resigning, yes. Kenner's staff are very loyal. Trust me. I've been trying to corrupt them for years.'

Delphine lifted a glass teapot, pear-shaped with a narrow swan-necked spout. She tilted it until a column of umber-red liquid flowed into her cup. The ritual helped steady her nerves.

'What if we don't go in at all?' she said.

Everyone turned and looked.

'What do you mean?' said Butler.

She poured tea for Alice and Martha. Her pale, lineless hand was marked with tiny red nicks and scratches. Though she could ball it into a fist and haul rope, it looked weaker than her old one, the one with liver spots and raised tendons, veins showing through loose skin. That had been the hand of someone with stories. Someone who didn't give a damn.

'Didn't that, whatever her name was, say that he'd given all his notes to a lawyer for safe-keeping?' Delphine said.

Patience glanced at Butler. 'What's this?'

He sniffed. 'Yes, something like that. To be destroyed if he's bumped off. What's your point?'

'Why don't we just go straight to the lawyer?'

There was a long silence. She sluiced hot tea through her teeth. It had a floral, fruity smokiness, with a bitter tang at the finish as a palate cleanser. All in all it was a bit busier than she preferred.

Butler looked down at the stub of his cigarette. 'That sounds . . . almost not stupid.' He looked to Patience. 'Can we do that?'

'If we can find out who they are . . .' She stroked her angel-arm like a hunting dog. 'I can send out some feelers. You should all get some rest. There are bedrooms all over the place. I hardly use them. Just take one. The cleaners only come every few days and they're off for the festival.' She sniffed. 'I'll have us a name by morning.'

Delphine walked the full square of the corridors, gazing down through tall, glassless windows into a courtyard full of plants in neat rows. Couldn't be easy, growing stuff with such poor light.

She found a room facing east, out across the ocean. There were heavy rugs across the stone floor, and dressers with statuettes of odd sea creatures in pastel-coloured stone. The bed was a wide, square hammock, big as a king-sized bed, stretched tight across six curving wooden posts carved into spirals and stained a deep red. It was heaped with round pillows, a silky fur blanket folded into a triangle in one corner. On a bedside table was a small stoppered flask. She opened it. It smelt like some sort of alcohol, but creamy.

She walked to the barred window.

Outside, the moon was low across the water. She could hear waves crashing on the cliffs below. The wind smelt fresh and keen.

She felt hands on her shoulders. Thumbs pressed under her trapezius muscles, turned slow circles. A chin settled against the curve of her neck.

'We've been sent to prison,' said Alice.

Delphine fought the impulse to withdraw. Ever since they had encountered Reggie she had been feeling bruised, fearful in ways she had not let herself experience for years. She could not admit as much to Alice, of course. It was utterly stupid. Why was she so scared of letting herself feel? She had tried the other thing. The slow hunger strike. The locked room. The deep freeze.

Feeling as if she were dropping from an aeroplane, she tilted her head back. 'What are you in for?'

'I beat a man to death with a chair leg.'

Delphine tutted. 'You're supposed to say something titillating.' A glow was spreading through her upper back.

'You weren't there to see it.'

'Alice . . .'

'Well, you name a sexy crime, then.'

Delphine rocked side to side as Alice's hands moved down towards her waist. 'Jewel heist.'

Alice blew a raspberry.

'What?' said Delphine.

'So much planning.' She began steering Delphine towards the bed. 'My crime was wild . . . impulsive . . .'

'It sounds deranged.'

'Yes! I'm a monster!'

The huge hammock shook as Delphine fell onto it; the cushions bounced. She was laughing. Alice stood over her, undoing shirt buttons, her hair all messy.

If only they could hold onto this. If only they could dig their fingers into time and scoop it up and hoard it. Delphine felt herself standing outside the moment, terrified. This joy was temporary. It could not last. They could not last. The one she loved was mortal. They would age, they would sicken, they would die.

She wished dearly, intensely, that it were otherwise. What a fearful thing it is to be alive. What agony to be truly awake. And as they fell together, hot and free and breathless, she clung on, tight as she could.

'Advocate Ashesh-Ro,' said Patience, walking into the side room where they were eating a late breakfast. 'Her chambers are opposite the spire.' She slid a piece of paper across the table with a scribbled map and an address.

Delphine was eating a flatbread from the evening's meal, and drinking cold tea. She was ravenous. Martha was sitting on the floor, sorting through various objects she had retrieved from the foot of the cliffs before sunrise.

'Temperament?' said Butler.

'Hard worker. Model of integrity.'

'Bribes are out, then.'

'New lover every week but admirably reluctant to reveal trade secrets during pillow talk.' Patience looked Butler up and down, disguising a smile with her teacup. 'Though you never know . . .'

Butler emitted a low, disapproving growl from the back of his throat. 'Absolutely not.'

'Oh, you wouldn't need to *bed* her. If you didn't want to, that is. Just . . . keep her away from her chambers for an hour. I'm told when she's not working she likes to frequent the Salon Au Delà Du Temps in the high town. She's a rum drinker.'

'No.'

'But you look so smart,' said Alice.

'I prefer the murder option.'

'Butler!' said Delphine.

'I've found you all outfits,' said Patience. 'Legal vestments, and some costumes for the festival. You'll be able to move through the high town with reasonable anonymity.'

'What about getting in?' said Butler. 'If it's on the esplanade we can't very well go kicking down the front door.'

Patience cocked her head and smiled at him. 'Well, Butler, once again you'll have to rely on your legendary charm. There's a young fellow who works for her I think you ought to talk to . . .'

Children played in the frothing run-off from a burst water pipe – harka, vesperi, human – while in the adjoining alley Butler pinned a vesperi to the wall by his throat.

'Did you get them?'

The shadows were lengthening and the alley was dark. Delphine glanced about for peace officers. Butler placed his free hand on the young clerk's cheek, running the back of his fingers down the soft, grey fur with gentle, proprietary strokes. The clerk's eyeball was swollen and blood-glutted, trending orange down to a capillary-mazed red. He sucked in his chin and nodded.

Butler cast an idle glance towards the children as they squatted on their hams, racing little boats made of dry grass in the haemorrhaging flow. Delphine stood behind him with Alice.

'Give them to me,' said Butler, mildly.

The clerk closed his eyes and delved into a pocket of his oversized jacket. His hand withdrew clutching a bunch of large iron keys.

'Venner,' said Butler.

Delphine stepped forward and took them. They jangled and the clerk flinched.

She understood his anxiety – there was something disturbingly polished about the way Butler operated, a clinical edge to his menace. She recalled something of the awe she had felt when she first encountered him, sitting across from her in the van – he exerted a kind of gravity, as if all his years had accumulated inside him, gaining weight and pull.

'And you're sure you told no one,' said Butler.

The clerk nodded frantically.

'This is your last chance to own up if you did. It would be better for you to be honest. If I find out you've lied to me, I shall skin you and kill your family.' Butler relayed this information with horrifying blandness. Delphine was in no doubt as to his sincerity.

The clerk shook his head. 'I . . .' He could barely croak out the words. Butler relaxed his grip a little; the clerk inhaled sharply. His bulging eye lent him a manic look. 'I said nothing. I swear. I wouldn't . . . I wouldn't dare lie to you, sir.'

Butler smiled broadly. 'Good boy.' He cast a last glance over at the children, who continued to play, oblivious.

He slammed the clerk into the wall. Delphine jumped. He raised his other hand; braids of vapour rose from his fingers. A sharp odour hit the backs of her nostrils, like chlorine.

Butler clamped his steaming palm onto the clerk's scalp. The clerk's ears splayed; his eyes rolled back in his head. He writhed. His wings pumped, scraping against dirty red brick as he slid down the wall. Butler drew himself up to his full height, taking on a regal disdain in counterpoint to the clerk's cowed submission. In that moment, there really was something monstrous about him – a hunger in his gaze, in the way he seemed to feed on domination.

Butler let go. The clerk slumped. Delphine ran in and caught him under the armpits. He was surprisingly light, but it was a job to hoist him back upright, his head lolling against her shoulder as he murmured dazed nonsense in her ear.

'Let's go,' said Butler. 'He'll never know he met us.'

He walked out of the alley to the burst pipe, where he knelt and began to fill a leather waterskin. The children became wary at his approach, their laughter tailing off. Butler stood and glared at them. The children fell silent. Delphine's heart tightened; she hurried towards him. Butler pressed his taloned foot to the mouth of the pipe, spraying the children in a rainbow blast. They shrieked, giggled, scattered, then rallied, scooping up handfuls of water and flinging it at him. He shielded himself with his wings, then theatrically stumbled, fell, and lay supine while the children ritually soaked him, crowing their triumph.

He returned to Delphine dripping, his white tunic translucent and creasy, his dark fur flattened round the contours of his bones. He handed her the waterskin.

'Drink up.'

She accepted it numbly. The water had the faintest tang of blood.

'Gosh,' said Alice. 'Wow, you look so . . . fancy.'

Butler was wearing a sheer silk scarf with an open, embroidered jacket over a sort of maroon sarong. He had combed sweet, musky oil into his fur and above his long, taloned toes hung a pair of bronze cuff anklets set with polished opals.

'It's done, all right?' He flourished his jacket sleeves. 'I'm meeting her at the bar in an hour.'

'You've got a date?'

Butler scratched at the backs of his ears. 'Can we please get moving?'

Vesperi could not blush or sweat, but the way he was trying to hunch down into himself reminded Delphine of Algernon.

'Of course,' she said. 'We'll be done before you know it.'

The sun was setting by the time they reached the high town. Half the street was in shadow, the other half drenched a delirious red. Delphine began to feel nervous, her belly tensing. She kept focusing on the back of Alice's head, on locks of white-gold hair curling in the heat.

They entered the cobbled esplanade from the south end. Lamplighters were using poles to light paper lanterns hanging from trees. At the centre was a tower of sheer red stone, perhaps a hundred feet tall, capped with a silver turret that tapered to a shining needle.

Banners fluttered from the top and what looked like strings of fireworks hung around it.

Trains of big, ostrich-like birds stood in the shade of the trees, their long, ribbed beaks daubed with glowing paint, bells jangling from their leather harnesses. Here and there stood big wooden carvings of animals, most of which Delphine did not recognise. Folks were gathering around the barrows of food vendors, or watching acrobats, a harka axe-juggler, a bird trainer, and a long-haired, squat old woman who sucked coloured smoke from tubes attached to a series of large glass cylinders, blowing elaborate shapes for the delighted crowd.

Butler led Alice and Delphine off into the shade of a tall, spreading tree. 'There.'

He nodded towards a row of buildings. There was a display window full of tinted, abstract glassware, lit by oil lamps with spiral mantles that turned slowly as she watched, giving the impression that molten glass was flowing down out of thin air. Next door, separated by an alley, was a smaller mullioned window, then three stone steps leading up to a black door. From a metal bracket hung a sign depicting a balance scale holding an eight-pointed star and a mountain, around which was written: *ASHESH-RO – A Member of the Noble Southern College of Pandecti.*

Butler leaned in and spoke in an undertone. 'Remember: once you've got your robes on, get in, find the lockbox, get out. The clerk said it's probably upstairs. Best to get it now while there's plenty to distract everyone.'

Delphine tensed. 'There are people everywhere.'

'They don't care. They have their own stories. Trust me. Act like you've every right to be here and no one will notice.' He turned to Alice. 'Cross. You're playing lookout. Stand guard on the ground floor. If anyone enters who isn't me, shoot them.'

Alice bit down on her bottom lip, frowned. 'Won't that just attract more attention?'

'Of course. But it'll buy you enough time to run.'

'I don't want to kill anyone.'

Butler adjusted his collar. 'Then I suggest you work quickly. I'll do my damnedest to keep the Advocate occupied. If you hear my signal to get out, I don't mean in thirty seconds. I mean now. Got it?'

'Got it,' said Delphine.

'Right.' He slapped her on the shoulder and she winced. 'If we get separated, meet by the volunteer fire wardens' clubhouse down in the stilt city. Don't die.'

Five minutes later she rounded the corner in her dark blue robes and half-cape. Alice marched by her side, looking brilliant, professional – perhaps laying it on a bit thick. They were supposed to be junior clerks, after all, not high-flying barristers. Even so, Delphine walked briskly, keeping her head up, as Butler had instructed her. She was on her way to retrieve some documents. She had every right to be there. She was probably in a rush, put out at having to perform her duties on festival night.

Delphine checked her reflection in the window of the glassware shop, experienced the brief, thrilling shock of seeing a young woman staring back from beneath a coarse-knit woollen hood. It was still odd, this body – electric with otherness. She would never quite belong in it, but the body she had left behind in England felt foreign too. Nowhere was truly home. She was an expat of the flesh.

She climbed the three rounded steps to the advocate's door, inhaling the aroma of frying dough, gunpowder and a sourish funk that came off the tethered birds. Beneath the door's polished upright handle was a brass keyplate in the shape of a pair of latticework wings. She took out the bunch of keys, selected the largest, and inserted it into the lock. Inside her felt gloves, her fingers were sweating.

The key caught, refusing to turn. Shit. She rattled it. Stay calm. No one's watching. She tried again. The tumbler clicked; the key rotated. She pressed down the thumb-plate and heard a latch rise on the opposite side. The door swung open. They were in.

The hallway floor was made of coloured glass beads sunk beneath some sort of clear resin, as if one were walking upon the surface of a frozen lake, filled with gems. She passed a ground floor reception room and a parasol stand. A carpeted staircase climbed past mounted carvings of robed vesperi in dark wood. She waited until she heard the door close. She held her breath, listening for movement. After five, she nodded back at Alice and headed up the stairs.

The first floor smelt of varnish and stale smoke. She opened a glass-panelled door with one of the smaller keys and entered an office. Red evening light bled through locked shutters. There were two desks, some cabinets and several leather chairs. Beneath her feet was a blond rug made from the pelt of some kind of hexapodal feline, complete with claws and a gaping, toothless face. Through the shutters came the rising pound of drums, the occasional echoing bang of a firecracker.

It seemed to take forever to work through the various shelves and drawers. Some locks she had to force with her penknife. No time for disguising the break-in. Documents were in English, an odd, archaic variant of French, and at least one language whose alphabet she did not recognise. Anything she wasn't sure about, she stuffed into the satchel under her robes.

She came out onto the landing and signalled down to Alice, then headed to the top floor. The stairs were covered in a finely braided mat of silk ropes. Unlit oil lamps sat in wooden sconces with chamfered edges. The landing outside the Advocate's room had a lacquered wooden bust of a vesperi with wide, triangular ears, a round jaw and a prominent, lupine noseleaf.

The door was stained black, with an oval doorknob of smoked blue glass. She stopped outside and listened. Her heart was pounding from the climb. Time was running out. From outdoors came the faint jangle of bells.

She tried several keys, wincing each time. Finally, the spindle slid aside. *Click.*

A stained glass skylight threw a collage of shapes against the east wall. Beneath elegant sloping eaves, the room's centrepiece was a pentagonal desk with carved wooden bosses on the corners. A set of bookshelves took up the entirety of the back wall.

Delphine rounded the desk, pushing aside a low-backed chair of chocolate brown leather. Its feet scraped with a harsh grating. She winced. She had left the door ajar in case Alice called. Through the closed skylight, dull discordant clanging was rising with the thump of drums.

She worked systematically through the bookshelves. Most were dry legal tomes with minute printed type. She wanted to be thorough in case something had been slipped between the pages – that's where she would have hidden documents. She felt so tantalisingly close.

She moved to the cabinets, opening drawers in turn, removing documents separated by card dividers and rifling through them with gloved fingers. Here her search grew more promising – every so often she would stumble across a floorplan, an architect's pencil sketch, tables of numbers. Some documents were obligingly annotated in all three languages.

It was hard to read in the failing light and she didn't think she could carry it all. Delphine dumped a pile of papers on the desk, sat in one of the chairs and began searching through the drawers for something she could use to light the large oil lamp. Up close, she could see the ornamental bosses on the desk's corners each depicted a thick-lipped fish swallowing an orb.

Two drawers just contained paper and what looked like templates for form contracts or documents. One was locked. Delphine tried the smallest of the keys on the bunch on the lock. It did not fit.

She rattled the handle. She took out her pocket-knife. The lock gave with a snap. Inside was an engraved silver dip pen, a small hinged notebook with a brass lock, a one-shot derringer-style pistol, a pipe, a flint and steel, a pendant with three red gems set in its face, and a strip of firecrackers.

Delphine pocketed the firecrackers, took out the notebook and broke the lock with her knife blade. The cover was black leather, with an embossed monogram in the bottom right corner: *CN*. Inside was just handwriting, using the strange alphabet she had seen elsewhere. There were sketches of humanoid profiles, lines showing approximate height. Some pictures appeared to be in sequence, showing what looked like crude blobs growing into people. Bloody hell. Was this it?

She tried the flint and steel, creating a shower of blue sparks. She lifted the frosted mantle from the oil lamp, lit the wick, and wound the key in the base. A clockwork mechanism began puttering, drawing oil from the reservoir in the clawfooted base.

In the improved light she flicked through the notebook, her heart beating faster with every page. There were detailed sketches of a black, winged insect she recognised as a godfly, studies of its stinger, its dissected venom sac. The paper crackled beneath her gloved fingers, stinking of solvents. She was almost sure this was what they were looking for. Her time had to be up. She should leave. She glanced up at the door and the skylight caved in.

She fell backwards. A shower of coloured glass struck the desk. Someone dropped from above and landed in a crouch.

Delphine slammed flat against the bookshelves. Standing on the table was a child, a little girl in boots and a black hat. Straggly blond-brown hair fell to her shoulders. She wore a jacket of faded brown leather that came down past her knees. Little boxes hung from her belt, chattering softly. Her underlit face was both youthful and strangely haggard, red marks underscoring her eyes as if she had been crying.

Delphine stared. A line ran from the skylight down to the girl's belt. The girl grinned. One of her top incisors was missing. She looked about ten. She threaded her fingers, stretched her arms leisurely.

'Fair tides, Advocate,' she said. Her voice was hoarse.

Delphine glanced down. Oh God, she had dropped the book. It lay beside one of the table legs. Had Alice heard the crash? Should she call out?

The girl's smile vanished. 'You're not the Advocate.' She stepped forward. 'Where is she?'

Delphine straightened up. Shit. It was a trap. Shit.

'Who are you?' The girl took a step closer. '*Qui êtes-vous?* Are you a *thief*?'

As the girl talked Delphine traced the trailing rope up through the skylight. Had she been lying in wait?

'Well, yes,' the girl was saying, 'I may be responsible for some tortious malfeasance.' She knelt and began to pull a thin stiletto dagger from her boot. The blade kept coming.

A silver ashtray stand stood to Delphine's right. Solid. Tall. She braced herself. She was not above walloping a child.

The knife danced in the girl's gloved fingers. She gripped it by its needle tip.

Delphine glanced towards the open door. 'I hope you brought a second knife for him.'

The girl turned to look. Delphine snatched the ashtray stand and swung for the girl's ankles. The base was good and massy. It connected and the child fell. Delphine went for a decisive downward blow. The stand struck the table with a wrist-jarring bang. The girl was up, gone. Papers flew in a blizzard.

Delphine dragged the stand off the table and switched to a double-handed grip. The girl threw her arms out in a combat stance, empty palms tightening into fists. This was no ordinary child.

Her gaze dropped. Delphine hurled the ashtray into her chest. The girl caught it, pivoting. She brought the stand round in a sweeping stroke. Delphine dropped and the heavy base swished overhead.

She saw the notebook lying under the desk and crawled for it. Footsteps thumped against the tabletop overhead. She shoved the book under her robes. Something smashed. Christ.

She scrambled from under the desk. The girl was blocking the door. She held a wire taut between her outstretched fists. Smoke. Something was burning.

'I don't want to kill you,' said the girl. 'I'm on a mission of peace.'

A fishy stink was clogging the air. The girl was talking. The wire slackened slightly. 'We may have a common goal.' Her tongue worked a gap in her teeth. 'I want nothing to postpone the Grand-Duc's arrival.'

'Who are you?' said Delphine.

She regretted the words instantly.

The girl narrowed her eyes. 'Where are you from, child?'

Butler had explicitly told her not to speak.

Footsteps coming up the stairs. Alice.

The girl sidestepped and put a finger to her lips. Alice was on the landing, creeping towards the door. Delphine glanced at the girl. The girl shook her head.

The footsteps stopped. The doorknob began to turn.

'Run!' yelled Delphine.

The girl slapped down a bar latch. The smoked-glass doorknob shook.

'Delphine?'

Her cry seemed to distract the girl. Delphine reached into her robes and pulled her machine pistol.

The girl saw the gun and froze. Delphine's finger quivered on the trigger. One squeeze and they would have an easy exit. The desire to kill rose in her like lust.

The door shook as Alice pounded the other side.

Delphine fired at a glass ornament bracketed to the wall. It blew apart with an almighty report. While the girl was still reeling, she hauled herself onto the desk. She tried the rope, and started climbing.

Splinters of glass dug into her palms. She gritted her teeth and dragged herself upwards. The rope shook; the girl was trying to make her fall. Fear and pain drove Delphine higher.

The evening smelt of bonfires and red meat. She clawed at the warm tiles and hauled herself onto the roof. A sharp metal strut caught her stomach. Her robes tore; she cried out as it broke skin. She kept pulling; her holster snagged and bent the strut back on itself. She got a knee onto the window frame and was out.

From here she could see everything: the spire, dark streets mazing down into the bay, a galaxy of lanterns burning all across the stilt city, the jungle, the ocean, the last sliver of sun blooding the horizon.

The roof sloped gently. There was blood on her hands. Her stomach throbbed. She saw the rope trailing across the alley to the rooftop opposite. Needs must.

Minutes later she was on the adjacent row of buildings, shuddering with adrenaline. She had just kicked the girl's grappling hook loose from where it had been attached to a little stone statue. The roof's hipped end dropped two storeys to the cobbles. The whole world felt spongy and dayglo.

She had to get away. Gritting her teeth, she shuffled on her backside down the esplanade side of the roof. She peered over the guttering. A sheer drop to the street below.

She clambered back up to the roof ridge and worked her way down the seaward side. A block and tackle hung from a wrought-iron bracket. The street was deserted, the drop substantial.

She tucked her robes around her and pulled her hood down. She felt her belly lurch as she rolled onto her front and began lowering her legs off the roof onto the bracket. Gingerly, she straddled it, letting it taking her full weight. It held. She raised the running block and hook. Dismounting the bracket sent another blast of adrenaline through her. With the hook as a foothold, she grasped the rope and lowered herself all the way down to the street.

She jumped the final few feet to the cobbles. Her hands were smeared with blood and grease. Without thinking she wiped them on her crushed silk robes. Ah well, her disguise had served its purpose anyway. She pulled the robes down over her shoulders, fabric ripping, and let them fall to the ground.

She began making her way up the street, back towards the esplanade. Hopefully she had provided enough of a distraction for Alice to get out. They could signal to Butler to bail on his date.

The houses here were all semi-timbered, the upper storeys leaning over the street on jetties. A candle flickered in a bottle on a sill. She stopped to check her reflection in the window.

It was very queer – she could see the old her gazing out from beneath the squashed, pink, features. This bland, unstoried doorknob of a face.

She removed her machine pistol from its holster, ejected the magazine and stuffed both down the front of her shirt. This was an uncomfortable arrangement, but she didn't want to carry it about in public. She adjusted her hood, poking strands of grey hair back underneath. Her hands stung – she had cut herself badly – and the cut in her stomach pulsed with a cold ache. Jangles and bangs echoed down the street.

As she turned from the window, a crowd of revellers rounded the corner, dressed in masks and furs and feathers. Torches dripped with fire, bell-cuffs jangled, giant painted heads thrashed side to side as feet stamped in time to the drumbeat. At the head of the procession, a great barrel of burning tar rolled over the cobbles, garlanded in orange flame, sending up a river of sparks.

Delphine turned and ran the opposite way. Shadows flashed by. She heard the *rat-a-tat* of firecrackers behind her as she fled downhill.

She was walking down the moonlit wharf when she realised someone was following her. She put her hand to her pistol, glanced back and the figure was gone.

Someone tackled her from behind.

Her head cracked off the boardwalk. The street went blurry. Someone was shouting her name. She groped for her gun.

A hot sting in the meat beneath her shoulder. She caught hold of a wrist. Christ, it was the girl. Delphine elbowed her in the throat. What the hell was she doing here? Hadn't that fall broken her legs?

She tried to roll clear and there was a biting pain as the knife slipped deeper. She roared. It echoed off the cabins. She channelled all her anger into her arms and shoved. The girl was light; she went skidding backwards on her arse.

Delphine stumbled to standing. She fled towards a heap of cages.

A blow to the nape of her neck. Her head jerked upwards. Stars bled into white streaks. The clank-clatter of metal. She fell. The second blow was a crack—

—she was sinking, drowning. Oh God, she was underwater.

Her clothes clung in a sucking skin. She made powerful, cleaving strokes in the direction she hoped was up.

The wound in her shoulder ached. The desire to breathe built to a desperate need, pale light spreading in the darkness behind her eyes.

One hand broke the surface. Her fingertips brushed planks' slimy undersides. With a final effort she clawed at them, caught hold of a joist, and hauled herself, gasping, spluttering, to the surface.

She was clinging to a small wooden platform, somewhere in the gloom of the undercity. Shafts of moonlight broke through here and there, frosting the outlines of stone pilings. Some hundred yards away was the glow of the wharf. She must have fallen. A strong current dragged at her legs. The tide was coming in.

She clambered onto the platform and knelt, shivering. Saltwater stung her shoulder wound. She touched it and her fingers came away bloody.

She felt very cold. As she stood, something cracked beneath her shoe. She glanced down. Ice.

'Hello, Delphine.'

The voice came from no particular direction. It sinuated into the hollow of her ear, like a tongue.

A chill on the nape of her neck. She turned.

And there he was. Standing slightly askance in a shirt with the sleeves turned up, his hands by his sides.

And she *knew*. Right away, she knew who he was.

She took a second to find her voice.

'Arthur.'

'I'm afraid we haven't much time,' he said. 'I must tell you everything.'

CHAPTER 14

MY SON WAS DEAD, AND IS ALIVE AGAIN

(Ninety-one years before the inauguration)

The rod cracked Hagar under the jaw, driving her spine-first into the bridge's stone parapet. She pirouetted left and backflipped; the follow-up strike swished through the space where her skull had been. She landed in a wide stance, straddling two stone balusters, her back to the ravine.

Canoness Limitless-Grace gritted her teeth against the sleet scything across the bridge. 'Did it never occur to you, sister, that this body might be a blessing?' She drew her rod back for another sacramental blow, snowflakes sticking to the shining ribs of its weighty iron head.

The balusters were glassy with ice; Hagar felt her bare feet slipping on the frictionless surface. She spread her arms to balance herself, eyes watering. Behind her, the drop was almost a mile. Her fingers and toes pulsed with a crushing heat.

'Form is burning,' said Hagar. 'Feeling is burning. Perception is burning.'

The Canoness lunged, testing the proposition. Hagar allowed her soles to slide in opposite directions. Her body dropped sharply. The rod swung over her shaved head. She grabbed its christwood haft and let it whip her away from the precipice, back onto the bridge's freezing grey flagstones. She spun out of range, one heel sliding back, arms rising up into fire stance.

Canoness Limitless-Grace turned to face her, rolling the sleeves of her gown up over her thick shoulders, exposing her votary tattoos to the wind. The scars were deep trenches of rubbery keloid, a livid glossy blue-black against the dark brown of her triceps.

'Through pain, we become disenchanted.' She advanced, tossing her rod from palm to palm. 'Through disenchantment, we become dispassionate.'

Hagar vacillated between breaking right and trying for a strike at the windpipe. She knew this slow approach was a trick, but she could not decide which mistake the Canoness was trying to goad her into. Damn the woman's stolid, doctrinaire self-confidence. Hagar broke right.

The Canoness did not react. It was as if she had not noticed. Hagar found herself on an exposed flank with a chance to go for a kidney, an ankle, the back of the skull. No. It had to be a trap.

The Canoness turned. 'Through dispassion, we are liberated.' She opened her arms. Her callused fingers relaxed, the rod dropping to the bridge with a decisive clunk.

Hagar could not help herself. The smugness was too much. She darted in, feinting low with a kick to the shin while driving her palm into the Canoness's face. Her hand connected with that full, self-satisfied jowl, then kept going as the Canoness twisted with the strike. The Canoness grabbed Hagar's wrist. Hagar tried to counter with a flat-palmed thrust from her opposite hand but the Canoness spun, pivoting at the waist and ankle, flipping Hagar head-over-heels and slamming her belly-first into the opposite parapet.

Hagar twisted her wrist free and staggered back towards the centre of the bridge. The impact had knocked the wind out of her. The Canoness came in with a blur of punches. Hagar sidestepped, turned one aside with the hard bone of her wrist, jinked within her billowing robes so the Canoness struck empty cloth, ducked, then came up inside the Canoness's guard with a two-fingered strike to the soft palate behind the jaw. The Canoness flung her head back; Hagar's fingers struck taut muscle, buckled.

Hagar pulled her hand away just in time to see the rod's iron head arcing towards her. How had she had time to pick it back up? It smote her cleanly across the temple. The world spun – sky, mountains, the grey bastions of the abbey – then the Canoness sweep-kicked Hagar's legs out.

Hagar fell from the bridge, dropping through cold air.

A wrenching pain across her sternum. The line securing her to the Canoness jerked tight. She swung into the shadow of the great weathered masonry arch that held the bridge aloft, the ravine rushing by sickeningly below, then back out. The rope creaked as she swayed to a halt.

Canoness Limitless-Grace leaned over the parapet and began hauling the line back in. As Hagar reached the top, the Canoness held out a rough, warm palm for her to take.

Hagar felt nauseous from the blow to her skull. The flagstones seemed to tilt beneath her feet. When she looked up, the Canoness was smiling.

'Good,' she said, rubbing her throat. 'Your rebuttals grow more convincing by the week.'

Hagar bowed. 'Thank you.'

'Remember, the kata aren't truths to be defended. They're organising principles to be compared and exploited. They are, by their nature, incomplete. If you fail to recognise this, your training will remain very limited.'

'I will contemplate your words.'

'The purpose of these drills, our chanting, our repetition, is not to instil dogma, but to alert us to the rote, arbitrary, automatic nature of normal existence. I applaud your discipline, dear sister, but we expect you to rebel – indeed, we're counting upon it.' She socked the rod into her palm. 'And don't scorn the physical world. Its challenges are a chance to act with true virtue – to choose kindness in spite of our experiences, to choose kindness though it may not be rewarded. It's easy to be compassionate in paradise. I suggest you reflect upon that.'

Back in her little dormitory, Hagar cleaned her cuts with water from the abbey spring and rubbed balm into her bruises. A weak glow emanated from a nook in the stone wall. The nook contained a shallow depression filled with oil, of which each sister received a small ration each month.

Theological debates left her restive. There was something oddly bloodless about each thrust and counter-thrust, as if the result did not really matter. She did not mind the harsh mountain winters, the hardship, the repetition. She had retreated to the Sciamachian Order to chastise herself, to prevent her weakness inflicting more suffering upon the world. The sisters followed a syncretic creed derived from a mix of old world religions, and in their blending of physical discipline with intellection and long periods of solitary repose, Hagar had found a measure of meaning, if not solace.

But lately, doubt had begun creeping into her prayers, the way water seeped into cracks in the abbey walls, freezing and refreezing over successive winters till ancient stone blocks split. She contemplated what the Canoness had said regarding paradise. They were safe up here. But were they serving a higher purpose?

She tested a bruise with her thumb and winced. She was probably just cross at having lost the debate. The new Canoness Umbra Prime invested the theodic kata with a dizzying spontaneity, each argument flowing naturally from the last. Hagar examined her soul and found more than a little envy. To know what to do, moment by moment. To be so *sure*.

A horn sounded throughout the abbey, low and resonant. Hagar unrolled her prayer mat and knelt at the foot of her wooden bunk to begin evening prayer.

As she lowered her head, she felt a frosty prickle across her fingers. New draughts were constantly finding routes into the dormitories, insinuating through gaps in the storied grey stone. Another breach to find and plug up with whatever she could scavenge.

Her nostrils twitched. A sharp, unfamiliar fragrance. Incense was strictly forbidden in the dormitories. Was Sister Ragarda still making clandestine offerings to her village's ancestral spirits? Hadn't she learned from her last rebuke?

Hagar was trying to swallow her irritation and return to contemplation of the ineffable when she heard a gasp and opened her eyes to see, for the first time, the angel.

He lay facedown on the stone floor – a man, by the look of it barely into his twenties. Slim, his brown hair ruffled. His whole body faintly luminous.

He lifted his head. 'Am I . . .' He glanced around with jerky, hunted movements. His skin was deathly pale. He wore strange foreign clothes.

On reflex, Hagar threw herself into one of the core stances: the querent. She glanced at the door. Still locked and bolted.

The man rose to his hands and knees. His outline was curling at the edges, licking back on itself like smoke.

'Wait,' he said. He touched the floor. His fingers sank into the flagstone as if it were quicksand. She realised his body was not quite flush with the floor. He appeared to be suspended one or two inches above it.

Hagar held herself utterly still. Was this a vision? She had heard of sisters hallucinating whilst in ecstatic states. Was this divine?

Something in his manner tempered her awe. He did not fit her idea of a celestial herald. He seemed bewildered.

She dropped her arms and took a step forward. 'Who are you?'

He looked up. 'Hagar?'

She had not told him her name.

He rose, not as a human would, but flowing upwards like a gas, until his image reformed in the semblance of a man standing. Where he had touched the stones, they were crusted with ice.

'What happened to your hair?' he said. He glanced around. 'How long has it been? Did it work?' He took a deep breath. 'My mind's a damn blank.'

'Who are you?' she said.

'You *are* you, aren't you?' His eye twitched. 'Hagar Ingery?'

His accent and his peculiar clothes, long mud-brown trousers and a brown waistcoat over a white shirt and black tie – they reminded her irresistibly of the other lands.

'You're English,' she said.

His mouth broke into a smile. 'Are you teasing?' He looked around. 'What is this place? Have you gone back to the convent?'

A crawling sensation spread down her spine. She thrust a palm forward and dropped her body into an aggressive stance: the inquisitor.

'Tell me your name. I command you!'

'Do you really not recognise me?' He pressed a palm to his chest, eyes widening. 'However long can it have been? It's me. Arthur.'

The name meant nothing to her.

His smile began fading, replaced by a look of concern. 'You came with Grandmama and dear Gideon.' He took a step towards her, vapour wafting from his shoulders. 'I was awake. I saw it.'

'I don't know what you're talking about.'

'None of it? Fat Maw, burning? Morgellon, weeping at your feet?'

A cold thrill washed over her heart. 'What do you know of my master?'

The man frowned. 'You have no master.'

Hagar felt strangely unmoored – poised upon the brink of something too momentous to comprehend. The expression on the young man's face suggested he too was groping for meaning.

'What do you think you saw?' she said. Every pore across her body tingled. She could hear the soft lapping of flames in oil.

'You freed yourself.' He smoothed a palm over the buttons of his waistcoat. 'Wait . . . how old are you?'

'I couldn't say, exactly. Around three hundred.'

He touched a thumb and forefinger to his closed eyelids. 'It hasn't happened yet.'

She sensed it would be useless to strike him. She should run.

The man threw open his arms. 'This is it. This is where it starts.' He clutched at his ruffled hair. 'Oh Hagar. I saw it all.' He looked down at his vaporous body. He pressed his palms to his stomach; they shifted through. His image began to break apart and then, like water pouring into a channel, his edges sharpened and he became clear, discrete. 'And this is how we meet!' He laughed. 'Gosh, I'm so clever.' His eyes became distant for a moment. He winced. 'So much is missing. It's like my mind couldn't hold it. I knew *everything*. Time was meaningless.' His smile returned. 'But we did it. We *won*.'

'Won *what*?' She momentarily forgot her astonishment in a flurry of impatience. The feeling was oddly liberating – in the abbey, she had grown used to keeping her frustrations compressed within a corset of sororal courtesy.

The man lifted his hands to Hagar's cheeks. He did not cross the room; he was simply there, before her, his gelid aura bringing her neck out in gooseflesh. Hagar had a sudden flash of Morgellon standing over her. She recoiled, twisting away, lunging to snap his wrist.

Her hand passed through the spectre's forearm as if through a dusty sunbeam. She darted back, panting.

'You do . . . not . . . *touch* me,' she spat.

The angel became solemn. He placed his palms over his heart and withdrew, floating backwards until he stood beside the small walnut chest containing her robes, Bible and wooden Christ child.

'Sorry,' he said. 'I was excited. I lost myself.'

Hagar relaxed her shoulders just a little. 'Speak.'

'Hagar. I know this must seem strange to you.'

'I've lived a long time.'

The angel nodded. 'Perhaps that's one of the reasons I chose you. I knew you might accept what others can't. Listen: what if I told you that together, we could end death?'

They talked for hours in her dormitory, Hagar and the angel. He told her his story.

His name was Arthur Stokeham. He was the grandson of a Welsh countess called Anwen Stokeham and her husband's butler, Rutherford Cox. Arthur's family had guarded the threshold that linked England with Avalonia for at least four generations. His grandmother styled herself Lady Dellapeste and became a peer in the perpetuum, taking Cox as her ageless valet. During a Great War in the old world, Arthur had been fatally wounded when an eighteen-pounder misfired. His father, Lazarus Stokeham, arranged for him to be rushed back to England to receive the honours.

'It went badly. I think because I was so close to death. My body sort of . . .' He made a squeezing motion with both fists. 'And they weren't sure if I'd died. I could see and hear and feel, but I couldn't answer.'

His devastated father had Arthur's body transported to Avalonia, where Lady Dellapeste and Cox had agreed to make every effort to see if he could be restored. In fact, they sequestered his body in one of their plantations outside Fat Maw, and did nothing.

'They probably considered you a threat,' said Hagar, sitting on her bunk. She had not engaged with real politics for years and the stench of intrigue stirred old appetites.

'They considered everyone a threat,' said Arthur. 'Love can do that to you.'

Arthur had spent months trapped in his useless, immobile body – free from pain, but unable to do anything except look, and listen, and think. He had feared he would go mad. But then a very strange thing happened. He discovered he could leave his body behind.

At first, he could only travel a few yards, rising as a faint copy of himself. With practice, he learned to project himself miles, and eventually great distances at the speed of thought. The time he could spend outside his body was limited, but finally he had the freedom he had craved.

Sometimes he went to cities and towns and watched, invisibly. But more and more, he found himself drawn to empty expanses – the eerie beauty of a world without people. So much of the planet was uninhabited. He would glide low over midnight deserts, or across the grey, ice-brindled ocean beyond the southern floe. Tall, isolated pillars of black volcanic rock filled him with a weird elation – not at the prospect of discovering something, but at their profound emptiness. Standing alone, the only sentient being for hundreds of miles around, he would lose his sense of self, merging with the sea, the sky.

'But when I flew, sometimes I felt this . . . I'm not sure how to describe it. Almost a yearning.' He pressed a palm to his heart. 'But a *physical* thing. Something calling out to me. Oh God.' He pulled a face. 'I sound like I'm writing a poem. It was more a *magnetism.* A force pulling at my etheric body, resonating with it, drawing it in. It was a bit like the feeling I'd get just before I had to return to my physical body, but . . . stranger.'

'Like hooks,' said Hagar.

'Yes,' said Arthur, 'exactly. Hooks. Some intuition – I don't know what – made me resist it, until one day, I wondered what would happen if I just . . . gave in.'

Instantly he had found himself propelled through the air in a blur of colour and sound, pulled towards the source of the signal. He resisted, felt a wrenching at his core, as if he were being twisted apart. Finally, exerting all his will and focusing it in a single direction, he broke loose.

He found hc was underwater, gazing down into an ocean trench – a vast canyon into which the seabed collapsed, a bottomless pit. From its depths, that strange resonance beckoned him, his etheric body vibrating like a cello string.

'And I had to know,' he said, with a note of melancholy.

As he descended, the light filtering down from the surface grew dimmer and dimmer, until he was alone in the soft nimbus of his etheric body. As if the universe had died, and here he was, at the end of all things.

Down, down, and all the while this feeling of yearning, of impending union. Time grew uncertain. Had it been minutes? Days? His mind wandered, looping back on itself.

'I had the strangest intuition that I'd been there before. Like I'd always been there, like I was returning to the beginning. Sensations were flowing into me: voices, gunshots, pipers playing, the crash of a waterfall. Wet mown grass, lemons. I was cutting into a steaming gammon. I was back in the trenches, smoking a cigarette. I was listening to Papa cry through the study door. I was a pike, oozing over the soft mud at the edge of the lake, I was the reeds caressing the white scales of its belly, the cold clear water that held it.

'I passed through a layer of ice. Things inside it called out to me. I could hear them singing.'

As Hagar watched, a ripple pulsed through Arthur's body. He seemed to lose his thread for a moment; strange trails rose from his edges. He snapped back to awareness. 'Sorry . . .'

He had continued to sink, though he sensed he was no longer heading down so much as *inwards*. His surroundings became liquid once more. Through the darkness he saw gnarled towers the colour of dead leaves coiling towards him over vast distances, forming immense contorted spirals that glowed with a faint smoked amber light. They loomed bigger, gaining texture and depth, until their scale began wearing on his composure.

Now he perceived threads of piercing black against the amber

– inky helixes, visibly flowing – hundreds, thousands of strands. The strands wove into lattices, complex geometric shapes rising from a sea of shifting lines then sinking back into chaos. He followed them, though they had no perceivable beginning nor end. The lattices showed him petals, crescent moons.

Deeper, deeper. The yearning rose to a kind of glorious agony, and was all twisting together, the amber and the black. Great snaking arms of midnight sprawled across a copper vastness. An axle turned at its centre – the heart of it all. The farther he fell, the larger the formation became, until he could no longer see it, until he understood it was bigger than he could possibly imagine, until he felt himself come up against an invisible threshold.

And he pressed himself into it. And he felt his mind brush against what lay beyond.

'I knew everything. The colourless dreams of hunching foetuses. The rich-rotten heat of deep-sea sulphur vents. Sunlight turning to sugar in a fig leaf. How it feels to be buried alive. The pull of moon on ocean. The pull of heart on heart. The treasures of the snow. The treasures of the hail.

'I saw through billions of eyes. I heard the hidden music. I touched the darkness upon the face of the deep. The source of the honours.

'And I understood.

'It *lives*.'

Hagar gazed down at her soft leather slippers. Odd notions were stirring at the corners of her mind.

Arthur had spent the past few minutes pacing the dormitory, lost in contemplation. She understood that he was a mere product of the godfly parasite – no more miraculous in origin than her. All sentient beings were dispossessed angels. Could this really be the hand of providence?

'It's no good,' he said. He shook his head. 'Most of it's gone.'

'Most of what?'

'The future.' He flicked a hand through his skull, hair wafting and reforming. 'It's like trying to hold the ocean in my hands. But I knew it. It was all there, laid out for me to read.'

She sighed. The boy seemed bewildered. Whatever wisdom his

experience might have granted had been squandered on his callow dullness.

'Don't you remember anything?' she said.

'That's what I'm trying . . . I can't explain. I don't have the words to carry it. Time was meaningless. I saw billions of futures branching out.' He squinted at an empty section of wall. 'You left this place. Took back your old position with the palace.'

'I'm in disgrace. Morgellon refuses to see me.'

'True, but he'll let you serve him. He thinks it's the natural order of things.'

'But why should I leave?' she said. 'To what end?'

'In a few years, Grandmama and Grandpapa conceive a little girl.'

'Impossible. A peer can't give birth. Their body purges the foetus as if it were a tumour.'

'But it's happened before, hasn't it?' Arthur inclined his head meaningfully. 'And Grandmama's gifts have never been entirely clear. Perhaps one of them is fruitfulness.'

'The honours manifest in different ways.'

'But you know the sort of powers the offspring of a peer and her valet is likely to possess.'

'I've heard the legends,' said Hagar.

Arthur took a step towards her. 'You've lived so long. You've watched the endless war, the suffering, the ignorance.'

'No one learns. It repeats.'

'And *why* don't they learn, Hagar?' He made a fist. 'Because death snatches memory. It robs us of wisdom. It dooms us to this endless cycle. That's what I touched beneath the ice. A god grown from mortal pain. It drinks our suffering. We sustain it.

'But what if we could undo death? What if we could connect all sentient beings in a great cradle of kinship and mutual reliance?' He held an open palm out towards her. 'The bond that ties you to your master. We could use my god's powers to grant that to everyone, only more so. Connecting with it projected me through *time*, Hagar. Imagine what would happen if it amplified mental gifts like Morgellon's and Grandmama's. We could directly access the minds of all sentient species, suppress the impulse towards murder, rape, destruction. We could link everyone with maundygrubs. Imagine. No old age. No sickness. No death.'

'You want to take away their power of moral choice,' she said.

He looked down at his open hand. 'No. *More* than that. I'm not proposing a mere negation. I'm talking about creating a world of love, brotherhood, harmony. People will be free to think their own thoughts – I've no desire to reduce everyone to cattle. It might sound funny to you, but war showed me the very best of mankind. Selfless sacrifice. Tenderness. Courage. A goodness that survives in even the bleakest of circumstances. A goodness that's worth protecting.'

Hagar thought of how the centuries had changed her and Morgellon. She imagined billions of souls, trapped in the material world forever. Without death, there would be no redemption, no chance to return to the Kingdom. Without the freedom to choose evil, there would be no true virtue. A great revulsion welled up inside her.

What the angel described was hell.

Arthur smiled. 'Ah, I wept too. It seems too beautiful, too perfect. Just thinking of it is a kind of torture. But we can do it, Hagar. You must find Auntie Sarai, and bring her to the city of Fat Maw, and face your master in the place you last met.'

'Impossible.'

'I didn't say it would be easy.'

Hagar laughed. 'You have no idea what you're asking.'

'If you prevail, you'll travel with Grandmama, and my old friend Gideon, far across the water.' By now, the flagstones around Arthur's feet were furred with rime. The water she had drawn from the spring for morning ablutions had frozen and split its wooden pitcher. 'You'll need Gideon to guide you. I don't know where I am, but we have a bond. He feels the same pull I did. When you reach me, you lift the darkness from the deep. Like Auntie Sarai, it feeds on suffering, only more so. She can speak to it directly, I think. I can't see her there, at the end, but she must be. My god will rise and drink our sorrows and use pain to reshape reality. Godflies rise in a black cloud. And my mind and Grandmama's mind and Gideon's mind, all our minds merge. That's the last thing I remember. The great rapture as we're finally joined.'

'So it happens.'

'Nothing is inevitable.' He looked at her with a sudden intensity. 'All I'm saying is that it *can*.'

'You overestimate me. I've no influence, no resources.'

'You've many lifetimes' experience. A singular will. My physical interventions must perforce be rare and small. I haven't the strength to do more than guide you. Oh!' His image fluxed, fraying at the edges.

'What's wrong?'

'It's calling me back.'

'What about your physical body?'

'It perishes.' His voice wavered. 'Dies and rots. It's still there, back in Avalonia. Grandmama and Grandpapa don't find out for months. They cover up the whole business, of course. A peer, dying in his sleep? Shakes every certainty they believe in. Ugh.' His left arm withered into mist.

Hagar lowered her head and closed her eyes, as if in prayer. Arthur's plan was monstrous, obscene. She did not yet know what God intended for her, but she sensed this angel had been sent to her for a purpose. Not the purpose *he* envisaged, naturally. But perhaps he was a raft, and her task, a river. Already, she was turning his proposal over in her mind. What if there was another way? Something better than eternal deathless purgatory. What if she could use the power of this child he claimed would soon be born, and turn it to more noble ends? The end of the perpetuum. A bringing down of the ancient order. The final sundering of the cage. Deliverance.

She could not lie, of course. Her vows were still binding, even if she left the convent. But she did not have to tell the truth either.

She breathed in. Her flesh prickled. As she lifted her gaze, she felt as if the great abbey were breaking loose from the mountain and sloughing into the ravine.

The angel was fading.

'Very well,' she said. 'Tell me what to do.'

CHAPTER 15
LE MORTE D'ARTHUR

'I won't insult you by asking you to trust me,' said Arthur.

Delphine shook water out of her machine pistol. His body gave off a blue glow that reminded her of Martha's eyes. Threads of vapour wicked up from his shoulders.

She had never seen a picture of Arthur. Yet she *knew*.

He stood with one hand in the pocket of his roomy tweed trousers, his hair side-combed, his caramel leather golf shoes bone dry. He was like a cinema projection, but three-dimensional. Her wet fingers ached in the coldness radiating from him.

'It's about your father,' he said.

Delphine dropped her shoulder and tackled him. Freezing air rushed over her body. She passed through as if he were smoke. Her heel slipped on the ice and momentum carried her off the edge of the platform.

Cold fingers gripped her wrist.

She swung out over the water. Arthur yanked her back onto the platform, then his fingertips slipped through her arm. She gasped; her blood felt like it had turned to ice.

Arthur stepped back – or rather, *flowed* back, his image receding and reforming. She staggered, rubbing her arm.

He examined his hand. His fingers smeared together at the tips like alcohol flames.

'I can't do things like that often,' he said. 'Now our time is even more limited.'

'What are you doing here?'

'Do you know who I am, Delphine?'

She lashed at his head with the pistol. It wafted through harmlessly.

'That won't do any good,' he said.

Adrenaline thundered through her body. She thumbed the pistol's safety catch to auto.

'Look.' He raised his palms with an air of weary indulgence. 'I'm not here to beg your forgiveness. I doubt you'd give it and, with respect, I don't need it.'

'What are you?'

Arthur looked down at his shoes, making little effort to disguise a smile. 'I am but a man. I've come to help you.'

'Fuck. Off.'

'For what it's worth, I'm sorry about your father. Truly. Poor Giddy wasn't ready. Thought I was dead, only to have me popping back like Marley's ghost. I thought I'd ease his suffering, but I made it worse.'

She pulled the trigger. Bullets ripped through him. She pissed through the entire twenty-five-round magazine in under two seconds. Reports echoed off the roof and pilings.

She stood, panting. The hole in his chest drifted shut.

'I can't keep this form much longer. Please. I've come to stop you making a terrible mistake.'

'Is he alive?' Her voice broke as she yelled, her words ringing in the darkness. All that time, Father had been trying to tell them. Arthur really had appeared to him.

Around them, the wind was picking up. 'Of course. He's in the summer palace. He's in terrible pain. He never took a valet or handmaiden. That's why Sarai can use him.'

Waves lapped over the platform, washing round Delphine's ankles. 'What do you mean, "use" him?'

'Poor Giddy suffers more than most. He burns.'

She winced at the memory of her father's flesh shrivelling and blackening, chunks dropping from his jaw. The thought of that agony persisting for seven decades.

'You did this to him.' Her voice was cracking. 'You drove him mad.'

Arthur closed his eyes. 'Oh, he's not mad. Quite the reverse. Giddy's problem is he's too awake. He feels God tearing at his heart.'

Delphine tried to suppress her rage and think. Waves slapped the stone pilings, sea spray cresting over Arthur, turning to ice dust.

'Listen,' he said, turning aside and running a fingertip down the bridge of his nose, 'a great change is coming to the world. I want you to live to see it. Gideon helps Auntie create paradise. It gives all his suffering meaning, you see. You wouldn't deny him that, would you?'

'How can you just *use* him? If you love him so much, why don't you bloody save him?'

Arthur gazed at her sadly, his margins fraying and collapsing. 'This *is* me trying to save him.'

'I don't believe you.'

His narrowing eyes blurred like a long-exposure photograph. 'I think you do, Delphine. You don't want to give me the satisfaction of saying so, but you do.'

She shrieked and lashed at him, again and again. 'Give him back! Give him *back*!'

Arthur's body withdrew effortlessly. Her foot slipped; she dropped to her hands and knees.

'It's taken such a lot of puff to get me here.' His voice was steady in her ears. 'Let me say my piece.'

She glared at the frozen boards, at her shivering pale hands.

'Turn back, Delphine. If you interfere things will end badly for you.'

She glanced up. 'Is that a threat?'

A wave broke with a crump against the lee of the platform, framing him with spume. 'What could I possibly do to you? I'm just a shade.' Froth crashed through his body and pelted her. 'But I've touched the god beyond time and I remember pieces of things yet to come. You can't save your father – you'll only add to his burden. And if you oppose us, when the Grand Duc arrives, the city will burn.'

Her wet hair whipped the sides of her face as she shook it. 'How can you be so fucking calm?'

Rain began pounding the boards and roofs above. Rumbling spread like thousands of boots stamping.

'What would anguish achieve?' His voice cut through the thunder. 'You think I don't care?'

'I think you're just like your grandmother. It's all a bloody put-on. You don't care who dies as long as you're at the centre of things.'

Arthur slipped a hand into his pocket. 'She cared when you killed Grandpapa.'

The jibe entered so cleanly it took her a moment to feel it. She saw Anwen standing over Mr Cox's body, saying his name over and over: *Rutherford. Rutherford. Rutherford.*

She dipped her head. When she looked up, he had vanished.

'Hey!' She stood, casting round for him. 'Hey!' Rain streamed through gaps in the boards above. Everything was drumming, thundering.

Oh God. She had to get back to the others. She had to warn them.

A swell was rolling down the undercity towards her. It drove a gondola into one of the pilings with a booming crash, blasting it to matchwood. She jumped just as the wave reached her. The cold shock of immersion. The wave lifted her up and back; her head went under. She surfaced a few yards from the platform, treading water.

'Hey!'

He was gone.

She made for a stone piling with a vigorous front crawl. Without Arthur's light it was difficult to see. The current sucked at her legs. Fighting against the waves, she managed to reach the base. Rungs led up towards the rafters. The bottom few were slimy with seaweed. She hauled herself up out of the water, nearly losing her grip, and climbed. Her injured shoulder smarted something rotten.

There was a hatch in the roof. It took a couple of slaps to work out which end had the hinges. She shoved. Instantly rain was pelting her face and the howl of the storm filled her ears.

Grimacing, she hauled herself out onto a narrow side street between two single-storey houses. It was blocked at one end by an upended canoe, rain hammering off the prow and wooden outriggers.

Netting hung overhead, threaded with vines on which pebble-sized yellow fruits danced as water pelted them.

The sky was roiling with thick dark clouds limned with moonlight. She crept to the end of the side street and looked out across an empty boulevard. Edges blurred in the rain. The wind lifted panels off roofs, tarpaulins snapping.

She recognised nothing, but the wind was coming in off the ocean, so she turned into the storm and started up the street, towards the wharf. There, she could get her bearings and find the meeting spot Butler had described to her.

A shape flashed out of the rain. She dropped behind a barrel. Christ. Christ. Christ. She was full of adrenaline. Her machine pistol had taken a drenching. She ejected the empty magazine and slotted a new one in.

Maybe she had imagined it. She couldn't go firing blindly. She clicked the safety onto semi-auto, counted down from three.

She rose and turned.

The street was empty.

A shadow slipped from behind a tumbrel blown over by the wind. It was the girl who had stabbed her. The girl feinted left; Delphine fired and missed. The girl covered the open ground between them in a few strides, lifting her knife.

A figure dropped from a roof and clattered into the girl, sending them both tumbling across the boardwalk. The girl rolled clear quickly and was back on her feet. The figure rose, spreading his wings. Butler! The girl flung her knife and hit him in the throat.

Delphine tried to back away. The girl charged her, dropping her shoulder and tumbling so Delphine's second shot blew splinters out of the boardwalk. The girl jumped. A roundhouse kick cracked Delphine across the jaw, throwing her head left. The girl tripped her. She landed heavily.

When she looked up, the girl was standing over her, rain drumming the brim of her black hat.

'I don't want to hurt you, Delphine,' she said. 'I just want to know why you're—'

A fist connected with the girl's head. An instant later someone dived on her in a flurry of blows and curses.

Alice.

Delphine rolled onto her front. The girl had Alice pinned prone against the floor and was pressing her face into a puddle. Delphine raised her gun; the girl kicked it from her hands.

Out of the rain burst Butler, vapour streaming from his hand. The girl saw him too late; he slapped a palm on the back of her scalp and she dropped, slack.

Alice hauled herself up, hacking and spluttering. She scrambled over to Delphine's side.

'Are you okay?'

Delphine let Alice help her sit up against the wall of a building. 'Oh, bloody . . . peaches and cream.' Her shoulder throbbed with her hammering pulse.

Butler tugged the knife from his neck and gazed down at the unconscious girl.

'Ah, Miss Ingery,' he said. 'Not a second time.'

Delphine followed Butler as he carried Hagar back to the wharf. Alice helped Delphine walk – now the adrenaline was tailing off she realised she was in quite a lot of pain. Her wound burned on the surface and ached inside. They moved under porches and awnings. The rain was easing to a steady shower.

'I wonder if it would've been kinder to take all her memories,' said Butler. He was cradling Hagar like a baby, her head tipped back in the crook of his arm, straggly wet hair hanging down to his knees. Her hat rested on her stomach.

When they got to the wharf he laid her down on the boardwalk. He wiped her knife with a rag and slotted it into her boot.

He stayed at her side for a few moments.

'I've washed her memory of the last ten minutes or so,' he said. 'That's about right, isn't it?'

Delphine nodded.

Alice picked something up off the boardwalk. 'What's this?' She held out a leather notebook, dripping from the rain.

'Oh God.' Delphine grabbed it from her. The book. The notes from the advocate's chamber. In all the havoc she had forgotten about them. Thank God she had dropped them. She pressed them to her chest. 'This is what we were looking for. I . . .' She glanced at the prone girl. 'We have to get back.'

Butler held a palm over the girl's head. He kept it there for a while. No glow emanated from his fingertips. He just looked at her. Then he nodded. He stood.

'Right,' he said.

Delphine held up the book. 'I got the—'

'I *know*. I heard you. Come on. Let's go before she wakes up.' He glanced down at his soaked, stained clothes. 'Another outfit ruined.'

CHAPTER 16

THE END OF THE WAR IN HEAVEN

Two hundred and seventy-eight years before the inauguration

Hagar stood on Fat Maw harbour and watched the smooth sculling of softshell turtles big as hayricks. Beyond the shadow of the hill, dawn light danced on the water in blazing golden sickles.

Her cowl was soft and warm. Every so often, she stole glances at the young man beside her, who stood with his cloak unfastened and his head tipped back, inhaling long draughts of sea air. His eyes were closed. He was smiling.

She could not recall ever feeling so happy.

'It's a miracle,' said Mitta.

'It is.'

'We're on the brink of a new age.' They spoke in Masillian French, with its softened consonants and proliferation of loan words. A breeze caught his hair and pushed it back from his brow. He looked vulnerable and awed.

'I'm not sure I believe it.'

'Believe it. Lord Cambridge arrived yesterday morning. Parmaran Koi and her retinue have taken up all three floors of the Korppi Inn. This city is full of old enemies, ready to make peace. The War in Heaven is over.' He turned to her, beaming. 'And tonight, at the ball, you and I shall dance.'

Hagar dropped her gaze, feeling her cheeks colour. Schools of black fish darted through the clear water.

'All our vanities will dissolve in the tide,' he said. 'You know, before the perpetuum's founding, peers lived two centuries then voluntarily gave themselves back to the source. Imagine.' He shook his head. 'Relinquishing *this*. How well they must have lived, knowing their time was short.'

She loved Mitta when he held forth like this, all wild poetic rapture, his eyes bright as flames. She had never heard of this 'source' he spoke of – he had served Morgellon far longer than she, and knew much she did not. How odd, to claim to love the world, yet advocate letting it go.

'How can mystics struggle to hear messages from the creator? Listen, Hagar!' Mitta laughed and spread his arms. 'God's singing to us!' He clapped and danced on the quay. Hagar shrugged down into her robes. She felt shy and unworthy of his joy. 'Come *on*,' he chided, capering to her side. 'What if today were our last together? What would you do?'

He reached under her hood and ruffled her hair. She winced, pulled away, but a warmth spread through her scalp, her shoulders, her whole body.

A flock of pink birds flew across the bay, like blossom caught by the wind. Round the mouth of the river, fishing boats sat waiting for the tide to fill their nets.

Mitta was right. This day was a miracle. Everything would be transformed.

Back in her little chamber in the east wing of the summer palace, Hagar took a box from beneath her bed. Her hands were trembling. Mitta had been joking about the dance. Hadn't he? What *would* she do, if she knew she would never see him again? The skin on her crown was still tingling from where his palm had brushed her scar.

She felt drunk with anticipation. After over a century of internecine strife between the great immortal powers of the perpetuum, a truce had been brokered. That evening, the peers would come together to celebrate the new peace. She was worldly enough to recognise that, for all the talk of harmony, this reconciliation had been brought about by the war with Hilanta and a succession of bad harvests – but if pragmatic self-interest succeeded where high ideals had failed, she was all for it. There would be uprisings, certainly – small pockets of resistance unable to relinquish blood feuds generations in the making – but the very real prospect of Hilantian invasion would soon unite former foes under that most stirring of banners, self-preservation.

Hagar sloughed off her robes. She took the gown Morgellon had chosen for her and laid it out on the bed. It was a modest, rather functional garment of light grey that fastened up the back with three hooks. The skirts were ankle-length and finely pleated, and a small spidersilk peony was stitched into the left shoulder.

She checked that her door was locked, then rotated the looking-glass on her dresser so it faced into the room. She pulled the dress on over her shoulders. The material felt funny against her skin – tickly and cold. She looked at herself in the mirror. Still the same callow child, skinny, shapeless. She tugged at parts of the dress, trying to get it to look right on her undeveloped body.

She examined her face. She pressed her top lip where the eye tooth was missing, watched flesh collapse into the socket. She practised smiling without opening her mouth. No, she mustn't thin her lips – that was a sneer. She compressed her mouth into a little rosebud. Now she looked like a pouting child. She let her mouth relax into a neutral line. There. That was the least ugly option.

Hagar tilted her head forward and examined her bald patch – a raw pink scar against her sandy hair. She opened the box. Inside, on a lining of red felt, was a long-toothed rosewood comb. It was perfectly symmetrical, with smooth curved edges and a handle that extended from the centre, tapering to a sharp point. She had spent weeks rubbing oil into it and the wood had a subtle dewy sheen. Gingerly, she lifted the comb from its box. It gave off a fragrance of autumn forests: rain and sap and leaves.

She had never bought herself something like this before – Morgellon gave her a small clothing allowance, but she always spent it on functional or ceremonial wear – her librarian's gown, her surgeon's gloves and apron. In the last few years, the young ladies of his court had started wearing combs – more ostentatious than hers, made of jade or ivory, studded with gems. She had seen the way Mitta's gaze lingered on such women, how they pretended not to notice.

As she had practised, Hagar folded her hair sideways over her scar, fixing it in place with the comb. She studied herself in the mirror.

The comb held her usually draggled hair in a controlled, flowing sweep. It complemented the silk peony just below it, accentuating a pleasing, even provocative asymmetry. Tingling spread down the nape of her neck. How utterly odd. She looked almost becoming.

She turned this way and that, sure it was a trick, frightened by her rising feeling of hope. Might Mitta be as surprised as she was? She knew he could never look at her in *that* way, that, in her perpetually arrested body, the strange violent appetites of adulthood would remain forever a mystery to her, but might he not one day feel a brotherly fondness so very far from romantic love?

Hagar watched her reflection, tried to see herself as others did. The ball was still six hours away. Her face looked like a word she had reread over and over, until it seemed misspelt, an error.

Guards stood either side of tall, curving sandstone pillars, dressed in ceremonial full-face helms, single-breasted green coats with silver buttons, white cuffs and collars and white leather crossbelts. Each carried an elaborate cavalry sword in a scabbard at their hip – silver ball pommel, spiral basketwork and a cartouche incised on the hand-guard depicting the Jejunus crest: a wheatsheaf surmounted by a marten *courant*. The blade itself was long and curved with a sawback edge terminating in a wicked barbed fluke. As Hagar understood it – from her studies of military manuals – the standard-issue version of these swords was less about stabbing, more about slashing, rending and bludgeoning. The hooked tip was intended for disarming an opponent or snagging their clothing and dragging them from their mount.

Their nation's military paradigm had grown out of civil war and assumed humanoid opponents with similar tactics and weapons. In her darkest moments, she worried whether their generals were prepared for the Hilanta. Perhaps she was being silly. Morgellon knew best.

Hagar pictured the notched steel ripping someone's throat and gagged. She had cut flesh living and dead during her training at the École, had witnessed the terrible diversity of mortal ruin while practising field medicine during the Atmanloka campaign, but the idea of striking to maim, to kill? What horror.

As she walked between the guards, she shivered. Perhaps one day, swords would exist only as odd relics of a crueller time.

As she stepped into the courtyard she heard the keening, watery strains of lantian flussmusik.

The courtyard was broken up into small terraces of different heights, with canals and ornamental bridges. The effect was of a grand, surreal vista of mountains and valleys. White marble fountains sprayed over gleaming rockeries. Guests in their feathered short capes, tightly-laced gowns and cinched silk trousers were enjoying the disorientation as they negotiated the maze, stepping on and off gondolas poled by veiled servants and waving to one another with tasselled fans from opposing terraces.

She kept to the courtyard's perimeter, following a veranda lined with smooth stone archways. They were lit by jars of luminous blue algae harvested off the Sinpanese coast. Waiters sashayed past with wine, spiced rum, nectar (a disgusting, mildly alcoholic slop of Avalonian provenance), soused decapus hearts, ganu-ganu cakes, little fish and crustacean medleys on wooden skewers, ripe Nautican cheeses and roasted chubmice stuffed with cherries. Several waiters gave her curious half-glances. Most ignored her.

She took a shortcut, ducking through a service door. A stone corridor led past a series of storage rooms. Light streamed through slatted windows. In the cool, dim passage, she felt calmer. She hated the pomp and subtle knifing guile of social occasions. People's motivations were alien to her, their tastes unfathomable. She only felt like herself when she was alone, free from the disfiguring influence of strangers.

She reached the kitchen and recoiled at a blast of noise and wet heat. Cooks bellowed at assistants who peeled vegetables, turned meat on spits and thickened sauces. She wove between them, the head cook's screamed orders ringing out over the clatter of spoons and knives.

She cut through the scullery, where an army of under-servants scrubbed and scoured mountains of pots and dishes. The air had a sharp, alkaline tinge that made her breath catch. The door to the cleaning cupboard was ajar. She tutted and tried to close it, but it wouldn't shut. Someone had dumped several empty sacks of Ado's Salts on the floor on the other side. Hagar sighed. Were he here, Mitta would have rounded on the staff, yelling, breaking things. He said it was the only way to make them pay attention – anything less was futile, because by the time they learned, they had been replaced by the next generation and the lessons needed teaching all over again. She wished she had half his passion, his decisiveness.

She kicked the empty sacks under the shelves and left. Such carelessness was a safety issue. The crystals were useful for unblocking drains clogged with fat, but just a sprinkling could give you a nasty burn if it mixed with your sweat.

As she followed another passage, the sound of flussmusik grew louder. She touched her fingers to the comb in her hair, checking it hadn't fallen out.

She stepped out into the northeastern courtyard. Slender neren trees (imported at great cost) dipped shocks of branches into the canal. A tunnel led to the steps of the pavilion, made of archways wrapped in lianas. The pavilion's grey stone roof tapered to a silver shaft pointing skyward, a spear thrust towards heaven. The palace spire had always looked rather martial to her, a symbol of aggression, but today, at the birth of this strange new era, the tower in all its improbable grandeur seemed to represent something quite different: hope.

She crossed the polished white flagstones, ducking under fragrant tresses of narrymere and sea poppy. A group of guests squealed delightedly, jumping back from a cage. Inside, a simarak beat upon the steel mesh with all four of its powerful fists, hissing and flaring its spinnerets in a show of dominance. Its luxuriant mane of flame-orange hair spilled down its back to the leathery sack of its abdomen. For the ball, Morgellon had insisted on having cages placed all round the palace. Simaraks were his latest obsession; he had had dozens imported from the northern jungles, and a whole enclosure constructed, with trees draped in rigging from a scuttled clipper. Hagar had watched them descend on gossamer cables to consume live prey at feeding time, extending venom-filled spines from their wrists, parcelling paralysed, half-eaten creatures in sticky silk and stowing them in bushes for later. Once again, Morgellon's instinct for spectacle served him well; simaraks were a thrilling hint of the brutality that lay beyond civilisation.

Gondolas emerged from the tunnels that ran beneath the palace, passengers blinking in the sunlight. The pavilion's huge doors were flanked by glass statues of Okap, the fish god. Serving maids in hoods held out trenchers piled with liquorice sticks and little sugared cheeses.

Within the pavilion, conversation and music echoed up towards the distant vaulted ceiling, where murals depicted savage beasts enthralled by Orpheus playing his lyre. The rendition of Orpheus looked very like Morgellon, from the beard down to the telltale kink in his smile. A dazzling abstract mosaic spread across the floor, depicting spirals rendered in red and black and gold. At the northern end, a balcony sat on helical columns striped with golden fluting, while in the centre of the room, steps led down into a huge swimming pool, which had been emptied to serve as a sunken ballroom.

In one corner, three lanta musicians with green-gold carapaces stood surrounded by black webs of godstuff, their domed eyes glowing as they manipulated it into unsettling matrices that tricked the eye into perceiving three-dimensional shapes when viewed from certain angles. Strands linking the shapes vibrated, producing shivering, spectral notes. It was a characteristically daring choice of entertainment by Morgellon, given the rising threat from Hilanta. Perhaps he sought to remind his guests that they were at war with a nation, not a species, and that not all lanta served the dark battalions of the mycocorps. On the other hand, perhaps their presence served the same purpose as the simaraks; a tactical disruption of the pampered calm, a demonstration that the world outside the palace walls – beyond the ramparts of mutual preservation – was alien and disturbing.

She hung at the edge of the vast room, conscious of her peculiar clothes, casting about for Mitta. Three big sluice gates were set into the southern wall, allowing the pool to be filled rapidly and dramatically via grille-covered channels that ran across the floor. And ah, there was Mortifer Bechstein, 1st Lord Cambridge, resplendent in a flowing diaphanous gown from which his wings spread, decorated with iridescent feathers and supported by a crosspiece of lacquered bamboo. About his ears he wore a ringleted copper wig that came down to the fat golden links of his necklace. His hands sparkled with gemmed rings – two or three to a finger. A retinue of cowed vesperi maids followed in his wake, while his retainer Kizo – a grey-furred vesperi with keen, lupine features from one of the long-defunct noble families – walked at his side in full ceremonial cuirass of hardened leather scales, one hand on the hooked pommel of a sword in a mammoth-bone scabbard that hung from a ring at his hip, the other clad in a gauntlet from which a sleek taldin launched and wheeled through the air, provoking gasps from the balcony.

Bechstein watched and nodded approvingly. Hard to believe this was the same person under whose command thousands of suspected rossi-ka militia had been taken out to sea and drowned. The fellow who fought for the vesperi liberation forces then turned on his own people in return for endless life and a seat at the perpetuum ganzplena. Skinning, disembowelment, decades of confinement in dark, cramped cells – the cruelties he stood accused of inflicting upon his enemies were stark in their lack of imagination. Notwithstanding his dress sense and legendary appetites, there was no theatre in his wickedness. It was brutish and functional. He intimidated, he tortured, he killed and he wasted no time inventing bogus justifications before he did so. In such a way, he had managed to bring the long defiant continent of Thelusia to heel, crushing incipient uprisings by turning dissident factions' paranoia upon one another.

As he breezily engaged with various guests of lesser status, she saw how Kizo's gaze was constantly roving, his weight shifting from foot to foot. Surely he could not suspect an assault here, at her master's ball, during a celebration of peace? A substantial coalition of elite soldiers from across the perpetuum stood on watch outside the palace walls, with more patrolling the city. Within the palace, many of the soldiers were from Lord Cambridge's personal guard. All guests here were safe. With Morgellon's powers, how could they not be?

A group of high-caste harka were talking to Lord Alderberen of Avalonia, their horns etched with intricate clan insignias. Servants stood by with tithing bowls into which the heavy-set dignitaries could ostentatiously tip a measure of local wine before imbibing. Lord Alderberen himself was a mild, whelpish sort of man with a thin nose and rounded back who looked perpetually as if he were trying to recall the second half of an adage. He had not long been in the position, having travelled, so they said, from the old world. If this was England's best she was glad she had never set foot there. He appeared unassuming to the point of feeble-mindedness. Apparently his arising had granted him the ability to make plants grow, a knack which brought him great pleasure but hardly bespoke authority. He seemed constitutionally unsuited to leadership and Hagar worried that, despite his pliability, Morgellon would have to replace him if he wanted to bring stability to this region.

No sign of Mitta. No sign of Morgellon, either. She fiddled with her silk peony. A big gong hung at the deep end of the emptied pool. Morgellon had hinted he planned to make a grand speech at some point during the evening – perhaps he meant to do it here, in the pavilion.

She was jolted from her reverie by a group of stunningly beautiful, richly attired young human girls standing beside a giant hourglass. They wore glossy silk pantaloons that stopped just below the knee, covered in gilt or silver filigree, their hair cut short or shaved to just above the ears, the rest swept forward in a dramatic wave that framed the face. They did not quite fill out their blouses – Hagar was poor at guessing ages, but she put them at around fifteen or sixteen. Dust poured through the huge hourglass in a silver cascade. A clockwork mechanism cunningly concealed within the frame drew the dust back into the upper bulb, so it never ran out. The girls stood with their backs to it, glancing round while holding their faces in looks of studied boredom.

As Hagar walked past, one of them looked at her askance.

'Where's the skroon fight?'

Hagar blinked. 'I'm sorry. I don't know.'

The girl gasped, snapping her paper fan shut. She was tall, with a wide, mobile mouth and gold cufflinks finished with two colossal pearls.

'What do you mean, "I don't know"? Look at me when I'm talking to you. What's your name?'

'Hagar.'

The girls laughed into their fans. The tall girl smirked.

'Isn't that a man's name?'

'No.' Hagar's throat felt tight.

The girl looked her up and down with cool derision. 'Well, Hay-garr, I want a drink.'

Oh no. They thought her a servant. Hagar glanced around the room, mortified. Where was Mitta?

'Are you simple, child?' The girl clapped out syllables. 'Get. Me. A. Drink.'

Hagar clapped once. 'No.'

The girls all stared in stunned silence. The ringleader lunged for Hagar's hair. She grabbed it and wrenched Hagar's head side to side.

'Yes . . . yes . . . yes.' With each syllable she yanked Hagar back and forth. 'Don't you *ever* talk to me like that, you nasty . . . vulgar . . . little . . . beast.'

Hagar tried to grab her wrist but the girl yanked her head left and right. She felt the comb slip loose, heard it clatter against the floor.

The girl pulled her hand back. 'Ugh! She's infected.'

Warm air tickled Hagar's bald spot. She tried to drag the matted lump of her hair back into place.

The girl scowled. 'Moths have eaten your wig.'

Hagar looked around for the comb. She spotted it on the polished tiles. She stooped to pick it up. The girl stepped on it. It cracked with a singing report.

Hagar felt a chill wash through her. The girl gazed down, the embroidered toe cap of her boot pressing on the comb. Hagar looked up, trembling. The girl smiled, as if daring her to take it. Hagar looked into the girl's eyes, and saw cold triumph.

An instant later, she lost interest. A friend exclaimed: 'Ah, Sabine!' The group moved off.

The flussmusik rose to a piercing, glassy crescendo. Hagar scooped up the pieces of her comb and fled.

Hagar found a storage space far from the main hallways – an awkward void between two rooms that few staff knew about. It was full of ladders and old garden ornaments under dust sheets. She lit a candle, cleared a space on top of a crate, and laid out the pieces of her comb.

It had split and several teeth had fallen out. She had to keep wiping away tears. Her fingers were trembling. No good, no good. She studied her reflection in the belly of a big glass vase, piling her hair up, trying to make it look like it had before, but without the comb it would not stay. Her appearance was no longer pleasing – just hopelessly ugly.

God, she wished she could slam that girl's face into the floor until it came up busted and bloody. What use were all her years of education if she couldn't defend herself? She would make physical training part of her daily regime. She would seek out instructors. She would never let herself be humiliated again.

Hagar pictured the girl ageing, her skin slackening and mottling, her hazel eyes turning milky, her limbs becoming infirm. All our vanities shall dissolve in the tide. The fantasy was strangely unsatisfying – it made Hagar pity her, not hate her. The girl was destined to rot, surrounded by people who would despise her for it. Perhaps cruelty was inevitable when life was so short.

How silly she had been, to think anything could come of this evening. It was a celebration of peace, not a pageant for her impossible fantasies. What had she ever done to make her think she deserved Mitta?

Morgellon had always said she was greedy, wretched. However much he had given her, she always wanted more. She was lucky he continued to tolerate her.

She squeezed between sheeted stacks of iron lawn chairs and sat against the wall. It was caked with dust but she no longer cared. She would never preen and fuss again. Today marked an end to all that. Let today be about peace.

An empty sack rucked under her heel. Underneath, the floor was covered in blue crystals. A caustic scent hit her nostrils – Ado's Salts. There was another sack beside it, and more piled up beside that. Ugh! Such laziness! Someone had clearly been dumping their rubbish in a little-used room rather than walk all the way across the palace. She grabbed a sack from the pile, ready to march to the head butler and excoriate him the way she imagined Mitta would.

A dust sheet slipped. In the corner of the room was a man. He was stripped to his underclothes, his windpipe neatly slit.

The copper band on his left wrist marked him out as a member of Morgellon's elite garde du corps. Dark blood on his undershirt was still wet and scintillating. She felt for a pulse. Nothing. She touched his cheek. Warm, clammy. She manipulated his wrist, his arm. Loose. No rigor mortis yet.

She stood, not wanting to move. Any reaction felt like it would make the situation more real.

Crashes rang through the palace. Servants were striking the gongs in the pavilion. It was almost time for Morgellon to give his grand speech.

Hagar sprinted through the palace, jinking round hooded maids and drunk dignitaries. Guests frowned and tutted. She had to warn Morgellon. She ran down a long hallway, while overhead lean vesperi acrobats painted silver and decked with ribbons and bells hung upside-down from metal hoops, very slowly opening and closing their wings.

When she reached the pavilion guests were loitering beneath the marble architrave, smoking pipes with long curved stems. She found a gap in the crowd and barged through it, wincing as she clipped an elbow and heard someone curse.

The pavilion was not yet full – guests were evidently still making their way from various diversions around the palace, moving at the stately pace appropriate to those with one eye on eternity. She slowed to a purposeful march. She did not want to embarrass Morgellon, or cause a panic. Servants moved from group to group, offering vivid berry liqueurs and golden nests of spun sugar set on little biscuits topped with soft sweetened cheese. Harka peer Parmaran Koi of the Balada Dynasty stood in purple robes amongst her entourage of priests, attendants and professional greeters who performed deep, ritual bows to any guests who drew near, offering gifts of cherries, votive dice and little scrolls bound with silk ribbons, containing extracts of Koi's poetry.

She felt Morgellon an instant before she saw him. Some valets and handmaidens claimed a bond with their master or mistress that went beyond pain. Some claimed to share emotions, even thoughts. Hagar could not boast of such a rapport with Morgellon, save for a sharp premonition, almost a shock, whenever she was about to encounter him.

Their eyes met. He was immaculate. He was dressed entirely in white – white robe, white cross-belt, white trousers and white boots. His dark hair was threaded with pearls. He was talking to a man in a colourful shawl and a tall woman in a sheer gown finished with golden chains. He raised a palm and smiled.

'Ah, *bichette*! You've come! I thought we'd never drag you away from your books.' He gestured around the room with a glass of port. 'What do you think?'

'I need to speak to you.'

'Of course, of course.' He handed his glass to a waiting maid and placed a palm on Hagar's shoulder. 'You know . . . I couldn't have done any of this without you.'

'Uncle.' She used the Low Thelusian term *oomkah* – it emphasised the warmth of the relationship while jettisoning the semantic cargo associated with literal family. She disliked hypocoristic terms of affection but they were useful for getting his attention. 'I know this will sound rash, but—'

'Did something happen to your hair?'

'Please, I—'

'Would you like ten minutes with one of our hairdressers? Honestly, carbuncle, you're a perfect dream but you don't help yourself.' He glanced down. 'And whatever's that in your hand?'

Hagar hid the shattered comb behind her back. 'I need to speak with you in confidence.'

'Can it wait until after my speech?'

She moved in closer than anyone except Mitta would be publicly allowed and whispered in his ear: 'I've found a body.'

The grin vanished from his face. 'Now's not the time for pranks.'

'I'm serious, I—'

He flashed a beaming smile at a passing guest, then said in a firm, clear voice: 'After. The. Speech.'

'My lord.' They both turned to see Mitta. He wore a mantle of dark grey cloth that came down to his calves, closed at the breastbone with two circular silver clasps. His hair was swept to one side, revealing a spiked silver ear cuff.

Morgellon cleared his throat. 'Is all well?'

Mitta blinked. 'Of course. I simply came to wish you good luck before your address.' Though his expression was neutral, his tone was calm, almost serene. 'Perhaps you should listen to Hagar. You said yourself you wouldn't be here without her.'

Morgellon raised his hand until it was an inch from Mitta's cheek. He stroked the backs of his knuckles down an imaginary aura.

'Ah, you're right.' He turned to Hagar. 'I'm sorry, *bichette*. The weight of the occasion has made me short-tempered. Come close. Whisper to me.' He beckoned, then went down on one knee with a practised ostentation, bowing his head as if capitulating.

Hagar leaned in. She could feel dozens of pairs of eyes upon her. Shards of comb slipped in her sweaty fingers. Her resolve weakened. What if the news broke his spirit? What if she ruined his speech, shattered the accord?

'Uncle.' Her throat was scratchy and dry. 'I've found a body.'

Morgellon was silent for several seconds. She sensed him stiffening, the way he did before he flew into one of his rages. He dug a manicured nail deep into his palm. She winced at the pain he did not feel.

'An unwelcome development.' Wine was heavy on his breath. 'Please – we are being watched. Maintain an easy smile and tell me more.'

As best she could, she let her jaw relax, and murmured to him where she had found the corpse, the nature of the injuries, the estimated time of death. All the while, she smiled, and Morgellon nodded, occasionally chuckling as if she had whispered an amusing morsel of gossip.

He patted her heavily on the shoulder and said, loud enough that the guests around them could hear: 'Wise words indeed. I'll see to it that your wishes are honoured, little one.'

'Thank you, Uncle,' she said, unsure if she understood.

'Now, will you do me a favour in return?'

'Anything.'

'Retire to your chamber and sleep, *bichette*.'

'But your speech—'

'Is nothing but a bit of dry politicking!' He swatted a palm at her and laughed. 'The work is already over. Please. You look exhausted.'

He was right. She felt bitterly fatigued.

'Go,' he said. 'I relieve you of all duties until further notice. Take to your bed, and rest assured I'll deal with your request.' His stare hardened for a moment.

She bowed deeply and began to retreat. 'Of course, Uncle.' Mitta had already slipped away. She glanced around the pavilion. Lord Cambridge was reclining on a low-backed chair while two slender vesperi dressed in half-capes contorted before him, performing a rapid and elaborate sword dance. His valet, Kizo, was nowhere to be seen, which Hagar thought odd given the proximity of the peer to several gleaming butterfly swords.

The gongs crashed again. Ushers urged guests down the steps into the huge empty pool, ready for Morgellon's historic declaration of peace. Hagar turned and pushed against the crowd, heading for the exit. Her heart felt crushed and small. The new age would start without her.

Hagar trudged through a cool, empty hall, her soles ringing on the marble floor. She still felt uneasy, but Morgellon was right. She should rest.

He would have this small calamity discreetly dealt with. The pressures on palace staff over the past few weeks had been considerable. She could very well imagine an argument escalating to something graver.

Life had taught her that peace was illusory. Perhaps that was why, now peace had arrived, it felt unreal. On the battlefield, silence was ominous.

She still had the broken comb clutched in her palm. She looked at it. Her fingers were tacky with black blood.

She followed a corridor to the eastern guest comfort rooms. Behind a tall door with woven rush panels was a softly-lit room containing a lavatory, basin, a fur rug, a selection of soaps, perfumes and pomades, and a dish-shaped mobile hanging from the door, laden with bells and glass chimes, that could be operated via a clockwork motor attached to the wall. When the motor was activated, the mobile turned and let out pleasant, melodic music, masking any noise made by the occupant. It was a fashion that had started in the upper-class bathhouses and arenas of the capital, where space was at a premium and elite members of society conspired in the mutual fiction that they did not defecate.

The water from the pitcher was silky and cold. She lathered up soap and washed her hands, over and over, lacing her fingers, scrubbing under the chipped nails. She rinsed them off, pulled the plug and watched blood drain over speckled volcanic stone. The whirlpool made her think of the great sluices in the pavilion. Her skin was raw from scrubbing. *All our vanities shall dissolve in the tide.* As the last of the water swirled away, she felt a sinking sensation in her belly.

She stared into the basin. She thought of all those dignitaries, paraministers, servants and peers descending into the empty swimming pool, filling it with bodies. The idea of being crammed in there with them made her shudder. No wonder Kizo was casting round for threats – that many people in one place was enough to make anyone edgy. As the last of the water belched down the pipe beneath her, she caught a burning whiff of Ado's Salts.

She glanced up into the mirror. Revelation hit her.

She ran.

In a low-ceilinged room, a figure in green garde du corps uniform emptied the last sack of Ado's Salts into a water tank sunken into the floor. Crystals sizzled as they dissolved, giving off a ghostly white vapour. The figure kept a wet cloth pressed to his face. The air was thick with acrid fumes that caught in the throat. A slatted window in the corner provided the only light and ventilation.

The figure took a heavy leg of mutton filched from the kitchens, and held it out above the water. His gloved fingers relaxed.

The mutton struck the clear water with a plop, then a fizz, white froth encasing the raw, marbled meat as it sank. Halfway down it simply sloughed away into nothing – even the bone dissolved.

Test complete, the figure moved to a huge pipe topped with an iron wheel valve. The pipe ran from the tank, through the wall, down to the sluices in the pavilion. Opening the valve would flood the empty swimming pool. The figure grasped the wheel, and threw his shoulders into turning it.

Hagar saw all this from her vantage point at the partially shuttered window. Her eyes streamed from the fumes. A guard's corpse lay slumped beside the hatch in the floor that allowed access to the pumphouse. A length of lead pipe was wedged under the handle, holding it shut. A dozen sacks lay empty. The figure had their back to her now, straining to turn the wheel.

She eased open the shutter, and slid, feet first, through the narrow gap. There was a six-foot drop to the floor. Holding her breath, she dropped.

Her shoes rang against the tiles. The figure spun round.

He whipped a dagger from his belt and flung it at her. Hagar threw herself aside; the blade clanged off the whitewashed wall and skidded into the water, where it immediately began to fizz.

She staggered to her feet. The figure was watching her, panting, a damp rag clamped over his face. He peeled it away.

Hagar squinted. Her vision was blurred, his features dim and indistinct.

No.

'Hagar?'

That voice. She hacked as fumes hit the back of her throat.

'Mitta?'

Tears streamed from his eyes. 'Get out of here!'

She took a step forward, taking shallow breaths. 'How could you?' She had expected Kizo, Lord Cambridge's retainer. 'Peace, you said!' She tasted blood. 'A new age.'

'Yes.' Mitta held the rag to his mouth. 'Born from . . . death.'

'No!' She could barely see. Her skin was tingling. 'Morgellon . . . trusted you.'

Mitta grimaced. His eyes were red and weeping.

'You. Don't. Understand.' He grabbed the wheel valve with both hands.

She lunged at him. His elbow smashed into her jaw. Ceiling tiles flashed past. Her head hit the floor.

The pain in her jaw was intense. Her throat and sinuses burned. He had *struck* her. The wheel valve squeaked as it began to yield.

Mitta was not going to listen. He had lost his reason. She staggered to her feet.

Hagar thought of her training in the École. She took a moment to appraise his body from an anatomical perspective, picturing the radius of each limb, the position of organs. This time, as she dived at him, she anticipated the blow, dodged just out of reach. His elbow swung through air. She punched him in the kidney with her non-dominant hand. The strike was weak, but enough to make him retaliate. He spun round, flailing at her. Hagar staggered back.

'Stop.' He stopped to hack up a string of bloody sputum. 'I. Don't. Want. To. Hurt. You.' His hand went to the sword at his hip.

She glanced at the sword, then into his raw and streaming eyes. 'You already have.'

'Join. Us.'

She edged back, seething water an inch to her left. What could she do? She had no hope of overpowering him.

'Why?' Her exposed skin stung as it began to blister. 'Mitta!'

A sudden sharp sting in her left palm. It repeated twice more, three brief, piercing jabs. Mitta winced too – which meant the sensation must not be hers, but Morgellon's.

'Hey!' she yelled. Mitta's image blurred and separated. She was going to pass out. 'Answer me! Does Morgellon's love mean *nothing* to you?'

He drew his sword.

'It. Means. *Everything.*'

He raised the serrated blade high above his head.

She stamped on an empty sack and kicked sharply sideways. It slid from under him. He stumbled. She ran and shoved him square in the chest. He threw his arms out for balance, dropping the sword. An instant later, he lunged forward and clamped his hands round her throat.

He bore her up off her feet and thumped her into the wall. His thumbs crushed her windpipe. She sucked for breath but her throat was shut. She pounded on his ringed fingers, kicked him in the stomach. He held on. He was far stronger.

He gritted his teeth. 'Close. Your. Eyes.'

Air would not come. Her lips worked uselessly. Her vision narrowed.

'Sister.' His voice seemed far away. 'Say . . . you renounce . . . the world.' He dissolved into another fit of coughing.

Her slick fingers fumbled for something tucked into the hooks on the back of her dress. Her palms were tingly. She could not feel her fingertips.

His grip tightened still further. 'Please. Let. Go. Willingly.'

Through gummy membranes of rheum, she saw his face, almost touching hers. She laid a palm upon the warm hands locked around her throat. She stroked her thumb across his knuckles. His breath felt hot against her lips. She tilted her brow till it came to rest on his.

With her free hand, she drove the spiked handle of the comb into his neck.

His head jerked back. He let go of her and she dropped to the floor. Mitta clutched at the comb, coughing, rasping. She punched him hard in the groin. He buckled. She shoulder-barged him. His head clanged off the valve wheel. He dropped to one knee, his eyes unfocused. He toppled towards the pool.

She caught him. His head lolled inches above the water. She had him by the collar. Her fingers trembled. She could not bear his weight.

'Mitta!' Her throat was burning. 'I can't . . . hold . . . you.'

He hacked up a grot of blood. It rolled from the corner of his mouth and dropped into the pool, where it fizzed and dissolved.

'Please!' Her tears hit the smoking water. 'Help me . . . pull you up.'

She was burning all over. Her ears were aflame. Her nostrils were aflame. Her tongue was aflame. Her body was aflame. The world was aflame.

Mitta twitched. His swollen eyes focused on her. He grinned, blood on his teeth, and took a deep breath.

He dunked his skull back into the pool.

She cried out. She tried to haul him back in, grasping at his cross-belt, his soft dark hair. The pool scalded the backs of her palms. She smelt her flesh burning. She did not care. She dragged and pulled and with a final broken shriek, swung his limp body onto the tiled floor.

'Mitta . . .' Already the name was bitter in her mouth, drowning in blood and bile. She choked it out. 'Mitta . . . Mitta . . .'

The body convulsed beneath her. Brain matter oozed from the smoking hole in the back of the skull. She pressed her face to the still-warm chest.

Together, they danced.

CHAPTER 17
LABYRINTH

Back in the old jail, Delphine told them everything she could remember about what Arthur had said. She described his appearance, the freezing pain when his fingers passed through her, the way his voice seemed to come from inside her head. She told Butler where she knew Arthur from, and a little of his background.

'He said my father's in the summer palace.'

Butler glanced up from his notebook. 'Well, that can't be true.'

Delphine inhaled sharply as Martha dabbed at her puncture wound with cotton wool dipped in alcohol. 'Why?'

'Morgellon had it buried nearly three hundred years ago. His valet died after an accident there. I suppose the memory was just too much. Always had an eye for the tragic, Morgellon.' He took a slug of a cloudy white beverage from a large mug. 'The spire's what's left.'

'You mean it's *here*, in the city?'

Butler hissed peevishly and turned a page. 'It was. Unless your Arthur's being deliberately obfuscatory the *only* place he could be referring to is the Grand-Duc's old summer palace.'

'Maybe he is, then,' said Patience.

'How?' said Butler, his eyes bulging with annoyance. 'I just *told* you, it's gone.'

'I was very interested in civic history once upon a time. I've collected a lot of maps over the years. Maybe we should investigate for ourselves.'

Up in Patience's library they took a huge book down from the shelf. It contained street maps of the high town drawn on thin onionskin paper with the houses and roads on one sheet and the sewer system on another so you could overlay them and see how they matched up.

'This is from around twenty-five years ago,' she said, smoothing the page down with her human hand, 'so I don't know how . . . ah, see here.' The paper crackled as she pointed to an open rectangle. 'This is the top of the high town. That's Mitta's Spire in the centre of the esplanade there.' She lifted the page to show a blocky rectangular area plotted underneath, more or less conforming to the dimensions of the esplanade. 'Could this be part of the palace? It's just marked here as . . .' She squinted at a tiny marginal annotation. '"Subterranean structure".'

'Let me look at that.' Butler shoved in beside her and started scrutinising the page. 'Hmm . . . I mean it could be *anything*. Let's see – what's the page reference here . . .' He flipped between leaves and spent some time comparing sections of map. He snapped his fingers. 'Pencil.' Patience rolled her eyes but got him one anyway. He spent the next couple of minutes jotting things down.

Delphine sagged into a deep rattan chair. She sipped at the cup of heady dark liquor Patience had poured for her. Aah, that was good. The funny thing about getting stabbed was it still felt better than rheumatoid arthritis. Nothing worse than that gnawing ache, deep inside your bones. Being old was like getting beaten up every day of your life. Mugged by time. Christ's sweet tree. She cackled quietly to herself, a little manic from fatigue. Perhaps a little drunk.

Butler got up and paced the library, scanning the shelves. He took down a book with a partially disintegrated spine, set it down on the desk. He pumped his wings to blow away the dust, and flipped through until he found a page that unfolded once, twice, into a floorplan.

'Here it is.' He tapped the page with the back of the pencil. 'Look.'

Delphine hauled herself out of the chair to come and see what he was referring to. Patience stood alongside her. Butler laid the map and the foldout floorplan side by side.

'This is the design for the summer palace.' He pointed to the floorplan. After so many years folded up, the page resisted lying flat, and he had to put candlesticks and an ashtray at the corners to weigh it down. He ran an index finger down a key at the top right, written in the same foreign alphabet Delphine had seen round the city. '"Steam Chamber East", "Fencing Court", "Royal Canal South". Hm! It's all coming back to me.'

'You've been there before?'

'Naturally. Before it was buried, of course. But look.' He pointed to corresponding sections of the two maps. 'The references here match up.' He flipped between several pages of the big city maps, pointing out further undefined structures on the underground layers. Their shapes corresponded to the plans in the second book. 'The spire's part of the old pavilion. It looks like they've preserved the internal structure. It's been sealed up, like a tomb.' He flipped between pages. 'It would have to be heavily reinforced, what with the weight of earth and buildings. These tunnels look like passageways linking sections across what would have been open courtyards. And here.' He perched a cigarette in his mouth and indicated a series of linked concentric circles on the city map. 'The spillways from his stupid canals run down into these old smugglers' tunnels that go right through the hill. Which in turn,' he turned to another sheet of paper, 'should be accessible where the high town sewers meet the undercity.'

'So we can get in?' said Delphine.

Butler unscrewed the glass mantle of an oil lamp and lit his cigarette off the flame. 'In theory.'

'Right.' She stood. She felt a twinge in her shoulder, tried not to let it show on her face. 'Let's tool up.'

'Sit down.'

'He's my father. He's in pain.'

'A fellow appeared to you and claimed to have seen the future.' Butler sat back and blew a plume of smoke. 'And you're just going to take him at his word?'

'He was warning me off. So I'm going to do the bloody opposite.'

'Wait, wait, wait. What was the part about an "auntie"?'

'He meant Anwen. Lady Dellapeste.'

'No, she was his grandmother. His auntie would be Anwen's daughter.' He looked at Delphine. 'She and her valet conceived a child. But then the baby was kidnapped. No one knows what happened to her.'

Delphine shivered. 'She came to England. I knew her.'

Butler's eyes widened. 'Goodness.' He tapped three fingers on the cover of the notebook Delphine had recovered from the advocate's chambers. 'I need more time with this. He uses a lot of abbreviations, words that are probably personal idiom or codenames. In places the handwriting is almost illegible, but . . .' He curled the fingers of his right hand into a fist, rested his noseleaf against his knuckles. 'A large portion of it is given over to a subject S. It's more like a personal diary than scientific notes. She was held in some sort of testing facility. And she could shape her surroundings just by willing it.' Butler opened the book and flipped through some pages. 'Some of the later entries are utterly deranged. He starts suspecting she's feeding off his emotions, claims he's losing the capacity for grief or regret.'

Butler looked up. 'There's another thing as well. It mentions a subject whose body produces flames. He's kept with S. The author thinks their powers may balance one another.'

'That's my father. It must be.' She felt dizzy and sick.

'If Anwen's daughter is still alive, and she's half as powerful as these notes claim . . .' Butler took another hit of cloudy white booze. 'And the Grand-Duc arrives in less than two days . . .'

'And the cliques are arming themselves to rise up against the perpetuum,' said Patience.

'Or each other,' said Butler.

'The idea Fat Maw might burn doesn't seem so far-fetched,' said Patience.

'Then let's go!' Delphine banged her fist against the desk. 'We can get in there and stop this atrocity before it starts.'

Butler eyed her up and down. 'You need food, rest. And a bandage round that stab wound.'

'I'm fine.'

'You'd be surprised how often I've heard that from someone just before they die.'

'Here's your chance to get rid of me.'

The old vesperi narrowed his eyes. 'Patience needs to transfer the last of our gear from the boat to the jail. I need time to look over these maps properly. Take some painkillers. Sleep. You look your age.'

'Thank you.'

'I don't think you appreciate the gravity of the situation. The cliques are on the verge of civil war. Infiltrators on our own side want us dead. Someone may be preparing to unleash the single most powerful weapon since the Hilanta Wars. Why on earth would you want to step into the middle of that?'

She necked the last of her booze. She shivered as the burn washed through her.

'People I love are still alive.'

Delphine swallowed a couple of ibuprofen and codeine with a tumbler of dark liquor that Patience called it 'killdevil', then smoked a pipe before bed. The storm passed and the air grew stifling. She couldn't lie flat – her shoulder hurt too much, even under the numbing layer of booze and medicine – so she made a nest of pillows in a big chair next to the hammock and settled down to doze.

Alice lay sleeping on her front with her arms spread cruciform. Delphine kept drifting into murky half-sleep, her thoughts growing gnarly and surreal. She and Martha had some fruit picking to do – they had to fill the baskets and drag them down to the storehouse, which was Delphine's shed, only inside it was colossal, and there was a vending machine with tea and coffee and hot rolls.

Sometimes, when she woke, her heart was racing for no reason. Sometimes she thought she heard footsteps in the hall. Once, through the fog of sleep, she thought she sensed a pale light, and a touch on her wrist, but when she opened her eyes, she and Alice were alone.

The next morning, she washed in seawater brought up by bucket and windlass. Salt stung her wound. Martha helped her change the dressing. She ate a breakfast of scrambled eggs, smoked fish, and soft pale kernels soaked and boiled into a spiced porridge. She took a pot of coffee up to a room in the east wing and drank it all and smoked three cigarettes and listened to waves crashing against the rocks. She had woken late. The cigarettes were bent and damp and tasted rank.

When she glanced out the window, Alice was talking to Reggie in the courtyard. She felt a little jolt; her stomach clenched. Why was she feeling strange? They were only talking.

She took her mug down to the scullery then descended to the dungeon room, where their recovered equipment lay in messy piles. Working one-handed, she unrolled a tarp and set the machine pistol and Remington on top. Her wound ached under the bandage. She felt a bit queasy.

She pulled out a carton of 9mm cartridges and rattled it – still half-full. She tipped them out onto the tarp and began checking each in turn, standing it on its end when she was done.

Facing death crunched one's life down to an almost monastic simplicity. No time to worry about letters that needed sending, or hospital appointments, or looming environmental catastrophe. She found her sickle under some mooring ropes. She knelt and rifled through the toolbox for a whetstone, trying to ignore the nauseous, worming doubt in her heart.

She wondered what Alice and Reggie had been chatting about. Alice had been looking up at him, squinting against the sunlight. She had passed a hand through her hair, nodding.

She sat down on a plastic crate and began sharpening the blade's inside edge. Did she secretly crave it? The urgency and pain? The way adrenaline emptied her mind? Algernon had once admonished her that she would hate war: *It's ninety per cent waiting around, ten per cent doing what you're told.*

Certainly she had not envied anyone fighting in the North African campaign, nor at Normandy. But war is a subtle paramour. Her experience on the Home Front had been a strange blend of absence and abundance. Long days in the fields, working till her arms grew hard, her palms rough. Heady, vivid trysts with homesick Land Girls. Hunger. Death the gap between breaths. Windfalls. Ice cracking under boots at dawn. The Apocalypse hunched amongst red-drenched aspens come sunset.

She continued working the whetstone over the curved steel; the motion and sound were calming.

She held up the sickle. Candlelight picked out a thin milk-white crescent. She tested it in either hand, practising hammer-swings, parries, backhands, sometimes thumbing the button so the shaft snapped out to full length.

After a time, she became aware that someone was behind her, watching.

'What?' she snapped.

Footsteps scraped on the gritty stone floor. Without turning round, Delphine set the sickle down and began searching through the equipment for batteries for her Maglite. 'If you've come to make one last appeal to my pragmatic self-interest I'm afraid you're out of—'

Rik-ik-ik.

Delphine turned. Martha stood in the doorway, her eyes pulsing a soft marine green.

'Oh,' said Delphine. 'Sorry, I thought you were Butler.'

Martha walked into the room. She was holding a mug of coffee which, judging by the sickly sweet aroma, was thick with honey. She stood and looked at Delphine.

'I'm just getting ready,' said Delphine. 'You all right?' She felt oddly self-conscious. She went back to digging for batteries, not so much to find them as to distract herself. 'Didn't get much sleep.' She talked to fill the silence, her voice echoing off the stone walls. 'Shoulder hurts like the Dickens. Alice said . . .' Her throat dried and she coughed. 'Mm. Well.' She took a pack of Duracells out of a zip-up toolbag.

Martha flipped open a crate and took out a spiral pad, yellowed and corrugated from repeated soakings. The paper crackled as she flattened it out with her thin, twig-like fingers, and wrote in pencil.

hagar was here

Delphine read it a couple of times and frowned. 'What? When?'

Martha took the pad back and wrote again.

today. patience saw her coming & locked the dungeon door so she wouldn't find you. they talked. i watched

'And?'

Martha wrote furiously. She produced several pages of exchanges, marked *p:* and *h:* respectively, then slapped the pad into Delphine's hands. Delphine was used to Martha's prodigious powers of recall, though she used them for the oddest things – writing takeaway menus from memory, or recording barcode numbers in a red notebook.

Delphine read the contents. Without any inflection or context the conversation was difficult to parse.

'Did she seem . . . hostile?'

Martha shook her fist for no. Then she wrote:

p says it's best we leave soon. if h has visited it might not be long before the cliques follow

'Right. Thank you, Martha.' Delphine turned back to the equipment. Her heart was racing. They were going in.

A tap on her arm. She turned and Martha was holding out the pad.

delphine. i am getting the sense again.

'What sense? Oh.' Delphine shook her head. 'Martha, with the greatest respect, now is not the time for one of your existential horror jags.'

he was here. in the city

'Who?'

Delphine knew from the first pencil stroke. Down, then an arc. She felt the name in her stomach, felt as if she were writing it herself. Martha held up the pad.

henry

They ate a patchwork meal of soft cheese, olives and salty little fish the pink of sticking plasters. Delphine did not feel hungry but she knew it was best to set off on a full stomach. Alice was there, and Butler and Martha and Patience and Reggie. She avoided catching Reggie's eye, but snuck glances. His face had a few days' beard growth. He did not speak. He ate heartily.

She spent a long time over her final fish, picking tiny translucent bones from between her teeth, chewing slowly, savouring the briny, slimy, if she was honest not-terribly-pleasant flavour. At last, she pushed her plate back.

Patience used her teeth to pull a white cotton glove over her human hand. She spat a thread.

'Now,' she said. 'Reggie has procured a boat. He's going to wait in the south quay.'

'What do we need a boat for?' said Delphine.

'To escape. We can't just come back here.' She smiled as if she thought Delphine was joking. 'You do realise that, don't you? If your father is there, or Anwen's daughter, and we rescue them, we'll be pursued relentlessly.'

'What do you mean, "we"?'

'Oh. I'm coming too. You didn't think I'd let you attempt such a stupid thing alone, did you? Leaving this island is a violation of my house arrest. Once they notice I'm gone, I'll be a fugitive.' She glanced around at the silk hangings and wrought-iron lamps. 'Can't say I'll miss the place. Oh God, it'll be good to stretch my legs.'

'You'll forgive me if the prospect doesn't fill me with enthusiasm. Last time I tried to save someone you put a gun to my head.'

'Then let me put things right.'

'You can't!' Delphine thumped the table. 'What's done is done. There's no fixing it.' She winced at a twinge in her knife wound, sat back. She looked from Patience to Butler. 'All we can do is save the future.'

'Where will we go?' said Alice. Reggie glanced at her and Delphine felt sick. So stupid.

Patience and Butler exchanged a look.

'That's . . . still a live question,' said Butler. 'For now, the threshold is off-limits. It's unclear what allies we have left.'

'A problem for tomorrow,' said Patience, guillotining a pickle with her incisors. 'For now, let's focus. I'll help Reggie transport some of our belongings to the ship. Then, we go.'

In the deepest part of the dungeon, ochre water stood ankle-deep. Granite blocks lay piled in one corner of the room. Patience's angel arm split into a web of gummy pink strands. She opened a black portal in the floor beside her. Another began to form beneath the blocks, bubbling and smoking. The blocks began sinking into the godstuff. One by one, she dragged them out the other side, until she had cleared the way to a hidden passage behind.

'This will take us beneath the bay to the undercity,' she said. 'Be careful. In some parts the water gets deep.'

Butler pulled up the hood of his long black cloak, his pistol in a shoulder-holster. He lit an oil lamp with a rush taper, fixed the glass mantle in place and trimmed the wick. He was grimacing, his ears pricked.

Delphine's stomach was turning over. Pragmatism be damned, Patience's presence made her uneasy. She took a swig from a plastic bottle, swilled water round her mouth and spat. She had the Remington hanging on a sling-swivel, solid slugs in the stock mount, shot shells in the sidesaddle. The sickle was in a sheath in her backpack, blade down, along with water, dried fruit, a plastic bottle full of paraffin and a blister pack of codeine. The air from the tunnel was musty and cool.

'Ready?' Alice stood beside her in boots and a light shirt, her white hair tied back, a velcro ammo belt strapped round her and the machine pistol in a hip holster. She looked martial and out-of-place and so, so young.

'You don't have to come,' said Delphine.

Alice nodded. 'I know.'

Martha walked up to Delphine and raised her hand. She was clutching what looked like a desiccated tangle of rust-red seaweed.

Delphine took it a little uncertainly. The tiny lobes felt prickly and strange.

'Thank you.' She tied it to the barrel of her shotgun. It hung there like a foxtail.

Delphine gazed into the darkness of the tunnel. *We shall have to go soon*, she thought to herself. And she stood, and she savoured each breath.

CHAPTER 18
THE DAY OF THE INAUGURATION

Rough hands forced Hagar down onto her knees. Her breaths were hot and moist inside the leather hood. She felt sick and thirsty, a pulse pounding in her temple.

No ambient noise. She was probably indoors. Her wrists were bound behind her back, the air cool and still against her bare hands. The ground beneath her knees was hard, with little ridges.

She remembered the hollow clatter of boots on boards, then the slosh of oars, the creak of a boat moving through the undercity. A handover. Shoved into a crate barely big enough to hold her, the lid nailed down. A long time waiting. Hot, cramped space. She must have passed out, because the next thing she knew was rocking, jostling, the clatter of carriage wheels on cobbles. The crate lifting. Knocks and thumps. Then a crack as the lid was levered off, and now this.

Her neck hairs prickled. Someone was watching her.

What if she had misjudged? No. Arthur had promised. He was capricious, insolent and gullible, but she did not think he would lie to her. Unless . . .

Footsteps. Coming or going? The hood made it hard to tell. She strained, heard only the rumble of blood in her skull.

She flinched at movement near her face. Someone gripped her shoulders. The drawstring slackened. The hood yanked upwards, sloughing off.

A river of stars in blackness.

She blinked. Cool air bathed her sweaty skin. She was in a huge open chamber, like a church, surrounded by hundreds of white candles burning in iron holders. The glow picked out spiral pillars twisting up into gloom. She looked heavenward, gazed into darkness.

A figure stepped into her field of vision.

'*Bichette.*'

Her breath caught. A tongue ran across wine-stained teeth.

Morgellon stood before her, holding a single fat white candle in his palm. He wore dark blue dress breeches fastened with silver buckles below the knees, a dark blue double-breasted waistcoat and a heavy black riding coat with long tails and a hood. The left side of his mouth wore that mischievous upward kink, the legacy – he had once told her – of a childhood broken jaw. He looked less like Lord Jejunus, the Terrestrial Grand-Duc, the Endless Sentinel, Guardian of the Free Peoples of the Perpetuum, and more like some cosseted civil servant from the capital.

'My lord.'

She invested the two syllables with all the scorn she could muster. It felt good, after all these years. The naked spite.

'So,' he said.

'So.'

Her eyes adjusted, revealing candles in a wide horseshoe shape, loosely conforming to the walls of a sunken section of floor. Behind Morgellon was a sarcophagus of black marble, haloed in soft orange light. An onyx statue rose over it, eighteen feet of exquisite detail – the soft pleats of the mantle, the embossing on the discs of his cloak clasp. She could not stop a sigh escaping. Almost three centuries had passed. And yet. Mitta.

Morgellon glanced past her. 'Ensure the doors to the surface are locked. No one is to come down here.'

'As you will it, my lord,' said a deep voice behind her. The sound of hooves on stone echoed away.

She waited, shivering in the chill. Morgellon's breath curled out in moustaches of vapour as he stood watching her.

She let herself examine him one last time. His hair was shorter, his beard trimmed and oiled. She marked the little flaws in her memory – how his eyes were smaller than she remembered, keener and more leonine. She realised the image in her head had been a composite, partly influenced by his portrait in the Library of the Six Bridges, which squared off his jawline and took considerable liberties with his hair, showing it flowing in great billowing foxtails, blasted by sea-spray and lit from behind by a great trident of white-blue lightning.

'You've achieved your purpose,' he said. 'You've drawn me out of hiding. What now?'

Hagar felt the impulse to dissemble, to flatter, still strong after all these years. Servility corroded the soul. *Lying is not merely a sign of weakness, Hagar. It is a cause of weakness.*

'I'm here to kill you.'

His upper lip peeled back from his teeth in a sneer. 'What a coincidence.' He brought the candle towards her. 'Ah. There you are.' His gaze crawled over the contours of her face, performing a slow inventory. His breath stank of wine. The bright yellow-white flame came so close she felt its heat against her cheek. She winced one eye shut, expecting him to set light to her hair.

He withdrew. She sagged – she could not help feeling relief, hated that already he was manipulating her emotions, punishing and rewarding.

'Did they harm you?' he said.

'No more than was necessary.'

'Good.'

A searing pain in the heel of her palm. She jerked, tried to twist her hands free, then saw the runnels of melted wax dripping onto Morgellon's open hand. He was aware of it, of course, but he did not experience it as pain – just information. She bit down on the inside of her cheek, trying to make space for the burning amongst the great range of sensations she was experiencing. The cool musty air of the pavilion. Coarse rope against her wrists. Her tongue against the backs of her teeth.

'Do you realise how far you were from succeeding?' he said, holding the candle so it lit his face from beneath. 'What was your plan?'

Hagar breathed, fury catching and kindling in her chest. She must not let him provoke her. She needed all her composure for what was to come.

She planted one foot on the floor and, staggering, rose. 'This *is* my plan.'

'Tonti was right. He saw straight through your lies. No wonder you despised him.'

'He was like a brother to me.'

'Abel, perhaps.' Morgellon stared into the white flame till his pupils shrank to dots. 'Do you think for a moment I don't know that you killed him?'

Hagar tried to hide her surprise. Morgellon kept his gaze on the flame. Her eyes stung. She blinked. Tears rolled down her cheeks. He dug in a pocket of his jacket and produced a square of white card. He thrust it before her. The card was glossy, slightly warped. There was a boxed image on it. Through tears, she picked out timbers, orange flames in a fireplace, and a pale, staring girl holding a black box.

Hagar gazed at the image dumbly. It was her, in Tonti's lodge. She had seen photographs before, but who had taken this? She saw bars of light, realised she was looking at her reflection, reversed, in a window. The box in her hands was a camera. She had taken the picture of herself.

He snatched it away. 'I've known for years. And yet, for the sake of national unity, for the sake of stability, I kept my counsel.'

It was Hagar's turn to laugh. 'For the sake of your empire, you mean. You were terrified the cliques would sense a palace coup was underway and rise against you.'

Morgellon looked her up and down. Hot wax oozed over his knuckles. She felt the searing pain of his skin blistering.

'That's all in hand.' His even temper troubled her. She could feel his control hanging slack around her thoughts like a noose. He knew the sisters had taught her to fight, and he was prepared. Any sudden movement, any hint of resistance, and he would try to take over her body. She had to delay that moment for as long as possible.

She glanced about the pavilion for something she might use to distract him, but the river of candles had made her night-blind. She saw only dust-covered tiles surrounding her, a hundred flames and the black sarcophagus. All else faded into darkness. It was as if they stood on a tiny island of light at the end of all creation.

'I was in love with him,' she said. It was the only thing she could think of. The words left a silence that hung between them like mist.

Morgellon raised a thick, oiled eyebrow. 'Tonti?'

'Mitta, you idiot. I loved Mitta.'

She watched the blow land. Funny how one who had lived so long was still capable of surprise. His fingers dug into the soft white meat of the candle haft.

'Impossible. You never knew him.'

Behind him, on the side of the sarcophagus, a long carved panel depicted a youth lying supine, a snake twined round his leg. To Morgellon, Mitta's memory was just another kingdom to annex. How dare he claim the right to grieve as his alone? The monuments. The renamed streets. The pornographic *excess* of it all.

'He tried to kill you,' she said.

Morgellon's jaw tightened in a rictus of disgust. 'You've no idea what you're talking about.' Wax dripped in gobbets from his fist.

'I was there. I saw.'

'You saw what you wanted to see.'

'Ha! You'd know all about that, wouldn't you?' She strained against her bonds. 'You can't bear that it was all a ruse. That he could lie to you so *casually*, that you understood him so little.'

'Nonsense.'

'He scorned your precious peace. He scorned the leaders you worked so hard to bring into the accord.'

'*I* scorned them, Hagar.'

His declaration rang over dust and stone.

'What? No, you didn't.'

'I scorned them and I scorned their peace.' Candlelight lit the slow motion of his lips.

She felt a wash of unreality. The burning in her hand brought her round.

'You're lying. The accord was all at your behest. You sent emissaries, held summits. You pulled troops out of Masakouri. It took decades.'

'How else could I get them all in one room?' His breathing took on heavy, guttural notes. 'Twenty-five years isn't so very long for me. You of all people ought to appreciate that. How long have you been planning your little power grab? Thirty? A hundred?'

'You wanted peace.'

'No, *bichette*. I wanted *liberty*.' The remnants of the candle slopped through his fingers and splattered across the mosaic floor. 'Not the false peace of surrender. Not the peace of the prison cell. Freedom for all species.'

'By murdering their leaders?'

'Koi tithes the Requen-Dar triple what she tithes her homelanders. She strips them of their lands when they can't pay.' He snatched emphatically at the air. 'Lord Cambridge ordered whole villages of his own people burned to the ground, then had their bones ploughed under. His *own* people. And you wanted me to honour them both as equals? That's your precious peace, is it?' At his feet, the fallen flame guttered and snuffed. 'We had a chance to save the world. Without the suffering of war. A new beginning.' His lower lip turned outwards and he looked down at her. 'And you destroyed it.'

'Mitta was going to kill you too.'

'I was delivering my speech from up there!' Morgellon pointed out of the pool, into darkness. 'I would have watched them all dissolve while I denounced their crimes. I would have forced anyone who tried to run to walk back in.' She felt him squeeze her mind, readying himself to take control. 'I dismissed you so you'd be safe. But you had to interfere.'

'You lied to me.'

'Because I knew you couldn't be trusted. You were barely a child.'

'I was over fifty years old!'

'Even now, you don't understand!'

'Oh, I understand.' She twisted her wrists within her bonds, working the rope against the back of her belt while keeping her gaze locked on his. 'You're a coward. You wanted them dead because you feared them. You're terrified of anyone you can't control.'

He spat on the remnants of the candle. 'I pray your insolence brings you comfort. You'll need it.'

He slapped himself across the face with such force that she stumbled.

She opened her eyes. 'Do it again.'

Morgellon hesitated. He balled his fist and clubbed himself across the jaw. Hot pain exploded through her face. She gritted her teeth, held her head still. *Not mine. Not mine.* It was an illusion.

'Again.' She presented her opposite cheek.

He punched himself in the face. A fourth time. Blood ran down his lip.

'Well?' said Hagar, her voice breaking. 'Did it work? Have you brought him back to life?'

Morgellon let his arm hang limp. 'Every day I wake, and I remember, and I feel the lack of him. It hasn't stopped, *bichette. It hasn't stopped.*' The jagged edge of his misery tessellated with something broken inside her. Maybe this was why he had kept her alive. She was the only one who understood.

'The honours are not a gift,' he said. 'They are an exchange. Something is given and something is taken away. What is given is time. What is taken . . . is everything else.'

He gripped the middle finger of his left hand and pressed it back against itself till it snapped. She screamed. He took the ring finger and did the same. Sharp, penetrating agony. Her vision doubled.

She shook her head. No more. No more.

'Are you in pain?' he said.

'Yes, Uncle.'

'No. *I* am in pain, *bichette.* Everything you have was gifted to you, by me. You feel because I permit you to feel. Where's your gratitude?'

His eyes misted with horrible, drunken sentiment. 'Once you were such an obedient child,' he said. 'You used to sit at my feet to receive instruction. You were appreciative when I corrected you. "Thank you, Uncle", you would say.'

Hagar felt the sting of a buried memory – the flash of a whip-thin switch across the backs of her legs, her bare shoulder blades. The acid in her belly, the humiliation of thanking Morgellon for thrashing her at fifty – at *fifty* – just to sate another of his rages. She had made herself forget these cruelties, but he – ah, her breath caught with indignation – he cherished such memories. They were when he had felt most powerful.

Hagar stiffened. She felt his serpentine authority coiling round her mind. He was about to try to seize control.

Not yet.

'Did you ever wonder why God permits suffering, Uncle?' she said.

In the darkness, Morgellon's expression shifted. He seemed confused, as if he could not tell whether she was mocking him, or insane.

'How could this existence be the work of a loving creator?' She shook her head. 'I say it is a trap. A false god lures us here and feeds on our pain.'

He chuckled contemptuously. 'You're babbling. Your time with the nuns has left you soft-headed.'

'All that is beloved and pleasing will become otherwise. All that we cherish will be separated from us. You and I know this more than most.' She felt the rope beginning to work loose. 'The world is very evil. The hour is growing late. With your help, I can free all sentient beings from the error of death.'

'And what on earth makes you think I would give you my help willingly?'

'Oh,' said Hagar, 'I never said willingly.'

Footsteps echoed through the pavilion.

Morgellon jerked round. '*Qui vive?*' His startled yell rang off stone and tiles.

The footsteps descended into the empty pool's shallow end.

'My lord.'

The roots of her hair tingled. She recognised that sonorous voice. Ha. Of course.

Morgellon resumed his default expression of composed disdain. 'Is he secured?'

'Yes, my lord.'

'Approach.' Morgellon gestured to the speaker.

Sheriff Kenner stomped into view, his hooves sending up little blasts of dust. He rotated to face Hagar. When he rolled his shoulders, a great ridge of muscle shifted beneath his tunic. His puffed-out chest was crossed with the green sash of the palace. Steam huffed from his nostrils.

This, she had not foreseen. And what was this feeling that gripped her heart? Could it really be disappointment? Perhaps a little. The boy was cannier than she had given him credit for. He looked very becoming, and almost she felt for him, because he believed his obedience would be rewarded.

Morgellon raised his hand and flexed his reknitted digits. 'The Sheriff allowed weeds to flourish in my beautiful garden. He failed in his duties. Do you know why I spared him, *bichette*?'

'Because you could still use him? Because your years inside the palace have made you isolated and weak?'

The jibe hit home; she saw a momentary flinch before he resumed his show of regal disdain.

'Because he begged my forgiveness. That was all it took, Hagar. Sincere repentance.'

He waited.

'You want me to ask your forgiveness, Uncle?' said Hagar.

He held his head still higher. 'Do you seek it?'

She closed her eyes, and lowered her head. She felt his mood bleeding into her – the sensuous craving. He ached to hear her say it.

'Uncle.'

'Yes, *bichette*?' His voice almost breaking.

'You deserve your suffering.'

The skin round his eyes tightened. 'As you wish. Sheriff Kenner will be my new prefect, and serve me as Tonti did. His first duty is executing you, for treason.'

'What about the election? The cliques will revolt.'

'To revolt, they would have to exist.'

A chill ran through her. Arthur had mentioned nothing of this.

'What have you done?'

Morgellon wrinkled his nose. He was growing tired of indulging her. For him to be this lucid, it must have been some time since his last dose of the black medicine. Soon, the cramps would hit her, but for now, he would be feeling the first symptoms – blurred vision, a sluggishness of thought.

'I pulled on threads that were already loose. My agents have been arming Lesang's butchers for months. Guns. Explosives. The hawsers and the bricks too. My spies have infiltrated the cliques at the highest level. The different factions already distrust each other. We'll throw the first stone – a bomb in the cellar of the brick clique's headquarters. It won't take much to turn their revolution into bloody civil war. I have five hundred loyal soldiers led by eighty of my elite garde du corps. We'll use the violence as a pretext to burn the stilt city to its foundations.'

Hagar could not find her breath. 'But . . . it's *your* city. And you won't kill the cliques. You'll kill civilians.'

'You're right.' His expression hardened. 'It is my city. Mine to protect, and mine to cleanse. The people here are maggots burrowing into rotten flesh. Ten thousand of their lives are nothing.'

Morgellon's image floated against the river of candles. Behind him, Mitta's black statue rose, immaculate, infinitely patient.

Morgellon looked askance at Kenner. 'Remember: your life belongs to me, now. Serve me faithfully, and I'll guard it as I guard all my possessions. Dishonour me, and I will end you without hesitation.' He smoothed down his waistcoat. 'Now kill her.'

Kenner slid his fingers into the flattened loop of his dagger's iron hilt. Slowly, he drew the long, recurved blade.

'Yes, Uncle.'

CHAPTER 19

CRAWL

Delphine hurried through the cramped and putrid tunnel clutching her Remington, her progress marked by the slosh, slosh of her legs through sewage. She was marching against the current. Torchlight picked out curving brickwork coated in fatty deposits, drooling pipemouths, and oil rainbows snaking across a torpid, oozing channel of shit.

She gagged into the neckerchief covering her mouth. Her shins dragged in a viscous grey-brown porridge. It had soaked through her shoes into her socks; she felt sludge squelching and separating under her soles. Submerged lumps broke against her ankles. A sour stench coated her tongue.

They were barely making progress. Already she felt worn out, her shoulder wound starting to tell.

Butler was out in front, crook-backed and furtive, his lithe silhouette cutting through the water. He did not seem to mind the stink; the half-eaten carcass of something dog-sized and leathery floated past with ribs jagging out of its chest, flies swarming over it in a glitching cloud. Every so often she heard the *puk-puk* of his speech-sight, as he sounded out the tunnel ahead. Funny how the noise which had once filled her with such horror now felt reassuring, metronomic – a heartbeat. His pops and clicks mixed with the slap, slap of rats scampering through the shallows or squeezing their fat, excrement-greased bodies into rusted pipes or cracks in the walls. A pack of the largest swam ahead of him, their slick fur sheened silver, their bodies leaving spreading chevron wakes.

At Delphine's right, Patience swayed above the water on gangling limbs. A trunk of knotted muscle curled from her angel arm, winding round her torso then splitting downwards into at least a dozen long, knuckled legs that picked their way through the slurry with eerie, arachnid precision. She wore smoked welding goggles over a white surgical mask.

Alice advanced on the left, her sleeves and trouser legs rolled up, her breath rising in puffs. She swept the torchbeam across sticky brickwork, one hand on the machine pistol at her hip. Behind her, Martha was jinking left to right, wings flicker-sparking in the darkness, her eyes a dreamy coral.

The sound of rushing water grew louder as they approached a four-way junction. Butler held up a palm.

'Wait.'

Sewage flowed from tunnels to the north, east and south, surging over a horseshoe-shaped weir. The weir was ten feet high, with no obvious means of scaling it. A scum of ochre froth trailed from the churning water at its base, drifting towards them, flowing past Delphine's legs.

Butler consulted a hand-sketched map, clutching a penlight between his fangs. He glanced back the way they had come, studied the junction.

'What's the hold-up?' called Delphine. The current was strong, and her feet kept slipping. Did Butler not know the way? Were they lost?

He walked to the centre of the crossroads, checking the map. He chitter-clicked something. Delphine heard a thrumming behind her head then Martha flew past, rising up over the weir and darting in and out of each of the tunnels. She landed on a narrow walkway running down one side of the southern tunnel, to their right.

Butler spat, folded the map and stuffed it into his trouser pocket. 'South.'

Patience anchored several tendrils to the weir, then grabbed Butler under the armpits and hoisted him over to Martha. Delphine was next. An unctuous tendril slipped round her. She rose suddenly, sickeningly, sewage dripping from her ankles, then her soles slapped down on brick.

The southern tunnel was narrower, the walkway a crumbling composite fill of cement and broken shells. Sections had fallen away completely, slowing their progress to a creep. Tangles of white mould hung from the ceiling.

She heard the spatter-scritch of things moving in the darkness, the plash of rapid paddling. Whatever it was, she was glad she could not see it.

Butler halted. He held up an arm.

'Wait.'

Everyone stopped. He tick-popped. Something brushed Delphine's leg and she gasped; a big, whiskery rat scampered through her torchbeam, into the gloom ahead. She held her breath, listening as its footsteps faded.

Butler held up an index finger. Martha's wings made a soft *ffffffrrrrrr*.

A rat ran out of the darkness. Two rats. A dozen. They skittered past, shrieking.

'Did you . . .' He threw his jacket open, reaching for his pistol.

Delphine glanced at the spot where her gunlight struck the water. The surface was rippling strangely, piss rainbows crinkling as if the flow were reversing. The nape of her neck tingled.

The water exploded. A hissing beast leapt at her. It slammed downwards with long dripping arms; she blocked with the shotgun but the blow was so hard it popped the sling swivel and knocked the weapon from her hands. Multiple red eyes flashed round a maw of flexing stylets. A second pair of arms lunged for her throat.

She twisted back, smacking her head against the wall. Rough fingers grabbed her windpipe. The thing's mouth dilated, then its face exploded with a bang. Butler stood with his handgun outstretched, a green laser sight cutting through clouds of vapour. The weight of the smoking torso dragged her forward. She felt the floor give way beneath her heel. With a crunch, part of the walkway disintegrated.

She clutched at air. Alice yelled. Delphine's chest slapped into warm sewage and she was under, submerged.

She clamped her lips shut, tore dead fingers from her throat. Her knee sank into slimy silt. A rubbery skein of something snagged across her face. She felt it stretch in the current, snapping. She planted her foot and pushed. As her head met the surface, instead of breaking, the water clung in a skin, yolky and amniotic. She tried to breathe. The skin formed a seal over her mouth, sucking in. She yanked the sickle from her belt and punched up. The sac slit with a gassy sigh. Voices were calling her name. She clawed the caul from her lips and breathed.

Shapes rose from the water. Sewage streamed from broad backs, down muscular torsos, each with four long arms. Their slick dark fur was clotted with shit and rancid fat, tangles of fishing line, small sharp bones. Red eyes blinked in bulging clustered tumours. She staggered back, up to her belly in warm, viscous sludge. Three creatures, nearly as tall as her. In place of heads they had smacking, sucker-like mouths lined with hooked stylets that wept slime. Sensitive hairs quivered across their shoulders and backs.

Lightning flashes. Bangs. Muzzle flare lit Alice and Butler up on the walkway, shooting back to back as more of the six-limbed creatures swarmed them from both sides.

Delphine raised the sickle.

The nearest to her spread its palms. Spines extruded from all four wrists like punch daggers. Its maw, red-pocked eyes and all, rotated through 180 degrees.

She sensed movement to her right. Instinctively she pivoted and cleaved. A creature broke the surface and she felt the blade hack through its shoulder. It rolled sideways with a slop of thick fluid.

The first beast flung itself at her, flailing its arms. She swung the sickle, thumbing the release switch; the shaft snapped to full-length, the crescent blade slicing through the creature's blistered abdomen. Still the thing came, thrusting at her throat with a wrist spine. Its midriff crunched; grey juice splattered from the long horizontal wound in its belly. The spine's tip juddered an inch from Delphine's eye. The creature burst apart and on the other side Delphine saw Patience, gripping the two twitching halves with pink ropes of muscle, her tendrils slamming another of the creatures against the wall, over and over, then punching through its chest with a bone spur. Another of the creatures latched onto Patience from behind and sank its hooked fangs into her scalp. She wrenched her mask down and yelled:

'Get out of the water!'

Breathless, Delphine began wading towards the walkway. The sewage was thick and her feet kept slipping.

'Quick! Quick!'

Alice had set her torch down and was leaning over the edge of the walkway with her hand out. Martha swooped in, grabbed Alice's hand and extended her own, forming a chain. Delphine lunged for it, missed, then on the second attempt caught hold and Alice and Martha hauled her onto land.

She dropped to all fours, coughing, spluttering. She tasted shit and retched. Bangs filled the tunnel.

'Can you stand?' said Alice.

Delphine retched again, her back arching. Her hair was slicked into an oily kelp. She wiped and wiped at her lips but could not get rid of the slimy film.

She nodded.

Bangs.

She grabbed her shotgun from where she had dropped it and staggered to her feet.

Ahead, muzzle flash illuminated a bright cylinder of tunnel. Butler was on one knee, shooting. She ran to him, swung her gun light up. Her breath caught; hanging across the tunnel was a huge, sagging net. It blocked the walkway. Wet ropes dripped with a substance like congealed fat; at the base, sewage sluiced through a dam of refuse and carcasses. Flies buzzed in a black mist. More of the creatures were crawling all over it, now picking their way like spiders, now swinging like monkeys. The stench was horrendous.

One of the creatures threw itself at Butler with a screech. He blasted it in mid-air. Its swollen hindquarters blew open in a pulp of innards and the body thudded into him. He grunted and shouldered it into the water. One of his ears was missing. His shoulder was slashed through to the bone.

He spotted her. 'Venner! When I say break, we push forward.' He ejected a magazine, pulled a fresh one from his holster. She worked the Remington's pump action, chambered a round. Still dry. Thank God.

Pale strands twitched. More of the creatures were plucking their way across the sticky net, heads swivelling. She saw now she was looking at a colossal web. Mouldering, limbless carcasses hung wrapped in what looked like dozens of layers of cellophane.

She took a step and fired, blowing one creature clear into the water and making a second hiss and shield its face.

'Ready!'

More were wriggling from a fissure in the ceiling. Patience had anchored several long ropes of tendon to the garbage dam. She glanced at Butler. Butler pointed. Patience wrenched. The web ripped from the black bricks, creatures splattered into the water, and the entire dam gave in a sucking cascade.

'Break!' said Butler.

Her gunlight swayed, her shoes slapping stone. Adrenaline made everything pulsing, technicolour. Multi-limbed shapes flashed out of the darkness, scuttling, flanking them.

One dropped from the ceiling; she slashed at it, felt the sickle cut fat and muscle. She clipped her head on a low pipe; Alice tackled her from behind, forcing her onwards.

Her trousers were wet, heavy. She could hear the beasts hissing, shrieking. More were joining the chase.

Butler swung left, up a sloping side tunnel where the floor was curved and slippery. After a few yards, they reached a chokepoint where the roof had partially collapsed. A big slab of rock created a triangular void under the dirt and rubble. Butler turned and fired into the pack pursuing them. Martha went into the crawlspace first, then Delphine, Alice, Patience. Delphine had to drop onto her belly, scrambling over cold damp soil.

As she pulled herself up on the far side, Butler had almost crawled through. As he emerged he swatted at her angrily.

'Don't just stand there! Move! M—'

There was a thump and loose dirt fell in showers. His face contorted. He clutched at the earth beneath him.

'Butler!' Patience wrapped a tendril around his arm. There was a wet scratching sound behind him, then a huge beast, the biggest yet, slammed through the gap and sank its teeth into his legs. Its corpulent, furry body wedged beneath the rock slab, fat bunching around its shoulders. Patience turned her angel-arm into a bone-blade on the end of a fleshy lash and began slicing at the creature. With two muscular arms it pinned Butler down and with a third it ripped the wings from his back with a *krrrrakkk.*

He glowered at Delphine. 'Go!' He thumped the floor. 'Would you fuck . . . off?'

Delphine chambered a round and charged. Butler yelled, 'No!' then one of the creature's stinking arms swung round, extruded a two-foot spear of bone and thrust at her chest. She threw herself flat against the wall. The spine struck stone just left of her ear, raking downwards with a screech. She sidestepped, cleared the last few feet and fired point blank into the creature's flank.

Flesh cratered, splattering her legs with blood. Loose skin hung in bedraggled rinds. Yellow fat oozed over exposed bone. She could see Butler's shattered legs inside its oesophagus. Patience yanked; his torso tore loose. She dragged his mutilated upper body free.

Bloodied, the creature's rage turned to panic. It tried to withdraw, shoving backwards with its piston-like arms; the slab holding the gap open tipped.

'Get back!' yelled Alice. There was a great crash as tons of rubble slid into the passageway. Dirt billowed up in a smothering cloud.

Delphine fled, stumbling, blind. She slumped against a wall. As the dust thinned she saw the glow of a torch. Alice was standing a few feet away. She shone the light back in the direction they'd come. A landslide of dirt and rubble completely blocked the passageway.

'Everyone okay?' Patience stood beside the upper half of Butler. His arms were limp, his head sagging to one side. A length of intestine trailed from his pelvis.

Alice swung her torch in the other direction. The tunnel continued for approximately thirty feet before terminating in a dead end – a flat wall of amber stone.

Patience looked a little unsteady. Her angel-arm lay puddled on the ground, dissolving into a pool of fizzling godstuff. Putty-like flesh hung from her shoulder in strands. 'I'm all right,' she said, slurring her words a little. 'It just . . . takes it out of me, you know?' She yawned. 'Give me a . . . moment.'

Delphine was still trying to catch her breath. 'What . . . the hell . . . were they?'

'Simaraks.' Butler rolled himself onto his back. Little shoots of cartilage were pushing out from the lower half of his body, bone accruing in milky deposits. 'One of the Grand-Duc's old . . .' He tilted his head to one side and spat out broken fangs. 'One of his old manias. Evidently they've found an ecological niche.' He hauled himself up onto his bloody buttocks. 'What the hell were you doing, Ms Venner?'

'Saving you.'

'I told you to *leave*.' Networks of bone and tendon branched behind him as his wings regrew. 'You nearly got killed.'

'You're welcome.'

'No.' He slapped the ground. 'No! This isn't some condescending lecture from a . . . some blustering authority figure you have to prove yourself to. You. Will. Get. Killed. I've watched people die and die and die, and you know what? They're always surprised. All of them. It's not a moral failing. It's not a competence issue. You're immensely skilled. There? Is that what you wanted to hear? You're up there with Judge Easter. Doesn't make you impervious to traumatic amputations. I am.' He gestured at his coagulating legs. 'Not a virtue. Not proof of my superior skill. Just a fact. Putting yourself on the front line places us all in danger. It's poor tactics. And if you ignore a direct order one more time I'm aborting the mission. Do you understand?'

Her face felt hot. She folded her lips over her teeth and pressed them together. She nodded.

'Yes, Butler.'

Tendons were tightening, hoisting bones into position so meat could set around them. He watched her a moment longer.

'Um.' Alice cleared her throat. 'We're trapped.' She shone her torch at the dead end.

Butler click-popped at it. He squinted.

'Hold on,' he muttered. 'Let me check the map.' He tilted to one side and reached into his trouser pocket. His slim fingers emerged through a ragged hole several inches down, where the leg had been bitten away. 'Oh for *pity*'s sake!'

As Butler cursed and punched the ground, Martha approached the wall at the end of the tunnel, her eyes burning fuschia. *Rik-ik-ik.*

Delphine went after her. 'Martha?'

Up close, the stone had a glassy lustre, cloudy and semi-translucent. It was completely smooth, lukewarm to the touch.

'Do you recognise this, or something?' said Delphine.

Martha pressed her bristled fingers to the wall. Her eyes shifted down through the spectrum to a warm amber-gold. Her body began to vibrate.

'Martha?'

Slowly, her fingertips sank into the stone.

'Martha!' Delphine reached for Martha's arm.

Martha withdrew her fingers. Her eyes fluxed back to a soft mauve. Her antennae were trembling.

She turned back down the tunnel, riffle-clicked something. Butler replied, and they had a short back-and-forth.

'She says she wants us to take a few minutes to rest,' he said. 'She needs time to talk to the wall.'

Delphine threw away her shirt and hacked out the claggy parts of her hair with the sickle. Her rucksack was ruined, clumped in shit and dust, but the water bottle inside was still sealed. She took out a little set of tools, sat crosslegged in her vest and stripped the shotgun. Using Patience's face mask as a cleaning rag, she cleaned out the chamber and wiped down the cartridges before she reloaded.

The ritual was grounding. She was quick, precise. Her hands knew what to do without her thinking. She tested the slide action, pumping shells through the chamber until the magazine was empty. Her system was still flooded with adrenaline. She reloaded, did it again. *Ka-chuk. Ka-chuk. Ka-chuk.* The pain in her shoulder faded into the background.

Meanwhile, Martha stood with her arm plunged up to the elbow into the amber stone, eyes pulsing sympathetic hues, body blurring with resonance.

Alice swept her torchbeam around the tunnel. The walls were

rough-hewn grey stone, the few flat patches covered in carvings and chalk pictures. Little ideograms were accompanied by scratchings that might have been text, and stylised pictures of lanta riding on what looked like ostriches, lanta on huge boats, giant monstrous lanta with horns and pincers, pictures of birds and spiders and fires between pillars, and an image of a tall tree with figures apparently spitted on the branches. Some of the pictures were quite accomplished, intricately etched and shaded with hundreds of tiny, stippling strokes; others were crude and juvenile – some of the chalk images had been drawn directly over the carvings.

Delphine was starting to feel faint. She swigged her water. She wondered how much air they had left.

Martha stepped back from the wall. For a moment, Delphine thought she saw the stone yield like treacle, then Martha's hand was free, the surface perfectly flat.

Alice walked up behind her. 'Did it work?'

Patience was squatting on her hams by the oil lamp. Her angel-arm had coalesced into a lump of grey flesh. She pushed up her goggles.

'Doesn't look like it. I could try to dig us out the other end.'

'That'll take hours,' said Butler. He dropped onto his palms and began dragging his half-formed legs towards them. 'There are still simaraks on the other side. And it's the wrong way. It'll be too late.'

Martha's antennae reared up and lashed in unison. The amber wall dented in, as if an invisible wrecking ball had struck a huge block of warm toffee. The centre of the dent sucked back towards them, thinning and turning translucent. It broke like a bubble in beer. A hole swelled wider and wider. Martha's antennae sagged, her eyes turned blue, and the stone fell still.

The wall now contained a four-foot opening, heading back ten feet into an open space on the far side. The edges of the hole had thick, wrinkled pleats. Delphine walked up and touched it. It was hard, faintly warm.

She looked down at Martha. 'Is it safe?'

Martha bopped her fist once.

They crawled through in turn. On the other side was a wide passageway with a low, curving roof. The walls had alcoves set into them at intervals, all made of the same amber stone. There were no bricks, as if the passage had been shaped from a single piece of rock, or melted together. The floor was crusted with grit.

Butler took some time looking up and down. He consulted with Martha. At last, he pointed off into the darkness.

'This way.'

Each of the alcoves was about three feet high, covered by diamond-shaped panels made of a clear substance like glass. Delphine shone her Maglite on the nearest. Inside were three smoked crystal statues of lanta, coloured green, red and blue respectively: a big one with broad, scissoring horns, one that looked like Martha, and a third, the blue one, with a narrow segmented body, elongated forelimbs, and a stunted, disc-shaped head.

'What is this?' she said.

'This is how you consolidate power.' Butler stopped beside her. 'Conquer people, bury their culture alive, then build your own history on top of them.' The statuettes seemed to drink light, a glow bleeding into the ribs of the thorax, the hooked mandibles. 'This place was a lantian temple-city, once. Morgellon stole it, and built his gaudy summer palace on top. And he wonders why the Hilanta don't like us.'

They pressed on through the tunnel, Butler leading in his tattered trousers. The diamond panels continued at intervals, the crystalline sculptures growing increasingly abstract: pyramids, concentric rings, whorls composed of dozens of tapering strands all twisting and pushing outwards. When the torch passed over it, each sculpture held its glow for a few seconds before fading, like the tip of a cigarette. A few of the hollows were empty, their panels staved in. One was flooded with turbid brown water.

'Morgellon used these halls for his underground boating canals,' said Butler, glancing at the damage. 'Wait.' He touched two fingers to his brow. 'I just . . . I can't remember how it was laid out on the map.' He took a deep breath, gasped. 'Ah, damn it all.'

While he was standing there, lost in concentration, Delphine felt a tap on her thigh. She looked down and there was Martha. Martha pointed to the sickle, made a grabbing gesture with both hands.

'Of course,' said Delphine, handing it over. 'What do you—'

Immediately Martha flipped it round and began scratching lines in the dirt. She worked with speed and precision, using the hooked tip to draw curves, parallel lines. Oh.

'Uh, Butler?' Delphine glanced up.

He snapped his eyes open, annoyed. 'What?'

She pointed down. Taking shape on the floor was a replica of the palace floorplan, approximately 4:1 scale. Delphine could not say for sure if it was accurate, but it was *detailed*, complete with text, crosshatched areas, and what looked like a rendition of a waterstain in the top right corner.

After a few minutes' work, Martha stopped. She handed Delphine the sickle.

'Thank you,' said Delphine, a little taken aback. 'I'm remembering why you and I stopped playing cribbage.'

Butler studied the sketch from various angles. 'Incredible. Look.' He tapped with a taloned toe at a long passage in the bottom left. 'Here we are. And we want to get . . .' He scraped a line east, then north. 'Here. That'll get us up into the old prayer caves. Excellent. Follow me.'

Perhaps half an hour later they reached a round opening in the wall with a sculpted stone gutter leading out of it, covered by an iron grille.

'Patience,' he said.

Patience let her angel-arm flow in through the grille's rusted bars and, with a crunch, tore it from the wall. Butler led the way. The tunnel behind was barely four feet high, so everyone except Martha and Patience had to drop to a crouch. Delphine felt the gradient in her calves. Grit crunched beneath their boots.

Martha's eyes lit their surroundings with a faint rose blush. A passage of smoothly hewn rock extended upwards.

The air was cold and musty. Dirt stung cuts on Delphine's hands. Eventually, the passage swung sharply left, then climbed steeply over crunchy, silty ground. Butler stopped. He turned, pressed an index finger to his mouth. He trimmed the oil lamp wick till it was barely alight. Delphine switched off her Maglite. Alice switched off her torch. Slowly, slowly, they ascended.

The tunnel came to a dead end.

Delphine's heart sank. Had Martha got it wrong?

Butler stopped and peered up. She shuffled alongside him, shaking with tiredness and nerves. She could not go on. God, she just wanted to sleep.

Above, she glimpsed the faintest hint of light. She was gazing at the bars of a drain cover, three horizontal and two vertical, over a hole the width of a person.

She felt a late surge of energy. Were they here? Had they made it?

She nudged Butler, jabbed two fingers at her eyes then pointed upwards. He nodded. Gingerly, she clambered to her feet. She straightened her legs until her face was pressed against the drain. She was peering into some sort of passageway. She could make out a rocky ceiling eight feet or so above her, curving down into cavern walls with doorways cut into them, covered by iron bars. Were these cells?

A meagre glow suggested a lamp farther down the passage. That had to mean regular occupants. She listened. She heard breathing, realised it was Butler. If there was anything to hear, he would hear it, wouldn't he? She curled her fingers round one of the drain's thick bars and shoved. It was securely mortared into the rock. A harka's face appeared inches from hers. They clamped a hand over hers and jammed a pistol through the bars, the muzzle pointing directly at her head. They squeezed the trigger.

CHAPTER 20

DEATH NEEDS TIME FOR WHAT IT KILLS TO GROW IN

Kenner's dagger shone with a liquid polish in the candlelight. Extending from beneath the rosette knuckle guard, the blade was curved like a horn, thinning to a narrow steel spike. The tip reminded Hagar of her old surgical instruments, and for a moment she saw them, laid out upon their bloodstained white cloth, a little garden of hooks and blades.

She took a step back. Morgellon did not attempt to stop her. His influence hung in slack coils around her mind, waiting to squeeze. He was well aware she had killed Tonti and his staff singlehandedly. When he chose to exercise his control over her, the charade would be over. Perhaps he wanted to see what his new servant was made of.

Or perhaps, as always, he merely longed for the distraction of a spectacle.

She slipped her wrists from their bonds. The surprise on Kenner's face was gratifying, but brief. She patted her jacket for her pistol. Gone. She reached for her boot. Her misericord was not there. She had expected that too. Without weapons, then. She spread her palms and flowed into the first pose of the theodic kata: the eternal question.

'Why?' she said.

Kenner dipped his head and charged.

He was startlingly fast. Hagar sidestepped and pivoted. Not enough – he was huge. She hurled herself backwards to dodge his sinistral horn, dropping into a defensive stance: the penitent.

Kenner turned to face her. He held his dagger out between them, its point curving upwards, a beckoning finger. He slid his left arm behind his back, as if they were on the Bataille court.

'Order,' he said.

A confident reply.

He advanced. His hooves moved with a familiar, limber poetry. Perhaps he had once been a player. She backed away, forced to take three steps for each one of his. His dagger swayed with sickening ease. She sensed the quickness under his poise, something keener and more decisive than cold finesse. Ah, that was it: *emotion*.

He feinted right – a short, testing jab. She resisted the bait, throwing her left shoulder back to narrow her profile. He thrust again, opening his guard, inviting her in. He was too smart to keep swinging for her like a brute. He was trying to provoke a mistake.

Hagar knew time was against her. Sooner or later, Morgellon would grow bored.

'He'll kill you too,' she said. She was backing up towards the river of candles – a faint warmth ghosted the nape of her neck. 'Not today. Years from now. He hates how much he needs us.'

Kenner tilted his head sideways till the joints cracked. The huge hump of muscle behind his shoulders tensed.

The strike came, dizzyingly quick. He punched the dagger at her jaw. She whipped her head aside; the blade swished over her shoulder, lopping the head off a candle.

She stepped back; her heel clipped a fallen candleholder. She had nowhere left to go.

He let the dagger drop to his hip. He approached with his guard down. If it was a bluff it was an exceptionally convincing one. Yet he did not strike her as overconfident, foolhardy.

She felt the initiative slipping away; her mind filled with memories of sobering defeats on the abbey bridge. He made another testing feint and even as she recognised the deceit she swatted at it, desperate to pressure him. She did not spot the hoof until it connected with her jaw.

The impact lifted her off her feet. Her skull bounced off the pool wall. Flames tumbled around her. She landed on her back, iron candleholders clattering on top of her. She caught one by the shaft. Kenner switched to a reverse grip and stabbed downwards.

She parried with the candleholder, turning his blade aside. It struck the tiles above her head with a crack. She kicked a burning candle at his face. It struck him square between the eyes and dropped to the floor. He snorted, raised the knife. She scrambled to her feet. He launched another kick square at her chest. Still dazed, she barely dodged, his hoof clipping a button from her jacket. She lashed out wildly with the candleholder, trying to force him back. He caught it by its curving base, and with a flick of his wrist, snapped the shaft. She was left grasping a metal strut.

The dagger came for her in big, cleaving arcs. She dodged left and left again. He was not tiring – on the contrary, he was warming to his task, each stroke invigorating him, feeding his power and speed. He knew time was on his side.

He was driving her back towards the sarcophagus. She tried breaking right; he aimed a couple of rapid kicks at her knees and she lost her footing trying to avoid them, stumbled. She was concussed from that blow to the head. Morgellon stood just out of sight, which kept distracting her.

She could hold off no longer. She was weary, losing her rhythm. One mistake could end her. She rocked onto the balls of her feet and took a few rapid steps backwards, raising her arms as she flowed into an outer circle kata: the apostate.

'If you kill me, I'll just be reborn,' she said. He sliced at her throat. She stepped into the blow then twist-dropped at the last instant, the blade rushing over her head. 'While there's delusion and clinging, while there are bodies to be reborn into, death is not enough.'

Kenner stamped. 'Till the next life, then.'

'May it bring you peace.'

As the words left her lips, she felt Morgellon grip her mind. She froze.

'I'm holding her.' His voice was utterly without emotion. 'She can't escape. Kill her.'

She could feel Morgellon's will enclosing hers, forbidding her to move.

Kenner rolled his shoulders, glowering. Clearly he had thought the fight was in hand and would have preferred to finish her off without help. Morgellon probably knew that – he no doubt thought it wise to deny Kenner that satisfaction, to make this new servant hungry for chances to prove himself.

Kenner recovered quickly. His gaze settled on her throat. He lifted his dagger. The blade caught the light and glinted. She wondered if he would offer some parting remark.

He brought the knife down, hard.

She did not move.

Then.

She moved like a gust, like a snatched cloth. The blade flashed through the space where she had stood. She pivoted on the ball of her foot, whirling away. Kenner was deft enough to keep his balance, but shocked enough that she got behind him before he turned. She flipped the snapped iron shaft to a reverse grip.

Someone with less anatomical knowledge might have driven it deep into the meat of his back, into that vast inviting hump of muscle, but Hagar's years of mortuary experience spoke to her now, even here, in this sepulchral gloom at the end of all things, whispering where the flesh was thick and where it was just a frail membrane of hide. Her chances of punching through all that muscle and splitting the spinal column were slight, so she came in low, lunging under his right arm as he swung at her. She drove the thin, splintered shaft into the soft fat covering his kidney. She felt his padded shirt resist and twisted her wrist to ease the tip through.

Kenner's moan was strained, almost sensual. He clutched at the shank. Before he could get a grip, she yanked it out, hot blood jetting over her wrists. A rose bloomed on his white tunic. He looked down, then back at her. His expression twisted into baffled reproach.

He lunged, a clumsy diagonal swing. She ducked inside his guard and drove the edge of an open palm into his wounded kidney. Blood splashed out. He grunted. His knee buckled.

Morgellon was yelling curses, unable to understand why she would not yield.

Kenner went for a grapple. She danced out of range with exultant ease. His other knee gave way, and he made a choked, expulsive sound, halfway between a cough and a sob. Black droplets splattered his chin. She could feel Morgellon squeezing at her mind, trying to restrain her.

She met Kenner's gaze. Steaming blood dribbled onto the pale mosaic beneath him. He looked down and moaned to see what he was made of. Too late, the boy was learning.

'*Bichette!*' Morgellon was shaking with fury.

Hagar cradled the underside of her left wrist, checking the lump through the sleeve of her jacket. The bracelet tick pumped softly, drinking her master's rage. She was not sure how long its protection would hold out. It had worked against Noroc's samples, but Morgellon's powers were without equal.

'Uncle,' she said.

He drew his shortsword. 'I'll kill you myself.'

No. It was still too early. Even if her protection held out, she could not fight him. She backed away and he advanced, lusty with rage.

He shook his head. 'You must know you can't escape.'

'Neither can you.'

He stopped dead, flipped the blade around, and pressed it to his stomach. He pushed it into his belly.

The pain was excruciating – the most terrible burning blossomed around a hot sharp sting as the tip broke skin and punctured the wall of his stomach. She doubled over – she could not help it, clutching at her midriff even as she knew, rationally, she was not wounded. *Not mine. Not mine.*

She searched for sensations in her own body, the moisture between her toes as she lowered her foot, the tightening of skin across the arch, the subtle pressure of the ball of her foot sinking into her boot's lambskin insole. This was real. Hers.

She began to rise. He twisted the blade.

Hagar dropped to one knee. Morgellon pulled the sword out, blood slopping down his front.

'Look at you,' he said, closing in. 'Ugly, broken thing.'

She felt him hurling himself against her mental defences, slamming into the walls round her mind over and over. Her vision blurred. Rage made him even stronger. He was breaking through. The tick on her wrist pumped, gorging itself, feeding off his power.

A whispering roar built in her brain. She had hoped his addiction would blunt his powers. Her left eye winced shut and refused to open.

Behind her, the heavy doors of the pavilion creaked open.

'*Qui vive?*' bellowed Morgellon. His challenge rang off stone.

Hagar's chest tightened. She flexed her fingers, fighting back the pain.

Footsteps. She risked a glance over her shoulder.

Out of the darkness came a detachment of eight green-sashed garde du corps soldiers, all harka, their lacquered horns etched with palace insignia and sharpened to wicked points. They carried no lamp. At their centre were two figures. The first was an old woman in a simple grey dress, walking with a hint of a stoop, a dark green hooded cape fastened about her shoulders with laces of brown leather. Her hair was white and straight and came down to her chin. The second was a naked man, lean and pale with messy grey hair and large, twitching hands. His eyes were glazed and steam rose from his shoulders and hair.

Morgellon's expression softened from alarm to irritation. 'All guards not on patrol were ordered to guard the esplanade entrance. What do you want?'

Fluxing velvet candlelight picked out long hair-like threads hanging from fissures in the guards' scalps. Their gazes had an unusual steadiness, almost a deadness.

'Bodies,' said the closest.

The old woman swept back her hair. One of her eyes was milky and blind. She looked at Hagar.

'Hullo. Sorry we're late.'

CHAPTER 21

THE PROUD HAVE HID A SNARE FOR ME

Delphine stared into the pistol muzzle. She could see the rifling inside the barrel.

The harka squeezed the trigger.

A noise from behind. Patience lunged over her shoulder with the angel-arm – a tide of raw formless flesh whirlpooled into the barrel. Strands flowed through the trigger guard, cushioning the trigger. More enveloped the exposed hammer.

The harka yelled, dropping his lantern. He tried to wrench his arm away. Stretchy tendrils of gut wrapped round his horns. Pink fluid oozed down his face, setting into translucent membranes that sealed his mouth, his eyes. He pulled his head back; the rubbery caul clung and sucked, conforming to the contours of his cheekbones, collapsing into his nostrils.

Patience yanked. He headbutted the drain. With each muffled scream the skin bag round his head inflated, then sucked tighter. He clawed at it. Ropes of tendon snared his wrists. Filigrees of nerves spread over his hands like lace gloves, plumping up into shiny puce keloid, healing his palms to his face.

His hooves scraped against the bare rock floor. The skin bag was filling with blood, bellying out. His shrieks turned to gurgles.

'Don't kill him!' said Delphine.

Patience blew a lock of hair up from her brow.

The sac split. Blood splattered through the drain. The harka gasped, fell forwards. Patience shot a tendril into his mouth. He gagged. White, living fat swelled behind his teeth, spilling out.

She looked up at him through the grate.

'Hello.'

His irises were chestnut, the whites around them mapped with burst capillaries. He breathed through his nostrils in shudders. His gaze twitched from Patience, to Delphine, to Patience. Blood slicked his black fur into peaks.

'Do you want to die?' said Patience. 'Blink once for yes, twice for no.'

The harka blinked once, twice, pinching out little dark tears.

'Good. Then I want you to answer my questions immediately and truthfully, otherwise the flesh inside your mouth will expand and burst your head. Do you understand?'

A single, emphatic blink.

'Good. Thank you. Are you the only guard?'

Two blinks.

'Thank you. How many are there, other than you? Blink the number.'

The guard's pupils twitched up and to the left. He breathed in. Blink. Blink. Blink. Blink. Blink. Blink. Blink. Blink.

'Was that eight?'

Blink.

'Thank you. Are they nearby?'

Blink.

'Thank you.' She glanced round at the others. 'Anything I've left out?'

'We're wasting time.' Butler shoved his way to the underside of the drain. 'Come on – we need to go.' He looked to Patience. 'Get us in.'

Patience turned out her bottom lip. 'All right. No need to be tart.'

'Wait,' said Delphine. She looked at the guard. 'Are any of the guards vesperi?'

Blink.

'So they've probably heard us coming.'

Butler unholstered his pistol. 'Fine. We'll fight our way in, then.'

Patience looked at the drain cover, her face tightening with concentration. Where her tendrils threaded through the iron bars, pale cysts fruited. They expanded to fill the gaps, bulging, tumescent with pus.

'Stand back,' she said. Delphine backed down the tunnel. Alice placed a hand on her shoulder. A crunch. Bars clanked down at Patience's feet.

A surge of vertigo. They were going in. Alice kissed Delphine's temple. Delphine flinched, then felt remorseful. Concentrate. She closed her hand around her shotgun's pistol grip and it steadied her.

Patience extruded a spray of tendrils and hoisted herself up through the gap. From above came a scrape, a thud. Butler followed. Martha unhinged her wingcases and flew up.

Delphine paused before she went through. What if she died, and her last interaction with Alice had been to pull away? She turned back.

'Sorry,' she whispered.

Alice prodded her with the side of the machine pistol and nodded up at the hole. Delphine could not tell if she was annoyed.

Delphine hesitated. She wanted to say something more. She knew it was the wrong time, which made her flustered. Her cheeks went hot; she cringed, flakes of dried shit cracking across her face.

'What?' Alice said.

Delphine dropped her gaze. She was only making things worse. Better to leave it. They could talk later.

'Sorry.' She turned away and hauled herself up into the passage.

The passage was long and damp, lit by the guard's dropped lantern. Crude timber supports girded the roof; water followed cracks in the floor. The walls opened onto dark, stinking cells.

Butler knelt over the supine harka guard, pressing a steaming, blue-limned palm to the ridge of bone between his horns. The guard shuddered and went limp.

'Better he never saw us,' Butler said. His ears swivelled. He rose sharply. 'Ah. They're here sooner than—'

His left shoulder blew open in a wet blast. He twisted with the impact, spread his wings and slammed flat against the wall.

Delphine threw herself against the opposite wall. Dazzling lantern light poured into the passageway from an opening at the tunnel's far end.

She pumped her shotgun's slide action, chambering a round: *ka-chuk.* The noise echoed. Oops.

She leapt into the middle of the corridor. A tremendous bang boxed her ears. She felt a puff of air against her left cheek. A screw of dust curled from the wall where she had been standing. She dropped to one knee, lifted the Remington and fired towards the light source.

The gun kicked. The far lantern shattered and dropped. She threw herself flat. Had she hit anyone? She fought for breath, her ears ringing.

Butler stepped away from the opposite wall. With a neat sweep of his taloned foot he kicked the unconscious guard's lantern into the busted drain. The passageway went pitch black.

A scrape. Muzzle flare lit a staccato sequence of poses, Butler seeming to teleport down the passage, first close, then flush with the far wall, then ducking, then thrusting an arm forward, BAM – BAM – BA-BAM – no laser sight, just stark, decisive shots selected by echolocation: one, two, three-four, five, six . . . a lull, her heart thudding in the dark . . . BAM. Seven.

Delphine lay with her shoulder against the rock, panting. The nape of her neck was wet with cold sweat. Her eardrums ached from the bangs.

A light appeared to her left – Butler, touching a matchhead to his oil lamp, a splash of orange and blue bleeding outwards. Her hand shaking, Delphine clicked on her gunlight.

Bodies lay in the corridor. A human woman was slumped against the bars of a cell, her legs jerking, her head tipped back. The other bodies looked like waxworks.

Butler went cell to cell, peering in. 'The doors are all open.' He grabbed one and yanked it back and forth, the hinges squealing. 'If anyone was here they've been moved on.'

'There's more than this, isn't there?' Delphine heard the desperation in her voice.

'Of course. Pull yourself together. Martha – scout the nearest passageways upstairs. We're in the prayer caves – the main body of the palace is one level up.'

Martha's mandibles chewed the air softly. As she began to blur, she touched three fingers to the side of her head in a scout salute.

'Thank you,' said Butler. He popped the magazine catch on his pistol and inserted a fresh one from his black bandolier. 'Reload, if you need to. Breathe. Make peace with your creator. After this, we go in.'

Delphine popped a solid slug out her sidesaddle mount and slotted it into the magazine. 'Right,' she said, under her breath. 'Yours in Christ, etc.'

Delphine crept down a hallway of curving sandstone pillars, guided by the faint orange glow of Butler's lantern. The air tasted of wet earth and charcoal. Her boots scuffed channels in the dust. There were already tracks, leading into the darkness.

The walls were decorated with grand friezes, blistered and peeling with age. Images floated in and out of the lantern light – archers storming a beach, a bearded human declaiming to a mixed crowd in a village square, and a similar-looking fellow stripped to the waist, whipping an eel out of river spray, its thick silver body bucking on the end of a taut line beaded with droplets.

Butler stopped at a set of double doors with rusted iron ring handles. He put his ear to a big panel of dark, wide-grained wood. Above, a marble lintel featuring a carved lyre was furred with black mould. Delphine held her breath.

He looked round, nodded. He placed a hand on the iron ring, gingerly turned it. A heavy latch lifted with a *shhhhhhack*. He pulled.

The door gave with a resonant groan, the noise echoing down a narrow passageway on the opposite side. She winced.

The passageway was much smaller than the door. It had cement walls and a low ceiling held up by metal struts. Delphine wondered if it crossed what had once been a courtyard. Martha scouted ahead, then Butler waved them through.

They advanced at a creep, weapons raised. After a short walk, the tunnel opened out onto steps leading up to a grand portico of black volcanic rock fronted with sandstone pillars. Butler held up a finger. Treading lightly on taloned toes, he approached a huge set of double doors as Delphine and the others waited. The doors were ajar. A faint glow spilled from within.

He pressed his pistol to his chest, edging closer. The doors were flanked by statues of giant fish. The statues were caked in dust, which gave way in places to green-blue glass. Cobwebs hung between the fishes' full and open lips, salted with tiny bodies.

Butler's ears pricked.

He beckoned Delphine with the gun. Patience was unwinding the bindings from her arm. Together, they crept up the left side of the steps. Even in the misty cold, Delphine felt perspiration beading on her forehead, trickling behind her ears and down the nape of her neck. Nothing felt real. Her damp vest was chafing. Sewer stink rose from her clothes.

She lined up behind Butler. She pressed the Remington to her heart. She heard talking. Vertigo surged through her and she had to steady herself against the wall.

The air near Butler's leg rippled. Delphine heard Martha click-clicking a message. Butler glanced back and nodded. He set his lamp down and extinguished it. The portico fell into darkness.

Butler's slender profile moved into the faint glow of the doorway. He slipped round the jamb and was gone.

Delphine crept to the edge of the door. Her chest was so tight she could barely breathe. What was it like to die? Would she have time to realise if a bullet hit her head?

She stepped through.

She entered a vast, shadowed space with twisted columns, mosaic floors and a high ceiling that vanished into darkness. A sunken area of floor was lit by hundreds of candles in a huge glowing crescent. Their brightness made her eyes water. The air above them wobbled. She could make out silhouettes, blurred against the flames. Running on the balls of her feet, keeping her steps light, she dashed across the open floor and hid behind one of the pillars.

She pressed her back to the cold, curving stone. Staring at the candles had made her night-blind. She blinked back towards the double doors, saw only the faintest of outlines. Her mouth was dry. She rubbed her eyes and peered round the edge of the pillar.

Wide stone steps led gradually down towards a floor covered in an intricate tiled mosaic. Harka bodies lay supine or on their sides. Some were convulsing. Limbs were severed, heads stoved in. Jesus. They had been slaughtered.

A man in a bloodied suit was standing over a fallen child, pointing a sword at her chest. Behind him was some sort of monument – a black sarcophagus topped with a huge onyx statue of a young man in a cloak. An old woman with white hair and a split lip stood to the bloodied man's right. To his left—

As she stared, the whole great chamber shrank down to a narrow tunnel. At its end, slightly hunched, stood a naked man, wavy steel-grey hair framing sunken eyes and a stubbled chin. His arms were pale and wiry. Smoke twisted from blisters as they popped and closed.

It was him.

Daddy.

CHAPTER 22

THE FLESH OF KINGS

'Now!' cried Hagar, springing backwards.

The Mucorian-infused harka guards drew sabres and stormed down the steps.

Morgellon backed away, momentarily bewildered. How odd that a chronic paranoiac should greet the arrival of assassins – former trusted soldiers, at that – with disbelief. He had spent half his long life crushing imagined plots before they came to fruition, conspirators dragged from their beds in the dead of night, tortured, executed. But actual treachery?

He roared with fury.

The guards charged, swords raised, filigreed nets of fungus hanging from clefts between their horns. The Mucorians had come. They had come. Glory be.

The first of their number closed in on Morgellon. Morgellon glowered, evidently trying to seize control of the body – the guard tilted, her leg buckling, and fell sideways. Morgellon barely had time to look alarmed before two more stepped into her place. He pointed at one with his short sword. The guard went limp and collapsed face-first. Morgellon cursed, bringing the sword round to turn aside a blow from the second.

It was just as she had hoped. His talents were blunted against the Mucorian parasite – she hypothesised because there were two minds interwoven, one dominating the other. Dr Noroc had noted as much in his research notes – a 'partial immunity' to mind-affecting powers. Morgellon seemed to be able to disrupt their control over the host body, but he could not seize control himself.

She gasped as a searing pain penetrated her chest. A guard had thrust his sabre between Morgellon's ribs. Kenner, bleeding out on the floor, moaned too. Morgellon hacked at the guard's throat. Dark blood splattered down both of them. Immediately, a mesh of yellow hyphae pushed from the guard's wound and began knitting it up.

The two guards Morgellon had incapacitated were stumbling to their feet, more advancing behind them. Morgellon staggered back, swearing. A guard faltered, collapsed. Then another.

Not mine. Not mine.

Puffing, clenching her molars, Hagar fought against the pain. Some of it was hers, of course. The bruises from her beating. The friction burns round her wrists. But not the ribs. She felt two rough halves of bone scraping together, saw-teeth snagging sickeningly. No. Despite the pain, she laughed. She was winning. Now she must see this through to its appointed end.

She advanced on him while he was distracted. The wounded guard gripped the sword stuck in Morgellon's chest by its hilt and drove him backwards into Mitta's sarcophagus. She cried out, feeling the sabre-tip pierce his back. Morgellon hacked clumsily at the guard's throat and shoulder, working faster than the fungal parasite could seal the wounds, splitting bone, the semi-severed head lolling backwards obscenely. He shoved the guard with both palms. The guard tripped and fell, his head snapping clear as he hit the floor.

Morgellon grasped the sabre by its slick grip and drew it from the scabbard of his ribcage. Hagar clutched at her breastbone.

Not mine. Not mine.

He was panting heavily. Another harka guard thundered towards him. He closed his eyes.

This time, the guard did not fall, but trotted to a halt. With a sharp, decisive motion she swept her blade out sideways and severed her companion's arm at the elbow.

Morgellon's wine-stained lips cracked into a smile.

Even through the hot, kicking pain, Hagar felt the cold plunge of despair. She had underestimated him. He had adapted.

The dominated guard pivoted on her hoof and flung her sword at her comrades. A Mucorian in the body of a lean black harka parried, the blade glancing his shoulder.

Morgellon worked quickly now as his talents waxed – Hagar had seen him use this trick many times, leaping between bodies, controlling a guard for a second, making her strike her neighbour, then jumping into the mind of the guard she'd just hit, making them strike her back. Rapidly the guards lost track of who was controlled and who was not – even their passionless Mucorian demeanours were not enough to stop them hacking one another down in a tumult of futile self-preservation.

Morgellon's mouth hung open as he controlled and maimed; he lost himself to the ecstasy.

Hagar glanced around for Sarai. Her silhouette moved against the river of candles, away from the melee, edging towards Morgellon. No. Sarai was pressing ahead with the plan regardless. She did not realise how strong Morgellon was, how they had already lost. Hagar had watched him use the same tactics to take down whole battalions of mounted infantry single-handed, force ships to ram their allies and captains to disembowel themselves in front of their horrified crews. He had practically broken the Siege of Atmanloka single-handedly. His long survival was no accident, his glory and infamy thoroughly earned.

Morgellon wiped a grot of purple viscera from his waistcoat then, glancing down, impaled a fallen guard's skull with her own sabre. Yellow thread fungus began knitting over the wound with dying languor, binding the blade in place before crusting, splitting. The rest of the Mucorian-controlled guards lay massacred, or else so viciously butchered that they could do nothing but twitch as fungal strands knotted useless flesh to useless flesh.

Morgellon regarded them with the disgust of the sated. He glanced up and noticed Sarai.

His lower lip curled downwards. Here was an old woman – stopping her ought to be a perfunctory thing, almost beneath his powers.

Almost. The weak were his favourite targets. He had never been the sort to relish a challenge.

Glutted on death, and doubtless a little sluggish now that his withdrawal from the black medicine was kicking in, he tightened his hand into a fist.

Sarai stopped. She held out a hand. Little grey trails, like dirty mist, were rising up from the dying guards, collecting in her open palm. She bent down and pressed her hand to the tiles.

Hagar watched as a small section of floor pushed up and scattered. From underneath rose a stunted tangle of black briars.

Morgellon looked round at Hagar.

'This is her, isn't it? Anwen's child. She was alive all these years. Ready for when I came.' For a moment, he seemed too stunned to react. Oh, he had thought she was treacherous, but he had always believed he had the measure of her treachery. That she had acted beyond even the reaches of his rangy paranoia . . . He wiped his mouth with the back of his hand. 'Her powers are too slow. I could kill her with a thought.'

Sarai's fist rose, then came down and down and down again, pounding her in the mouth, the skull, the eye socket. Hagar winced, feeling the pain as if it were her own. He was supposed to have been distracted. Sarai stumbled as he released her from his grip. He looked her up and down. 'If you move, I'll make you tear your own eyes out.' He looked past Hagar. 'And who's this?'

Hagar felt an immense heat against her back. The air rippled around Gideon as Morgellon puppeted him. Gideon trudged past, coarse dark hairs continually growing and burning away all over his body. Morgellon licked his lips as he scrutinised the stranger, evidently evaluating him inside and out.

'Your mind is restless,' said Morgellon, bringing Gideon to stand beside him. 'I can tame it.' His jaw clenched; the heat warp around Gideon instantly cleared. Burns closed up. Smoke cut out. Gideon staggered, blinked.

Then he groaned as Morgellon let go. Fire broke out down his arm.

'But you must yield,' said Morgellon. He turned back to Sarai, and she shuddered as he dominated her again. She began drawing

Gideon's suffering into her, fine black cords that snaked into her nostrils.

Hagar dragged herself to her feet. She would not die kneeling.

'Hmm,' said Morgellon, his gaze distant. 'Never thought I'd live to see a second sorrow-eater. Shall we see what she can do?' He planted his boot on the dead guard's head and wrenched out the sabre. 'Here now.'

He pointed with the tip of the blade. The air around Hagar fluxed and sucked inwards. She tried to run.

She came round on her side, blood pouring down one side of her face. Her ears were ringing. Morgellon was advancing on her. She scrambled to her feet, stumbled dizzily.

He flicked blood from the sabre and moved to a run. She took a step back.

Morgellon balled his free hand into a fist.

Neatly, her leg swung out from under her. Her centre of gravity shifted. She tried to throw her arms out for balance but they would not obey. She toppled.

Her head smacked the tiles. She saw white flashes; icy pain forked through her skull. She got up. She took a step and her leg folded. She headbutted the floor.

Her ears were full of the rumble of blood. He had overpowered her protection. She lay on her back. He was toying with her. Killing was not enough for Morgellon. Humiliation. Supplication. Annihilation.

She was deadly afraid. But she would not give him the satisfaction.

He forced her to stand. Her limbs worked against her will, hauling her up, swinging her round to face him. Sarai stood at his side, cowed and compliant, her lip swollen, a mauve bruise blossoming round her eye.

Hagar fought for breath. Warm salty blood dripped from her nostril. She felt him burrowing through her brain, revelling in his conquest.

Morgellon eyed her with contempt. He said something she could not hear.

She felt as if she had been kicked in the chest by a mule. She doubled over. The pain was like crushing iron bands. And it was hers. He had seized control.

He was stopping her heart.

Nausea washed through her. Her vision smeared. She could not draw breath. She collapsed. She felt the smooth mosaic tiles against her cheek.

Father, into thy hands I commend my spirit. No, no. It was not finished. She did not want to die. Perhaps Morgellon would draw out her punishment. Perhaps his cruelty would override his judgement, and she would have a chance to trick him, or the parasite around her wrist would adapt to his methods, or—

Morgellon drove the point of the sabre into her chest. He pushed, twisting the blade. Excruciating pain. Burning. She convulsed beneath him. Sweat streamed down her brow. She tasted vinegar. The vice tightened on her heart.

He yanked the blade out. Through bleary eyes she saw him stab Gideon through the throat. Ah God, he wanted more pain. He was going to puppet Sarai for the final mercy stroke. Hagar felt his control on her relax but her throat was filling with blood. The tick on her wrist beat like a second heart. The world began receding.

It was over. Arthur had lied.

An almighty thunderclap. Everything went white.

CHAPTER 23
REUNION

Father raised his head and looked directly at her. His eyes widened. His mouth fell partly open.

The floor seemed to tip. Reality washed through her.

He lifted a hand, reaching for her.

The bloodied man turned and drove the sword through Father's throat. Father jerked to the side. The blade emerged from the other side of his neck, steaming. He convulsed, transfixed, and the man beside him began to laugh.

Delphine decided in her heart and her body took over. She broke cover. She sprinted across open ground, closing the distance between her and the target. Black strands were curling from her father, rushing into the old woman. Delphine swung the muzzle up, keeping her arms loose. She felt the sweet spot as a warmth in her belly.

She squeezed.

A kick-bang. The slug punched through the bloodied stranger's skull, tossing him backwards in a spray of dark blood. His legs bucked and he backflipped as he fell, skidding across the floor, arms splayed, until he came to rest at the foot of the sarcophagus.

Delphine chambered another round and ran down the steps. She swung her shotgun about, hunting for targets. Everything was still. The candles burned with a soft fluxing light. She heard a yell from behind her and ignored it. She ran towards Father, who stood clutching at the sword blade, moaning softly.

As soon as she got within twenty feet of him the heat rose sharply. She slowed down, out of breath. It was him. Her father. Daddy. Oh God.

Her vision blurred with tears. Jesus. Her hand was shaking so hard she could barely wipe her eyes.

Come on now. She punched herself in the leg. Come *on*.

She stepped up, heat washing over her face, drying her tears. She grabbed the sabre by its chain grip and pulled it out. She felt a pain as her palm blistered, but it was nothing, a vague sensation in the background. The blade clanged to the floor. Father swayed on his bare feet.

'Daddy. It's me.'

His eyes were closed. Blood bubbled through the hole in his neck, boiling away, leaving a black sticky resin.

'Daddy. It's Delphine.'

His eyelids flickered, just slightly.

Hands pulling her back. She twisted, struggled.

'Easy. Easy.' Alice's voice in her ear. 'You're too close. We don't know he's safe.'

'He's my *father*!' She wrenched her arm free. 'Daddy! Can you hear me?'

Butler was there. 'Venner, what the *hell* was that? What did I say? *What did I say?*'

'Oh my God.' The third voice was Patience's. 'Hagar.'

A concussion shook the chamber. Candles toppled. Something dropped from the ceiling.

Patience shot out a rigid canopy of skin and spines, shielding them all. Delphine ducked. Glass and debris shattered just above their heads.

Patience retracted her angel-arm. The pulverised remnants of a stone arch lay around them. Father was standing just as he had been, flesh smouldering softly.

'What the bloody hell was that?' said Butler.

A series of aftershocks made the floor shudder; dust fell in crackling showers.

'Someone just bombed the esplanade.' The white-haired woman in the grey dress walked towards the fallen child, limping. 'Many people are hurt.' She blinked, and tears rolled down her cheeks.

She knelt beside the girl, who Delphine now saw was Hagar Ingery. The girl's eyes were open, her face ashen beneath the cuts and bruises, a dark wet stain coating her chest.

There was something unsettling about the old woman. Delphine felt as if she knew her, and yet they had only just met. The face was eerily familiar.

Another surge of vertigo. This was Anwen and Cox's daughter. This was Sarai. Delphine had established a strange intimacy with these features as a child, spying on her in Alderberen Hall. Back then, she had studied them in fascinated horror – but here they were *animated*. The body was out of bed, moving around. No longer an invalid. Full of vigour.

Delphine approached her father. 'Daddy?' Did he even remember her? It had been more than seventy years. Everything was bright and unreal. 'Daddy, it's Delphy.'

Father opened his eyes. He looked around, then looked straight at her.

Her legs were weak. Her sight was failing. Her hands trembled. She had never felt so young.

'Please,' she said.

Father gritted his teeth, squinted. He shook his head.

'No.' His voice was so gentle. He screwed his face up. 'Sarai. I'm seeing her again.'

'One moment, Gideon.' Sarai rolled back Hagar's jacket sleeve. Attached to Hagar's wrist was a bloated tick the size of a tennis ball. It was shrivelled and dead, its thorax imploded in a crust of black blood. A substance like honey wept down her arm.

Sarai gripped the tick and pulled it out of Hagar's arm. A barbed stylet curved from its leathery head, several inches long and bloody. Sarai stood with some difficulty.

Grey filaments were forming in the air round her head – smoky threads which she drew into her eyes, nose and ears. Another detonation shook the chamber. The grey threads thickened to braids. Delphine staggered. A huge section of stained-glass window struck the floor just feet away with a crash.

'We need to leave,' said Butler.

Sarai gazed at the tick in her hand. The dark amber fluid

leaking out of it abruptly sucked back into the cracks, which sealed up.

The bloodied man sat up.

Sarai brushed her hair back and looked at Delphine. One of her pupils was obscured by a nacreous sheen.

'The world is very evil,' she said. 'Look after him.'

The air pressure dropped. Delphine smelt ozone. Sarai raised an arm. The space around her buckled like a ripple on a pond. Cobalt light enveloped her limbs.

A mass of dark thorns tore from the floor, snagging the man's arms and throat, hoisting him to his feet. Sarai bounded towards him and drove the tick's stylet into the centre of his chest.

A wake of blue energy bore her backwards. She stumbled, dropped to one knee beside Hagar. Sarai raised a palm, and beckoned to him. The tick's thorax began to pump.

It was like someone squeezing maggots out of a dog. His back arched. All over his face and hands, his skin was beading with black fluid. Godstuff welled in his eyes, ran as tears down his sallow cheeks. It streamed from his ears, flowed thickly from his nostrils. He coughed up throatfuls of dark liquid.

Delphine smelled that familiar hoppy, tarry, resinous stink. His cloak burst at the throat. Beneath, a great pullulating tumour was splitting and collapsing. Pale grubs dropped from the disintegrating flesh, writhing on the floor, smoking and gnarling.

Droplets of godstuff melded into a vinyl-black river, pulling away from him, flowing through the air. Like a liquid briar it began helixing up Sarai's arm.

It traced the curve of her throat, her jaw, her cheekbone, curled round her eye socket, then lifted away from the skin, snaking round on itself, before striking her in the centre of the forehead.

She stiffened. Godstuff poured into her. The front of her dress browned and rotted away. From her breastbone quested a silver cord, rounded at the tip.

The cord shot upwards, plaited over and around itself in a shining knot, then with a sudden hunger drove down into Hagar's skull.

Hagar's body bucked and convulsed. Sarai had fallen onto her hands and knees, her face contorting. Where the godstuff was entering her forehead, the skin was scarring and blistering in a radiating spiral, her white hair dropping out in clumps. Where the silver stream emerged, a blue-black necrosis was spreading outwards.

The channelled godstuff was eating her alive.

Delphine ran at her. An arm locked round Delphine's throat, dragging her back.

'Keep away,' hissed Butler in her ear. 'It'll kill you too.'

Sarai dropped to her knees. Godstuff poured into her, through her, alchemising, consuming.

A whipping black tail lashed from the bloodied man and sluiced through her body before it poured into Hagar.

Sarai slumped. A moment later the brambles holding the man crumbled and he dropped to the floor.

Delphine ran to her. Sarai's chest had a bullseye-shaped imprint of blue, mottled skin.

A foul, cloying smell struck Delphine's nostrils. She clamped a hand over her mouth. The front of Sarai's dress had completely disintegrated.

'I'll be damned,' said Butler. He touched two fingers to the back of his ear. Neither Hagar nor the bloodied man appeared to be breathing. 'I think she just deposed the Grand-Duc.'

A tremor made dirt trickle from the balconies.

Delphine looked to Father. He was shaking his head, pulling pained expressions.

'Daddy. Father.'

Nothing.

'Gideon.'

He twitched.

'Gideon. We need to go.'

He shook his head vigorously. 'I don't feel right. It's dreaming of me.'

Delphine looked to Patience and Butler to help her. 'Please, Gideon. It's dangerous here.'

He opened his eyes, casting around anxiously. 'Where's Sarai?'

'She's just here.' Delphine glanced at Sarai's slumped body. 'We're going to take her somewhere she'll be safe. Will you come with us too?' She just had to get him out of here. Then he would know her. Then she could help him.

Flames broke out along his arm and he moaned, flailing. 'Ice! Salt water!'

'Of course, Gideon.' Patience spoke in a loud, confident voice. 'We'll take you there now. Everyone's waiting. Come on. This way.'

She signalled to Butler, who hoisted Sarai's lifeless body onto his shoulder and began leading them back towards the steps. Delphine followed, watching Father stumble in a groggy, semi-oblivious trance. She would save him. He would recover, just like Alice. She would take away his pain.

Martha was waiting by the big doors, standing watch. Her antennae were performing rapid, quivering sweeps. Her eyes had turned a delirious sunset red. Butler click-chirruped at her, and they had a quick exchange.

'What's wrong?' said Delphine.

'Heaven knows,' said Butler. 'She says someone's . . .' He circled his hand. 'Present? Aware? It doesn't translate exactly.'

'Where?'

'She doesn't know.' He peered round the door, popping, range-finding. 'Not outside, apparently.'

'It's not another of your intuitions, is it?'

She bopped her fist once for *yes*.

'*Please*, Martha!' Delphine found herself making a fist. 'Would you just . . .' She stopped, took a couple of deep breaths.

Alice knelt and laid a hand on Martha's back. 'We'll stay alert. Tell us if you feel anything else.'

Delphine was about to say something – Father was beginning to worry at his scalp with his fingernails – but Alice flashed her a look. Come on, now. Keep your head, Venner.

Butler nodded towards the door. He slipped outside, and Alice followed.

Before she left, Delphine threw a final glance across the pavilion. The candles were distant lights in windows. Dust was falling in shining sheets, like snow.

CHAPTER 24

THE SECOND DEATH HATH NO POWER

Hagar Ingery blinked and opened her eyes. Mitta was gazing down upon her, diademed with light. She felt an extraordinary ecstasy.

And God shall wipe away all tears from their eyes; and there shall be no more death, neither sorrow, nor crying, neither shall there be any more pain.

No pain in her shoulder. No pain in her heart. Just a hot, rushing sensation, the quickening spirit.

She thought, for a wild, delirious instant, that she was in paradise. Then she felt the gap in her teeth, the blood turning tacky in her palm.

She placed a hand on the tiles and attempted to stand. She did so easily. Incredible.

All around her, an unearthly quiet, as if the pavilion were holding its breath. She felt an expansive calm. The slightest tilt of her head, the turn of her wrist, felt like the execution of a command, an expression of deep axiom.

At her feet lay Kenner, curled up like a child.

Hagar felt an unexpected sorrow. She was acutely aware she had destroyed something of beauty, one of God's creations. All those times he'd warned her to leave the city. Perhaps he had been trying to save her. She found herself wishing she could hug him, and tell him she loved him.

She knelt. She was used to the smells of death, and though she did not find them pleasant exactly, there was something in the sweet, ripe scent that felt like home. She ran her thumb over his fingertips. Still warm.

She looked around the sunken pool. Candles lay in burning pools of wax. Chunks of masonry had buried themselves in the floor. Flames backlit the red mound of his corpse.

All this sadness was the very reason she had set out upon this journey. To end it. To break the cage.

A few yards away, Morgellon lay on his side.

'Uncle.'

He stirred, mumbling, grinding his shoulder in the dirt. His fine cloak and breeches were torn and soiled; one of his silver buckles had torn loose and hung by a length of fabric. He looked as if he had been on one of his revels. She cleared her throat. He snapped awake.

'Wha, ah . . . uh . . .' His chest rose and fell.

'Uncle. Get up.'

Morgellon looked around, his eyes wide. 'What . . . what's happened to . . .'

'Uncle. *Get up.*'

It felt rather like drawing a noose tight. She sensed his mind, weak and jittery, and she simply closed her will around it. She did not see through his eyes, nor did she think specific instructions – it was more intuitive, a gentle exercise in resolve. She was able to think and breathe and adjust her own hat, while simultaneously directing him to stand, take his shortsword from the floor, and approach her with his head lowered.

She had him hand her the sword, then, with the slight reluctance one feels when tossing a fish back into the ocean, she relinquished control. No sooner had she done so then Morgellon hurled himself at her.

He threw a right hook at her jaw. His fist connected. Both their heads snapped sideways. Hagar let the momentum spin her, then she threw a leg out behind her as counterbalance and pirouetted to a crunching stop.

Morgellon staggered back and fell. He lay there, staring up at the ceiling.

Hagar stroked her cheek, full of wonder. She had felt his fist strike her face, had felt the flesh compress under his knuckles, could even feel a faint warmth where her cheek was swelling, but of pain she knew nothing.

A soft rumble passed through the chamber. A few candles toppled.

'Shh, shh, shh.' Hagar walked to his side. She bored into his mind and made his muscles go slack. His head lolled to one side. She made him take some slow, deep breaths, feeling his will struggle beneath hers, the way the horse in Lesang's slaughterhouse had kicked after its throat had been slit. At last, she felt him yield. She gave him control of his head and throat, allowed him to breathe by himself. 'Now. How are you feeling?'

He stared up, eyes bloodshot, teeth chattering. 'What's . . . happening to me?'

'Pain.'

His face contorted. Tears trickled down either side of his steep nose.

'Oh. Oh, Hagar. Please help. Something's happened. Something's gone wrong.' He clutched at his curly hair, screwing his eyes shut. 'I don't . . . I don't feel right. Please help me, *bichette*. Help your uncle.' He used the Low Thelusian *oomkah*, investing the first syllable with a plaintive moan.

She hiked up her sleeve. *Surely a bloody husband art thou to me.*

Turning his sword's serrated edge downwards, she began sawing through her wrist.

It was a fascinating sensation. She watched the curved teeth drag across the skin, ripping its stitches, revealing the red muscle beneath. She was not numb – she could feel it, it just didn't hurt. Morgellon howled. She willed him to stay in place, granting him his voice and nothing more. She worked the blade back and forth, gnawing through arteries. Her fingers convulsed as she slit the tendons. She felt the blade resist as it met bone. She lost sensation in her fingers. Blood pumped to the rhythm of her heart, splattering the tiles. So this was what had lain hidden all these years. How few knew themselves with such splendid intimacy.

The hand fell and hung swinging by a flap of skin. She tossed the sword to the floor and ripped her hand off.

Morgellon writhed and gaped. His voice was hoarse from screaming. Her severed hand was clammy, pale fingers drooping like a dead spider. She tossed it down in front of him.

His eyes were closed. He whimpered and rocked.

'You said you liked me to suffer,' she said. 'You said it was good for me. That you were teaching me.' She put on the haughty, pedagogical voice he used to use with her. 'For what is more injurious to the obedient spirit than self-love? What is more proper than mortification of the flesh?' She picked up the sword with her remaining hand. 'I'm returning your kindness, Morgellon. I'm educating you.'

'Oh *bichette* . . .' he gasped, '. . . I always did . . . what I thought . . . was best. Always. If I seemed cruel . . . it was because the world . . . was cruel to me. I . . . saved you. Aren't . . . you . . . grateful?'

Hagar turned the sword around so it was pointing at her stomach. She stabbed herself, again and again.

'Thank you, Uncle. Thank you, Uncle. Thank you, Uncle.'

His screams rang off the pillars.

She did not stop. 'Where's your clipper?'

He howled.

It was very peculiar, feeling the sword inside her, the busy, tingling sensation of her stomach wall closing up. The blade snagged on white fat and she had to yank it to get it out. 'Come on now. You must have some plan for getting away. If you expected war you wouldn't drop anchor in the bay.'

He was gibbering, rubbing his cheek against the tiles.

'Morgellon.' She paused, gave him time to gather his wits. 'I know you have a ship. Where. Is. It?'

Morgellon lay panting, moaning. He was in denial. He thought he could hide and this would all go away. She lifted the sword and prepared to stab herself again.

'North.'

'What was that?'

'North!' He clutched at his belly, his face screwed up with pain. 'A lagoon about twenty muh . . . twenty miles north!'

'You know if you're lying to me it doesn't matter how far away you run – I can still hurt you. I'll rip my eyes out.'

'I'm not lying!'

She looked down at the creature beneath her, wretched, craven, utterly selfish, and felt only disgust. Killing him would be a kindness. The centuries had left him hungry and deformed. She raised the sword.

And hesitated.

While Morgellon lived, he bore her pain. There was work to complete. Until she found a suitable replacement, was it wise to throw away such power?

He cowered in her shadow. She tossed the sword to the floor. She had no appetite for vengeance.

She turned away and left him. She could hear rats pattering amongst the bodies. Sarai had delivered her from her suffering. Now she must recover Sarai and Gideon and make her escape. It was not enough to merely free herself – she must liberate everyone. The work had to be finished.

No matter the cost.

CHAPTER 25

BURNING AS IT WERE A LAMP

Through dark palace hallways they ran, down into the prayer caves, through the open drain where the harka guard lay unconscious and down into the wide amber tunnels of the old lanta city. All the way, Father staggered and mumbled, clawing at himself like a caged circus bear.

'Come on,' said Delphine, beckoning. 'Just a little farther.' That was a lie, of course. Her feet were blistered, her limbs rubbery with fatigue. Every time he stopped, or looked behind him, or started punching himself, she wanted to cry. Black, greasy smoke wicked off his body, his shoulder spitting and popping like pork fat.

They stopped at the map Martha had drawn in the dust. Butler set down Sarai, spent a moment checking her over.

'There's the faintest of pulses,' he said. 'We need to get her out of here, fast.' He nodded at the map. 'The route we entered by is blocked, and even if we clear it, there's a simarak nest on the other side, so we need another way down to the sewers. There's this room to the east.' He tapped the floor with his toe, indicating three concentric circles linked to the main body of tunnels by a short passage running east to west. Little squares like gear teeth came off the largest circle. 'It was my original choice for getting to the palace. It appears to have lots of small rooms attached to it. Might have been a communal living space of some description. It looked like there was some sort of opening in the east wall.'

'Or maybe you could do your wall thing, Martha,' said Alice.

The comb-heads of Martha's antennae were quivering to a blur, her eyes a piercing ruby. She bopped her fist once. She was rarely this edgy. Delphine bit back her misgivings, pushed on.

As they continued the hall narrowed, the architecture taking on strange, captivating geometries. Reliefs showed Fibonacci spirals like giant nautilus shells. Curves tessellated and intersected in a way that confused her brain, making her misgauge the hall's dimensions.

With Sarai slung over his shoulder, Butler led them into a series of cramped, winding corridors where the path split and split again. The ceiling was low and Delphine had to stoop. She glanced down and saw the floor was incised with complex mandalas, shapes within shapes, many-petalled lotuses locking together like a vast chain. Looking at them made her nauseous. Father was running his fingers along the grooves, muttering to himself.

'No mud, no lotus,' he said, nodding, wincing. 'The great wheel turns in the ocean.'

Butler clicked and walked, clicked and walked, his pistol drawn, his lantern swaying in his grasp. He never tired, never slowed, pausing only to consult with Martha. Presently, the winding, branching paths straightened out into a short corridor with a sloping floor and a gutter running down the middle. The desiccated bodies of tiny insects crackled under her boots. Things moved in the darkness; eyes glinted, paws skittered. She spotted rat runs in the dirt, shallow trenches close to the walls. The sound of running water grew louder.

They emerged in a wide, echoing cavern. Butler's lantern glow rainbowed in a fine mist. The air was warm.

Lamplight picked out splashes of an amphitheatre-like chamber. Huge cobwebs lay in thick membranes over everything, but unlike the web in the tunnels, these looked dry and ancient. Delphine and the others were standing on a narrow walkway that ran east to west over a deep, bowl-like depression in the floor. Giant gnarled fungi grew around a bubbling pool covered in red algae, spilling from the edges in crusted heaps.

Delphine moved her Maglite across the far wall. All round the room were circular openings, each about four feet wide, shrouded in webs. What looked like rotten tapestries dangled from hooks. She swung the light up to the ceiling. She could make out a pattern etched into the amber stone.

Overlapping circles created geometric flowers or stars that bulged out like flesh straining against a net. There were eight discs made from dark and light woods fused together, each about twelve feet in diameter, appearing to represent the phases of the moon. From the sunken star in the centre, four black arms spiralled out in perfect golden ratios, spreading, consuming the pattern.

A strange sickness came over her as she looked – a crawling sensation inside her throat. This image was just like the one that used to cover the ceiling of the banqueting hall at Alderberen Hall. Only much bigger.

Butler was crossing the walkway. 'There's the bugger.' He pointed his gun at an archway in the opposite wall, about ten feet across and six high, and blocked with rubble. The archway itself was made of wood, the amber stone around it bulging oddly. He turned to Patience. 'Think you can shift that lot, DeGroot?'

Patience patted her angel-arm. 'Depends how far back it goes. I'll need a few minutes, at least.'

Father grabbed his scalp and let out a moan. Smoke rose from between his fingers, his hair twisting away to ash.

The temperature dropped. The air thickened with white mist. Delphine knew what was coming. Oh no.

Arthur walked through the rubble as if it were smoke, his head down, his eyes fixed on Delphine. Stark featherless wings spread from his shoulders, trailing vapour.

'I warned you,' he said.

'I ignored you,' said Delphine, chambering a round.

'Yes, I thought you might.' He smiled. 'That's why I told you.'

'What?'

'I hoped you'd interfere,' he said. 'I wasn't sure *what* you'd do, exactly, but I'd seen the pattern. I knew you were essential. And you hate me, so it made sense that if I begged you not to do something, you'd do the opposite.'

'Liar.'

'Yes, well. You killed my father, my grandfather, you tried to kill my mother and you tried to kill me. By comparison I've always treated you pretty decently. But I said it would end badly for you, and I meant that. You've served your purpose. I can't have you robbing the world of its last chance for peace. Sarai is coming with me, and your father is coming with me. Heaven is more important than your hate.' His jacket flared as he turned. 'Gideon!'

Father jerked alert. 'Arthur?'

'Bearing up all right, old stick?'

Father's eyes were wild and bloodshot. 'Where am I? Is this real?'

'Afraid so.'

'Where's Sarai?'

'Auntie? Bad news on that front, I'm afraid. She's dead.'

Delphine had to shield her face from a great wave of heat that pulsed from her father. Sheets of cobweb above him fluttered in the updraft.

'No!' he said.

'Killed,' said Arthur. He pointed at Delphine. 'It was her fault.'

Father gripped his skull. 'No!' Skin blistered beneath his palms. 'No!'

'Stop it!' yelled Delphine. She turned to her father. 'Daddy, it's me. Don't listen to him. She's just hurt, that's all. He's lying!'

'She died in terrible pain, Giddy. She won't be able to help you any longer.'

Another blast of heat forced Delphine back. 'No! No! No!'

'Please!' Delphine waded into it, striding towards him. 'You have to believe me. We're getting her to safety.' Her skin was burning. 'Daddy! It's me. It's Delphy.'

Butler shot him through the head. The bullet punched a neat hole between Father's eyes. He dropped with a whump.

The heat dissipated at once, replaced by lukewarm mist.

'Sorry, Ms Venner. New strategy.' He turned the gun on Arthur. 'Do fuck off.' He fired. A puff of dust went up from the rubble in the doorway.

A green laser sight cut through Arthur's head, lighting up the mist curling off his side-parted brown hair. Delphine stared, stunned. Father lay crumpled on the ground.

Arthur glowered. 'You're not very bright, are you?'

'Don't try to intimidate me, boy.' Butler fanned his leathery wings in opposition to Arthur's. His lips peeled back, exposing purple gums and a maw full of needle fangs. 'I've faced peers with powers that far exceeded your own. Ask me how many still live.'

For a moment, Arthur's glare faltered. Delphine snapped awake. Without thinking, she ran to Father's side.

'Father!' She touched him. His skin was warm, not burning. The hole in his brow was filling with dark, clotted blood.

'Delphine!' Arthur flicked his arms outwards and a perfume of ice joined the mist. 'You wilful, spiteful little brat. I *told* you this won't do.' He began marching across the walkway towards her. Ice marbled the stone. 'I'll kill you myself.'

CHAPTER 26

A FOUNTAIN OF WATER IN THE WILDERNESS

Butler set Sarai down on the walkway and in the same fluid movement sidestepped to block Arthur. 'No.'

Arthur did not break stride. He stepped through Butler, their forms briefly merging before his nose, eyes and mouth surfaced from the back of Butler's head. Hoarfrost crusted on Butler's fur and the tips of his ears.

Arthur was grinning, the fingers of his right hand performing predatory arpeggios. 'Now, you little canker,' he said, 'I may not be strong, but I'm sure a few fingers briefly manifesting in your brain will be quite sufficient to k—'

Butler turned and lunged at him with a hand trailing blue smoke. His fingers wafted into Arthur's head. Arthur's neck snapped back.

Cobalt vapour tongued off Butler's fur. Arthur gaped in frozen horror. Butler licked his fangs, seething with appetite.

Arthur's eyes went blank. He curled in on himself and was gone.

Butler stumbled forward, closing his fist on nothing. 'Damn!' A twist of smoke rose from his fingers. 'I almost had him.' He sniffed, looked up. 'I took at least an hour.' He examined his fingers, shook his hand out.

Delphine felt a sudden heat rising from Father. The wound in his head had sealed up.

'He's waking up!'

Butler shot him again, the exit wound splattering black blood and bone fragments across the floor. Delphine and Alice both jumped.

'Stop that!' said Delphine. 'What are you doing?'

'Keeping us and him safe,' said Butler, holstering his pistol and picking up Sarai. 'DeGroot – get shifting those rocks. Cross. Venner. We need to keep Gideon unconscious. It's for his – and our – own good. Use your guns if you have to, but a blade's better. Don't waste ammo.'

'I'm not . . .' Delphine was shaking. Oh God, tears? Not now. For Christ's sake.

'Delphine.' Alice put an arm round her. 'I'll do it. He's right. It's what's best. You . . . go and help Patience.'

Delphine pinched the bridge of her nose and tried to suck the feelings back down. She let Alice bring her in for a hug, slapped Alice on the back and disengaged.

'All right,' she said. 'Let's bloody finish this.'

Hagar sprinted through the dark of the lanta city, clutching a candle in her gloved hand. She ran as fast as she could, and though her breath grew short, her legs did not ache, and her lungs did not burn.

Testing her new powers, she felt about for a mind, something to sinuate round, to slip inside. The action was unfamiliar – at first, she sensed nothing amongst the dust and blackness, save her own clumsy attempts at connection. Dominating Morgellon had been an instinctive act – she knew his mind as she knew her own. Learning how to exploit her powers to their fullest with strangers would take practice.

She slowed down as she followed the tracks through branching tunnels. Instead of grasping at random, she let her mind relax, allowing her consciousness to swim in the still, dark passageways. After some time, she became aware of a second presence. She resisted the temptation to lunge at it, instead allowing her thoughts to float wider and wider until they enveloped it. There. A mind. She allowed her control to tighten around it, until she could feel the flow of thoughts.

They burned.

Patience opened a godstuff portal in the floor. Fleshy limbs pushed out of it and hooked into the rubble blocking their escape, while Delphine loosened rocks with the pommel of her sickle.

'Okay,' said Patience. 'Get back.'

Delphine backed off. Patience heaved and wrenched. They repeated the process until, at last, a whole section of rubble and dirt collapsed into the portal, rocks spilling out the other side. Several large rats skittered through the gap.

Patience had cleared a hole slightly bigger than an adult. Delphine kicked away a few stones and shone her gun-light through the gap.

'Looks like another tunnel. Stone rather than this amber stuff. Can't see how far it goes.' The beam winked off dozens of rats' eyes. The rats were sitting on their haunches along the tunnel's edges, calmly staring. She was too tired to feel anything but a mild disquiet.

'One way to find out,' said Butler. 'Patience, would you mind carrying Sarai? I'll hold Gideon and watch he doesn't wake up.'

He hauled Father over his shoulder. Father's head flopped to one side and Delphine saw the bloody purple-blue hole in his eye socket.

She heard a noise, like the flapping of silk. Butler frowned, then his ears swivelled. He swung Father's limp body aside with one arm and with the other pulled his pistol. A blast of putty-coloured flesh rushed past Delphine and slapped it out of his hand. Butler pivoted with the blow and reached for his belt in one clean movement. A second tendril went for his throat. He pulled his serrated dagger and slashed in an upward arc, slashing the limb in half. The stump whipped about like a hosepipe. The flesh began peeling back, extruding a long blade of pearlescent keratin. Butler moved to parry and with a sharp flick it severed his head from his shoulders.

His body took a couple of steps and toppled from the walkway.

Delphine spun round. Patience stood there in the doorway, underlit by her dropped lantern. Her angel-arm slapped to the floor, a sticky liquid mess.

Delphine raised her shotgun. 'I *knew* it!'

Patience lifted a shaking hand to her own cheek, touched it. She shook her head frantically.

'It wasn't me!' She drew her liquefied angel-arm back up into an amalgamated lump. 'I couldn't control it, it just—'

Delphine fired. The noise was a thunderclap. The solid slug punched a hole in Patience's stomach, throwing her backwards through a veil of webs, into the heaped rubble. She dropped to her hand and knees. Delphine chambered another round and fired again, this time through the head.

Delphine looked down at the Remington. It shone with hallucinogenic clarity. She had not meant to do that. Her hands had acted on their own.

'Delphine?' Alice was staring at her.

'Alice!' Panic rose in a numbing rush. 'Something's wrong!'

Alice looked at something off to her left. Her face fell. Delphine spun round.

Standing in the western doorway was the little girl, Hagar.

Delphine dropped to a crouch. Hagar was wearing that familiar black, wide-brimmed hat. Her hair fell about her face in sandy tangles. She was grubby, splattered up one side of her face with gore, her shirt and gilet in tatters. She flicked something gummy off her fingers.

Delphine kept very still, her finger flat against the shotgun's trigger guard. She could see Alice and Father out of the corner of her eye. Best to stall.

'What do you want?' said Delphine.

The girl strolled out onto the walkway. 'Peace.' In her scratchy, ruined voice, the word sounded strangely melancholy. 'And for that I'm going to need your father.'

CHAPTER 27
EXTINCTION BURST

The girl with the gun crouched, waiting. She was crusted in filth, her clothes and skin shades of grey-brown, her hair stuck in stiff peaks. She looked like a member of one of the vesperi clans House Dellapeste had hunted down in the Avalonian jungle. Feral. Full of savage reproach.

To her right, a young girl with white-blond hair knelt at Gideon's side, holding a sophisticated-looking pistol from the other world. Gideon was rousing – Hagar dimly apprehended the tumult of his thoughts. Gently, she disengaged his body from the rush of feelings; the fires across his flesh cooled.

'Please bring Gideon and Sarai to me,' she said. 'I'll take care of them now.'

'They're hurt,' said the white-haired girl.

'I have a background in medicine.'

The white-haired girl glanced at Delphine.

'I'm his daughter,' said Delphine. 'He needs me. I'm going to make him better.'

'If I stop now, all his pain will have been for nothing. We're so close. He's going to help me save the world.'

'I don't care about the fucking world. Let. Him. Go.'

'He wants to help. He chose this.'

'Bollocks! He chose nothing! This was *done* to him. He's just a thing to you. A tool.'

Hagar took a step forward. Gideon's mind squirmed under her control. Even as she helped him suppress his torment, the proximity of his daughter was disturbing him. Sarai's consciousness was the faintest of stirrings, barely perceptible. The poor girl was probably going to die. No matter. She had played her part. It was Gideon who still had work.

'I'm sorry,' said Hagar, 'but it's for the greater good.'

Delphine grimaced. She hung her head.

'All right,' she said. 'I know you'll kill me if I try to fight. No more death. I want it to stop.'

'Then we want the same thing.'

'So no bloodshed. Please.' Delphine looked up. 'Let me help you.'

Delphine watched Hagar's expression shift – cautious but intrigued.

Alice threw her arms wide. 'Delphine! No!'

As Hagar turned to look, Delphine pulled the trigger.

The chamber rang with the report. The slug blew through Hagar's collarbone, blasting a hole in her shoulder. She spun and fell from the walkway.

Delphine stared into the space where Hagar had stood, panting. She walked to the edge of the walkway and peered down into a mass of old webs and fungi. She flashed her gun-light around. Rats scurried from the beam. She saw no sign of Hagar. The drop was less than thirty feet. They did not have long.

'Butler!' Her yell rang off the walls. Patience was still unconscious, slumped against the rubble, her gunshot wounds not bleeding but visible – ugly dark gouges. Delphine sprinted to Father's side.

'Are you okay?' said Alice.

Delphine nodded. She wiped her lips.

'We need to get him out of here.' She grabbed Father under the armpits. His flesh was frighteningly hot. 'Come on, help me!'

Father raised his head and screamed. Delphine nearly fell over. The heat beneath her palms surged.

She clung on till the pain was unbearable. She swore and let go. Gouts of flame erupted from broken flesh across his back. His hair blackened and crisped. He shrieked, thrashing.

'Hold on!' said Delphine. 'Daddy! Get up and things will be fine.

Just a little farther, I promise.' He writhed. 'Daddy, it's me. Daddy! It's me.'

'Please stop this.'

Delphine turned.

Round the edge of the chamber walked Hagar, gripping her wounded shoulder, holding it in place while threads of scar tissue relearnt its shape. 'Stop this, Delphine. You can't look after him.'

'*You* stop! He's *my* father!'

'What about your friend?' Hagar nodded at Alice.

Delphine turned. Alice was walking towards Patience.

'Alice!'

Alice did not react. Her eyes were glassy. Patience's eyelids flickered. Alice strolled up to her, raised the machine pistol and emptied the entire clip into her head. Patience's body jittered, sagged.

Delphine aimed at Hagar's head and fired. The shotgun's muzzle jinked to the left. The slug struck the far wall with a crazy ricocheting sound, slicing through cobwebs. She pumped the slide action and fired again. The muzzle jinked to the right. Both times, Alice lurched as Hagar briefly relinquished control.

'Look at yourself! Can't you see what this world makes us do?' Hagar smoothed a hand over her shoulder and, like a magic trick, the skin had sealed up. She poked at the waxy mass of keloid scars. 'We age and sicken and die. Suffering makes us afraid, which makes us selfish, hateful and cruel. Even a mother's love for her child . . . The desire to protect easily turns into a willingness to kill. This . . . *place* was designed to take every good emotion and poison it.' She crushed her fingers into a fist. Her left hand was pink and without fingernails, strangely oily. 'I'm going to undo that. I'm going to save everyone.'

'You can't.'

'I can. Even you.'

Delphine backed onto the walkway. 'I've killed a peer before.'

'Anwen?' Hagar smiled. 'Oh yes, she told me.'

Delphine had a moment of disorientation. Surely a lie.

Hagar spread her arms. 'Don't you think there might be a better way?'

'You are not a better way.'

'You don't think it's a horror, then? Babies turning to frail, broken husks?' She gestured at Sarai. 'Your father, trapped forever in that body, burning?'

'I'm trying to save him!' Delphine tried to fire but her trigger finger froze. She fought Hagar's control, but it was absolute.

'Sarai is the only relief he's ever known. She drinks his pain. Turns it into beauty. And just look what she could do when she had the suffering of a whole city to feed on.' Hagar patted her own chest.

Father howled. Flames were licking from his flesh, catching layers of cobwebs draped across the floor.

'Fight me,' said Delphine. 'You're a bully.'

'The Lamb was slain from the foundation of the world. We were created to suffer.' Hagar looked as if she were barely listening. She ran a thumb across her chin, examined the blood. 'We're food, Delphine. Fodder for the *rex mundi.* But there's a place beyond pain. Gideon is going to lead me to his earthly god. The beast of lies and shadows. Then I'll stop the wheel of birth and death. Smash it right off its axle. Not for some. For everyone.'

Delphine felt Hagar grip her mind.

Alice cried out: 'Delphine!'

Hagar glanced at Alice. 'I need to show you both, don't I?'

Delphine's hands chambered a round. Hagar made her rotate to face Alice.

'No!' yelled Delphine. She fired.

The slug hit Alice in the belly. The impact threw her back against the rubble. She slumped, limp. Blood flowed over her legs.

Delphine blinked.

'I'm sorry,' said Hagar. 'You need to understand.'

Delphine could not speak. She felt weightless. It was as if the room were a sketch drawn on paper.

'*All that is beloved and pleasing will become otherwise*,' said Hagar. '*All that we cherish will be separated from us*.' The air was rich with the scent of burning flesh. The squeak and skitter of rats grew louder.

Hagar brought Delphine back around, dropped her to her knees. Delphine's hands turned the shotgun round and thrust the muzzle into the soft palate under her jaw. Her thumb settled on the trigger.

The muzzle pressed against her tonsils. She tried to move her fingers, but they would not obey.

'Do you really want to cling on, Delphine?' said Hagar.

Delphine's body refused to struggle. It was over. She could not go on without Alice. She could not bear to face a world where Alice's death was a reality.

Hagar watched, trembling with anticipation.

Delphine looked into the face of death, and did not feel afraid.

Her thumb twitched. Slowly, deliberately, Hagar forced it down.

Delphine closed her eyes.

The hammer fell.

CHAPTER 28
PLAGUE

Clack.

Hagar heard the hollow punch of the hammer. Delphine knelt there, eyes closed. The shotgun was empty.

Flames spread from Gideon. Fire ate through cobwebs, illuminating patterns in the exquisitely carved ceiling, picking out hundreds of rats watching from the shadows, their shining eyes and whiskers. Hagar strode onto the walkway and moved behind Delphine. She whipped the garrotte from inside her sleeve and wound it round Delphine's throat. She pulled crosswise; the wire bit, the flesh beneath cinching like a corset. Delphine jerked and gagged. Hagar dug a boot in the small of her back and yanked.

Delphine's chokes echoed through the chamber. Hagar wished the stubborn girl could have understood. Heaven was nigh. It would be painless.

Something brushed her ankle. A second later she felt a mild pressure between her shoulder blades. She grabbed at it, releasing the garrotte. Her fingers closed round a hairy, squirming body. A rat.

A second one dashed up her leg and lunged at her throat. She snatched it off, shocked, and crushed its head in her fist, blood and fur oozing through her fingers, its pink legs convulsing. She flung the other rat against the wall. Another bit into her thigh, puncturing skin through her breeches. Tiny claws scrabbled up her back. One tugged on her bootlace. She stamped, punched.

Rats were streaming over the walkway, dozens, hundreds. She tried to drop into the theodic kata, but her training had no answers. She pirouetted, flinging rats in all directions, slammed herself against the wall, leaving an imprint of smashed, maimed carcasses. Still they surged, a deluge, two deep, three deep, springing up, gnawing her clothes, tangling themselves in her hair, scratching her skin.

She fled. They were on her back, her arms. In her eyes. The world went black. She stumbled – the weight of bodies brought her down. She felt tiny mouths inside her, fangs shredding sinew, working at her vertebrae. It did not hurt, and she could not make it stop. Shrieking drowned out everything.

Fear rose in a bewildering rush. What was happening? How could this be? She tried to find her feet, to resist.

But already, the wicked, fallen world seemed horribly far away. She tried to resist, but her limbs refused. Little tongues were lapping at her brain. Of course. How bewildered Noroc must have been, beneath that heap of gnawing, struggling bodies. How sorry.

CHAPTER 29

NOT TILL THE NEXT WORLD

Delphine lay rigid, windpipe crushed. Thousands of rats swarmed over and around her, and ate Hagar alive. The last Delphine saw of her was a child's bloody fingers, grasping at air. The wave rolled and she vanished. Fur seethed and churned. Rats burrowed between one another, bodies rolling off the walkway, fat and sated.

Father lay at the centre of a wheel of flame, burning. Dripping, golden strands of cobweb hung about his body. The fire was spreading fast; it had reached the big wooden discs in the ceiling. Smoke churned lower, thicker.

Delphine staggered onto all fours, struggling to draw breath. Rats flowed round her, rubbing against her wrists and legs but never biting. Some scampered through the flames and caught light, spreading the fire. Slowly, the throng thinned, sinking lower and lower until she saw a ribcage, the pale dawn of a skull. The rats were scattering. Stragglers squeezed in and out of the eye sockets, gnawed connective tissue from between bone splinters. Dead rats lay all about the bones, most stripped to skeletons themselves.

She watched in horror as the swarm bore away Hagar's ribs and skull and shins, drifting under the archway like sticks in a river.

Delphine staggered to her feet, hacking. She ran to Alice's body. Alice lay on a heap of soil. There was a purple mark on her forehead. Her eyes were closed. Blood covered her legs and pooled on the ground. Delphine dropped to her knees. Her legs would no longer hold her.

'Alice.' She could barely say the name. 'Alice. Alice. Alice.'

Firelight danced over the body. Delphine was so desperate to touch her, so scared to confirm what she already knew. She reached for the bloody patch on Alice's stomach.

Her palm stopped, halted by an obstruction. Beneath her fingertips was something smooth, hard. There were anomalies in the air over Alice's belly – places where the shirt behind seemed to warp, as if viewed through a lens. Delphine pressed against it, felt resistance, then gradually a shape began to emerge, a curve, a ridge, the comb-shaped head of an antenna.

She let out a moan.

Lying in Alice's lap, her armoured back shattered, was Martha. Blood and a yolky, pinkish bile flowed from the ruin of her wing cases. A single round was embedded in her back. She had curled her legs up into her belly. Her eyes were the colour of water.

Alice stirred, blinked awake. 'Wha . . . Where . . .' She looked at Delphine, then looked down at the body in her lap. 'Martha!'

One of the moons fell with a crash. It dragged down blankets of cobwebs. Fire and smoke woofed over the walkway.

All was lost. And yet. She snapped her fingers in front of Alice's eyes.

'Can you move?' The words came out as a rasp.

Alice tried to lift herself, winced. She shook her head.

'I think my leg's broken.'

'I'll help you. You'll be all right.' Delphine crouched, nearly swooning with exhaustion. She hauled Alice over one shoulder in a fireman's lift and hugged Martha's body to her chest. She staggered as she rose.

'Your dad!' said Alice.

God. She had almost forgotten. She cast around. Where was he? Smoke was thickening, stinging her eyes. Each step was agony.

'Father!' She could not speak above a strained croak. Was he back the other way? She started stumbling back across the walkway.

The heat was incredible. Sweat was dripping down her. Strands of burning web fluttered past on intersecting currents. A wind was beginning to roar through the gap beneath the western archway. What about Sarai?

Alice cried out. 'Ah! Delphine, it's too hot. I'm burning.'

Delphine squinted across the walkway, through the flames and smoke. There he was, in the doorway! She could barely see him, just the black outline of a man swathed in fire.

Another moon fell, smashing through fungi and sending up thick green clouds of spores. The crash made her ears ring. Father stood, just a few yards away.

She felt herself decide before she did it, felt her heart drop away.

She turned her back on Father, and began staggering towards the exit. Her eyes were streaming. The rubble and archway were a blur, lit golden by the raging fire.

Her leg gave. She dashed her knee on amber stone. Heat pounded against her back. She forced herself to stand. No. There was no power left in her leg muscles. She felt them convulsing as she strained to rise, to bear Alice up and to safety. Please God. Please.

Alice shoved herself free. She landed on her hands and knees, grunting with pain.

'Argh! Come on!' Her white hair hung in knotty strings. Her teeth were bared. 'I'm fine! Let's go!' She began dragging herself arm over arm towards the way out, kicking with her good leg.

Delphine staggered beside her. She focused on the archway. Every step hurt.

Beside the archway, Patience lay in the heap of debris, slowly coming round. As they reached her, she opened her eyes.

'What did I . . . oh *shit.*'

Delphine set down Martha's body. 'Take Alice and Sarai and *run.*' She turned. 'I'm going back for Butler!'

Alice grabbed for her ankle. 'Delphine! No!'

But Delphine was away, slipping off the ledge onto a ridge ten feet below, then from that down into the swirling wet heat of the basin. Crooked mushrooms with thick, cerise gills threw jagged shadows. The floor was choked with mulch that squelched and crackled beneath her boots. She flashed her gunlight around, trying to keep her balance.

His headless body lay at the base of a bulbous fungus, having smashed through the cap, wings crumpled. Flesh was threading up from the neck stump like the tentacles of a sea anemone. She dashed about wildly, hacking with her sickle. Where the hell was his head? Mushrooms were burning. The aroma was heady and stifling and her vision began to blur.

She slipped, landed flat in a bog of mulch and red algae. Her hand found something wet and sharp.

She dragged Butler's head out of the muck by his fangs. His eyes were open, twitching. She nearly dropped it in revulsion, but holding her breath, she managed to clamber back to his prone body. She pressed the head against the stump of his neck.

Ten seconds passed. Smoke swirled and thickened, blotting out the light. She tried not to inhale. Her eyes were burning.

His hand fluttered. Butler rose, gasping.

'Bloody hell!' He dragged Delphine upright. They ran for the side of the pit, Butler wafting a path through the smoke with his wings. The walls were smooth, greased with muck. Fire closed around them. Delphine jumped and scrabbled at the sheer wall. Butler got beneath her, tried to lift her.

Ropes of flesh whipped down through the smoke and lashed round their arms. Delphine rushed upwards through a hot wind; her feet hit the ground, then Patience was shoving her under the archway into the passage beyond.

Another moon smashed down behind them. Butler grabbed Alice, Patience carried Sarai in a mesh of shock-absorbent dendrites, and together they fled down the corridor, grit blowing in their eyes as the fire drank oxygen.

Delphine tasted blood and charcoal. She clutched Martha's broken body to her chest. *I'm sorry. I'm sorry. I'm sorry.*

For a time, all she knew was the rhythmic pain of one foot thumping into the floor, the other rising. She wanted to shrink herself down to that sensation. Hide in it.

A hand gripping her shoulder. Butler had stopped.

It took a few seconds for Delphine's eyes to focus.

At the end of the tunnel a figure waited, hunched in the dust.

He shrank from the torchlight. He was filthy, his clothes ragged tatters. He had a scraggly beard and matted brown hair.

'Hello?' said Delphine.

At his feet, spreading outwards in a sea, were thousands of rats.

They were eerily still. Some were sitting up on their haunches. Some were big as dogs.

'Who are you?' said Butler.

The challenge rang flatly off the tunnel walls, fading.

The remnants of Hagar's bones were scattered amongst the rats, skull included.

The figure looked from Butler to Delphine, sniffed. The rats parted and he began moving towards her with a strange, bent-backed gait, keeping low to the ground, sometimes letting the backs of his fingers drag along it, as if tasting its texture. He wore a backpack that swayed as he moved, its contents clanking softly. He seemed relatively young, just dirty, weathered, with long side whiskers. Butler moved as if to block him, but Delphine waved Butler aside. It was the oddest thing. She already knew.

The man stopped in front of her. He licked black grime off his palm. A swarthy grey rat was sitting on his boot. Another, smaller rat scrambled from the folds of his shirt, up into his hair. His sleeves were rolled up, his forearms lean. He gave off the sweet-sour stink of piss and sweat. A tumour the size of a peach clung to his neck. He scrutinised her without awkwardness. His gaze lingered on Martha's body for a time, then rose to meet Delphine's.

The eyebrows were thinner and browner, the hair thicker, the ears smaller in proportion to the face, but that look of disapproval was unmistakeable.

As she opened her mouth, his name turned in her heart like a key.

'Henry?'

It felt peculiar on her tongue – faintly blasphemous.

The young man narrowed his eyes. In the dark of the tunnel, ten thousand rats opened their mouths and shrieked.

He led them to freedom. Through the secret ways, the hidden paths beneath the hill. All the while they felt reverberations from the surface, the muffled concussions of warfare.

Delphine ran. And when she could not run, when her boots had filled with blood and her legs collapsed beneath her, Butler and Patience and even the rats carried her.

Colours bled together. Delphine flowed with them, down to the sea.

Reggie was waiting in the undercity. Gunfire rang through the boardwalks. By the time he was rowing them across the bay, the sun was setting. Stealthily, they cut between the shadows of larger ships, till they reached a twin-masted schooner with its sails furled. Reggie whistled; a rope dropped.

Once they were aboard, figures emerged from belowdecks. Delphine recognised the teenage girls from the boathouse. And here was Agatha, a pistol at her hip and a heavy red jacket slung about her shoulders, hissing orders.

Soon, they were slipping out of the bay.

Fat Maw burned. Fires raged across the high town, columns of smoke rising over the harbour like blood in water. The schooner headed west, out onto the heart-purple ocean.

Delphine watched from the taffrail as the devastation shrank and compressed, losing detail. The farther they travelled, the easier it was to think of it as history, rather than an event that was still happening, the suffering of people as real as her. Soon it was just a glow on the horizon.

They crushed Hagar's bones with a hammer and burned the fragments in a brazier. Butler did not think a peer could regrow from a skeleton alone – and the bones showed no signs of regenerating – but he was not keen to test the proposition. Her pyre sent up a pennant of oily smoke that smutted the mainsail with a yellowy resin. Butler watched the flames, mouthing words under his breath.

Delphine found Henry down in the hold. Rats scuttled amongst the cargo. He was squatting against a crate, tugging at his beard.

He was skinnier than she remembered. Far younger, of course. Odd to see him without his hat.

'I brought you a cup of tea,' she said.

He did not look up.

'No milk, I'm afraid.' Algernon had called milk in tea 'the English perversion'. She stopped a few feet from Henry and set his mug down on the floor. A heavy sadness threatened to swallow her. She took a deep breath. 'We held a service for Martha. Recited Psalm 23. She would have liked that, I think. *The Lord is my shepherd; I shall not want. He maketh me to lie down in green pastures: he leadeth me beside the still waters.*'

Henry stared off to the side. Rats came and sniffed the mug.

Well. She was expecting too much. She walked to the other side of the room and sat down on a plastic chest. She blew on her tea, watching it tilt with the movement of the ship.

When she glanced over a few minutes later, Henry was holding his mug in both hands. She did the same. She felt the sorrow welling up inside her, stronger. Something darker than the night, impossibly vast. She closed her eyes and let the heat from her mug bathe her face.

Till the next life.

Night fell. The wind picked up and the sea took on the shifting topography of mountains.

'Hey.'

Alice appeared by Delphine's side. She was wearing a waxed cloak with the hood up, and walking with a stick. Her ankle was sprained, rather than broken, though she was badly bruised.

'Hello,' said Delphine. She shuffled along and Alice joined her, leaning out over the rail. The boat left a frothing wake like a ploughed field in winter. Delphine felt as if she were watching from the window of a train. Glowing shapes bobbed just beneath the surface. Sometimes a fin cut laterally through the spume.

The ship was taking them west. Perhaps they would make for Gallia, perhaps Albion. Butler said Sarai was breathing, but she would not wake up. He had cleaned and dressed her wounds. He did not know if she would survive the next few days.

Delphine was beginning to realise she might never see England again. Even if Ms Rao solved the unrest at the camp and reopened the threshold, what would they be going back to? Old age, cancer, dementia. Martha was gone. There was no home to return to.

And what of Avalonia? The Grand-Duc had ruled for centuries. Butler thought the conflict in Fat Maw was just the beginning. Hilanta might seize the opportunity to invade while the nation was weak. Ms Rao said upheaval brought opportunity. Places to hide. Chances to help. Ways to steer history. Delphine and Alice were welcome to continue their work with *SHaRD*, she said. With the threshold closed, supply lines were temporarily cut off. But Butler and Patience had contacts in Gallia. Of course, Alice and Delphine were free. Once the ship made land, they could go where they pleased.

Delphine did not know what she wanted. Or rather, she did. But it was impossible.

'We're alive,' said Alice.

'We're alive,' said Delphine. She ran her palm across the grain of the wood and thought about what to say. She thought of Martha, and a wagon full of oddments, and the sound of rain on leaves. She looked down at their hands next to each other on the rail, fancied she saw the beginning of lines, the rising of veins, a hardening, a tremor.

She slid her hand over Alice's. A pulse socked her palm. It felt heavy and good.

She squeezed.

EPILOGUE

I manifest in the pavilion, folding my wings round Gideon. Ice meets fire. Steam rises from us in a column.

My memory has a hole burnt in it. An hour is missing. Sarai is gone. Ah well. What has happened is what must happen. Gideon is returned to me. All is proceeding as it should.

Morgellon is on the floor, screaming. Abruptly, he stops. Here we go. I withdraw to a safe distance. I know what's about to happen, and I want to watch.

A figure descends the steps from the balcony. She's beautifully dressed – wrapped in an ankle-length black cloak held fast by a lattice of embroidered punchwork and grey cotton cords, her face obscured by a mask. The mask is featureless white, save for two hollow sockets which appear black in the guttering candlelight.

She crosses the floor, stepping over shattered bodies. When she reaches Morgellon, she kneels. She pushes up her mask. Of course Grandmama is mesmerising. She wears her pale-daffodil hair fastened with an ebony clasp. Her skin is supple and flushed with colour. You'd never guess she spent decades buried alive, dreaming delirious, grief-filled dreams of her lost love. Madness is a cleansing fire. The Anwen who regards this scene is utterly hollow. Purified. Her hatred for the one who slew Grandpapa has undergone a radical diffusion. She no longer hates just Delphine. She abominates life itself.

She studies the prone body of her old benefactor. Her betrayer.

Lord Jejunus, the Terrestrial Grand-Duc, Gallia's Endless Sentinel, Guardian of the Free Peoples of the Perpetuum.

She touches him lightly on the elbow. She lowers her mask and rises.

'Gideon,' she says. 'It's time to go.'

Gideon nods in mute compliance, and begins to trudge towards the tunnels.

Anwen sifts through debris until she finds it: a child's hand, severed at the wrist. Sinew trails strangely from the wrist stump, like new shoots pushing out from a seedling.

She presses the hand to her chest, glances round a final time, and vanishes into the shadows.

The chamber shakes. A great stone lintel drops from the spire and bursts against the onyx head of Mitta. The lid of the sarcophagus cracks. The statue tilts. Morgellon lies motionless amongst the debris, his body grey with dust.

My god is calling me back. With the last of my strength, I drift behind the statue and give it the gentlest of taps. The stone lid gives way. Mitta falls towards his master.

A boom rings through the pavilion.

By and by, Grandmama will set sail to find me. Gideon will hear the song of the dreaming deep and guide them. The seedling will find a worthier servant than her former master, and, when they arrive, she will waken my god and reshape the world. Threads that were many and thin are now woven together into a single, unbreakable rope. My god will rise and transform our suffering. It can no longer be stopped.

An end to the error of death. Paradise on this world and on Earth.

These are the wonders I believe I am ushering in.

An end to the error of life. An end to the error. An end.

I start to fade, returning to my prison beneath the ice. In my innocence, I think we have won. My body unspools. It doesn't hurt. There is no pain.

Only love.

ACKNOWLEDGEMENTS

This was not an easy book to write, and I'm very grateful to everyone who helped pick me up and carry me when I fell down.

Firstly, I'd like to thank my dear friends Cleo Madeleine, Kieren McCallum, Beth McKenzie and Rachael Weal, for teaching me the meaning of companionship and adventure, and keeping the spirit of storytelling alive in my heart. I wouldn't have made it without you.

Thank you to Iain Ross and Hayley Webster for reading parts of my novel and offering reassurance and feedback when I needed them the most.

Thank you to the Society of Authors, who gave me a grant that helped me finish the book after life circumstances had made doing so look impossible.

Thank you to my agent Sophie Lambert, who has been supremely patient, insightful and positive throughout the long process of getting this novel finished. Thank you to my editor, Jo Dingley, for her advice, wisdom and support. I owe both of you such a lot for helping me find the story that needed telling and make it the best it could be.

Thank you to my parents, who are always there for me, and who have always made me feel very, very loved. I'm also grateful to my mother-in-law, Leena Horton, whose positivity, calm and good humour are a constant inspiration.

My greatest debt of gratitude goes to my wife, Lisa Horton, who has at various points encouraged, supported, hugged, tolerated and forgiven me while I siphon off the best of myself into an imaginary world. Thank you. I love you.

Finally, thank you to my daughter Suki, who was born during this book's creation, and who teaches me so much about love, bravery and joy every day. I would carry you down mountains, through jungles, over oceans, even unto the end of the world. I love you so, Suki. One person really can change everything.